But at this exact moment, sitti̶̶̶̶̶̶̶ the bar, what Topo fancied he s̶m̶e̶l̶l̶e̶d̶ ̶w̶a̶s̶ ̶m̶o̶n̶e̶y̶. not? Wasn't he one of the originators of 'The Tales of the Miracle and the Mystery' – much on a par with Leo Pizzola and Franco Fortino? In fact, if pressed, Leo Pizzola would have to admit that much of the original scheme had come from Guido's head. At least some of it . . . Or at the very least, a little of it. Yes, when it came to boldness and clever ideas, he and Leo were cut from the same bolt of cloth. That fact was proven, even now, by the birth of the excellent idea floating around inside his head.

How could he have predicted what terrible events this excellent idea would help to set in motion? How could he anticipate that such an innocent little thought would ever contribute to him becoming a criminal – a master thief? Who could foresee such a harmless notion bringing such a world of trouble?

The Miracles of Santo Fico

D.L. SMITH

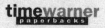

timewarner
paperbacks

A *Time Warner* Paperback

First published in the United States in 2003 by Warner Books Inc.
First published in Great Britain in 2003 by Time Warner Books
This edition published by Time Warner Paperbacks in 2004

A CIP catalogue record for this book
is available from the British Library.

ISBN 0 7515 3358 0

Illustration © Flying Fish

Typeset in Fournier by M Rules
Printed and bound in Great Britain by
Clays Ltd, St Ives plc

Time Warner Paperbacks
An imprint of
Time Warner Book Group UK
Brettenham House
Lancaster Place
London WC2E 7EN

www.twbg.co.uk

For Dorothy

ACKNOWLEDGMENTS

This is only a partial list of the people I would like to thank. Unfortunately to acknowledge all of the dear friends, family members, and colleagues who have encouraged my efforts over the years would require an additional chapter.

I want to thank Susan Amey for bringing that little newspaper article into class (and consequently getting this whole thing started in the first place). I want to thank Joanna Steinman and Victoria King for their generous spirits and encouragement. I especially want to thank my brother David for his tireless efforts, his discerning eye, and his unflagging sense humor.

I want to thank my wonderful agent, Liv Blumer, for her wise council and patience – and for inviting me along on this astonishing ride. I want to thank Susan Sandler for her literary wisdom and her steadfast optimism whenever I became discouraged. I want to thank my editor and friend at Warner Books, Caryn Karmatz Rudy, for her gentle yet determined hand, her vision, and her amazing serenity.

And I would like to thank my wife, Dorothy, for her days of diligent proofing and her months of encouragement and good humor. And finally, to her and to our sons, Matthew and Daniel – thank you for your years of faith, for being in my life, and for being exactly who you are.

One

*S*leep was the enemy. The old man knew that. The heat was merely its accomplice and these scorching days of August were particularly dangerous. He rebuked the little voice whispering in his ear that it would be all right to lean his head against the cool stone wall of his closet for just a moment. But the little voice insisted that a quick rest of the eyes might even help him to concentrate on Maria Gamboni's moans droning from the other side of the black lace netting.

The old man thought of all the years he had been hearing this particular confession and his mind couldn't help but wander to how many atonements this poor woman must have uttered over the years. Years became numbers that rolled around in his head like marbles in a bowl, brushing against his fingertips, always just out of reach, or a bit too slippery to grasp – and again the little voice suggested that maybe he would feel better if he just rested his eyes for a moment. Soon Maria Gamboni's muffled voice droned into some vague distance as the familiar blanket of heat and darkness folded over him and he wondered if this pleasant sinking feeling was what death was like. How fitting it would be to die in this little closet, he thought, while Maria Gamboni chants her sins next door. How appropriate.

Only when his white head finally plopped and his neck snapped forward and his skull conked against the hard stone did the old priest jerk upright.

'Oh, my goodness,' Father Elio Caproni mumbled as he tried to stretch his aching limbs, but there wasn't enough room in the cramped compartment. He sternly rubbed his craggy face with both hands in an effort to focus on his task. Sweat poured down his forehead, stinging his eyes, and that helped a bit. He tugged at his soiled white collar in an attempt to capture more air, but it did no good. How could anything as old and frayed as that collar be so stifling? He recalled his childhood daydreams of wearing the white collar. It never occurred to him, back then, that being a priest could ever be a bad thing. That came later. It wasn't until he was a young man of twenty-two returning home from Bologna, wearing the stiff white collar for the first time and for all the town to see, that he realized he had made a horrible mistake. Everyone was so proud of him that day, and yet he was so ashamed. God knew his lie. He swore that day to devote his life to serving his neighbors as the priest of the Church of Santo Fico. If he did that, he thought, God would have to forgive him for his terrible sin.

Now, Father Elio had been Santo Fico's priest for as long as anyone could remember, including Father Elio. For fifty years he kept his secret and devoted himself to his promise as he waited for some sign that God had forgiven him. But nowadays his faith was worn as thin as his frayed collar, and his heart felt as dry as that fountain in the center of the piazza. These days, if he dreamed at all it was no longer in hopes of a sign – these days he usually dreamed simply of an ending.

On the other side of the black veil, Maria Gamboni whined, '. . . and heaven knows that I deserve whatever punishment God chooses to inflict on me, because He knows all of my wicked sins against my beloved Enrico – God rest his soul if he be truly dead . . .'

It wasn't difficult for Father Elio to find his place. He had been listening to this same confession at least once a week for almost thirty years and he not only managed to catch up, but even inserted a comforting 'There, there . . .' right on cue. At least he hadn't fallen completely asleep and snored like last Thursday.

It had been almost thirty years ago that Maria's husband, Enrico Gamboni, had disappeared. One spring morning he walked down the steep cliff road leading southeast out of Santo Fico to catch the bus into Grosseto, where he was going to buy a new rebuilt oil pump for the engine of his fishing trawler. He was never seen again. The police combed the streets of Grosseto for weeks, but they never found a clue as to what happened.

Maria, on the other hand, knew exactly what had happened. She had driven the poor man away – probably to his death. Since the day Enrico disappeared she knew that God was punishing her for being a disagreeable wife. And Father Elio had to acknowledge that there might be some truth in this.

'. . . And Father, I swear,' Maria Gamboni whispered as if she were revealing a black secret, 'sometimes I feel like if God were to ask me if I should live, I would just say, 'No. Come ahead and take me.' That's what I would say. I would just say, 'Come ahead.' Is that a terrible sin? . . .'

Father Elio was prepared to answer, but he knew it wasn't necessary. Maria wasn't interested in replies.

'. . . I ask God to forgive those thoughts. But sometimes I wonder if God even hears me. Sometimes I think I should go to a big church in Siena and light a candle, because Santo Fico is so small I feel like my prayers get lost. No one ever comes here anymore; sometimes I wonder if God does. I know it's a terrible sin to say that, but I can't help it . . .'

Father Elio leaned against the cool stones and smiled. Maria Gamboni was not the first resident of Santo Fico to feel the frustration of insignificance. He recalled another confession along those lines – actually, it wasn't really a confession, not in any priestly sense. This confession was some years ago now and was actually more of an owning up to the truth. The disclosure slipped out quite accidentally over lunch one afternoon, when his niece Marta Caproni Fortino finally admitted the actual facts concerning Santo Fico's wonderful summer of miraculous arrivals.

Father Elio enjoyed recalling the days when Marta was young and carefree, part of a band of four that had a rare and special fellowship, one that transcended blood ties. There were Leo Pizzola and Franco Fortino – closer than brothers and rivals in everything, they seemed determined to set the world ablaze together. And then there was nervous little Guido Pasolini – Topo, or little mouse, as they called him – whose devotion to his friends made him everyone's Sancho Panza. And at the center of this golden circle was his beautiful niece Marta, younger than the others, but still wiser and stronger than her years. These four shared a bond that lasted . . . perhaps, lasted too long. The old man sighed. He didn't want to think about that part right now.

He could still see Marta's earnest expression as she explained, trying unsuccessfully to sound repentant. It seems that the four friends had been lolling about the church's bell tower one hot afternoon, fighting off the summer doldrums by inventing ways of getting enough money to escape Santo Fico. According to Marta, it had been Franco who first suggested that Follonica and Punta Ala had the right idea.

'Tourists!' cried Franco. 'Santo Fico should do something to bring in tourists.'

Marta swore that she wasn't trying to encourage anything illegal when she pointed out that 'those other towns have certain things that tourists want – attractions!'

'But Santo Fico's got attractions!' Leo almost whispered. 'The Miracle and the Mystery are attractions and I'll bet tourists would even pay to see them.'

Well, some things are so incredibly obvious that one wonders how they stay undiscovered for so long, and as Leo unfolded the clever scheme the others could only stare at Leo slack-jawed. Finally Marta (according to her, the only determined voice of reason) pointed out that they also lacked another basic ingredient – advertisements! Those other places had highway signs to entice passing travelers.

She was right. After a long collective silence it was a dejected little Topo who sighed, almost to himself, 'It's not fair . . . We should just go out to that highway and change those stupid signs!'

Marta assured her uncle that no one ever spoke anything out loud, but Leo's and Franco's eyes grew wide and the power of their silent resolve and the danger of such a wild plot frightened Marta and Topo. In fact, Topo suddenly remembered he was supposed to help his father with something. Within seconds he was gone. Marta also remembered certain non-specific chores and disappeared – but not before this ten-year-old girl had given both boys a stern lecture on the law and sin.

Leo and Franco brought their scheme to Father Elio. The two twelve-year-old boys sat with him in his kitchen and solemnly explained to him all the virtues of telling tourists the stories of the Miracle and the Mystery. Of course, he gave them permission to bring guests into the church – after all, they were his altar boys. But he warned them, 'Don't get your hopes up, boys. If anyone comes to Santo Fico, it will be a miracle!'

Imagine his amazement when the very next day two car loads of travelers on their way south to Riva del Sole suddenly found themselves in the piazza of Santo Fico by mistake. Father Elio was so proud of the way Franco seized the moment to convince the confused travelers to have lunch in the hotel across the piazza and then allow his good friend, 'Leo, the Altar Boy,' to show them 'the Miracle and the Mystery of Santo Fico.'

By the end of the first week, a half-dozen automobiles and a few small buses had unexpectedly found themselves in Santo Fico's dusty piazza. Father Elio had to admit he might have investigated this marvel with more vigor, but there was something so wonderful about the way Leo told those stories. Day after day, he found himself sitting with the pilgrims – who donated surprising amounts of money to the boys – listening to Leo's wonderful tales.

All that summer the procession of tourists continued and the boys always gave a share to the church. It was a happy arrangement for all. Until one day in the fall, the car loads and buses of bewildered tourists who thought they were headed for Piombino or Orbetello or Punta Ala suddenly stopped arriving in Santo Fico. Father Elio remembered when the man from the government drove into town, stopped his car in front of the hotel, and stomped inside. A lot of yelling was heard from within the hotel before the man from the government stomped back out to his car and roared out of town.

It seems that someone had gone out to the highway and changed a bunch of the signs. Travelers en route to a particular destination suddenly found themselves in the center of Santo Fico. It occurred to the man from the government, whose job it was to fix all of those signs, that the most likely candidate for this dastardly act was the owner of the only restaurant in town. It was later learned that he had threatened Father Elio's brother, Young Giuseppe Caproni, with jail if there was ever again any funny business with the signs. For his part, Young Giuseppe threatened the man from the government with immediate emasculation if he ever entered his hotel again . . .

Father Elio had to smile when he recalled how he had warned those boys, 'If anyone comes to Santo Fico, it will be a miracle.' How could he have known that what they had in mind was a whole summer of miracles . . .

Suddenly, Father Elio sat up with a jerk and held his breath. In the adjoining closet Maria Gamboni had stopped talking. The old priest had no idea exactly when her words had stopped, but he had certainly heard something that had abruptly caught his attention. Maria Gamboni had growled at him. It was a low, rumbling, menacing sort of growl and he found it quite unsettling. He strained to listen, but now all he heard from the other side was the sound of the old woman's heavy breathing.

In her adjoining cubicle, Maria Gamboni also strained forward with her eyes wide in both amazement and no small amount of fear. In all the years that she had been making her confessions to Father Elio, at no time, as far as she could recall, had he ever growled at her. But she had definitely heard it – a distinct growl. And now she too heard stirrings next door. He was leaving the confessional.

The old woman opened her door and peeked out and in the shadowed cathedral light she discovered Father Elio also peeking out of the adjacent door, staring back at her in a curious fashion.

'Excuse me, Father. Did you . . . ehh . . .'

Just as he was about to ask her a similar question, from outside the church came a low, rumbling growl. And it was getting louder. Father Elio, followed closely by Maria Gamboni, hurried down the empty aisle to the front of the church. Whatever grumbling beast was doing this growling, it was arriving just beyond the cathedral doors.

What greeted them outside was a blast of hot air, blinding sunlight, and the spectacle of a blue and white sightseeing bus straining up the last steep street leading into the center of Santo Fico. Its gears ground painfully and the engine groaned in anguish as the stunted little tour bus rounded the corner and drove past the church. The bus appeared to have been transported from a previous decade. It was too fat and too tall with exaggerated windows and it was only about a third the proper length. From where they stood on the church steps, Father Elio and Maria Gamboni stared dumbfounded into the vacant eyes of a dozen bewildered travelers trapped behind dusty windows.

The little bus made a slow exploratory circle around the piazza, using the empty fountain in the middle of the square as a pivot point. At one time the marble fountain was quite a centerpiece for the small piazza. The central pedestal was made of white marble and topped with a smiling cherub tipping some sort of jug that once poured an endless stream of water into the surrounding pool. But the cherub's bottomless jug had been dry for many years and the only water that graced the pool anymore came during the rainy season. Nowadays the monument best served as a turnaround point for lost buses and a bench for old men.

At that moment one old man sat on the edge of the fountain watching the one-bus-carousel revolve slowly around him. A skinny gray dog lay at his feet, and as the bus rolled by, raising a cloud of dust and diesel fumes, the dog lifted his head curiously. The old man scratched the white stubble on his chin and apparently decided that some greeting was in order because he offered them a friendly wave. The gray dog went back to sleep.

From their front-row seats behind the sun-baked glass the visitors had a wonderful view of all the high points of Santo Fico on their orbit around the town square. First, of course, came the blessed Church of Santo Fico, and standing on the church steps was an old priest with a wild shock of white hair and a bewildered smile that, like his hair, seemed to be gripped in perpetual surprise. It was sad, the observers thought, that there should be such a deformed lump growing out of the old priest's back, but on closer inspection the lump blinked two frightened eyes at them. Even though Father Elio was a short man, Maria Gamboni was shorter still and as thin as a weed. And since both she and her priest tended to wear the same shade of black, and because at this moment the old woman was clinging to his back like a growth and peeking around his shoulder, their mistake was understandable.

The bus continued its extended left turn toward Santo Fico's newest building – the Palazzo Urbano. Built before the turn of the century to house all the government offices, the faded two-story palazzo now stood empty and in disrepair. Most of the windows were locked and shuttered and apparently nobody had even mentioned the word *paint* in its presence for many years. One small room on the ground floor remained open to serve as a postal drop for the obnoxious young man who came over from Grosseto every Tuesday and Friday with the mail.

The rest of their quick expedition around the cobblestone piazza showed a jumble of small homes and shops crawling down the town's inhospitable slopes. Most of Santo Fico clung to the jagged cliffs above the sea by its fingernails, and many of the old buildings, like these newest visitors, seemed to be asking in surprise, 'How did I get here?'

In a matter of seconds, the bus's brakes screeched to a halt in front of a handsome old villa and the tour was complete. A weathered sign above the gate leading into the villa's courtyard announced in fancy letters of faded reds, yellows, and greens that they had arrived at the Albergo di Santo Fico. With a gasp of gratitude the engine died and, except for a distant dog that continued to bark its personal protest, the village was silent again. Shiny tourist faces peered through the glass as if they had unexpectedly landed on the back side of the moon. Although they had no idea where they were, it was a safe bet that this place was not listed in any of their glossy, tri-folded, four-color brochures.

Back on the steps of the church, the novelty of the bus passed quickly for Maria Gamboni. She was impatient to get to her atonement.

'I think fifty today, Father. Don't you think so? Don't you think maybe fifty?'

Father Elio felt her insistent tug at his sleeve, but he was preoccupied with the bus. What was this bus doing here? Of course, it must be lost, but how strange, after so many years to have a tour bus become lost again. And with Leo Pizzola returning to Santo Fico just six weeks ago – a suspicious coincidence, he thought. He sighed as he also thought of all the finger wagglings and forecasts of misfortune he could expect before this day was over – all because of Leo Pizzola's return.

Since his return, rumors and speculations about what Leo Pizzola would do next ignited faster than grass fires. Gossip of scandal and doom is always engaging and the villagers enjoyed discussing these rumors as if they were omens. Even in the best of times insignificant incidents were good for at least a casual debate among the 437 inhabitants. And why not? For some time Santo Fico had only grudgingly conceded the passing decades, and the second half of the twentieth century visited only occasionally – and then, like this tour bus, usually by mistake. The inhabitants of Santo Fico no longer concerned themselves with unimportant things like the future. They had better things to do – like spending a cool evening at a verandah table with a friend, a glass of wine, and domino tiles, debating winds and cloud formations – or like sitting at their open windows studying how distant lightning storms changed the blues of the Tyrrhenian Sea.

Father Elio finally had to respond to the insistent yanks on his sleeve and so he patted Maria's bony hand and said, 'No, fifty is too many. It's too hot. Ten is plenty.'

'Ten? Ten would be an insult to God!'

'All right, twenty. But no more than twenty.'

As he guided Maria back into the church where she could spend the next hour savoring every chastising moment of her penance, Father Elio stole one more glance across the piazza at the curiosity parked in front of his niece's hotel. He liked the notion of these tourists staying for lunch. It meant that Marta would dress up her menu and that prospect made his mouth water.

At that moment a wiry little figure came hurrying up the street, following the route of the bus. Father Elio couldn't help noting the appropriateness of Guido Pasolini's lifelong nickname. It was more than just Topo's short stature or slight build. It was also his gait; the way he moved with a comical jerking motion when he was excited. It couldn't quite be called running, but might best be described as scurrying – like an excited little mouse.

Guido Pasolini didn't notice Father Elio watching him from across the piazza. By the time the excited little Topo reached the hotel, he was dangerously out of breath. He'd run for almost a quarter of a kilometer up the hill and now his thin legs could barely hold him. But Guido Pasolini was not the type of fellow who failed to recognize opportunity when it presented itself and from the first moment he'd heard that diesel engine approaching, he was on the alert. When it rumbled past the open door of the Pasolini Fix-It Shop, it had taken him only seconds to abandon Signora Morello's broken record player, grab his hat, and race out the door in full pursuit. Now, staggering up to the blue and white bus, gasping for breath, he tried his best to look uninterested.

Strolling nonchalantly by the bus, Guido knew that they would have to be getting out soon and opportunities pass quickly. So he hurried across the verandah and disappeared through the front doors of the Albergo di Santo Fico.

Two

*T*he silence of the empty lobby made Guido nervous and he felt the anxious urge to urinate. It was more than just his reasonable fear of the proprietress, Marta Caproni Fortino. It was also the hotel itself. The high ceilings and colorful tile floors were much more in keeping with a grand estate or important museum, and the stately rooms always made him feel slightly out of place.

Once upon a time the Albergo di Santo Fico had been a magnificent villa that, along with the church, had dominated the town for centuries. The villa had been in the Caproni family forever – that is to say, there was no memory of it ever having belonged to anyone else. According to legend, the villa had been built as a summer retreat for Cosimo de Medici, but the Grand Duke thought it was haunted by the ghost of his dead wife, Eleonora, and he refused to ever live there. When and how it actually came to the Caproni family is a detail lost in time and murky fables.

In any case, recent memory is reliable only back to about 1873 when Old Giuseppe Caproni (Father Elio Caproni's father and Marta Caproni Fortino's grandfather) decided to turn his family's deteriorating villa into one of the finest hotels on the Toscana coast. It was certainly the most isolated, but the Albergo di Santo Fico occupied a prime spot on the piazza, directly in front of the juncture of two important roads. The smaller road bends around the hotel to a narrow cobblestone street that winds its way down to the sea. A wall of whitewashed shops and houses with terra-cotta roofs and colorful shutters lines one side of the street – and on the other side, a low stone barrier keeps the unwary or tipsy from plunging off the cliff-face road to the harbor below.

But it's that other road just outside the hotel's tall front doors – that road which the bus recently scaled amid a chorus of whispered prayers and curses – that has always been the more significant road. Centuries earlier it had been cut by hand through granite sea cliffs, and this is the road that leads inland away from Santo Fico, toward the Ombrone River and then farther on to Grosseto and beyond that, to the world.

Back then Old Giuseppe Caproni saw Santo Fico as a village with a future. He predicted that someday processions of holy pilgrims from all over Italy would trek to Santo Fico just to visit the Miracle and the Mystery of their blessed little church. Then his Albergo di Santo Fico would be a gold mine – as soon as the government widened that damn cliff road. But the old east road that was to bring the world to his hotel's doorstep was never improved and the main highway never came closer to Santo Fico than seventeen kilometers. Many said that the tragedy of Santo Fico was how little that road has changed in four hundred years. But that was all too long ago for most memories. The village eventually just abandoned her dreams, resolved that opportunity had simply moved on, and settled into a comfortable obscurity.

Opportunity, however, can occasionally pull into even the most insignificant village and on this particular morning Guido Pasolini had it in mind that it was parked just out-side – and the clock was ticking. He hurried through the lobby and directly into the restaurant. He wasn't surprised to discover the large room empty, but better safe than sorry – so he called loudly enough to be heard, but not loud enough to be offensive.

'Marta . . .'

Silence.

He peeked through the open doors to the verandah and, sure enough, inside the bus the tourists were gathering their belongings to exit. The grumbling roar of its diesel engine had already announced the bus's arrival to most of the village and Guido knew that shortly the square would be filling up with his curious neighbors. Guido also recognized the danger of venturing beyond the restaurant and into the kitchen without a direct invitation, but what choice did he have? If he was going to be the first to tell Marta of their arrival, he would have to hurry. It could be worth a reward – maybe lunch. The little man carefully stepped through the dining room's swinging doors and entered the forbidden kitchen.

On a large stove, two steaming pots of water were threatening to come to a boil and the room smelled of fresh garlic and basil and onions and oregano. The door to the back garden was open, as were all the windows. The floor was still damp from a mopping, making the burnt umber tile an even deeper red.

'Woo-Whoo . . . Anybody here,' he pretended to call cheerily, but really it was just a loud whisper. The room was empty.

'Marta . . . Hel-llooo . . .'

Silence.

He was wise to be cautious. Marta Caproni Fortino had firm rules about outsiders in her kitchen and childhood friends were no exception.

'Marta . . . ?' A little louder this time.

'Topo! What are you doing back here?'

The voice came sharply from behind and above and it spun Guido around on his heels. Standing at the top of stairs that led from the kitchen to the family's upstairs rooms, a young woman looked down on him with mild consternation as she carelessly wound her thick black hair into a yellow scarf.

Whenever Guido saw Carmen Fortino, the older of

Marta's two daughters, he always found it hard to breathe for a moment. It wasn't just because of her luxurious black hair and smooth olive skin or her dark eyes that seemed to bore through him or her red lips that never required paint. It wasn't just because of the way her full mouth always seemed about to either smile or sneer at him – he didn't care which. It wasn't just the haughty manner with which she carried her body or the way certain of her soft curves pushed and strained against her clothing. All of these things certainly caused his mouth to go dry and his stomach to tense, but there was also something almost mystical in her allure. Her mother, Marta, affected him in the same way and had since they were children. And really, it wasn't just Marta and Carmen. It was all beautiful women. Beautiful women made Guido feel both insignificant and thrilled to be alive.

Carmen knew the effect she had on the funny little Topo and she enjoyed it. It was essentially the same effect she had on most men, but with Guido it was a bit more obvious and his level of adoration was sort of endearing. She'd begun to notice her power when she was only fifteen. It had something to do with the way certain boys who had always been so bold before, even cruel, all at once began to stutter. Suddenly they were unable to hold her gaze, but the instant she turned away she could actually feel the heat of their eyes silently following her. After some months of initial confusion and anxiety, Carmen realized that she was developing siren powers. She'd spent the last two years practicing her skills and, sometimes, like right now with Topo, she felt as if her abilities already surpassed her mother's.

Carmen slowly descended the steps with her arms raised, now self-consciously working her black hair into the yellow scarf. She knew she should hurry, but she couldn't resist the helpless look on Guido's upturned face and she allowed her body to bounce slightly as she dropped methodically from step to step. Her voice was softly reprimanding.

'You know my mother doesn't allow anyone back here.'

'I know. I know that . . . Sorry. I was looking for her . . . Your mother. It's important. Where is she?'

To Guido, Carmen seemed to descend the stairs in slow motion, and the way she looked directly in his eyes with that slight smile of chastisement – slow hands weaving yellow scarf through black hair – it was all like a scene from a movie. Sunlight gleamed through the eastern windows and reflected off the thin film of water on the newly mopped tile floor. The light bounced off the sheen and enveloped Carmen in a golden haze and Guido couldn't help thinking, this is pure Zeffirelli . . .

Suddenly, an irritated question came from behind him and jolted Topo out of his reverie like a swat on the back of the head.

'Topo! What are you doing in my kitchen? Carmen, why aren't you in the dining room?'

Carmen's expression chilled faster than November frost. In an instant the yellow scarf was tied and she was down the stairs. Guido turned to greet the glowering eyes of Marta Caproni Fortino coming in from the garden carrying a basket of vegetables. Her tall figure was framed in the door-way and her skin glistened with sweat. The tousled waves of her thick black hair refused to be completely captured by her red scarf. Like Carmen, Marta had the brooding look of most Caproni women – dark eyes and high cheekbones, determined jaw and narrow nose and that smooth olive skin. But Marta was taller than her two daughters and possessed a powerfully sensual athlete's body that they did not. Right now, with the morning sunlight flaring white behind her, Guido couldn't help thinking that here was no colorful Zeffirelli nymph. Marta was earthy, with stifled passions that were best shot in black and white – much more De Sica or Rossellini.

'We need table settings. Now.'

'I'm going,' was Carmen's indifferent response as she made a pointed effort to slow her exit.

Guido had grown up an only son surrounded by five sisters, so he long ago recognized the edgy tension of unspoken antagonism that often roils between a mother and her daughter. He'd observed with his mother and sisters that these feelings of tension were usually because the two women were so much alike. And he also knew that if he were to helpfully point this out to these two women, they would both be so insulted at being compared to the other that they would immediately join forces to burn him down where he stood – so he said nothing. But in his mind Carmen and Marta were like two different bends in the same river. The difference was Carmen found her source higher up, near the headwaters, where the ravines are narrow and the river is young and anxious. A young river is fresh and fast, crashing and cascading impatiently through rocky chasms as if it can't wait to get to the next turn its course might take. That young river doesn't care where it's going. It just knows that it has to get away from where it's been and all twists and turns are filled with promise. Marta was the same river only wide and deep. Time had run a longer course with Marta and she had experienced enough unexpected turns and twists to stop counting on the promise of the next bend in the river. The river just was. Her waters appeared smooth and still, but for those who carefully studied the surface there were eddies and swirls that announced: this water is deep and unsafe. There were dangers hidden beneath this still surface – sharp snags and jagged crags and undercurrents best not explored. Only a fool would blindly dive headfirst into these dark waters.

'Is your sister back from the bakery with the bread?'

'No,' was the curt reply and Carmen disappeared into the dining room.

As Marta moved past him and set the basket on the counter, Guido caught the fragrance of her bath soap. It smelled like lavender and he took in a deep breath as his imagination smiled. He was reminded that for all of Carmen's intoxicating power, she was still just a facsimile of the original. Carmen was enchanting, but still so young and self-indulgent. Her mother was a woman. Everything about Marta was natural and genuine – her beauty, her grace, her sensuality, her passion, her temper, her bitterness. She never toyed with him or made him feel small and homely. Of course, she never made him feel particularly welcome either, but that was all right.

'I'm busy, Topo. What do you want?'

'I wanted to warn you, a sightseeing bus is here.'

'I know. I saw it from upstairs when it was still crawling up the hill.'

'It must be lost.'

'It must be,' she replied and casually picked through the tomatoes. 'So, what do you want?'

'I wanted to tell you. They might want some lunch.'

Marta stopped rinsing the tomatoes and stared incredulously at the short fellow smiling expectantly at her shoulder. He wore his smile like an apology, but his dark, close-set eyes were filled with expectation.

'You ran all the way up here, in this heat, just to tell me that?'

Guido's foolish grin grew even broader as his cheeks flushed. He shrugged and felt like an idiot, as usual. After a moment Marta went back to her tomatoes. That was it. Apparently the audience was over. Guido didn't know how to leave and still salvage any dignity, and as the silence became more embarrassed, his absolute belief in his own idiocy compounded until a blush crept down his cheeks to his neck on its way to his toes. Finally, Marta broke the awkwardness.

'Well, you must be hot.' And she called over her shoulder to the dining room, 'Carmen, give Topo a glass of wine.'

Guido moved across the kitchen toward the dining room. 'Oh, that's okay. You don't have to.' He had hoped for lunch.

'Go on. I have a lot to do.'

And she did. This would be the largest lunch crowd the

hotel had seen in months. And it wouldn't just be the bewildered tourists, but also all of the nosy villagers who would
show up to stare at the bewildered tourists. She had a lot to
do and Nina should be back with the bread by now.

In the cool dining room, Carmen stopped laying out the
folded napkins and silverware long enough to step behind
the marble bar and pour a glass of red wine. Guido noticed
the young girl's hand shook slightly as she poured the
Chianti and her eyes kept darting toward the empty lobby.

'Here, Topo. Now, stay out of the way.' She handed him
the glass with a nervous smile that told him that she didn't
have time to flirt right now, but maybe later.

He nodded and quickly surveyed the empty room. He
could already hear the jumbled voices of the tourists entering the lobby. Having tested the view from all of the stools
and chairs in the bar many times, he chose a spot at the shadowy far end where he would have the best vantage to
observe the action.

It began slowly, in the tentative manner of all lost and
confused foreigners afraid of invading the wrong space. But
the room eventually began to fill with a dozen sweating,
shuffling, middle-aged to elderly bodies grateful to Old
Giuseppe Caproni for his cool tile floors and stone walls.
They found their way to tables and chairs and collapsed.

Their portly young guide wasn't so lucky – he still had
much to do. He smiled at his grim group and said . . . well,
he said something. Guido had no idea what it was the guide
actually said, but he perceived two things: first, many of

the words he recognized as being English and second, whatever the guide's comments, they failed to impress his charges. This chubby conductor was feeling a heat that far surpassed the warmth of a Toscana summer. The poor guy was miles from where he needed to be, in a village he didn't know, in the midst of a heat wave with a group of discontented Englishmen and he alone knew their desperate fuel situation. Why had he sped by that last gas station outside Grosseto?

The bus had, of course, taken a wrong turn as the inexperienced guide/bus driver tried to invent a shortcut between Grosseto and Piombino. By the time he realized his mistake it was already too late. The narrow east road to Santo Fico abruptly becomes a tortuous climb skirting chalky coastal crags on one side and sheer cliffs that plunged to the sea on the other. And to add to the chagrin of so many innocent motorists, the route offers absolutely no place to turn around. Unwitting drivers must either put their vehicles in reverse and drive backward down the cliffs for some kilometers or continue on and pray that eventually the trail will widen before they either run out of gas or road. So great is the frustration and fear of what danger might lie around each hairpin curve that, by the time they finally arrive at the picturesque promontory of Santo Fico, most travelers are actually grateful. And so it was with this party of tourists and their baffled pilot.

Carmen was surveying the elderly assemblage of bloated English bodies and vacant pink faces when the poor guide started what he thought was charming repartee. But this was not the sort of invasion from the outside world a seventeen-year-old girl, sentenced to life imprisonment in Santo Fico, dreams about. With less than two words out of his mouth, Carmen scowled, turned on her heels, and walked back into the kitchen. What the guide did not need right now was some snippy waitress insulting him. His credibility with these pompous English was already dangerously depleted. He also wished the chinless fellow at the end of the bar would stop staring at him.

Guido, on the other hand, enjoyed Carmen's haughty display. He didn't like the arrogant confidence this stranger showed as he approached the girl. The guide leaned against the bar and offered Guido his smile.

'She's pretty.'

Guido nodded.

'Is she coming back?'

Guido shrugged.

'Do you know how far we are from Follonica?'

Guido shook his head and sipped his wine. He actually did know the exact distance, but he wasn't about to tell this guy anything – not after running all the way up the hill to get nothing more than a crummy glass of wine. The hell with him. Besides, he wanted to see this inflated sausage's reaction to Marta – and he wasn't disappointed. He knew, without turning, when Marta entered. If the guide had found Carmen attractive, he was absolutely alarmed by the voluptuous Marta and the intriguing animal glint of peril buried in her dark eyes. Guido had seen it all his life.

Marta was no stranger to the guide's predicament and she

quickly took charge, conducting their business swiftly and efficiently. He would need thirteen lunches. She would need forty minutes. The price was agreed upon. He asked about diesel fuel. She recommended a walk down to the harbor to see if any of the fishermen might sell him some. Then, just as Marta turned back to the kitchen, Guido perked up as the guide asked a significant question.

'Is there anything of particular interest here? Something that might help us pass the time?'

Marta studied him for a moment before replying, almost offhand, 'No, not really.'

Then she noticed Guido sitting in the back corner. She'd forgotten about him. She wasn't sure he had heard this last exchange, so she motioned toward his empty glass.

'Topo, you want another?'

Guido smiled broadly and shook his head. Marta returned to the kitchen.

He liked the way Marta called him Topo. It made him feel special. The casual way she said it re-enforced his own perception about his lifelong nickname. It had nothing to do with diminutive stature or mousy traits. To him it was a term of endearment and an indication of his cleverness. He was totally oblivious of the fact that his narrow nose was a bit too long and arched, his chin was a bit too weak, his large brown eyes a bit too close together, his mouth a bit too small, and his front teeth a bit too prominent. Occasionally, in just the right light, if he were to simultaneously smile and wiggle his nose, one would swear he had just smelled cheese.

But at this exact moment, sitting in the shadows at the

end of the bar, what Topo fancied he smelled was money. And why not? Wasn't he one of the originators of 'The Tales of the Miracle and the Mystery' – much on a par with Leo Pizzola and Franco Fortino? In fact, if pressed, Leo Pizzola would have to admit that much of the original scheme had come from Guido's head. At least some of it . . . Or at the very least, a little of it. Yes, when it came to boldness and clever ideas, he and Leo were cut from the same bolt of cloth. That fact was proven, even now, by the birth of the excellent idea floating around inside his head.

How could he have predicted what terrible events this excellent idea would help to set in motion? How could he anticipate that such an innocent little thought would ever contribute to him becoming a criminal – a master thief? Who could foresee such a harmless notion bringing such a world of trouble?

Right now, it seemed to him that his simple little plan was an excellent one; tried and true. How could he have been so shortsighted? Hoping for a free lunch! What had he been thinking? Where was his brain? Leo Pizzola was back! It would be like old times!

Topo pushed himself away from the bar, grabbed his hat, and was out the door. He knew what he had to do. He had to find Leo Pizzola – and quickly.

Three

As he raced down the gravel slope of the coast road north of town, Topo strained to keep his body at least one step ahead of gravity. Nobody could say that Guido Pasolini failed to recognize opportunity when it landed in his lap, and he tried to calculate how much profit there was to be made from his scheme. Unfortunately, he had no idea how much to charge. This was an area where Leo Pizzola shined – at least he used to. Of course, Leo was bound to be a bit rusty after so many years.

Topo arrived at an unassuming break in an old stone wall that bordered the road. The gap in the wall had probably once housed a handsome gate, but now it was just a broken spot in the undergrowth. He tried to make the turn, but his speed had finally combined with gravity to create an unanticipated inertia that carried him straight off the road. Like some runaway torpedo, Topo shot across a sea of brown thistles, accidentally kicking over a 'FOR SALE' sign that had been crudely painted in red letters. The makeshift sign disappeared into the weeds, but Topo couldn't worry about it now. His short piston-legs ripped through weeds and leapt over low cactuses and jagged boulders. Finally managing to slow himself, he turned back onto the rutted dirt lane and scurried on toward the Pizzola family's pastures by the sea.

Not far from the road and up a sloping meadow, buried in the shade of a grove of cork and linden trees, loomed the ghostly figure of a once admirable house now fallen into dreary disrepair. Topo thought the dark weathered stains on the plaster walls and the branches of neighboring trees twisting themselves into the terra-cotta roof tiles gave the place the look of an abandoned old woman with her make-up smeared and her hair tangled – and she seemed sadly confused by her loveliness lost.

He panted down a road that bordered neatly planted rows of muted green olive trees. Their gnarled branches were wild and unpruned and Topo thought of how annoyed old Signore Pizzola would be to see this. The branches should be heavy by now, weighted down with fruit bursting with oil and juice. But these branches bore only a slim scattering of tiny, rock-hard olives – not worth the effort to harvest.

He passed a neglected vineyard whose scant purple berries

struggled against the weeds and baked under an uncaring sun, and he kept his eyes on the path, trying to ignore the dying vines. It angered him to see the vineyard going the way of the olive grove and the house.

Puffing across a dry field inhabited by stray goats and sheep, Topo glanced nervously over his shoulder. The Lombolo family leased these fields from Leo to graze their horses, and horses made Topo nervous. The Lombolo horses were fierce and powerful Spanish thoroughbreds that, Topo was convinced, were also treacherous. Fortunately, he didn't see them right now, so he hurried on toward the only thing to break the landscape for some distance — a small stone dwelling surrounded by a half-dozen flame-shaped cypress trees.

To call this structure a house was flattery; it was little more than a large hut that sat on a rise overlooking the sea and when the wind was right you could hear waves crashing. Probably built by some ancient Pizzola ancestor many centuries earlier, the stone and plaster walls gave the impression of snug lodgings. But for all its quaint charm, it was still just a single-room stone hut with no electricity or indoor plumbing. Why Leo chose to live here rather than in the big house on the hill where he grew up was a question Topo would someday have to ask. He knew it must somehow be connected to why Leo refused to walk into the olive grove or tend the vineyard, and he was pretty sure it had something to do with why Leo mysteriously ran away to America eighteen years ago. Someday he would ask him, but not today.

He leaned against the door and pounded only once before opening it and calling.

'Leo!'

The room was empty. This was not just bad; this was a catastrophe. Where could Leo be in the heat of the day?

Of course! It was Monday! Topo's heart sank. Disturbing Leo today could be trouble, even dangerous. The secret that Leo had revealed to him about his Mondays was shared in confidence and no invitation had been extended. Leo was going to be angry.

'Well, let him be angry,' Topo huffed. 'This is business.' And he scampered across the meadow toward the sea.

Leo Pizzola struggled to pull his lanky frame forward through the tall razor grass with some sense of stealth and still keep his knees and elbows out of the dirt. Why the hell hadn't he changed his clothes first? It was so stupid to crawl across a field in a linen suit, and he was glad he was horizontal so he couldn't kick himself. He was the only man in Santo Fico with enough style to even own a linen suit and here he was . . .

A sand flea jumped up his nose and his whole body spasmed at the invasion.

'The price you pay for crawling through their neighborhood with such a big nose,' he told himself.

He flopped onto his back and beat his hands against the marks smudging his elbows and his knees. Fortunately, the pale sand and dust of this region were of a similar hue to the creamy suit so Leo was able to rationalize how the delicate shadings of dust might even enhance the casual nature of the rumpled cloth.

Too late now and it was his own fault. He'd once again lost track of the days of the week, and when he dressed this morning for his usual pointless trip into town, some unexplainable whim told him to put on his suit. He was all the way to the olive grove before he remembered it was Monday, and his run back down the dusty path and then the sprint up the coast had left him sweating and out of breath. Now, here he was, thirty-six years old with grass stains on the elbows and knees of his only suit, crawling through the tall grass like some hormonal schoolboy.

With one final grunt Leo pulled himself to the edge of a low bluff of sandstone boulders that joined a white beach and led down to a peaceful lagoon. Carefully parting the blades of razor grass, Leo peeked over the edge of the cliff toward the sea.

Across the white sand beach an attractive but rather ample woman lazed back on a smooth boulder at the water's edge. Her bleached tresses rested on a rolled towel and her thin cotton dress was hiked up revealing pleasantly plump legs. Leo realized that in his haste he was becoming careless. He still wore his soiled Panama hat and it stuck out like a white flag in the tall grass, so he swiftly swept it off his head in a strangely gentlemanly way.

At the water's edge Angelica Giancarlo was having trouble keeping the lids of her large brown eyes from fluttering closed as she baked under the August sun. She knew this much sun wasn't good for her skin, but at the moment her real concern was falling asleep. So she forced herself to stretch across the warm boulder in an effort to stay awake. Who was she kidding? It was obvious that Leo Pizzola had lost interest. He wasn't coming. In all the Mondays since she first noticed him spying on her secret swims, this was the first one he'd missed.

She was tempted to stumble back up the hill to town and take a real nap. There would be plenty of time for swimming later – perhaps tonight. Angelica liked to swim at night, under a full moon. When she looked at her naked body standing on the wet sand, the silver haze of moonlight and glistening water hid the tracings of time and her perpetual losing battle with gravity and she felt younger.

Just as she decided to summon enough energy for the hike back home, she saw a small rustling in the grass at the crest of the cliff. Then there was the swift flash of a familiar straw hat.

'Well, it's about time,' she mumbled to herself.

If this drama were something that either of them could acknowledge, she would certainly give him a piece of her mind for keeping her waiting in this heat. But her best opportunity for an indignant display was when she first saw him peeking at her through the tall grass over a month ago. She wondered sometimes why she entertained his childish peeping at all. It wasn't like she really knew Leo Pizzola. In fact, they didn't even speak. She wouldn't mind it if they did – but of course, that would be too awkward now.

With a somewhat ungraceful effort Angelica hauled herself from the warm rock, and this time as she stretched in the sun, it was more deliberate. Why did she even bother? She didn't even know him really and already he's late; probably getting bored – they all get bored eventually. But she knew why. It was vanity. There was so little that made her feel attractive anymore; or alluring; or desired. She quickly dismissed any notion of giving him a piece of her mind, and instead she unrolled her towel and placed it across the flat boulder that jutted out into the lagoon. Then she stepped into the shallow water and delighted at its coolness on her bare feet and ankles. Ah, this was what she needed to wake her. As Angelica slowly waded deeper into the inviting sea, she lifted her light dress a little higher with each step. She wore no underclothing. Underclothing was always so clumsy and ungraceful. This economy made the dance appear much more effortless. Finally, when she was deep enough to justify it, she pulled the dress completely over her head and held it high up in the air. She deftly rolled the colorful print into a tight ball and with a practiced flick of the wrist, the wad of still dry cloth flew across the water and landed perfectly on the edge of the boulder. Angelica held her unveiled pose for just a moment before diving beneath the surface of the cool blue water.

From behind his curtain of grass at the top of the bluff, Leo rested his chin on his hands and watched Angelica's smooth pink form glide through the translucent blue. Where Angelica Giancarlo was concerned Leo had never quite outgrown the innocent adoration he'd felt when he was a boy. Although she was only a few years his senior, how he had yearned for this full-busted 'older woman' of sixteen who was willing to occasionally indulge a twelve-year-old boy with her secret smile. As boys, Leo and Topo and Franco Fortino had been unable to hide their fascination with the voluptuous Angelica. When it came down to it, every man in the village noticed Angelica when she walked by and every woman hated her because of it. But these three boys loved to follow her just to watch the way her round hips swayed as she walked up the narrow streets, the way she tossed her bleached hair when she laughed, the way her eyes flashed like tiny signal lights as she raised or lowered them, or the way she would casually stroke her rib cage just below her breast. This was all great stuff and a tremendous education for three pubescent boys.

Leo was thirteen when Angelica left home. He and every other male in the village was sorry to discover her gone, but being the principal *femme fatale* for the village had probably become a little awkward for the bighearted Angelica – not to mention embarrassing for her mother and stern father. At seventeen Angelica left Santo Fico to find her fortune as a movie actress in Roma – so the story went.

About a year after she disappeared, Leo, Franco, and Topo hitched a ride into Grosseto because Topo swore that there was a movie playing that had Angelica Giancarlo in it and you could see her breasts!

The movie was about sheiks and sultans and deserts and harem girls and it was all pretty silly. But Topo swore that the plump blond harem girl was Angelica. If it was, you certainly could see her breasts and they certainly were beautiful. Unfortunately, all the harem girls wore little masks and Franco insisted it wasn't Angelica. Topo swore it was. Leo wasn't sure, so he sided with Franco just because that's the way things worked back then. Even so, Leo still managed to secretly hitch a ride back into Grosseto one afternoon before that movie closed, because the odds were that Topo was right. Even as a boy Guido Pasolini knew more about movies than anyone in Santo Fico. As Leo seated himself, he spotted Topo sitting a few rows in front of him. He didn't say a word because he suddenly felt embarrassed about being there. But also because, in the flickering shades of gray light bouncing off the screen he was startled by the expression of adoration on Topo's face as his little friend stared up at the giant image he swore was Angelica Giancarlo. Leo felt as if he'd invaded Topo's holy shrine and he sneaked out before the movie was over.

A rustling in the grass behind him disturbed Leo's meditation of Angelica gliding and turning in the cool water. He turned fully expecting to have to shoo away a sheep or a goat or at worst one of the Lombolos' horses. Instead, he discovered – a mouse.

'Topo, what the hell are you doing here?' Leo whispered angrily.

The little man could only wave his hands feebly as he tried to catch his breath.

'Get out of here. I knew I shouldn't have told you about this.' Leo made an ineffectual kick in his friend's direction.

Topo took an equally unproductive swing at Leo's foot and recovered his breath enough to gasp, 'A tour bus . . .'

Leo spun around in the grass as if he'd received an electric shock.

'How many?'

'I don't know. Over ten.'

'Back up, back up, back up . . .'

Feet were suddenly headed in Topo's direction for real this time, so he rolled to one side and let Leo scramble through.

For an instant Topo was alone with the notion that just beyond that veil of razor grass, Angelica Giancarlo's naked splendor glided through blue water. But he couldn't look. Some other woman, maybe . . . but not Angelica Giancarlo. Instead he sighed and followed Leo's disappearing rear end.

Staying on their hands and knees, the two men scrambled toward the path and continued their excited conspiring in whispers.

'Where are they?'

'The hotel. They're going to have lunch.'

'Marta hasn't served them yet?'

'Not when I left.' Topo was beginning to wonder if he was up to the return trip.

When they finally reached a path well out of sight of the beach Leo stood up, brushed himself off, and checked out the condition of his suit. A few grass stains, but nothing too drastic. Topo collapsed at his feet.

'Does she know you're telling me this,' asked Leo.

'Naw, I don't think so.'

He knew what Leo was thinking, and fearing. The hotel belonged to Marta and they both knew what her reaction would be to Leo Pizzola entering her restaurant. Since his return, Leo and Marta had kept their distance – like two animals who spied each other from across a plain and then watched tensely, almost daring the other to make a move. The thought of walking into her restaurant filled him with dread. He knew she had not forgiven him. She would never forgive him. But this tour bus held a potential for money and every day money became more critical.

Selling his father's farm hadn't been as easy as expected. Leo's plan had been for a quick trip back to Santo Fico, a quick sale, and an even quicker return to America. Instead he had watched his savings disappear in an assortment of airline terminals, train stations, bus depots, and bars – too many bars. He'd spent money for newspaper ads in Follonica and Orbetello. He'd paid ridiculous fees to real estate brokers in Grosseto and Siena. The reasons they all gave for why there was no interest in his 'OCEANFRONT TUSCAN ACREAGE W/ORCHARDS, VINEYARDS, VILLA' were as varied as the people who were willing to take his money. Some said it was too run-down. Some said Leo was asking too much. Others said the season had passed or the season hadn't arrived or his ad wasn't big enough. But they all agreed on one thing – it was too damn inaccessible. One had used the word *godforsaken*. Unless something changed quickly, Leo knew he could end up trapped in Santo Fico again – this time maybe forever. Money was the answer and to escape Santo Fico he would face a hell of a lot worse than the wrath of Marta Caproni Fortino.

'Tell me about the guide.'

Topo was still collapsed on the grass. 'He's a *pazzo*. He knows nothing. He asked Marta if there was anything of interest to see.'

Leo held his breath. 'And?'

'She said, "Not really".'

Leo laughed out loud. If Marta knew that that was exactly what he would have begged her to say, she'd never forgive herself. A thought struck him.

'Americans?'

'Could be. But I think maybe English.'

Leo's enthusiasm sagged slightly. He would like to talk to some Americans again. They could have talked about baseball. Here it was August and he had no idea how the Cubs were doing.

He shrugged and sighed, 'We should hurry.'

As they quick-walked back up the trail Leo tried to remember his lines. It had been years since he'd spoken them or even thought about them – but he knew they were still there, somewhere just slightly out of reach in that murky Italian haze near the back of his brain. Leo rubbed his three-day stubble and toyed with the idea of a quick stop at the shepherd's hut for a shave. No time. This would have to do. He optimistically brushed his suit and straightened his lime green tie. Wasn't it amazing that for some extraordinary reason earlier in the morning, on some whim, he'd decided to wear his suit? What good fortune. Some people are just born under a lucky star.

Back at the water's edge, Angelica Giancarlo stood by the smooth boulder clutching her towel and watched Leo Pizzola's white straw hat disappear up the trail. She sighed and dried her hair. There was a time when she had no problems holding an audience.

Four

The atmosphere in the kitchen of the Albergo di Santo Fico was charged. The counters were quickly filling with trays piled with plums, grapes, and sliced melons. At the large island stove in the center of the room, a great copper pot of water boiled frantically, as if it were running out of time. Simmering next to it were two sauce pots, one filled with a deep red sauce and the other a creamy white – both bubbling like primordial Tuscan magma. Next to these, a broad copper skillet held a brushing of olive oil and some diced garlic that hissed and snapped as it browned. Stacked inside the ovens were trays of sole and shrimp, chicken and sausage, each tray waiting for its own bath of steaming sauce. All these preparations filled the kitchen with incredible combinations of aromas that crept out into the dining room and set English stomachs grumbling and English mouths watering in anticipation.

Marta stood at the sink and sliced pears into a huge earthen bowl that was already filled with leafy *ruchetta*, walnuts, and chunks of feta. It was almost ready for the vinaigrette. Carmen was stationed beside her, slicing cheeses, salami, and radishes and then loading them onto antipasti trays next to near perfect rows of olives, peppers, and tiny yellow tomatoes. Across the room, Nina, Marta's younger daughter, having returned from the *panetteria*, now stood at a great wooden cutting board deftly slicing long loaves of fresh bread before piling them into small straw baskets.

The women worked silently, except for Nina's soft humming of a melody that only she heard. She loved working in the kitchen, especially on those rare days when they were impossibly busy – like today. Her older sister, on the other hand, considered this just another penalty of her loathsome and meaningless existence in Santo Fico and she filed it away as just one more stupid routine to someday escape. Marta didn't have time to think about it one way or the other. Like everything else in her life, it simply was. She moved quickly over to the island and stirred her locally famous red sauce with a wooden spoon. It was time. Pouring some olive oil in the great copper pot of boiling water Marta began working in handfuls of brittle pasta.

'We need the bread on the tables.'

Nina's hands darted around the large tray in front of her as she quickly counted baskets. There were enough. 'I'm ready,' she replied, trying to hide her excitement. She loved serving when the dining room was crowded. She nimbly carried the tray of breadbaskets through the swinging door.

A moment later Marta called over her shoulder to Carmen, 'Why don't you go in and see if they need more wine . . . And see how many gawkers have shown up who want lunch . . . And tell your sister that Uncle Elio's basket is almost ready.'

Carmen knew why her mother wanted her in the dining room. She wanted to make sure nobody said anything cruel to Nina. It was silly. None of these people would do that – they were English. Still, at least it gave her a chance to stop slicing vegetables.

When Nina carried her tray of bread into the dining room, it wasn't as if all conversation suddenly stopped. A general murmur did continue, but intermingled with it was the occasional soft but audible gasp as one guest after another beheld the young girl. First of all, it should be said that for fifteen Nina was uncommonly tall. Not as tall as her mother, but at least as tall as Carmen. She also had the silky, raven black hair of the Fortino women. But that was where the family resemblance ended. Nina was, well . . . Nina was a swan. Although her slender, graceful figure already hinted at womanhood, it was obvious that she would forever possess the body of a ballerina about to go on pointe. In truth, more than a few of the older English women who gazed at her long, graceful neck and her high cheek bones and narrow nose recalled a classic, enchanting face they'd seen delicately carved on some ancient cameo worn by their grandmother in a previous century. Indeed, this shy and unassuming serving girl would look quite at home fashioned in alabaster or milky porcelain.

But it was only when Nina crossed the room with slow and deliberate steps, and then stood at each table to serve them their basket of fresh bread, that the strangers discovered Nina's most remarkable feature. It was then that they could gaze into the most beautiful blue eyes any of them had ever beheld. Nina's remarkable eyes captured the color of a spring sky, only more distant; the color of the Aegean Sea, only deeper; the chilling watery blue of ice, only colder. But it was only as her hand nimbly crept around the tray searching out the next straw basket that they realized for sure that these remarkable eyes were sightless. Their initial reaction was shock, then embarrassment for themselves, and finally some vague anger at God for this profound injustice. Many found themselves politely thanking the cheerful girl with a catch in their throats.

Nina noticed the change in the attitude of the room, of course, but she just attributed it to the welcome arrival of the bread. She found everyone to be quite pleasant and courteous, and as she chatted carelessly with this latest bunch of strangers in a beautiful language they didn't understand, her voice was like music. Occasionally her laugh would ring like a small country bell and soon they all relaxed and resumed their conversations, secure in a quiet appreciation that they had experienced a blessing. Nina affected everyone that way, including her family.

By the time Carmen came in from the kitchen, the dining room had pretty much returned to normal. She counted heads as she walked across a room that was slowly filling with shy but inquisitive locals who came to see the curiosity – foreigners! And to her amazement almost all the locals actually ordered something; many even ordered a full lunch. This was going to be a good day. It took her a few minutes at the bar exchanging pleasantries with neighbors and pouring wine before she could take the large bottle of Chianti and move on to the tables. She carefully checked their small earthen pitchers to see if any required more wine, and through a series of gestures and noises (she, of course, spoke no English and the visitors grasped little Italian) she determined whether they wanted more. Carmen was unusually astute at keeping an exact tally of which table had how many small pitchers. It would be so easy to overcharge the silly foreigners who were always sleepy and slightly groggy after lunch, but if her mother ever caught her cheating a customer she would filet her like a carp.

Carmen moved past Nina as she finished bestowing her baskets of bread.

'Mama says Uncle Elio's lunch is ready.'

Nina's expression fell. Lunch with Uncle Elio was usually the highlight of most days, but not today. She loved the sounds of all the foreign voices, and the excitement, and the jostling of the crowded dining room. But her expression brightened again when she realized that if she hurried with

Uncle Elio, she could be back in time to help serve dessert. That was her favorite course anyway because everyone was always so happy and friendly at the end of one of her mother's lunches. So with a quick nod in Carmen's direction she headed for the kitchen.

By the time they had reached the coast road, Topo just wanted to get back to town without having a heart attack. So he sat on a rock at the side of the road and called up the hill to Leo, 'Hey . . . Wait a second!'

When Leo stopped, Topo waved, vainly trying to motion him back. But Leo knew what Topo wanted and he considered ignoring his old friend and just continuing on. He certainly wasn't going to walk all the way back down the hill only to haggle about money, so he simply called to the small figure plopped down on the rock, 'Ten percent!'

Topo was outraged. 'Fifty-fifty!'

This was no contest. Leo didn't have to give him anything and called to him again, 'Fifteen percent, or nothing!'

'Forty percent! You wouldn't even know there was a bus if it weren't for me!'

'Twenty percent. Or maybe you want to do it yourself.'

'Maybe I will. It's not so hard.'

'Well, come on! You do it. I want to hear you do it! In English!'

English . . . *Merda!*

Topo was dead. Even in Italian, nobody in the village could do it as well as Leo. Even Father Elio couldn't do it as well as Leo. Franco Fortino, maybe, but that was a long time

ago, and never in English, and besides, Franco was dead.
Topo tried one more desperate plea – his big gun.

'Come on, Leo. Thirty percent! Be fair!'

Leo's heart sank. He should have known it would come
down to 'Be fair.' In an instant they were nine years old
again – Leo was farther up the trail, Topo was left behind
with tears streaming down his dirty cheeks, demanding that
life, 'Be fair.' The only things missing were Franco Fortino
and Marta Caproni standing at Leo's side, chuckling at poor
Topo's grief.

'Twenty-five percent, Topo, and that's it. One more word
and you get nothing.'

Topo threw up his hands. After his patented plea for fair-
ness he knew twenty-five percent was as good as he was
going to get, and actually a little better than he'd hoped.

Leo started back up the trail, but after just a few steps he
called back to the little man, 'You okay?'

Topo nodded and gestured for Leo to go on. After all,
time was money.

Word spreads quickly through a village like Santo Fico. By
the time the breadbaskets were empty and the antipasti trays
were picked over, the hotel's dining room had filled with
curious townspeople either crowding up to the bar or quietly
elbowing into shadowed corners to gape at the strangers.
The air had become thick with a murmuring tension. The
exhausted tourists felt trapped at their tables on one side of
the room, staring uncomfortably at their tablecloths and
hands, while barricaded around them an invading army of

silent villagers stared at the uneasy foreigners with unabashed wonder. Occasionally, Carmen was forced to cross the hushed room with fresh supplies of wine or bread, and the sound of her shoes echoed off the tile floor like rifle shots. Even someone clearing his throat resounded like a mortar blast.

Finally, to the great relief of the English tourists, whose inborn sense of etiquette had been strained to the limit, the kitchen doors swung open and Marta charged out with steaming bowls and platters. Carmen quickly followed with fresh baskets of fettunta. Saved! In a matter of minutes, plates of tender pasta smothered with chunks of sole and shrimp swimming in creamy white sauce or red marinara with chicken and sausage, had effected a truce. All uneasiness quickly evaporated and both camps, the aliens and the natives, were soon chatting away gaily — within their respective ranks, of course.

As Leo crossed the piazza, he heard voices coming through the open verandah doors of the hotel dining room. He decided he had time to catch his breath and count his obstacles, so he sat down on the edge of the fountain just across from the old man and the skinny gray dog. The guide, of course, was an unknown factor, but Topo had called him a pazzo and he would just have to go with that. A more difficult matter would be trying to finesse the pazzo in Marta's hotel. He imagined the way Marta might treat him. She might throw a water pitcher at his head. It wouldn't be the first time. She might scream at him, point to the door and order him back out to the street like a naughty dog. She could make things complicated. His thoughts lingered on Marta for too long, remembering the disaster six weeks ago when he first returned to Santo Fico . . .

It was a long walk down the north coast road from Punta Ala. Exhausted from jet lag and bus rides and the weight of his battered suitcase, all Leo wanted was to get to Topo's house without running into anyone he knew – especially Marta Caproni Fortino. So, it stands to reason that the first person he should run into as soon as he set foot in the piazza was Marta.

It was a little after noon when Leo trudged into the piazza, just as Marta was lugging a large basket from the hotel to the church. Leo knew her immediately. But from across the square, Marta failed to recognize the tall stranger with the cardboard suitcase held together with tape and twine. He was just some outsider with a black mustache and a rumpled linen suit plodding into town, and she wondered if he would need a room. He certainly could use a bath and a shave, she thought. His long face and broken nose were familiar, but there was something about this fellow's sorrowful eyes and the way he watched her with a familiarity that was unsettling.

When it suddenly struck Marta that this was Leo Pizzola staring back at her she shrieked as if he were a ghost. She dropped her food basket right there in the street. Soup and bread, fruits and cheese, a pitcher of wine, plates and bowls, it all dropped and slopped and crashed onto the worn cobblestones.

'What are you doing coming back here?' Marta had screamed out across the cold stones of the piazza. 'You don't belong here . . . !'

Her voice bounced off the plaster walls and echoed off the red-tile roofs and proclaimed her indignation to the countryside. Leo stood in silence, offering no apology for his return. Tears welled up so quickly and so unexpectedly, Marta barely had time to run back into the hotel; abandoning the clutter that was to have been Father Elio's lunch.

Leo had hoped to sneak back, take care of his business, and then quietly disappear. He was going to be the shadow of a starling – gone before you see it. Instead he had been in Santo Fico less than two minutes and had already caused a mess in the town square, frightened a woman to tears, been cursed to the surrounding hills, and caused the village priest to probably miss his lunch. But at least one nagging question had been answered – Marta had not forgiven him.

Now here Leo was, six weeks later, once again wearing his linen suit and again wondering why the hell he ever thought coming home was a good idea.

'You know what time it is, Nico?'

The voice came from the opposite side of the fountain and it belonged to the old man whom everyone called Nonno. No response was necessary and so Leo ignored the question, but, as expected, Nonno continued anyway.

'I lost my watch when I made the water go away.'

Like so many old people who dress more out of habit than season, even in this summer heat Nonno endured a frayed coat draped over his bony frame and his tattered slouch hat still managed a jaunty angle. For as long as Leo could recall, he remembered Nonno sitting on the edge of the dry fountain. A confirmed eccentric, the old guy was always oddly selective in whom he chose to warm up to. Some people Nonno seemed to invariably regard with a mysterious affection and he sought them out whether they wanted it or not. Others, he would inexplicably shout at from across the piazza, calling them a 'Fascist' or a 'Nazi' or just ordering them to go to hell. Even as a boy, Leo had always fallen into that former category. Only now, since his return, for some strange reason, the old man had taken to calling him Nico.

Someone leaving the back of the hotel distracted them and Leo recognized the gracefully hesitant step of Nina Fortino carrying a basket of food across the piazza. He watched her softly count her way across the square to the church where she floated up the steps and disappeared inside. She was obviously carrying lunch to her great-uncle, Father Elio – which brought to mind another situation that Leo hadn't considered.

He not only had to face Marta in her own hotel and remember how to tell the stories of the Mystery and the Miracle in English – he also had to get Father Elio's permission. Leo seriously considered forgetting the whole thing and going back to the beach. Maybe Angelica would still be there, gliding and turning in the cool blue water. What was he doing trying to work a scam that he and Franco came up with when they were, what . . . twelve?

From the dining room, one of the English tourists must have said something amusing because laughter poured out the open doors and echoed around the piazza. There was a time, Leo recalled, when he was welcomed into restaurants filled with laughter and good-natured friends. Since his return to Santo Fico he'd lived like an outcast. Nowadays when he approached groups of people, conversation stopped. With the exception of Topo, no one visited his stone cell down by the sea and Leo certainly wasn't invited into anyone's home.

'Do you know what time it is, Nico?'

Leo looked over and discovered that Nonno had casually scooted himself around the edge of the fountain until he had finally arrived at Leo's elbow.

'No.'

'I lost my watch when the water went away.'

Leo nodded as if he understood. Nonno's constant companion, the skinny gray dog, joined them and plopped himself down at their feet.

'I made the water go away,' was the old man's whispered confession.

Leo nodded again, 'I know, Nonno.' But he wasn't really listening.

'I shouldn't have done it.'

'Some things we can't undo,' sighed Leo, still lost in his own regret.

The old man nodded and mumbled his agreement, 'Some things we just have to live with, I guess.'

Leo considered the truth of these last statements and nodded absently, 'I guess.'

It was true.

Leo rose and brushed himself off. He smoothed his thick mustache and recocked his hat at a rakish angle. He straightened his lime green tie, adjusted his pale yellow pocket hankie, and pointlessly polished each worn shoe on the back of an opposing pant leg.

'Wish me luck,' and he gave Nonno a quick wink.

'Sure, Nico. Why not? You're a handsome boy. All the girls will think they love you.'

Leo chuckled to himself at the old man's chatter. With Nonno, it was the thought that counted – although he did occasionally wonder who the hell Nico was.

Then Leo Pizzola marched resolutely across the piazza and walked right through the open front doors of the Albergo di Santo Fico for the first time in eighteen years.

Five

When the tour guide saw the tall fellow in a dirty linen suit saunter in and stand quietly in the shadows of the lobby, discreetly surveying the dining room, he knew immediately that there was something about this guy he didn't like – and it wasn't just his cheap suit. This guy wasn't some farmer, or sheepherder, or fisherman. The calculating way Leo inspected the room indicated a brain and a purpose. Besides, that broken nose looked earned.

And the guide wasn't the only one who noticed Leo's entrance – Carmen saw him the second he stepped in the doorway. Standing in the lobby was bad enough, but now

Leo Pizzola was actually daring to enter the restaurant and catastrophe was only as far away as her mother's entrance from the kitchen.

Certainly all the natives of Santo Fico noticed Leo and his disheveled linen suit, and a thrilling anticipation of something dreadful seized them. 'My God,' they all thought, 'Leo Pizzola is walking into Marta Fortino's hotel, in broad daylight!' This scandalous event promised a disastrous showdown – and they had ringside seats!

Fortunately for Leo, the English were too involved in their meals to notice all the elbow nudgings and head jerkings that accompanied his entrance as he strolled to a place at the bar right against the tour guide's elbow. They exchanged strained smiles and Leo watched the sweaty guide struggle to nonchalantly focus his attention back onto his lunch. How perceptive of Topo, he thought. This guy is a pazzo.

A glass of water suddenly pounded onto the marble counter in front of him and Carmen Fortino spoke to Leo for the first time in her life.

'What are you doing here?' she hissed.

Leo considered the glass of water she was offering and wondered if she intended him to drink it or wear it. He didn't know this older daughter of his dead best friend. Topo had pointed her out to him, of course – and her sister Nina too. He'd occasionally noticed her watching him from across the piazza or from behind a window, but he always tried to hide how much she fascinated him. It was like seeing her mother and yet at the same time it was also like seeing Franco – very strange. Now, facing her at the bar, he had to smile because he could see that her ferocity was still being learned. It didn't have the depth and lethal passion of her mother's. She was just a girl.

Out of the corner of his eye Leo caught the guide's leering smirk as he reacted to Carmen's presence – so Leo spoke what was on both their minds.

'Isn't she beautiful.'

His voice was soft and sincere and it wasn't a question, but a statement – he meant it. Carmen flushed and fought to smother an embarrassed smile. After six weeks of mystery, to now have such an excellent compliment be the first thing this notorious man said to her left the poor girl completely flustered. This was not the response she'd expected from this man her mother hated so perfectly; this stranger who had once been her father's best friend; this scoundrel who had somehow betrayed everyone. All her life she'd heard rumors of the exploits of her father and his comrade, Leo Pizzola, and about their sudden bad blood, and Leo's mysterious disappearance on the day of her mother's wedding. There had been a fight, and rumors of a robbery, and years of anger. It was all quite mysterious – and very romantic.

Leo nudged the oily stranger on his left as if they were old friends and pointed to Carmen.

'Beautiful . . . huh?'

The guide smiled awkwardly and a bit of white sauce dripped from his lip. He grunted agreement and grinned seductively in Carmen's direction.

She glared at Leo with all of her strength and tried to ignore his forlorn eyes and gentle smile. She heard herself

say harshly, 'You shouldn't be here.' But what she meant to
say was: 'Tell me about my father! Tell me why your name
makes my mother cry! Tell me about America! And tell me
how I can escape too!'

Leo downed the water without stopping. Then he put
down the glass and met Carmen's gaze.

'Where's your mama?'

'In the kitchen, but she'll be coming out here—'

Leo stopped her with a casual wave of the hand. 'Don't
bother her. I'll see her later. Could I have a glass of wine and
a refill for our guest here? My treat.'

What on earth was he talking about? Was he crazy?
Carmen was trying to offer a warning and he was acting
like he belonged here; like he owned the place.

In fact, Leo just wanted her to leave before she said anything more. He couldn't have this little girl challenge him in
front of the plump *raviolo* on the adjoining stool. Any talk of
Marta could only be dangerous.

When Carmen went off to get the wine, Leo nudged his
neighbor, 'She likes you.'

The guide almost choked again, this time on a combination of *fettunta* and shock.

'I don't think so.'

'I saw the way she ignored you.'

Leo watched a spark of fantasy ignite in the back of what
was probably the guide's tiny brain.

'You think so . . .?'

By the time Carmen returned with their wine, Leo and the
guide were laughing like old friends. And, as if that wasn't

bad enough, when she set the glasses down in front of them, the greasy guide smiled shamelessly at her and then, worst of all, he winked! She determined – For that insolence, he would pay.

Leo didn't care. Carmen had been a hurdle, but he'd bought a bit of time. And in less than two minutes he could tell that this pazzo would keep his group in Santo Fico for a week if he thought he had a chance with Carmen.

As Leo prattled and joked with the guide at the bar, his attention was actually tuned in on an interesting conversation coming from a small table near the verandah. A bony Englishman with a wild shock of salt-and-pepper hair and too many teeth was posing an interesting question to two older women who might have been his sisters, but undoubtedly weren't. The combination of food and wine, and their confidence in their alien language, had allowed the conversation an indiscreet boldness.

'It's really quite odd, if one stops to consider. I mean – Why? Every unlikely and inhospitable bend in the road seems to present these little villages that don't have any apparent, you know, reason for existing.'

Both women nodded in agreement. One sipped more wine, while the other added loudly, 'And it seems the more treacherous and uninviting the terrain the better. Hang them off the side of some cliff or perch them on some mountain-top, or something equally nonsensical. It makes you wonder what on earth those original peasants, I mean the . . . what-do-you-call-its . . . eh, founders of these little clusters were thinking.'

'Or drinking,' piped in her tipsy friend. The three joined in a laugh, and adjacent tables chuckled their agreement.

Perfect, thought Leo. Their conversation was just a bit too loud and with just enough mockery to embarrass them if they discovered they were actually being understood. Not only that, but the table was strategically placed so that all the tourists in the room could witness, and even be included in, their humiliation. And best of all, the table was occupied by a man and two women. Leo would approach the man first. That would be proper – a gentleman addressing a gentleman. But after a few moments he would shift his focus to the women and then to the whole room.

Leo abruptly left the bar and crossed the room to the table. He deliberately cleared his throat, bowed slightly, and spoke in excellent English overlaid with a charming accent and just a bit too loud.

'Excuse'a me. I could'a not help but'a overhear your conversation.'

'I . . . I beg your . . . your pardon,' sputtered the poor fellow, choking more on the moment than his lunch.

'I heard'a what you said about'a our town.'

The room instantly became as quiet as the proverbial tomb. Indeed, at that moment many English souls may have wished they were in their tombs and the expression of horrified mortification on the faces of the horsy-looking trio at the table told Leo that he had probably come off a bit less charming than he'd intended. In fact, what he saw was fear. He'd been told all this life that he sometimes affected people that way – it had something to do with his smile being too much of a sneer and his close-set brown eyes looking vaguely dangerous. The scar across his broken nose didn't help either. But it was all purely unintentional – he truly meant to be charming.

Now, all around the room, he recognized that same anxious reaction as English minds raced, straining to recall what they too might have said that may have been offensive. English eyes darted around the edges of the crowd, studied the weathered faces and rough farmer hands, the provincial clothes and the innocent stares – how many more of these enigmatic Italian peasants secretly spoke their language?

Then there was this tall, dark fellow standing at their table. To the English, Leo looked like he might be willing to hurt someone. Stories about hot-tempered Italians with their exaggerated masculinity, their fierce national pride, and their knives were common knowledge. Their congenial lunchroom had suddenly become uncomfortable and frightfully awkward.

'You all wonder why this'a village even exists at'a all.'

How mortifying to be overheard insulting their village. Still, the question was a fair one. Why would anyone choose such a remote and inaccessible promontory – surrounded on three sides by steep climbs of cactus and rocks and on a fourth by jagged sea cliffs – to build a town? Who, in their right mind, would ever build a village in such an insane place? It was all like some master builder's mistake – and it was.

One summer day in 1555, shortly after conquering his rival city-state, Siena, after a terrible two-year siege, Cosimo I de Medici, the Duke of Firenze, was playing with his children in one of the smaller fountains of the Boboli Gardens when a minister approached with some maps. The Grand Duke knew he had decisions to make about his new holdings in Toscana, but playtime with his children was rare. The minister pressed the point – if he would just decide where they should invest their efforts for a defensible port.

Whether the error was due to Cosimo's refusal to forgo his game of tag or bad eyesight or because he momentarily couldn't remember the name of the correct town – his finger slammed down on a spot on the map with a decisive, 'There!' To the minister's surprise the wet fingerprint was on the tiny promontory of Santo Fico. To the best of his knowledge all that was there was an insignificant monastery, and the befuddled minister politely pointed out that there were probably no reasonable roads to that spot.

'Well, there should be,' roared Cosimo as he leapt back in the fountain. 'And make it a fit place for my family. We want to summer there.' Then his wife, Eleonora, who was watching from the shade of a lime tree and whom he loved, teased him about the gray in his beard – and the splashing and laughter began again. So, without further protest, the adviser went off to write notes for the creation of a port, and a road, and a summer villa at . . . Santo Fico.

On that clean, warm morning neither the minister nor the Grand Duke realized his hurried finger thump missed the intended mark by a full two inches. But there was a day some years later when, exhausted with intrigues and worried about a war with France and an uneasy alliance with Spain, Cosimo requested a particular architect be sent to Livorno to inspect the harbor fortifications. When he was informed that the architect was unavailable because he was in Santo Fico picking mosaic patterns for the villa, Cosimo's reaction was unexpectedly confused.

'Where?'

'Santo Fico, sire.'

'Where the hell's Santo Fico?'

No matter how hard his memory was jogged, the great Duke could not remember giving any orders to build a road, or a port, or a summer villa 'on some godforsaken crag, on a totally useless stretch of Tuscan coast!'

On that day his irritation quickly turned to rage when he discovered that this project had been going on for three years. And he became almost homicidal when he was told how much had already been spent on one misdirected finger. Work would stop immediately. Buildings would be deserted before completion; roads abandoned before they could be widened or even arrive at a destination. But it would all be too late, because even as Cosimo canceled his orders, his little mistake by the western sea was already a reality. Destiny had decreed a small port with a fine road up to what might have been an excellent little cathedral, the beginnings of a handsome villa, and almost a road to the outside world . . . and houses, and people, and a village called Santo Fico.

Of course, Leo Pizzola knew nothing about Cosimo's inability to read maps. And even if he had he wouldn't have mentioned it, because his version served his purposes better. There's a time for facts and a time for stories. So, Leo let his observation 'You all wonder why this'a village even exists at'a all' hang like a shroud over the room, and he waited and tried out a couple of different smiles – hopefully something a bit less threatening.

At last the flustered Englishman he'd approached sputtered painfully for an apology and to his surprise, instead of pulling a knife, this dangerous-looking Italian stranger presented a generous smile.

'No, no. Please'a, do not apologize. You are quite'a correct. It is'a most odd for many of the villages in this region. Many times we also ask'a ourselves, how come?' And he threw his hands up with an exaggerated shrug and a laugh.

All of the relieved English visitors joined him in his joke as they realized his intention was not to brawl or even to rebuke. He was actually being congenial and the fact that he spoke English implied that if he wasn't completely cultured, at least he was civilized – and even possibly semi-literate. He was, after all, wearing a suit and tie – such as they were.

They quickly asked him to join their table, and just as quickly Leo declined. He wasn't about to give up his command position at center stage. He did, however, graciously accept their offer of some wine, and then right on cue someone at another table asked where he had learned such wonderful English. Leo explained about his years in America. He was disappointed that none of his audience had been to Chicago or knew anything about baseball, but he quickly reasoned that although talk of Chicago and baseball would be wonderful, it would only distract from his greater purpose. Business was business.

The older villagers had guessed where all this was leading when Leo had entered the room and it made them proud to see one of their own socializing with this battalion of strangers – even though they had no idea what was being said. Leo was speaking for them all and proving that they were smart and worldly and had good manners and some even wore linen suits and ties. Really, the only person having any problem right now was the guide. He was wondering why, if Carmen liked him so much, had she just poured a small pitcher of Chianti in his lap?

Leo addressed the crowd.

'I did not mean to interrupt'a your lunch, but I thought'a your question was a good one. Why? Why Santo Fico? Why here? Well, the answer is'a strange. It happened a long time ago, hundreds of 'a years. It is, in fact, a sort of . . . magical story about faith and blessed saints, and noblemen, and wars, and miracles . . . If you would'a like to hear . . .?'

The response was unanimous and sincere. Not only was this pleasantly disheveled character not going to make trouble, he was actually offering them a marvelous diversion – a history of the region.

Amid this hail of approval, Topo made his way to the last empty stool at the bar and gave Leo a quick wink and thumbs-up. It was just an instant of recognition, but Carmen noticed it and recalled how Topo had raced out of the hotel earlier. Something was going on and she didn't like it. Leo watched Carmen make her way toward the kitchen door and thought – Oh God, she's going to tell Marta. But there was nothing he could do now, as the room was already hushed in anticipation. Leo closed his eyes, took a deep breath, and became strangely distant – as if he was recalling some blurred memory.

'It was'a over four hundred years ago . . . this month. The great Cosimo de Medici was the Duke of Firenze, what-you-call . . . Florence. It was a time when Firenze was at war with the great city of Siena. Now, this'a war lasted many years and like all terrible wars, it was the cause of many regrets, many tragedies, and even a few miracles . . .'

Leo moved through the room, weaving a stirring tale of how the courageous Duke Cosimo was a flame that lit the fire of the final terrible battle of Siena. He described how Cosimo's exhausted troops, so far from their home and for so long chancing death, grew discouraged as, day after day, they threw their bodies against the stubborn walls of Siena. Leo thrilled them with his account of how, on one fateful day, astride his valiant white stallion, Cosimo inspired his forces with a heroic speech – though more than a few in this English audience found it surprisingly similar to Henry the Fifth's call to arms before the battle of Agincourt.

Leo described how Cosimo recklessly charged his proud horse ahead of his troops and, brandishing his broadsword as if it were a dagger, fought back the startled defenders. The hearts of the listeners pounded when Leo, as if he had been a witness to the fateful moment, described how a lone archer shooting from a distant tower loosed a shaft that caught the great Cosimo full in the chest.

Neither breath nor breeze dared to stir; all were captured by the mortal plight of the great Duke in the very city that they had visited just one day earlier. Many found it amazing that in their time in Siena not one tour or guidebook mentioned any of this wonderful history. Even the local villagers, who didn't understand a word of what Leo said, still recognized a few things – they knew he spoke of the great Duke Cosimo, they knew he spoke of Siena and probably a great battle, and they were sure he was telling a wonderful story extremely well.

Leo's voice became an emotional whisper when he told how Cosimo's officers carried their beloved Duke to the Siena Duomo and gently laid his dying body on the black and white marble floor beneath the great dome, so he could receive the last rites. But with a wounded gasp the noble Duke abruptly stopped them—

– And Leo also abruptly stopped.

From the back of the dining room two dark eyes burned into him like black firebolts. Without warning, Leo was facing the glare of Marta Caproni Fortino, and he knew instantly from the set of her jaw and the curve of her brow that her quiet fury was profound. Like a frozen Medusa, lightning shot from her dark eyes, seared his brain, and for a moment he was turned to stone. His words became like dazed soldiers who stumbled into one another as they scrambled to rediscover their place in the line of his story, but mostly he was just drowning in her sea of fury. As an Italian, Leo understood Marta's seething rage – but he'd been living in America for so long that he was unused to it. Americans have never learned what the Italians have perfected — that is, the value of full-blown, for-all-the-world-to-see Righteous Indignation. And because, at that moment, Marta was boiling over with it, Leo was almost knocked to his knees by its full force.

Meanwhile, his rapt English audience was oblivious to his dilemma. In fact, most found Leo's hesitation poignantly dramatic. The poor man was obviously quite moved by Duke Cosimo's plight. On the other hand, the moment was not lost for the natives of Santo Fico. They were silent witnesses to an intense battle of wills that was both frightening and fascinating.

Finally, when the tension between the two contenders was pushed so far that half the room was ready to scream at them to stop and the other half was ready to scream at him for the end of the story — Marta blinked. Then she sighed. She would allow him to continue.

For his part, Leo recovered as deftly as a cat that had slipped from a table. He knew exactly where he was in his improbable fiction, and like any great actor, he knew just exactly how to turn this awkward moment to his advantage. He simply began his description of the dying Duke's last wish with a slight catch in his voice — and suddenly that long pause, which had actually only been a few seconds, took on a whole new meaning. This sensitive storyteller had needed that moment to master his emotions — and in a twinkling, Leo was rolling again as the tragedy of poor Duke Cosimo continued to unfold. He was so relieved that he even allowed himself a fleeting smugness that he was so much better at this than he was at hanging drywall.

Marta, of course, knew nothing about his years in Chicago hanging drywall (whatever that was). She was only thinking, How dare he do this in my hotel? How dare he wait until my restaurant is crowded with customers and then play his childish scheme?

Although none of the townspeople were foolish enough to openly stare at her, Marta could feel their eyes nonetheless, and so with a practiced response that she was no longer even aware of, she automatically closed off her heart and her mind to any feeling. She allowed nothing in and nothing was allowed to escape, because she knew what they were waiting for, what they wanted – and she was pleased that they would not get it today. This was not the day she would confront Leo Pizzola. Besides, too much of her life had already been a topic for their gossip. Too many times her grief had become nothing more than another whispered scandal or exaggerated rumor for the amusement of her neighbors. They acted as though they understood her life better than she did – and perhaps they did. They certainly knew enough secrets about her and Franco, and maybe even Leo too. But there would be no show for their amusement today – not unless Leo Pizzola cost her business. Then she would pound him like a cheap steak and she didn't care who saw.

As for the English audience, they fully expected to hear about Duke Cosimo's last moments on this earth, but it seemed he had another destiny . . .

'Like everyone in'a those days, the Great Duke had heard the tales of the tiny monastery hidden somewhere on'a the coast of Toscana. This monastery was'a built because so many miracles happened on that spot, and according to legend, a certain, powerful miracle still lived there – along with a wonderful'a mystery. And Cosimo sensed that if he could'a only stay alive long enough to get to that blessed site, he might'a yet live.'

Leo told his enthralled audience how a devoted squad of anxious soldiers rode for three days through the heat of the Toscana summer while the poor man's life teetered between this world and the next. Finally they arrived at the blue Tyrrhenian and climbed the steep cliff crags to a tiny, almost inaccessible monastery perched on the farthest point of a sheer promontory.

'When the humble Franciscan monks saw the Great Duke, of course they took'a him in and gently laid his'a weak body on a cot in front of their hallowed shrine – the Miracle of Santo Fico. But poor Duke Cosimo, even in his'a feverish state, he was able to look across the courtyard and'a there, shining out of the darkness, as if it had'a some Inner Light, was the Mystery of Santo Fico. And all through that long night, with the divine Miracle on'a one side and the beautiful Mystery of Santo Fico on'a the other, the holy friars held their vigils with prayers and secret medicines.

'Can'a you even imagine,' Leo sighed, 'how shocked those loyal soldiers must'a have been when they came into the church in'a the morning and found that their Duke's fever was all gone and the infection of his wound was'a healed? He would live! Well, maybe that was'a miracle enough for his soldiers, but not for a Great'a Duke who had

just returned from the brink of 'a death with . . . a vision!'
With a sense of quiet wonder and awe Leo told them how
the blessed Saint Francis had come to Duke Cosimo in the
night and gently kissed his fevered brow and touched the
fatal wound. Leo allowed his voice to lift in exaltation as he
told of the Duke's resolve to create a town on that very
spot . . .

'. . . So weary pilgrims from around 'a the world, like
yourselves, could come and witness the shrine of the Miracle
and the splendor of the Mystery of Santo Fico. And that
was 'a how Santo Fico came 'a to be.'

The room was silent for a long time. To Leo's way of
thinking, perhaps too long. After all, he hadn't told the story
in many years, and never in English. He may have lost his
touch. But, at last, a universal sigh was expelled. Then someone was inspired to applaud (actually it was Topo) and the
ovation quickly became enthusiastic. Leo smiled and offered
a modest bow – quite pleased with how much he'd remembered of the original version and also how many poignant
details he had been able to fabricate on the spot.

There wasn't a lot of time to bask in the afterglow. He
caught a glimpse of Marta marching in his direction so he
hurried back to the bar – away from his fans. Carmen was
refilling his wineglass when suddenly her mother was at her
shoulder, and it took only the slightest jerk of Marta's head
to make her daughter disappear.

Marta looked Leo up and down – this would not be like
their first meeting in the piazza six weeks ago when she'd
been so shocked at seeing him. That day she hadn't been

prepared and her emotions had attacked her with a ferocity that she couldn't control. This was different. This time Leo was in her hotel and this time she was in control.

For the first time since his return, she had a chance to look closely into Leo's face. He'd changed. This was a man's face. There were more lines and more scars – probably from fights. The eyes were the same even with the wrinkles, but now the nose was broken in a different way and a jagged scar crossed the bridge. Marta wondered if she'd done that the night before her wedding when she had grabbed up a water pitcher from off the nightstand next to her bed and hurled it at him. She had intended for it to crash into the wall next to him, but in the darkness of the night and blinded by her own tears, she missed. The water pitcher smashed into Leo's face and knocked him backward out of her second-story bedroom window. He came to earth in the garden below, among the radishes . . . Marta remembered thinking he was lucky. He barely missed landing in the tomatoes where he would have been impaled on the stakes.

She had watched him from her window as he limped out of the moonlit garden holding his face . . . Eighteen years ago last month. That broken, scarred nose may have been her work, she thought – at least, she hoped it was.

For his part, Leo had never considered landing in the radishes a particularly lucky break. He often felt his life would have been so much simpler if he'd just landed on the tomato stakes and that thought occurred to him again as he too had a chance to study a face he hadn't been close to in eighteen years. The girl he grew up with was gone. It was a woman's face that stood before him now, but it still took his breath away. It was a face that should have been chiseled out of stone centuries ago and celebrated through the ages as beautiful. There had always been that beauty, Leo thought, but now there was something more. Around the corners of her dark eyes and taut mouth were the tracings of small wrinkles some people call laugh lines, but Leo had a feeling that they weren't caused by years of excessive joy. Marta had always been filled with a certain intense determination and there was no denying it was still there, but that wasn't all Leo saw today. He also recognized regret and resignation. He knew them because they were such old companions in his own life.

From his place at the bar, Topo prayed like a zealot that Marta wouldn't spoil everything – they were so close to success. Even now a few members of the English tour group were asking their guide questions and pointing at Leo. It was going perfectly, and now Marta was going to spoil everything because of some silly . . . What? Even he didn't know. He, Guido Pasolini, who'd been there eighteen years ago still wasn't sure what had happened to drive such a terrible wedge between his three best friends. He just knew that after the night of Franco's awful bachelor party he was never allowed to mention the name Leo Pizzola to Marta again. He'd discovered that much the next day at the wedding. Franco was angry too, of course, because of the fight in Grosseto the night before. But eventually Franco had let go of his anger. Once, when they were drunk and melancholy, Franco had even confessed to Topo that it had been his fault. Sometimes he and Franco would reminisce and wonder what Leo might be up to. They knew he was in America . . . somewhere, and they would occasionally pretend that someday they would get out of Santo Fico too. They would join Leo in America, just like they used to dream of doing when they were boys . . . someday. But they could never talk like that when Marta was around. When Marta was around, Leo's name was not to be mentioned. Neither Topo nor Franco ever knew about Leo standing at Marta's window the night before the wedding. She never told anyone. So, of course Topo didn't understand. He just knew that the English tourists were now talking among themselves and pointing at Leo and nodding. Sometimes Marta's bitterness made things damn inconvenient.

Leo and Marta continued to stare at each other in silence. Leo was waiting for Marta. It was her hotel, after all. But at that moment Marta was busy hating Leo's battered Panama hat, and his wrinkled suit, and his stupid mustache, and everything else about him. He looks ridiculous, she thought, in that shabby suit, with that ugly green tie, and that stupid yellow hankie – he looks like a faded Italian flag.

Marta called down the bar, 'Carmen, did he pay for this wine?'

'Yes, Mama,' Carmen lied without hesitation.

She eyed him for another moment. 'Nice suit.'

He nodded a bit too smugly, and for an instant thought he was about to get slapped as Marta's hand shot toward him. But, to his embarrassment, she merely pulled a long blade of razor grass out from under his coat lapel.

'What've you been doing, crawling through a field?'

His common sense argued with his panic – there was no way she could know about him crawling through the field! Leo struggled to control the nervous twitch at the corner of his mouth as Marta pressed on.

'Have you asked Uncle Elio about this?'

From the cloud of guilt that crossed Leo's expression, Marta read the answer. The idiot hadn't so much as spoken to Father Elio. He'd simply plowed ahead with this whole elaborate thing without having spoken even a word to the old priest.

'I didn't think so,' she chuckled mirthlessly – and Leo fought the image of Marta cackling with laughter as she gleefully shoveled dirt on his grave. In less than a minute and with about three short sentences, she had established her authority over him, identified a secret sin, and pointed out the major flaw in his scheme. The thought occurred to him that if it were only a hundred years earlier, he could have her burned as a witch, no problem. She was frighteningly correct about one thing though – there was a chance Father Elio wouldn't give his permission.

Fortunately for Leo, the guide was approaching and their exchange was to be cut short. Marta spoke quickly, biting her words under her breath.

'I know what you're doing and I don't like it. If I didn't have these people . . . I'd tell you how much! You've got two minutes, then you get the hell out of my hotel.' She turned smoothly and smiled to the guide just as he stepped up, 'Signore, the desserts are ready. Zabaglione and coffee. We'll bring them right out.'

'Good . . .'

And Marta disappeared into the kitchen without giving Leo another look.

The guide was delighted to hear about the desserts, but that wasn't why he'd come over.

'It seems that some people in my party liked your story.' He smiled broadly and quoted Leo, *The shrine of the Miracle and the splendor of the Mystery of Santo Fico* – That was good. These people, they're interested in seeing these sights . . . If you're not too busy . . . Maybe you could give them a personal tour?'

Leo's brow furrowed with concern. He rubbed his unshaven face wearily and sighed. 'This is difficult.'

The guide leaned in and whispered, 'I think they'd be willing to pay . . . Maybe a few hundred thousand lire?' and he encouraged Leo with a sly wink.

Leo raised himself to his full height of indignation (which was actually quite tall) and fixed the guide with a glare that struck the poor man with cold fear to his very bowels. It was obvious to everyone in the room that Leo was deciding whether or not to strike this impudent rascal. Those locals who remembered the wild days and the violence that often surrounded Leo and Franco recognized the potential seriousness of the guide's situation.

In truth, although Leo really didn't like this pazzo, his mind was racing. Until that moment he hadn't given any thought to exact figures. The guide's approach and subsequent proposal were, of course, expected, but now Leo was thankful for this moment of bluff because he had to do some fast calculating.

He glared at the round man like the great Duke Cosimo himself and frantically tried to work out the numbers in his head . . . *Twelve people . . . maybe 20,000 lire a head. That's, eh . . . 200,000 lire and . . . something. But, twenty-five percent to Topo, and another twenty-five percent to Father Elio . . . that means about 100,000 lire and, eh . . . something . . .*

His brain longed for a pencil and paper and just one minute alone. Should he ask for 400,000 lire . . . *400,000 lire! Too much!* He tried to remember the rate of exchange for a dollar and his brain screamed, *Who cares about dollars? You need pounds . . . !* He lost track of what he was trying to figure out and now people were staring at him. He needed to have an amount in mind before he spoke and everyone was waiting.

The tourists could not, of course, discern the meaning of the unintelligible Italian words that had passed between their cloddish guide and this congenial native. But, to every English eye it was obvious that this good-hearted man who had enthralled them with his story had again been offended – and again it was their fault. The poor British invaders felt a massive stab of national shame for the distress that they seemed to continually cause these kind people.

The local villagers, on the other hand, felt a huge surge of communal pride at how well Leo was directing the ebb and flow of this scene, especially after so many years with no practice. And although they had absolutely no idea what he had said to the English or what was going on right now, they supported his current mood by politely lowering their eyes in respect of the monumental faux pas – whatever it was.

Up to this point everything had gone perfectly. Leo couldn't recall it ever going this well – even when he and Franco had worked together as boys. But now he needed someone other than the guide to speak, and yet the room remained silent. It occurred to him that maybe he'd overplayed it. Maybe all those years ago it had only worked because he was a child.

At the bar Topo wiped his sweaty forehead on his sleeve and also prayed that someone would speak. Leo might actually have to slap that fellow or worse – leave! What was wrong with these heartless English? But the silence remained abysmal.

Leo had just concluded that he would have to cut his losses when the two horsy ladies at the table he'd first approached prompted their gentleman companion and Leo heard the sound he'd been longing for. The man cleared his throat.

'Excuse me, sir, eh . . . signore . . .'

Leo turned.

The Englishman stepped forward and stuttered, 'Signore, I, eh . . . that is, we aren't quite sure what the . . . difficulty is, but we certainly did not intend to give you any offense. Please, accept our apology.'

'No, no, no, no, no, my friend. *You* did not offend.' Leo gave a certain edge to the word *you* and turned a special frown toward the confused guide. The English tourists turned and frowned at him also. Then the villagers turned and frowned at him. But, for the first time all day, Carmen smiled at him. The poor guy stared dumbly at them all.

'I'm afraid you do not'a understand, signore,' said Leo. 'Our village is poor, but we are also proud. We do not'a have much in the way of, how you say it . . . *opulenza laica* . . . eh, worldly wealth. What we do have are two gift-s'a from'a God. To pay to see them seems like a, eh . . . the, eh . . . *sacrilegio*?'

'Sacrilege?'

'Si, the sacrilege. Our priest, Father Elio, a pious man, he would never allow it. I am sorry.'

The faces of the English tourists fell, but suddenly Leo had a brainstorm. He gasped and held up his finger as if to point at the wonderful idea floating over his head. 'Unless . . .' he whispered to himself.

He crowded in on the Englishman's elbow and spoke in a conspiratorial manner – but loudly enough for all to hear.

'Of course, there would'a be nothing wrong with'a my asking Father Elio if I could bring a few of my good friends into the sanctuary and'a share with them our Miracle and our Mystery. Then, if you would'a like, you could'a make a . . . a . . . what do you call . . . a donation . . . to the church! Then I could pass it on to Father Elio, after you have left. Once you are gone, what'a can he say? That is not'a like selling tickets, is it?'

'Certainly not. Nothing like. Just some good friends exchanging . . . gifts.' The horsy Englishman turned to the group and they all nodded affirmatively. A few older men even, 'Here, here'd.' What clever ducks they were.

'How much would you think is . . . I mean, what might be an appropriate . . . donation?'

Now, it is possible for things to go too well. Continued good fortune can often lull a man into carelessness and by this time Leo was feeling almost intoxicated. He had a plan. He had determined a good price. He had done this many times before, and even though he hadn't practiced in years, some things you just don't forget. This was no time to improvise. So he couldn't believe it when he heard those terrible words come pouring out of his own mouth.

'Oh, whatever you think would'a be fair.'

He almost shrieked! He wanted to scream! He wanted to jump up and down and tear his hair! But instead he froze a smile to his lips and waited.

From the end of the bar Topo caught his eye and gave him a wink. Leo thanked God that his friend didn't understand English because if he knew what Leo had just said, he would be on top of him and ripping at his throat.

The Englishman turned back to his group and there was an interminably long moment of hushed whisperings, nods, grimaces, and secret signs. Leo was tempted to reiterate the poverty of the village, or the piety of Father Elio, or perhaps even his own desperate yearning to escape Santo Fico – but he had to wait it out. He'd rolled the dice – let them fall. Finally, the tall man with the big teeth and wild hair turned around almost apologetically.

'Would, eh . . . five hundred thousand lire be acceptable?'

Their worst nightmare was that they would insult Leo yet a third time, and his reaction frightened them. But, when he was able to breath again, and had recovered control of his sagging jaw, he whispered words of gratitude with complete and genuine sincerity.

'That is . . . too much.' And he meant it.

There was almost a cheer of relief from the English. 'Nonsense,' was the cry as the jovial Brit clapped him on the back.

Leo's head was spinning. He couldn't seem to catch his breath, but the sight of Marta stepping back in from the kitchen quickly returned him to reality with a sudden urgency. Marta was right. He needed to talk to Father Elio, and quickly. Without Father Elio's blessing, this magnificent castle he'd just built could abruptly return to sand. So Leo hastily explained to the English that he would go over to the church and make arrangements and when they had finished their desserts, they could join him.

And with a cheerful wave to all, Leo hurried out of the dining room, across the tiny lobby, and out the front door. Within seconds Topo scurried after him.

Six

*T*he smells of the old church overwhelmed Leo when he first entered – the musty stones, the ages of incense, centuries of smoke from perpetual candles. He stood at the back and leaned against the cool plaster until the light-headedness left him and soon he found himself comfortably anonymous in the dim shadows, as if protected from the outside world by a shaded cloak of invisibility. Was this what a priest felt?

Many times since his return from America, he'd been struck by the plainness of Santo Fico. When he was growing up here, he hadn't realized how meager everything was – but now it was more than just that. For instance, everything in the village was so much smaller than he remembered and that included this church. As a child, the size of the sanctuary had always impressed him, but years of wandering had taken him to some of the great cathedrals of the world and now he saw everything around him through those experienced eyes. He'd discovered the insignificance of Santo Fico within the first month of his exile. At only nineteen, working in Milano so he might earn enough money for a ticket to America, he saw the white marble spires of the Milano Duomo at sunset and it made him weep. And then in America, even the public shrines of Chicago confirmed the irrelevance of his home . . . After you've been to the top of the Sears Tower . . . Why, the entire village of Santo Fico could fit inside Wrigley Field, including this church and its dwarfish bell tower.

America had been the cure. Once he got to America, and especially Chicago, Santo Fico finally became some distant dream that faded over time. For over sixteen years he worked as a drywall hanger for his mother's brother's wife's son, Steve Costello.

The work was hard, but the pay was okay and it wasn't long before he could afford his own place, and new clothes, and a used car, and finally bars and even dates with women for dinner or a movie. Most important, he could afford to buy tickets to Wrigley Field. Cousin Steve made it perfectly clear that Leo was going to have to learn English and baseball – and for Cousin Steve, baseball meant the Chicago Cubs. With much painful effort Leo did learn English, and discovered, to his delight, he also loved 'base'a-ball' and the

Cubs. And soon, without even noticing, Santo Fico faded like a morning mist.

But there had been one exceptionally bone-chilling morning last winter when all that he had given up was driven home with biting clarity. The wind blew off Lake Michigan with a special ferocity that day and he spent the morning battling awkward sheets of drywall, first against the wind and then up three flights of stairs. This wasn't unusual. But on this day, along with the heavy sheets of plaster, he also carried Father Elio's terrible letter crumpled in his shirt pocket. It was already a year old when it arrived. It had taken his Aunt Sofia that long to track him down. The letter – read and reread throughout the day – told him that he was too late. He had failed. His father had been dead for almost two years and he hadn't even known. Father Elio's awkward letter told of how the farm belonged to Leo now and it needed care. Leo didn't want the farm. He wanted ten minutes with his father. His fellow workers thought his eyes were watering because of the bitter wind.

Now, standing in the shadows at the back of the sanctuary, Leo thought, it's not just familiarity that breeds contempt – it's also time. He wondered how he could have ever been impressed with this church. There was nothing remarkable here, and he should know. He recognized every hidden nook and passage in the building. How many times had he darted into the dark passage to his right and clambered the winding stone stairs to the top of the bell tower? As a boy he had loved to explore the world from the open porticoes surrounding the top of the tower. He, Franco,

Marta, and Topo spent hours sneaking around the tower, hiding from the adults in the piazza, having spitting contests, but mostly just daydreaming about what lay beyond the edge of their horizon. On some especially clear days, when Isola d'Elba shimmered against the northwest rim of the world, they pretended it was America and devised schemes on how to get there . . . America!

That brought Leo back with a snap. To hell with his childhood. The problem was Father Elio. Of course, he'd seen the old priest a few times since his return and they had talked. Father Elio was friendly enough, but he always seemed to want to say something difficult to Leo or maybe he wanted Leo to confess something painful to him. In either case, he made Leo uncomfortable. But that didn't matter now.

It took only a quick glance to see that the old priest wasn't in the sanctuary and Leo would have to search him out. Within arm's reach was a carved stone basin and its shallow splash of holy water. Leo considered performing the ritual before entering the sanctuary, but no one was watching, so what would be the point.

Walking quickly down the middle aisle, Leo glanced up at the ceiling – always his favorite part of the sanctuary. Surrounding the long inner chamber and supported by opposing rows of brawny stone piers, high walls held a series of leaded windows placed in such a way as to capture the best light of the day. He stopped in front of the familiar altar that rose modestly above the smooth, worn benches at the heart of the chamber. A simple chandelier of candles and cobwebs hanging from the ceiling haloed the altar. At the eastern end of the room a semicircular apse was high-lighted with five soiled, but colorful, stained glass windows. Below the windows reclined a small Pietà statue, crudely carved from laminated layers of cedar some hundreds of years ago.

Leo stood midway between two small transepts that invited parishioners in for solitary meditation. To his left, the northern transept was a small alcove buried in shadows and guarded by a crude wooden railing. Leo deliberately ignored it. He knew that hidden behind the shadows of the piers – shrouded by both the darkness and probably one of Father Elio's old blankets – was the Mystery of Santo Fico. He hadn't seen it in eighteen years, but he'd thought about it. Now, standing this close to it again, he silently cursed him-self for his thoughts – and cursed God for tricking him into returning to this place. If he really wanted to get out of Santo Fico, there was his ticket. Could be worth a fortune, the man had said. He'd just need a truck. He could steal a truck. Yeah, all he needed was a truck . . . And a day or two when no one would notice him removing a small portion of the church's northern wall! Pointless! He needed to find Father Elio – and fast.

Two oak doors mirrored each other from their opposite sides of the nave. The northern door on his left led to a garden that was part of the original monastery. Although, for many centuries now it had been less of a garden and more a courtyard designed to protect the Miracle: the blessed Shrine of the Withered Fig. Leo knew how much time

Father Elio spent in prayer before the shrine – the old priest might be out there.

To his right was the vestry door where he and Franco had spent so many hours as altar boys preparing Father Elio for mass. In America, sometimes when he'd been drinking, he used to joke about being 'the best damn altar boy in Santo Fico.' And it was true. Father Elio had told him so.

Beyond the vestry was a low corridor that led to the kitchen and Father Elio's rooms and it was through the open stone passageway that Leo heard voices and he recalled seeing Nina carrying lunch across the piazza.

Lunch was Father Elio's favorite meal. Breakfast was just a cup of coffee and some fried bread with honey or butter. Dinner too seldom varied: hot tea, fruit, cheese, bread, sometimes an egg. These two meals he prepared for himself, but lunch was a different matter. Not only was it the largest meal of the day, but it was also prepared by his niece, Marta, and her cooking was famous in the region.

Exactly when meals started arriving at the back door of the church was something that neither Marta nor Father Elio could recall specifically. Marta's mother, Katrine, swore she only cooked for her brother-in-law because watching him slowly starve himself to death with his own cooking was just too cruel. Eventually Marta took over the responsibility and Father Elio never questioned her arrival, because Marta was family, the youngest daughter of his only brother, Young Giuseppe. For the girls, cooking for Great-Uncle Father Elio was not something Carmen or

Nina ever wondered about either. And while Father Elio loved the meals Marta fixed, he could have cooked for himself if necessary, but this was family. Besides, the food was not the best part of the arrangement. The best part was that Marta or Carmen or Nina brought it to him, and each was his favorite for a different reason.

Elio liked it when Marta brought the basket because she was old enough to remember family things. Most of his family – brother, sisters, father, mother – were all dead. The three women of the Albergo di Santo Fico was all the family that remained and Marta was the only one old enough to share some of his memories. When she brought lunch they chattered about her parents and grandparents, or people and happenings from their past. Although he did wish she wasn't always so serious. A few older villagers occasionally mentioned her seriousness, but only because they remembered her as a child – a high-spirited, beautiful girl with boundless energy and an infectious laugh. Someone who knew her then would have a hard time recognizing the humorless, slightly dangerous woman of today. It had to do with disappointment and Father Elio understood some of it.

There had been the death of Elio's older brother, Marta's father, Young Giuseppe. He was called Young Giuseppe right up until his death at seventy-one. He died on a Sunday morning in late spring while weeding a bed of ripe parsley. Elio often thanked God that his older brother had lived such a full life and died such a tranquil death. Marta was grief-stricken, of course, but her mother, Katrine, was desolate. From the day Young Giuseppe died Katrine began making her own funeral plans and in less than a year, showing commendable determination and resolve, Katrine did precisely what she intended. She followed Young Giuseppe. Although Marta was profoundly saddened by her mother's death, she certainly wasn't surprised.

Franco was a story that Elio didn't understand, but whenever the subject came up, such a dark cloud crossed his niece's already dark eyes that he knew this was not something he should explore.

Franco died two years after Katrine and three years after Young Giuseppe. Carmen was six and Nina was only four. It all happened so fast. Everyone knew Franco was too wild on his motorcycle, but it still came as a shock – in the middle of the night, Franco was drunk, and then there was that woman with him. She died too. For months, Marta looked as if she'd been run over by a truck or crushed by some great weight. Everyone in the village expected Marta to crumble to pieces, but she didn't. Instead she turned to stone. To the best of anyone's knowledge, she didn't even weep and this is something that the women in the village look for and expect. Most of her neighbors attributed it to the fact that she had a hotel and restaurant to manage, and two small children to care for and what with the little one going blind. People told each other that she didn't have time to weep or that the shock had not hit her yet. In six months she would collapse. But six months had come and gone many times and Marta still did not weep.

Father Elio also liked it when Carmen brought the lunch because Carmen was young and vivacious. She was like a breath of fresh air, although he did occasionally catch a faint scent of brimstone on the breeze. There was that touch of wickedness in Carmen that all men immediately recognized and Father Elio was no exception. He was her great-uncle, and a priest, and an old man, but he was neither a fool, blind, nor dead. He saw the way she greeted the men of the village as she passed them in the street; the way she tossed her hair and laughed and smiled at them, her dark eyes peering slyly out from beneath her brows. He saw the way the young men, and many older ones too, reacted to his great-niece's charms and he was grateful that the fountain in the center of the piazza had long ago gone dry. If it were still filled with water, he was certain that some local idiots would be in serious danger of drowning as Carmen glided across the square.

But he wasn't worried. Father Elio loved his great-niece. She reminded him so much of Marta in her younger days, when she was the one catching the attention of every man on the coast and, as he recalled, even those strangers from Milano who were considered authorities on beauty. Although unlike Carmen, Marta had never seemed aware of her charms. But he wasn't worried. What Elio saw as Carmen's playful wickedness he never associated with evil; rather he attributed it to youthful exuberance. It was something he had witnessed many times before and was fully confident she would outgrow. He wasn't worried. Besides, he prayed for her continually.

Father Elio liked it best when Nina brought the lunch because Nina was the quietest and the deepest. She seemed to have a special sensitivity toward whatever he was thinking and feeling and although this sometimes frightened him, it was never in a bad way. It wasn't just as if her hearing was more attuned, although it was, or her touch more sensitive, although it was — it was more than that. Nina felt more deeply. Everyone recognized her as a remarkably sweet-natured girl, but Elio recognized in her the hand of God.

She was also filled with questions and starved for answers, and he liked that. And so often her questions challenged him on so many subjects: the meaning of life, the form of the universe, the duality of nature, varying perceptions of God. Father Elio often felt like he was back in a classroom at the university in Bologna with a shrewd professor who hid behind a cloak of innocent curiosity. He knew the strategy of Socrates; how the old philosopher would befuddle his students by his continual amazement at their astute perceptions, asking them more and more questions, begging them to teach him their wisdom, until at last they crumbled under the weight of their own ignorance. When Nina questioned, Elio considered his answers carefully.

Although he enjoyed those times of discussion that often turned into philosophical debates, those were still not his favorite times to be with Nina. His favorite times were when they didn't speak at all — when she was doing some simple task like picking up the dishes or darning his clothes or petting the cat. She tried to be quiet, certain that Father Elio was either reading his Bible or some other great spiritual work or he was meditating or he was deep in a profound prayer. But he wasn't. Most often he was watching her. When he watched her, when he listened to her soft, unconscious humming, when he observed the grace of her soul surround even the simplest, meanest task, it brought serenity to his heart.

Everyone knew that Nina was different. Most people in the village felt she was limited because of her blindness. Some silently thought she was slightly simple. Others thought she was so childlike and innocent because Marta and Carmen were so zealous in their protection of her. But even Marta and Carmen didn't truly understand Nina and what it was that made her special. Elio knew. He alone recognized the truth. Nina lived a life of grace; a grace he did not possess. And lately, more and more often, it frightened him and made him angry. Not angry with Nina – never with Nina. Nor did it make him angry with God. It wasn't God's fault. He was angry with himself. After all these years of struggling to atone for his sin, he only had to see the grace of God's hand on Nina to recognize his own failure. And recently, something new had begun to gnaw at his heart.

He'd begun to feel mortality. He knew instinctively that time was shortening, and the day was approaching when he was going to have to pay for his arrogance and deceit – and he was afraid. He'd known for years that this time would eventually arrive and he was willing, almost anxious, to have it over and done with, but he was afraid his retribution was spilling beyond himself. He didn't want the price of his sin to touch those he loved, those he wanted most to protect and serve, but he couldn't shake the premonition that the village of Santo Fico was going to pay.

It was Nina who first heard Leo's footsteps. Father Elio was far too interested in his remarkable plate of pasta drowning in a sea of creamy white sauce and swimming with shrimp;

and he was still chuckling at Nina's account of the morning's excitement with the tour bus. It was because of the tour bus that he was feasting on white sauce and shrimp. Monday was usually pasta with pomodoro and salsiccia. When Nina raised her hand to indicate the steps in the distance, Elio knew who was walking down the stone corridor toward his rooms. Earlier, watching the tour bus, he'd thought of Leo Pizzola.

Last month, less than an hour after Leo trudged up the north coast, no fewer than eleven concerned neighbors ran to the church with the news that 'Tony Pizzola's trouble-maker son' had returned from America – probably 'looking to make more trouble.' But Father Elio knew what this pilgrim was looking for, even if he didn't. It wasn't trouble. But Leo would have to figure it out for himself.

Father Elio even went out to the Pizzola farm and discovered that Leo wasn't living in the house. He'd taken up residence in an old shepherd's hut down by the cliffs. The priest had hoped that he'd returned to put the farm in order, but Leo only wanted to sell it all and go back to America. Their conversation was polite, but not friendly. Elio wished it had been friendly, but he made Leo uncomfortable – probably because Tony Pizzola had been one of Father Elio's best friends from childhood. But Leo was a good boy . . . an idiot, but a good boy. He was the best altar boy Father Elio'd ever had . . . and the magical way he told those stories . . .

'Hello.'

Leo stood framed in the low door of the kitchen wearing a wonderful facsimile of a smile he'd created as he walked down the passageway. He was even prepared with a couple of spontaneous quips, but even as he was still offering his hesitant greeting, the old priest was already shuffling across the kitchen. Father Elio wrapped him in an enthusiastic embrace and pulled his head down to kiss both his cheeks — it was the same *return of the prodigal* greeting he'd given Leo the first time he saw him at the shepherd's hut.

Leo had always considered Father Elio to be God's hand on earth; he'd certainly felt that hand across the back of his head and regions farther south enough times. In his mind's eye, the face of Father Elio belonged somewhere on the ceiling of the Sistine Chapel — perhaps imperiously reaching his finger out toward a drowsy Adam's languidly outstretched hand. Father Elio's hair turning white by his forties reinforced this image, and so Leo had *always* considered Father Elio old. But now when he embraced him and felt his small, frail body beneath his baggy black jacket Leo realized he hadn't correctly perceived the old man. Why had he remembered this priest as being large? He was a small man, a full head shorter than he was. And his frame was skin and bones. Father Elio was just a man, unexpectedly aged and surprisingly fragile.

Father Elio performed a short introduction of Nina to Leo, and then Leo hemmed and hawed impatiently as she gathered up the lunch dishes. He understood that she was blind, of course, but he did wish that she would hurry up because there was something about the girl that disturbed him. On the surface she appeared to take no notice of him and simply went about her business, but Leo couldn't shake the feeling that she heard him – not what he spoke, she heard his thoughts, she heard his heart. That was unnerving enough, but now, seeing Nina beside Father Elio as she cleared the table, Leo felt a chill run down his back – it was their eyes. They had the same startling pale blue eyes. To be confronted with one set was unsettling – but two sets of those haunting eyes, side by side, was downright spooky.

Father Elio could sometimes be surprisingly astute. He knew Leo had come for a reason and he had a pretty good idea what that reason was. Leo wasn't going to be able to get down to business until they were alone and even he finally recognized that Nina was obviously stalling. So, as they chatted, he began casually pushing plates and bowls in front of her groping fingers.

When Nina understood what her great-uncle was doing she picked up her pace, but she also showed her displeasure by loudly dropping things into the basket with a pointed indifference that made the old man fear for the crockery. She wanted to stay and listen – not because she was interested in anything Leo had to say, but because of his voice. It was musical and filled with secrets and such an unusual accent after his years in America. But mostly she wanted to listen because his voice was like diving into a deep pool of mysterious water. She sensed that no matter what Leo actually said, it was rarely connected to what he was actually thinking. If she could listen to him long enough, if she could swim down into that dark water, she could perhaps glimpse his secret. She had no way of knowing that this was precisely what made Leo uneasy about being around her.

Once Nina was packed and out the door it took Leo little time to get down to business. Father Elio listened patiently. When he was done, Leo waited silently while the priest carefully brushed breadcrumbs across the wooden table and into a tiny pile. Finally after some deep contemplation, Father Elio spoke.

'So, they're English.'

Leo nodded and waited some more. Some things never change. Even as a child Leo was aware of Father Elio's legendary pauses. The old priest didn't rush into anything, and the length of his contemplation was entirely dependent on how weighty he considered the situation at hand. Those who wanted Father Elio's blessing or opinion were best armed with a full complement of patience. Leo concluded that either his current proposal was especially weighty or, because of his extended absence from Santo Fico, he owed a big backlog of missed pauses. After a bit it became hard to tell if Father Elio was still awake – or breathing.

At last, 'Are they Catholic?'

Leo was delighted that he could answer in all honesty that he did not know, but he silently doubted it. He knew now that it wouldn't have made any difference. Father Elio was going to acquiesce and the English tourists being Catholic would have just been frosting on the cake – kind of like Chicago or baseball. Then, out of the blue, Father Elio shocked him with a remarkably straightforward and mercenary question.

'How much are they going to pay?'

Apparently some things do change. The old priest shot

that one in so quickly that Leo was caught completely off guard. He didn't have time to think.

'Four hundred thousand lire,' he lied.

Why did he lie? He hadn't planned on lying. Why did that figure pop out of his mouth? Where did it come from? Unfortunately, there'd been that split second of indecision. Had it given him away? But he couldn't take it back now and say he was mistaken, so he smiled.

Father Elio looked back down at his small pile of bread-crumbs. He didn't care about the price. He wasn't thinking about money or even the English tourists. His mind had again drifted to that first miraculous summer and the two twelve-year-old boys sitting with him at this wooden table. Father Elio brushed the breadcrumbs across the table and sighed, 'Four hundred thousand lire. That's a pretty good price.'

Leo smiled, nodded. 'Yeah, it's . . . pretty good.'

He heard his own voice affirming their good fortune, but Leo imagined he saw judgment staring at him from the old man's twinkling blue eyes and he was once again a little boy caught in a fib. His stomach turned sour with guilt and the muscles in his face ached from the pressure of his forced smile – he hated himself for ever thinking this would be a good idea.

Seven

*T*he English tourists had already visited the great cathedrals of Milano, Firenze, and Siena and were scheduled to be in Roma in three days, where they would tour Saint Peter's Cathedral. So, although no one was openly rude to their horsy companion who had negotiated this deal, upon entering the remarkably unimpressive church of Santo Fico they all certainly gave him looks that seemed to say, 'Five hundred thousand lire, indeed!'

As Leo observed them from the shadows of the narrow passageway it was obvious, even from that distance and in bad light, that they were feeling distinctly disgruntled and he wished the church weren't so damn dingy. He didn't remember the windows being so dirty, or all the dust and cobwebs on the candleholders, or the altar looking so shabby, or the transept being so dark. He was suddenly reminded of Father Elio's frugality and he turned to the old priest, who was at his shoulder straining to see how many visitors had made the pilgrimage.

'Are there light bulbs in the lamps for the Mystery?'

Father Elio chuckled, 'Light bulbs? In the lamps? Of course.' He chuckled again and patted Leo on the back, but even in the shadows Leo could see the old man's mind racing. Finally, 'I don't know . . . Maybe not . . . I don't think so . . . No.'

'We'll go out to the garden first, to the Miracle. See if you can find some light bulbs.'

Father Elio nodded. 'It's better when you go to the garden first, isn't it?'

Leo shrugged in a way that seemed to say, maybe, but what's to be done. Father Elio nodded his agreement and returned his shrug. Leo stepped out of the hallway and Father Elio followed him into the nave. For the first time the priest saw the size of the group waiting – there were about a dozen strangers and at least twice that many villagers. Apparently when the tourists departed the restaurant, the curious villagers followed them and those who were mid-meal just brought their plates of food and glasses of wine with them. So even though the natives were becoming friendlier toward the foreigners, smiling and nodding at every opportunity, the strangers still wore the frozen gaze of those who wished some giant elevator doors would open and they could gratefully step off onto their floor.

As Leo moved up the center aisle he smiled broadly and with a generous wave of his arm he called, 'Welcome to the Cattedrale di Santo Fico!' It was pushing it a bit to call this mishmash of incomplete architecture a cathedral, but he was counting on poetic license. With another sweep of his arm he directed their attention toward the timid little shadow standing behind him, grinning self-consciously and fidgeting like a schoolboy.

'And'a this is Father Elio, who has been the priest of Santo Fico for . . . oh, at least two . . . three hundred'a years now.' For their part, the tourists were Christian and the old man was, after all, a priest, so Leo's little joke received polite nods and chuckles. Their predicament wasn't his fault and he looked like a nice enough chap – besides, he seemed so anxious to please.

'*Benvenuto!*' Father Elio wanted to kick himself. He knew the English word once, what was it?

Leo called to them, 'He says welcome.'

Father Elio clapped his hands and pointed at Leo. That was the word! And he called again with almost frightening enthusiasm, '*Si! Si!* Wel'a-come! Wel'a-come!' He took a deep breath and tried to settle down. He knew he was too nervous. It had been so many years since he'd seen this many strangers in his church. In fact, he rarely had this many villagers in his church, apart from certain high holy days, or weddings, or christenings, or funerals.

Leo spoke to the group again in English and Father Elio

had no idea what was being said, but he could occasionally pick out certain words. He clearly understood references to Cosimo de Medici and so he knew that Leo was telling them something about the history of the little church and the foreigners actually seemed to understand him! Like the rest of the village, Father Elio was proud of Leo's mastery of this strange language.

Leo chattered away as he conducted the group down the center aisle, turning them toward the door by the northern transept – and as they disappeared out into the courtyard, he quickly hissed a harsh whisper at Father Elio.

'Light bulbs . . .!'

Light bulbs? Ah! Light bulbs . . . Yes! Father Elio knew for sure that there was at least one by his bedroom and another in the bathroom.

The sunlit courtyard was a small rectangular affair, probably fifteen meters in width and not much more than that in length. Two of its walls were the exterior side of the northern transept and apse, while the other two borders were exterior courtyard walls obviously built after the original church, but still hundreds of years old. There wasn't much in the small enclosure to distinguish it as even a garden, much less a shrine to some miraculous event.

The visitors shuffled along a stone path that trailed through clumps of herbs, always pressing forward – trying to make room enough for everyone to fit into the modest space. Fortunately, for some lucky ones there were a few stone benches placed rather haphazardly. In the center of the courtyard was an olive tree that bestowed a surprising amount of shade. The combination of the tree and the fact that they were on the north side of the building made the rustic courtyard a shady and not wholly unpleasant place. It was a simple arrangement; paths, benches, random clumps of rosemary, basil, sage, lavender, lemon balm, thyme, the olive tree – and in the farthest corner of the exterior walls, surrounded by a low border of obviously ancient stone, was a withered and blackened tree stump. The dead stump was no more than two meters at its highest point and from all appearances it should have been pulled up years ago. A little more than halfway up two split and warped branches reached painfully upward and had the surprising effect of making the entire area seem more untidy than it actually was. That awkward twist of dead wood, like some mummified, agonized letter *Y*, gave the space a disheveled appearance and all of the fastidious English gardeners in the tour secretly longed for their trusty garden shears and pruning saws. It was obvious even to the most horticulturally obtuse that the trunk was dead, but few would have guessed its demise was counted in centuries. Leo sat on the low wall that surrounded the dead tree and absently pulled at a brittle weed as his odd mixture of soft, pink English tourists and sturdy, tanned villagers worked their way in. When finally he cleared his throat the courtyard became silent. His calm voice drew the listeners in as he outlined the history of this promontory, before there was a Santo Fico, before a small band of Franciscans built a monastery sometime in the thirteenth century. It wasn't difficult to imagine this craggy point overlooking the sea prior to that time – with pastures and shepherds, and fruit trees growing every-where.

As Leo spoke, few of his listeners noticed that his thick Italian accent, before so quaint and charming, began to thin. Leo had spent enough years in America that his English was actually quite accomplished, but he'd found early on that there were occasions when it was beneficial to play the role of the simple *paesano*. It had gotten him out of more than a few tight spots and occasionally saved him some money. In the restaurant he had laid the accent on a bit thicker than nec-essary for the sake of rural charm, but now the story was taking on a life of its own and he couldn't be bothered.

Leo told them of Saint Francis. Of the weary and pious saint plodding the Italian countryside with a loyal band of friars who had heeded his call and followed his vision – trav-eling on foot to palaces and hovels, no matter the season or inclement weather. Leo told of how, one warm spring day, the good saint found he had occasion to travel south from Livorno along the coast on his way to Roma.

'It was the spring and everything was beautiful as the blessed saint and his disciples followed the same road you traveled, along the cliffs above the sea – they too were on a journey south. Now in those days, there was a shepherd that had his home somewhere near this spot. He used the pastures down by the sea for his sheep and his goats.

'It so happened that Saint Francis and his companions, walking along the road, passed by this shepherd's cottage. The shepherd did not know who they were, but wandering

monks and holy men were not uncommon. The good shepherd apologized for his poverty and welcomed them to his
little home. He offered to share all he had with them. This
blessed Saint Francis, who was'a both tired and sick . . . He
asked the shepherd, if it might not be too much trouble,
could he and his companions stay and rest for a few days
before they continued their journey? The shepherd said he
would'a be honored. Well, can you imagine that poor shepherd's surprise when he discovered that the man who was
sharing his cottage was'a none other than Saint Francis of
Assisi? Of course, he wasn't a saint then, not'a yet, but even
in his own life he was famous and many people knew his
miracles.

   'Now, not far from the shepherd's cottage, up on top of a
hill that overlooked the sea, there was a beautiful fig tree.
Every day Saint Francis would walk up that hill, sit beneath
that tree, and cool himself in its shade. He would look out to
the sea and watch the gulls swoop around the cliffs and dive
into the ocean. He would'a watch the winds wave the pines
on the hills behind him or blow great white clouds over the
distant mountains. And, every now and then, he would reach
up and pull a fig off'a that beautiful tree and he would eat it.
And so, he rested and prayed, and slowly his strength began
to return – and it's a good thing too. Because, it didn't take
that shepherd long to tell his neighbors who was staying in
his little hut. And those neighbors told their neighbors.

   'It started'a slowly, just a few peasants hoping for a
benedizione . . . sorry, a . . . blessing. But soon people were
coming from all over for the blessings from'a the man who

was touched by the hand of God. Saint Francis did not mind. He was so full of love. He loved the people. He loved this spot high above the sea. And, he loved the fig tree.

'But one day he was saddened to see that there was no more fruit on the tree. Between himself and his companions and the many visitors – they had picked the poor tree clean. The story goes that Saint Francis sat on the ground beneath the branches and he embraced the tree, tenderly – like a papa would hold a child or a child would hug its mama and he thank'a the tree for its generosity. And he apologized that they took all the fruit and left none for the birds.

'The next morning, when Saint Francis returned to his spot beneath the tree there was already a big'a group of pilgrims waiting for the blessing and prayers of the humble man. But, there was also something else. The fig tree was full of fresh fruit. Overnight the tree had'a borne fruit and it was ripe. Well, as you can guess, that morning, among his morning prayers, Saint Francis offered a special prayer for his'a new friend, the *santo fico* . . . the blessed fig tree.

'And so he stayed here at this place for many days and in that time pilgrims from all over came to this place and there were many miracles. People who could'a not walk, left here leaping for joy. People who could'a not speak, left here singing hymns'a to God. People who could'a not see, left here wondering at the glories they beheld. And every day, throughout that whole spring all of the people would eat'a the fruit of the fig tree. And every morning they would find its branches filled with new, fresh fruit.

'At last Saint Francis had'a to leave for Roma. Even saints

don't keep'a the Pope waiting too long. But, he left something behind. The fig tree, she continued to bear fruit. And in the years that followed, no matter what'a the season, no matter what'a the weather, the tree kept offering its fruit. It was a miracle for sure.

'But, people are *strani*, eh . . . funny. When a miracle becomes'a *ordinario* . . . ordinary . . . eh, common . . . it'a stops being a miracle. And so, after a while the people made up their own reasons why the tree bore the fruit. 'There must'a be something wrong with the tree,' they would say. Or 'It's something in'a the dirt,' or 'The stupid tree is'a just confused!

'In time, the people forgot about the tree and its miracle. But not the old shepherd. Every day, first thing in the morning, he would walk up the hill and thank'a the tree for its fruit, and he thank'a God for his blessing. And the old man always shared whatever he had with his neighbors and he even look'a for the poor so he could'a share with them.

'One cold morning, when the frost was on everything, the kind old shepherd came out of his cottage and hiked up the hill as usual. But he discovered that the tree was not just bare of fruit, it'a was bare of leaves. Overnight the tree had withered and died. The old shepherd blamed himself and he wept over his tree.'

'It was weeks later that some travelers told him the news. On'a the third day of October that year, Saint Francis had'a died. When he heard'a this news, the old shepherd went to what was left of the tree, and knelt before it, and thanked his old friend, the withered fig, for being faithful to the end.'

Leo turned and for the first time gently caressed the smooth, dry trunk of the blackened old stump behind him.

'. . . For, you see, the third'a day of October was the very day the blessed fig tree also had died.'

The courtyard was hushed. A few of the English tourists shivered off a wave of goose bumps. Some of the older ladies quietly dabbed their eyes. The locals studied the sky or their own hands. They judged from the silence of the foreigners that Leo had told the story well – although many were sure that he had undoubtedly left out important details.

Leo sat on the low wall and fiddled with the lichen on the stones. He was quite proud of himself; he had recalled many of the touching details and phrases, even a few dates, although he hoped no one wanted to check on them.

The sound of someone politely clearing her throat brought him back. He could gloat more later – right now he had to finish up; it was hot and he wanted a cold beer.

Leo looked up to meet the watery gaze of an elderly woman whose voice barely rose above a whisper, but she asked the question that was on everyone's mind. Leo knew the question before it was asked and it astounded him how some things refuse to change. He felt that he had, as always, made himself perfectly clear, but here was that maddeningly predictable first question.

'Is that the, eh . . . That is to say, is that what's left of the . . . ?' For some reason she couldn't bring herself to say fig tree – as if uttering the name would be some sort of desecration. Leo nodded, smiled, and finished the phrase for her. 'This is all that remains of the blessed fig tree.'

With that, he stood up – because now two things were going to happen rather quickly. First, someone would venture the alternate most popular question, to which he would nod and step aside. Then, as they all pressed forward to touch the sacred stump, maybe on some spot that Saint Francis had once touched, other questions would begin – slowly at first, but they would quickly pick up pace until they began to overlap. He had barely gotten to his feet when, as if on cue, a tall large-boned woman (who might have been the blue-haired twin of the horsy gentleman) spoke out boldly with the alternate most popular question.

'May we touch it?'

Leo nodded and stepped aside. So the ritual began. The English tourists politely shuffled forward, patiently waiting their turn to reverently caress the smooth dark wood. Many were surprised when their turn arrived – the wood felt like it had been varnished. In fact, the old stump and broken branches bore many coats of shellac going back hundreds of years. This was the only way to protect the wood from the wind, the sun, the rain, and mostly the bugs.

As Leo worked his way through the crowd, answering their questions as he crossed the courtyard, he thought – amazing; so many years and yet it was like riding a bicycle.

But as well as things were rolling along, it was time to get on to the Mystery – there was no avoiding it. As he worked his way through the crowd, trying to get back into the church, an odd thing happened. Many of the locals, neighbors he had known all his life and who had gone out of their way to ignore him for six weeks, now nodded to him. A few even lightly patted him on the back. Considering the way they had shunned him as a leper, this was like a testimonial dinner.

From the garden door he called out in his most endearing accent, 'Ladies and'a gentle'a-men, if you would'a step this'a way,' and he moved through the low doorway leading back into the cool shadows of the nave. It would be some minutes before they would abandon the Miracle, so Leo found a bench near the door and, sitting in the cool shadows, considered his next challenge. The Miracle had been simple, but the Mystery was difficult. The story wasn't harder to tell. In fact, in many ways it was easier. It was certainly shorter. But Leo didn't like the way the Mystery made him feel and he didn't like the thoughts it made him think.

Topo was the first to re-enter the church and he almost danced with excitement. Leo was reminded of when they were children and Topo would occasionally get so excited or scared that he would wet himself. It had been many years since he'd been around his friend and he hoped that that particular problem had been corrected. Topo seemed unaware of Leo's presence as he placed himself next to a pier that was both strategic and yet out of the way. And from his shadowed bench, Leo observed something that he hadn't expected. As Topo stared into the darkness at the back of the transept Leo recognized an expression that startled him, partly because he would never have guessed it of his old friend. But also because it put a face to what he felt in his own heart – greed. It passed like a blurred cloud across his friend's face, but there it was. Then, as if his soul felt his sinful thoughts being observed, Topo turned and faced Leo and for an instant the little man looked ashamed. Then the others began filing back inside and the moment was gone – but Leo had seen the secret in Topo's heart and they both knew it.

The sanctuary echoed with the sound of scuffling feet and reverential murmuring as the chapel filled and the strangers tried to sense where they were expected to stand and which direction they should look. Leo caught a glimpse of Father Elio returning from the garden with Marta. They were whispering about something that made them both smile. It lasted only a moment, however, before Marta discovered Leo watching her and then her smile vanished. But for Leo the damage was done – for an instant he'd seen her eyes shining and her white teeth flashing. For the first time since he'd been back, he saw her as she used to be and he wished she weren't here.

When Leo stood, the room became hushed and even though he spoke quietly, his voice echoed around the vaulted hall. After telling the stories of Cosimo's miraculous healing and then of Saint Francis and the Miracle of the Santo Fico, Leo liked to keep the story of the Mystery brief. In fact, the story was almost superfluous – the power of the Mystery was in the viewing. So it didn't take him long to tell about the rich patron whose libertine son was killed in some frivolous war or other. Then he told about a Beautiful Lady who mysteriously appeared, late one night, at the front door of a Great Artist. Sometimes the unnamed Great Artist lived in Siena, sometimes in Firenze, but on this occasion he lived in

Roma. The Beautiful Lady spoke for the grieving father of the dead soldier and she offered the Great Artist a generous sum of money for a painting dedicated to the lost son. The Great Artist refused because, as he explained, he was scheduled to leave on a trip. The Beautiful Lady came to his door every night at the same late hour for a week, begging him to reconsider. And nightly he refused, until at last he left on his trip.

It was supposed to be a simple trip concerning a rich commission for some obscure and forgotten work. But throughout the day the artist's horse continually turned down a wrong path, or strangers gave him inaccurate directions, or road signs were strangely missing. By evening he was completely lost and wandering along an inhospitable section of the Tuscan coast known as Santo Fico. To make matters worse, a violent storm blew in off the sea and the Great Artist was forced to take shelter in a small monastery atop a rocky promontory.

'Even from within the stone abbey the Great Artist could hear the wind howling, the thunder rumbling, and the rain beating'a down outside. But he did finally manage to drift off'a to sleep.'

Leo's voice became a hushed, secretive whisper as he told them that, 'It'a was in the middle of the night that the terrible storm suddenly stopped and it'a was the frightening silence that caused the poor man to wake up. But can'a you imagine the Great Artist's amazement when he opened his eyes and found, standing before him, glowing like'a the sun, the same Beautiful Lady that had come to his door so many times. She was an angel. Not'a far from her was a handsome soldier, also with'a golden hair, and even though his'a body was covered with the wounds of a terrible battle, he too shone with a heavenly'a light. And standing between them, shinning like a brass trumpet, was'a the blessed figure of Saint Francis.'

Leo told of how the Blessed Saint commanded the astounded Great Artist. 'It was'a God's will that he should create a fresco in memory of this Handsome Soldier — for the youth had been a bad'a boy, much like the young Saint Francis. But just before a terrible battle, the young man had renounced his evil ways and asked Saint Francis to bless him. To honor this conversion, the Great Artist was to depict the miracle of the blessed fig tree.

'And so, the next day this Great Artist, inspired by his late-night vision, painted a miraculous picture. Then he just disappeared — gone without'a payment or even leaving his name. The painter of this'a masterpiece of Santo Fico remains forever . . . a mystery.' At this point, Leo nodded to Father Elio and the old priest plugged in the lamps attached to the backs of the piers. Audible gasps accompanied the dazzling lights, not from the sudden glare, but from the power of the fresco finally revealed.

Nobody ever seemed to notice that Leo's story absolutely defied reason. It didn't matter where he set the home of the Great Artist — Siena, Firenze, or Roma — the man could not possibly have gotten to Santo Fico in one day, especially considering all his mishaps. And what was even more glaringly impossible was the notion that anyone could create a fresco in a single day. And, why would humble Saint Francis want a depiction of himself and the fig tree to commemorate some repentant soldier's conversion? The only fact that Leo got correct was that for at least four centuries the identity of the artist had remained unknown – 'a mystery.'

There was so much that just didn't make sense, but none of it mattered once Father Elio plugged in the lights. Any concerns about facts and fanciful tales were forgotten against the brilliance of the fresco.

A dozen English tourists and many more villagers stood in awed silence. It wasn't as if these people had never seen a wet-plaster wall painting before. In the past week alone these foreigners had probably seen enough frescoes to last them some years. But this fresco was different. What they had seen were innumerable wall paintings that were chipped and decayed, rendered in colors that had faded and were then coated with centuries of grime. This wall was smooth and even, unmarred by time or man. Also, there's a wondrous chemical reaction between pigment and lime-rich wet plaster that gives the colors a luminous richness not found in other forms of painting. These colors still possessed their amazing original hues. This fresco might have been created four months ago, not four centuries ago. Hidden in this obscure little corner, there was no harsh sunlight to fade the colors. And since the odd little cathedral had been essentially ignored by generations of villagers, the tincture was not muted by continual candle and incense smoke.

The second and most remarkable feature was the soul of

the scene depicted. The focal point was, of course, a magnificent tree filled with leaves and an abundance of ripe figs.
Reclining beneath its shaded boughs, his back resting comfortably against the smooth trunk, was a youthful and
surprisingly pretty Saint Francis. One arm reached up, fingers poised only inches from the ripe fruits. This recumbent
figure of the saint was an odd mix of sensual yet innocent
paradoxes. He was, all in all, a middle-aged man, yet still
strangely youthful and delicately boyish. Most startling was
his childlike face. Although his hand reached up for the fruit,
his eyes were almost shyly cast down, not quite meeting the
gaze of the viewer – and they were filled with both gentleness and profound sadness. His small, well-formed mouth
appeared on the verge of a smile: either amused understanding or resolute acceptance. Every part of his
countenance embodied both joy and lamentation.

Leo stared into the face of that paradoxical boy/man,
saint/God, and his heart raced. He had dreaded this moment
since his return. It was that face that had kept him from
entering the cathedral for the past six weeks. That face, and
the fresco. Now it was in front of him, and again that wondrous face of Saint Francis took his breath away. He stared
into those radiant eyes that refused to look at him. They
were inviting, confirming, accusing. That damned enigmatic
mouth that seemed to be smiling just at him, as if they two
were sharing a secret. But Leo smiled back as if to say, 'I
know you. You're no mystery to me.' Then Leo took a deep
breath and forced his gaze away from the saintly face. He
and Topo and Saint Francis shared a secret and there was

nothing to do about it. So, he studied the rest of the picture that he knew so well.

Gathered around the fig tree were seven other figures: four characters to the left, three to the right. Of the four on the left, one was a beggared supplicant who knelt, reaching out to Saint Francis. Behind him, three disciples huddled together and conversed in an excited, expressive way about things that were undoubtedly profound. Leo guessed they were disciples because they wore the same robes of brown homespun material as their master and their hair was cut in the same saintly tonsure.

To the right of the tree, three other figures were likewise occupied. One appeared to be a shepherd, for he held a crook in his hand and two sheep were at his feet. An aged man with snow-white hair and beard, an unpretentious face, and pale blue eyes looked upward in astonishment and adoration. The other two figures at his side appeared to be more poor supplicants awaiting an audience and probably, hopefully, miracles from Saint Francis. One leaned painfully on a crutch and the other, with rags covering his eyes, appeared to be blind. And in the cobalt sky above this assemblage was a tight array of three angels with golden robes and white wings. This was the apex of the triangle that surrounded and pointed to the blessed saint beneath the blessed tree. And beyond the angels, seven silver stars twinkled in the night-blue sky.

It's hard to say how long the group of cultured English tourists and uncomplicated villagers stood together in whispered silence in front of the fresco.

Fortunately, while the English tourists stayed occupied with the Miracle and the Mystery, their beleaguered guide had also been successful. A hurried run down the winding street to the harbor had led him to Carlo Serafini, captain of the trawler *Emilia*. The old fisherman, who hadn't been more than a mile out of the harbor in years, could still tell when something swam into his net. He charged the desperate guide an outrageous amount for two big buckets of diesel fuel and then charged him again for a ride back up the hill in his old truck. By the time the troop of English pilgrims finally left the coolness of the church, they'd almost forgotten what was awaiting them. Stepping out of the quiet shadows into the blazing afternoon sun, the blast of heat almost roared at them.

The tour group noticed that their bus driver was a bit greasier than usual and reeked of diesel fuel, but they didn't care. It was enough that they were finally going to be on their way again. They might even be in Piombino in time for a cool bath, a change of clothes, and an evening stroll along the bay before dinner.

Leo stood at the door of the little bus bidding farewell to his new friends and accepting their thanks and good wishes. At last the tall Englishman with the large teeth and wild shock of salt-and-pepper hair stepped forward, placed one hand on Leo's shoulder, and thanked him heartily. As the two men shook hands Leo could feel a wad of bills being pressed into his palm. How discreet. How tactful. How British. With sincere thanks he prudently slipped the money into his trouser pocket without counting it. Trust was a valued thing in such an arrangement.

Then, with the transaction complete, the tall fellow climbed on board and the door closed. With a cough of foul smoke, the bus roared to life, circled the piazza once, and headed down the bumpy street out of town. The few locals that had stayed to watch the spectacle to the final curtain waved farewell as the bus disappeared down the hill. At Punta Ala they would pick up a comparatively decent road that skirted the Golfo di Follonica all the way to Piombino.

After a moment the dust settled and even the rumble of the engine was gone. All that remained was a silence broken by the distant yapping of startled dogs protesting the bus passing their yards. Then even the dogs went back to sleep. People returned to their homes and humdrum returned to Santo Fico.

Leo was finally able to count the cash. Trust is a valued thing, but so is accurate bookkeeping. In a quick check he discovered an extra two hundred thousand lire. A mistake? A tip? It didn't matter – they were gone. Leo quickly glanced around. Marta was eyeing him from behind the hotel's dark windows. Father Elio stood on the steps of the church waiting for him, and Topo was already scurrying across the piazza for his cut. He quickly shoved the extra bills in his pocket and hoped the surreptitious move wasn't noticed. It wasn't like he needed to hide anything, but why raise questions?

From inside the hotel, Marta watched the bills disappear into Leo's pocket and sighed. 'Typical.'

Why had he returned to Santo Fico? She'd reached a point in her life, after years of hard work and denial, where her disappointments had almost stopped hurting. She had carefully closed door after door to her heart, shutting out things, memories, and people who were reminders of her mistakes. She had embraced a kind of gray numbness that was preferable to red rage or black despair. And she certainly didn't need this memento of her greatest blunder walking back into town.

She watched Topo run over to his old friend and banter about something – probably the money. Suddenly the small man's face fell and then turned crimson. Marta knew this exchange by heart, but she hadn't seen it played out in many years and she couldn't help smiling. Leo was telling Topo that the cheap foreigners shortchanged them, or that Topo misunderstood the fee, or that he'd expected too much, or that Topo wanted more than his share – anything to torment the little mouse. And with each irritating claim Topo became more agitated, dancing around an unruffled Leo, who remained seemingly unaware of his friend's dilemma. She laughed in spite of herself when Topo finally stomped his foot and she saw him mouth those familiar words, 'Be fair!' That was the finale. Leo handed his friend a wad of bills and after a quick count, Topo's whoop for joy echoed around the piazza. Marta even heard it from behind the glass in the still messy dining room.

Topo waltzed around him as Leo walked across the piazza to the steps of the church and when Father Elio received his share, he first slapped Leo on the back and followed that up with a warm embrace – which irritated Marta even more. All of these people being so nice to Leo was only encouraging him to stay longer.

The sound of Carmen's laughter in the kitchen pulled Marta back to reality. To hell with Leo Pizzola. He wasn't going to spoil her day. It had been a good afternoon. She'd made enough money to take the pressure off for some weeks, but more important, she'd had Carmen and Nina working by her side in the kitchen and they'd even laughed together a few times. Marta allowed herself to hum a small tune as she returned to collecting dessert plates and coffee cups. Why not hum? The lunch had been a victory. They made money. She and her daughters had laughed together like the old days. The afternoon had been quite a success.

Father Elio was having similar thoughts as he returned to the coolness of his sanctuary. What a wonderful afternoon, he thought. First the strangers arrive, which forced Marta to change her lunch menu. Then Leo brings the foreigners in to see the Miracle and the Mystery, which hasn't happened in many years – even since before Leo ran away. And so many villagers came too. And finally, what a nice surprise it was that the English paid Leo more than they agreed on. But really, 700,000 lire was too much.

The old man made his way down the northern transept to the Mystery and switched off the lights. He considered returning the light bulbs to his bath and bedroom, but decided not yet. He wouldn't place the blanket back over the fresco either. He would leave it uncovered and tonight he would turn the lights back on so everyone could see the Mystery again.

Yes, the money was a wonderful blessing, but it wasn't

the best part of the afternoon. The best was that his old
church had been filled with people. Well . . . maybe not
filled, but there had certainly been more people than he'd
seen in a long time and many of them were villagers. True,
they were a bit sheepish about missing church for so many
months – or years. But had he gone too far? Had he become
too swept up in the excitement of the moment? As the foreigners were departing, he'd announced to all of his
neighbors that there would be a special mass this night.
Why did he do that? What had possessed him to say that?
The words just came flying out of his mouth before he
could stop them. The amazing part was they all promised
they would return . . . sort of. At any rate, many of them
did . . . or rather some of them nodded and said they would
try to attend. Now, wouldn't that be wonderful – to actually
have people attending mass again. This was the kind of
afternoon that made him think that someday God might
actually forgive him.

It was a rare occasion when Topo found himself in complete
accord with both Marta and Father Elio, but that was the
case today – what a wonderful afternoon. This was the first
time since Leo's return that he felt their old kinship. For six
weeks, the talk in the village about 'that young Pizzola's
return' had been generally unfavorable. Most people found
him 'standoffish,' or 'arrogant,' or 'dangerous,' or filled with
'stuck-up American ways,' or he just 'talked funny.' Topo
knew differently. Leo was unhappy. He was homesick and
talked incessantly about selling that run down farm and

going back to Chicago. But today was different. Today was like old times, only much better. In the old days Topo was on the perimeter watching Leo and Franco. Then he was an outsider who could only watch as they split the money. But today, he had performed Franco's job . . . sort of. It didn't matter if he didn't do all that Franco used to do, he sure received more money than Franco ever did. One hundred thousand lire!

And his joy was increased by Leo's joy. This was the first time he'd seen his old friend really happy since his return. Until today, he'd forgotten how infectious Leo's smile could be. His sad eyes and long face tended to occasionally make him look like he was trapped somewhere between being dangerous and dull-witted. But when he smiled, Leo's face exploded with such sincere innocent pleasure that any observer was forced to smile too. And that's what had happened to Topo. After Father Elio had disappeared into the church with his share of the fee, Leo had turned to Topo wearing a grin so expansive that at first it actually frightened the little man. But Leo just hooked his arm inside Topo's and suddenly pulled his small friend around in circles, dancing a clumsy yet spirited jig. Their whoops echoed around the piazza as they shook their respective wads of bills in each other's face. Topo relished that moment of gaiety more than he could say.

From their trusty places by the fountain, Nonno and the gray dog watched Leo's and Topo's antics as if the revelers' brains had gone sour.

But Topo's joy at their renewed camaraderie really only

lasted until Leo abruptly stopped dancing and announced enthusiastically, 'I have a great idea!'

It was impossible for Topo to hide his fear. From earliest memory, Leo's great ideas – in Topo's considered opinion – were often ill conceived, usually impetuous, and almost always dangerous. He also knew that he was ultimately going to go along with it. He couldn't resist that smile. He couldn't resist the enthusiasm. He couldn't resist the brotherhood. He was doomed.

His heart sank even deeper when Leo followed his announcement of an idea with a joyously loaded question. 'Does your truck have gas?'

Doomed!

Eight

*T*he western horizon still clung to a warm orange glow when Marta finally finished her preparations for the next day and turned out the lights in her spotless kitchen. Things would be back to normal tomorrow – six or seven lunches not counting Uncle Elio, then beer in the afternoon and wine in the evening. As she climbed the stairs to the bedrooms she heard music; Nina was listening to the radio. An orchestra was playing a song that Marta knew once upon a time. It was a familiar melody attached to some pleasant memory – what was it? She couldn't recall.

When she reached the hallway and turned the corner, she

was hit with a wall of hot, stale air. The kitchen had been warm, but compared to the stifling upstairs the downstairs was balmy. Sleep was going to be difficult tonight. She remembered nights like this when she was a little girl. Her father, Young Giuseppe – sometimes with the help of Uncle Elio – would haul old mattresses up from the basement and spread them across the grass in the backyard. As soon as those musty mattresses were on the grass Marta and her sister, Rosa, would be leaping from one to the other, pretending they were islands of safety in some magical sea of boiling acid or craggy mountaintops surrounded by plunging chasms. In either case, one misstep meant certain death. Then their mother, Katrine, would scold them – but always Rosa more than Marta because she had fourteen more months of good sense than her younger sister. Katrine was convinced that those old mattresses were filled with every disease of every former guest that ever spent a night under the hotel's roof dating back to whatever Caproni ancestor had made this villa his own – not to mention the legions of bugs that lived in the basement. Until all those filthy mattresses were covered with clean sheets, Katrine insisted that everyone stay off!

Those were wonderful nights. Marta's father would build a fire and neighbors would come over and drink wine and sing. They would play bocce until it was too dark to see and then play some more. Then the whole family would lie out under the black sky waiting for shooting stars and talking far into the night.

After Young Giuseppe and Katrine died, and Rosa had

married and moved to Cecina, when it was just herself and Franco and the girls, sometimes, on hot evenings, Marta would try to convince Franco that they should sleep in the backyard. But he only complained that dragging those filthy old mattresses out of the basement was too much work and they would only regret it when the morning sun shone in their eyes. Then later, as Marta and the girls lay upstairs tossing and sweating through the night, she would hear Franco's motorcycle start and then disappear down the road. Apparently Franco had his own solution for beating the heat. But all that was a long time ago and Marta was too tired to think about Franco tonight.

There were no lights on upstairs as she poked her head in Nina's bedroom and her eyes quickly adjusted to the glow of the radio on the other side of the room. Marta could make out the silhouette of her younger daughter sitting by the open window. This night wouldn't offer much relief from the heat for some hours yet, but by the window there was at least a little breeze coming in off the sea. Nina sat there in her thin nightgown, diligently working at her tatting and she spoke without breaking the rhythm of the little needle.

'Are you going to bed?'

It always amazed Marta that no matter how silent she attempted to be it was never enough.

'Yes. Where's your sister?'

'In her room I think.'

'Don't stay up too late.'

Marta looked down the hall. The living room was dark and silent. It was strange that at this time of the evening, in the summer, Carmen wasn't lying on the cool floor in front of the television. Across the hall, the door to Carmen's room was shut and there was no light showing, so Marta quietly opened the door a crack and peeked in. The moon was rising in the east and in the pale blue light streaming through the open window Carmen was visible in her bed. The sheet was pulled up and her thick black hair spilled across the white pillow. Her breathing was deep and steady.

Marta silently closed the door and walked on down the hall. She considered watching some television herself, maybe something that might make her laugh. But she was too tired. Instead, she went into her bedroom and dropped back onto the bed without turning on the light and she was immediately sorry she had done that. It was going to be difficult getting back up again. The day had been so busy that she'd forgotten to open the upstairs windows in the afternoon and that's why it was so stifling.

Forcing herself off the bed, she opened both sets of tall windows and welcomed a soft evening breeze. She stood for a moment allowing the cool air to wash over her. Maybe she should draw a bath. A bath would be wonderful. Maybe she should just shed all her clothes and sit in front of the dark window. Or maybe she should just run naked through the streets of Santo Fico until she reached the harbor. Then she could dive into the sea and swim and swim toward that dark crimson line in the west. She didn't have the strength to laugh at her foolishness. Besides, she probably couldn't even run all the way to the harbor anymore. The bath was a better idea.

She wondered how Carmen could possibly sleep under that sheet. Her room was every bit as hot as Marta's was. She must have been tired. She'd worked hard all day and had been especially helpful in cleaning up this evening, but still, to sleep under that sheet . . .

Her musings were disturbed by an almost comically familiar sound from off in the distance. An old motor scooter was painfully making its way up the steep road. It sounded like Salvatore Puce, that unpleasant young man from Grosseto who brought the mail two times a week, but what would that greasy little *porco deficiente* be doing here now? She didn't like the way that pimply little pervert looked at Carmen, but more than that she didn't like the way Carmen insisted on flirting with him.

The sound of the scooter stopped not a hundred meters down the road.

It was a good thing Carmen was in her room so early . . . asleep . . . with the door closed . . . and with the sheet pulled up to her neck!

Marta leapt away from the window like a bolt of lightning and was across her room and down the hall like rolling thunder.

Throwing open Carmen's door she discovered the bed empty. Since the hallway was clear Marta concluded that her idiot daughter was by now on the ledge outside her window, around the corner, and headed for the empty rose trellis.

Carrying her shoes in a small handbag, Carmen worked her way along the wobbly old tiles of the narrow overhang that skirted the back of the hotel as quickly as possible, but every time she stepped the tiles slipped or cracked beneath her bare feet. Her escape route was less substantial than she remembered. The roof gave an odd moaning sound and it occurred to her that if she fell she could be seriously bruised or even scratched, and her best skirt might be torn. She just needed to get over to the trellis by the kitchen door, and then she could climb down it like a ladder.

When she had imagined this evening's escapade, it had not included danger, pain, or ruined clothes. The prospect of an evening with Solly Puce wasn't even all that appealing, but Carmen had her reasons. It wasn't like she didn't know what Solly wanted – at least, she thought she did. She had seen enough kissing in the movies, and her girlfriends certainly talked about it enough. Carmen knew what Solly had in mind – and he would just have to learn to live with disappointment. He promised to take her to Grosseto and Grosseto had movie theaters and nightclubs and bars where people danced. It shouldn't take her long to dump Solly for some rich man with a nice car.

Scrambling down the bare rose trellis, she heard Salvatore Puce stop his ridiculous scooter down the bottom of the road as agreed. His timing was perfect. At the far end of the flagstone path she could see a moonlit figure step out from behind the stone wall. Of course, it was too dark to actually make out his face, but even in the pale blue light of the moon there was no mistaking Solly Puce's twitching.

Solly had an unpleasant quirk that was more than just a series of disturbing twitches, it was more like an eerie ritual.

Without warning, in mid-sentence sometimes, he would suddenly jerk his head backward as if tossing thick locks of luxurious hair off his forehead. He would then roll his head to the left and rotate his right shoulder in a great circle, like a stretch designed to relieve tension in a muscular neck or shoulder. This sequence happened dazzlingly fast and was followed up by an abrupt shake of his whole torso – much as if his body were a sack of randomly disconnected bones – and this tremor put everything back in proper position. The truth was, Solly didn't have luxurious locks. His black hair was piled and greased into a pompadour of preposterous proportions that wouldn't budge in gale force winds. And he certainly didn't need to relieve tension in a muscular anything. He was not only shorter than Carmen, but one of his most amazing features was that anyone could be that skinny and live. Actually, this whole series of bizarre spasms and tics that Solly performed with clocklike regularity found their origins in old American rock and roll movies of the 1950s, and if the routine weren't so weird, it would have been comical. But, in his mind, his moves projected a powerful and dangerous virility, and he knew that women found his contortions irresistibly sexy – witness Carmen Fortino hurrying down the flagstone path toward him.

As she drew closer Solly started to speak, but his eyes suddenly became wide with terror. Then, even more unexpectedly, he performed what seemed an odd variation of his predictable twitch. His new little dance followed a strange moment when Carmen could have sworn she saw something like a rock bounce off Solly Puce's pimply forehead with a surprisingly deep thud, but it was hard to tell in the moonlight. For some reason Solly's legs did turn to jelly and he staggered around in a complete circle with both hands gripping his forehead. When he finally wobbled back into place and looked toward Carmen, his face was white as a sheet, except for a large dark smudge in the center of his brow. Then he shrieked in terror and Carmen turned in time to see a giant apparition striding toward her with what appeared to be an ax raised in the air – or perhaps it was a scythe. This shadowed Grim Reaper was moving fast and its obvious intent was death. Carmen's scream mingled with Solly's girlish shriek and she stumbled backward into the herb garden, landing painfully in a prickly rosemary bush.

Marta swung her shovel at Solly's head with all her might, but the little weasel fell backward into the dusty road as her shovel crashed against the stone wall with the resounding clang of an alarm bell and a surprising flash of sparks. As quickly as she could recover, the shovel was raised over her head again and, this time, directed down at the terrified boy screaming in the dirt. But he was already twisting and spinning down the road like a top, and by the time the shovel landed he'd rolled away. Marta strode forward to get a better swing at his backside, but by now Solly was crawling down the lane faster than most people could run. So Marta shouted something indistinguishable after him. Even she had no idea exactly what she said, but her intent was clear – 'Return and die!'

By now Carmen was on her feet and screaming at her mother for this attack on her independence, but all of the adolescent outrage in the world was no match for Marta's wrath. When her mother turned on her with the shovel still held high, still eager to dig someone's grave, Carmen discovered how seriously she was overmatched. Marta's voice was so swift and intense, her threats so honest, her daughter was chilled with fear. In the distance poor Solly Puce yelled some frightened vendettas and sobbed a feeble promise of vengeance as his old Vespa putt-putted down the hill and Carmen listened to her chance for bright lights and a reckless night disappear into the darkness. Amid a hail of curses and tears Carmen retreated into the house.

When she was alone, Marta dropped the shovel and sank to her knees on the path as silence enclosed her. Marta didn't cry often, but when the river overflowed its banks it was usually a flash flood. The deluge passed as quickly as it came and when she was finally able, she looked into the dark sky and said simply, 'Help . . .'

That was all. Help. She hadn't intended it as a prayer. She hadn't even intended to say it, but within that simple plea her splintered heart spoke of regret and fears and questions. It was a plea for solutions to terrors so thick and knotted that words tangled inside her like matted hair and couldn't be spoken, only felt.

Father Elio was tired, his chest hurt, and he longed for his bed, so progress around the empty sanctuary was slow. He shuffled around turning out the main lights, unplugging the extension cord, and rehanging the old blanket over the Mystery. He managed to do all this without once meeting the eyes of the figures that watched him from the wall. It was a practiced procedure. The light bulbs were hot and he was too tired to juggle with them tonight. Everything he needed to do in his bath or bedroom he could do in the dark. Nina did everything in the dark every day and she lived every day with grace.

He extinguished the altar candles he had lit earlier in the evening and the room was finally dark. Moonlight through the upper windows spread a series of small silver pools down the center of the sanctuary and Elio sat on the stone floor in one of those small pools of moonlight thinking about his special mass. No one had come. Not one person. He had donned his robes alone, but with expectations. He had prepared the Eucharist alone, but with hope. He had knelt alone at the chancel for over two hours, praying softly and straining to hear the sound of someone entering the vestibule. No one came. Tonight he had discovered a new depth of being alone. It wasn't loneliness. He was well acquainted with loneliness and it no longer bothered him. This was different. For the first time he felt abandonment.

Angry voices shouted somewhere off in the night. Women were arguing somewhere about something, but it was all too faint to make out and he was glad when they stopped. It was only people arguing. People argue. People fight and they say things they don't mean, but they say them anyway. When he was a young man living in Bologna, late at night he heard people fighting all the time. Sometimes he heard them scream. It was awful when he heard distant screams. He was studying to be a priest because he wanted to

help people and angry shouts in the night meant people were
suffering. Priests were supposed to make things better.

He was startled by the sound of his own moan echoing
around him and without warning his tears washed the
ancient stones. A prayer escaped before he even knew he
was going to pray.

'Help . . .'

Help whom? Help him? No. He was a failure and he knew
why. God had rejected him – to deny him the privilege of
the Holy Spirit was only justice. Elio had perpetrated his
monstrous sin every day for almost fifty years. No, this was
a prayer of bewilderment he felt for the people of Santo
Fico. They hadn't sinned and yet they were the ones who
were being punished. They hadn't even lost their faith. They
simply no longer cared. Apathy wasn't rejection. But it was
as if God had also abandoned them, and so it was for them
that he prayed for help.

In his little room down by the pier, Nonno had just finished
supper when he heard what sounded like the postal boy's
motor scooter headed south out of town and he wondered
who might be receiving a letter at this time of night.
Actually, the gray dog heard it first, and when Nonno saw
him suddenly perk up, he paid special attention too. Time
had taught him to pay attention to his companion. He wasn't
really Nonno's dog, but for many years now they'd lived
together in this shed down by the wharf. The single room
had once been a part of Angelo de Parma's house, but the
connecting door had been mysteriously sealed off in some

previous century and Angelo had allowed Nonno and the dog to live there for so many years they'd both forgotten what the original arrangement was. Neither cared anymore anyway. The walls and roof, like so many ancient buildings, were thick and snug, but Nonno particularly liked the room because he was just across the harbor road from the bay and he loved the ocean. The dog never complained either.

Nonno had no idea why he so loved the sea. It probably had something to do with his past and so he resolved that he would never know. There was so much in his past that was blank he'd finally stopped questioning – not because he didn't care, but because it was too frustrating. It was like trying to fill your hat with fog. You think you have some until you go to check it in the sunlight – then it's gone. So much about him had evaporated under the Tuscan sun. Like his name – everyone had called him Grandfather for so long his real name was probably forgotten forever. But he didn't care anymore.

The old people still remembered him wandering into town in the dead of winter, starving and delirious with fever. Even back then he wasn't sure of his name or where he was from. He knew he had a wife and three sons, but to the best of anyone's knowledge Nonno's family were all dead, probably killed. No one knew for sure because too much war, too much killing, and too much grief had jumbled Nonno's senses. Back then he talked angrily about killing Germans – not prudent talk in Italy during World War II. But the villagers of Santo Fico took him in and now the old man's mind wandered around his memories much in the same way he wandered around the village – like a man lost in the clutter of his own house, searching for something significant that can be known only when discovered. Why he bore a personal guilt about the fountain's missing water was a mystery, but most of Nonno was a mystery. He often spoke cryptically of misplaced times, or of soldiers and battles, or war in the mountains. He would ramble on about women he had known, or his lost pocket watch, or his lost sons. Nonno knew that he got confused sometimes, but then at other times he couldn't understand why those around him were so confused.

'Like this afternoon with Nico,' he thought out loud as he wiped his dinner plate with a dirty towel. 'Nico's a good boy, but he's so unhappy all the time,' he said to the gray dog sleeping in the corner.

As he sat on the edge of his bed and pulled off his shoes he confessed to his dozing companion, 'I don't understand why he acts like he doesn't know me sometimes.' But it was enough just to be around him after so many years. Nico was all he had left, so it didn't bother him too much when sometimes the boy acted like he didn't know his own name. Leo just passed off being called Nico as some obscure term of affection, and unfortunately there was no one in the village who knew the name of the old man's youngest son. Nor was there anyone able to recognize Leo's resemblance to the sorrowfully handsome boy that Nonno had buried with his own frozen hands forty years ago in the snows of the Dolomites where he and his two brothers had died fighting the Germans.

As Nonno put out the light and lay back on his cot he determined that what he should do is pray more for the boy. And so he did.

On the plains south of town, Topo stood by the side of the road and peered into the moonlit darkness trying to see if Leo was still conscious. But the star-filled sky and the low moon weren't offering enough light, and he shuddered with a nervous chill. At least Leo's revolting gagging had finally stopped, but now the eerie silence was bothering him. He considered moving away from the safety of the truck to search for his friend, but there might be snakes out there. So he just called again, 'Leo?'

Silence.

His little truck was parked just beyond where the road turned out of the trees and then curved west across flat fields that ran on toward the ocean. From this spot to where the cliffs met the sea was only a few kilometers of dry plains filled with weeds, cactus, and rocks. The road then turned north at the headlands and ran along another kilometer of treacherously narrow cliffs to the top of the promontory until it reached Santo Fico. Topo could see a few random lights in the distance and could almost make out the bell tower silhouetted in the moonlight. He could be home and in his bed in minutes if Leo would just come back to the truck. This had not been a merry night and now it refused to end.

Topo hated Grosseto – not the whole city, just the places that Franco and Leo liked. When he allowed Leo to convince him to take their new wealth to Grosseto for a good time, he also made Leo promise that they would stay away from Il Cavallo Morto. Topo hated that place most of all.

They tried numerous bars, looking for someplace that Leo felt had the right mix of noise, smoke, and congenial company. And Topo noticed that Leo became increasingly irritated with their inability to find that perfect spot. So they kept bar hopping, always drawing nearer to where Topo feared they were headed even before he reluctantly left Santo Fico. By the time they did finally arrive at Il Cavallo Morto, Leo was not only drunk, but also generally belligerent.

It had been eighteen years since their last visit to the rough bar on the edge of Grosseto's railroad district. In all the years since Franco's terrible bachelor party, the seedy little saloon hadn't changed – the clientele hadn't improved, nothing had been cleaned, and Topo still couldn't figure out why anyone would name a bar after a dead horse. But Il Cavallo Morto had been Franco's favorite watering hole and now for some reason Leo was drawn to it.

It sure isn't the happy memories, Topo thought, and their last visit burned in his mind. The night before the wedding . . . They had sat at a big round table in the back for hours, eight or ten friends – all drinking and singing. Then it got to be late. Sofia de Salvio was sitting on Franco's lap crying and begging him not to get married and Franco was laughing. And the more he laughed, the more she cried. Then Franco said something to her – Topo couldn't hear, but it made Sofia de Salvio laugh too. Leo was across from them with his head on the table and everyone thought he was asleep, but when Franco whispered that thing to Sofia and they both laughed, Leo was suddenly on his feet. He roared as he leapt completely across the table at Franco. The three of them – Leo, Franco, and poor Sofia de Salvio – all crashed to the ground, and then they were brawling on the filthy floor. Leo and Franco battled for almost twenty minutes and pretty much destroyed the bar, not that there was much in this bar to destroy. It was the only time Topo saw Leo win a fight with Franco, but Leo's rage was fearful to see. When it was over Franco lay in the street and Leo took Topo's truck. Franco and Topo had to hitch a ride back to Santo Fico. The next day at the wedding Franco walked with a limp. One of his eyes was puffed shut and his jaw was so swollen he couldn't say 'I do.' He had to nod. Topo's truck was abandoned outside town and Leo had disappeared. Topo had to be the best man and he lost the ring. Marta couldn't stop crying. Later in the afternoon it rained. What a terrible wedding.

Now, standing in the dark field, waiting for his friend to stop throwing up, Topo realized that tonight had already turned out more like 'the good old days' than he had hoped for. The drinking, the singing, the reminiscing had been good – but by midnight the liquor in Topo's stomach had turned sour, he had a headache, and he wanted to go home. That was about the time that Leo decided to join a card game in a back room. He was going to win enough money to 'get the hell outta this piss hole.' At least, that's what his garbled slurs sounded like to Topo. Later there was the pushing and the shouting at the card table after he'd lost all his money. Next came the punching and the falling down in the street when they were tossed out of the bar. Then there were the protests about being cheated, followed by the bumpy ride home filled with angry threats against every male child ever born in Grosseto. Leo finally reached his peak of self-pity with a demand that Topo stop the truck, and even before the truck came to a complete halt, Leo was out the door, staggering and vomiting his way into the darkness. That was twenty minutes ago.

'Leo?'

Silence.

Straining against the moonlight, all Topo could make out were mounds of shadowy boulders and cactus. He knew that one of those motionless lumps was Leo, but since the retching noises stopped he'd lost track of which one.

'Leo? Are you okay?'

Silence.

Leo struggled to his knees and was glad it was dark. He looked terrible, that was for sure. He remembered the jacket ripping in the fight and one of the knees tore when he fell on the greasy pavement. All his money was gone and his suit was ruined. With one hand he checked the top of his head – at least he still had his hat. He tried to climb up to his feet and failed.

Topo called again from the truck. Kneeling against the low boulder Leo let out a sound. It was supposed to be a word, perhaps a phrase – something to let Topo know that he was all right. Instead what came out was the cry of an animal in pain – something terrified and trapped. Leo moaned angrily to the sky; it was as close to a prayer as anything he had uttered in years. Why had he returned? Why had God trapped him in this place again? Why did God continue to humiliate him and mock him? It may have been a prayer of sorts, but he was surprised to discover that it was also a challenge because as he knelt clenching the boulder, he felt defiance growing in his heart. No words, no real thoughts, but abstractions of anger raced in his mind and he tossed his contempt into the teeth of God. He would not accept this fate – a lifetime of disrepute in Santo Fico. No matter what it took he would escape and this time he would not be tricked into returning. He dared God to stop him.

Struggling to his feet, he searched out the faint silhouette of the small truck back at the road.

'I'm okay. I'm coming.'

His words were still more slurred than he intended, but some dignity had returned. Brushing himself off and straightening his tie, he took less than a dozen tentative steps across the field before he tripped over a tall thin boulder that was standing oddly on its end and he fell into a small cactus. The stinging nettles gave him new incentive to quickly find his feet, accompanied by a hail of painful curses. In a matter of moments he was again staggering across the field toward the shadow of the little truck.

Leo didn't bother to notice the tall, thin stone that had tripped him and he was certainly far too drunk to see the bright glint of metal that the moonlight revealed buried beneath it.

Nine

*A*fter their long day sweltering in the kitchen and then the violent rendezvous in the garden with Solly Puce, Marta and Carmen were both exhausted. They barely had enough energy to fight for a full hour before retreating to their bedrooms where each cried herself to sleep.

At about that same time, Father Elio finished his prayers and made his way back to his dark rooms. He got all the way to the bathroom before he was reminded that there were no light bulbs. He was so exhausted from his unusually active day, he didn't mind ignoring a few of the usual ablutions.

What was absolutely necessary was performed in the dark and he was asleep by eleven.

Down the road, in the cluttered rooms behind the Pasolini Fix-It Shop, it was almost 2:30 by the time Topo was finally able to climb out of his clothes and slip peacefully between his cool familiar sheets.

Topo loved his house and his shop. He had inherited the building, the business, and much of the debris that filled all the rooms from his father. He even inherited his talent for tinkering and his reluctance to throw anything away (or put anything away for that matter) from his father. Cans of discarded screws, countless bolts without nuts, twice as many nuts without bolts, washers, wires, tubes, and cords, boxes of parts, parts without boxes – anything that his hand or the hand of his father had ever touched, but didn't use, remained in the shop; shoved, stacked, and crammed into every room, closet or cubbyhole available. To call the Pasolini family pack rats trivializes an art form.

The whole lot of it had been passed down from his father – that is, all except the 'Pasolini Classics of World Cinema.' That was Topo's doing. He began collecting old films as a teenager when a movie theater in Castiglione went out of business. When he was older he discovered a distributor in Livorno who would sell him discarded or damaged prints. Now, after almost twenty-five years of collecting, he had over sixty films. The large tin spools were all categorized and filled special shelves that covered the walls of his bedroom. Some years earlier he'd acquired a broken projector and repaired it himself. Often, on

Saturday nights, when the weather was fine, Topo would set up his projector in the town square and show his films on the side of the church. He didn't make any announcements. He had no schedule – he just set up when the spirit moved him. But when word went out that Guido Pasolini was stringing extension cords across the piazza, you could be sure that as the sun went down the square was going to be filled with blankets and chairs.

Topo could hear Leo already snoring in the front room. The thought of any further trek to Leo's stone hut had been too daunting for either of them and Leo quickly accepted Topo's mumbled offer to spend the night. He sprawled across his friend's couch and the discrepancy in length between Leo's lanky frame and the short sofa was no deterrent. In a matter of minutes, first Leo, then Topo drifted off and, at long last, everyone in Santo Fico was finally asleep.

When the earth began to rumble, sunrise was still over two hours away. It began when the ocean floor buckled slightly some fifty kilometers out at sea and it rolled quickly north past the small island of Montecristo, heading for the coast just south of Santo Fico. As earthquakes go, it wasn't much. The next day newspapers in the region would mention the event, noting some minor damage to a few older buildings in Grosseto, Follonica, and Massa. News accounts would assure the readers that, 'Fortunately, the moderate tremor missed major cities and caused relatively no damage.'

But while the citizens of Grossetto to the south and Siena

to the north barely rolled over in their collective sleep, to certain small and forgotten villages it was serious business.

It was 3:47 when the gray dog stirred. Of course, Nonno had no way of knowing it was 3:47 because, as he repeatedly reminded people, he lost his watch when he made the water go away. He knew it was early since through the room's only window he could see that it was still dark outside. The scratching at the door at such an hour troubled the old man because the dog always slept through the night and it was a little upsetting to suddenly have his mangy companion whining as if the earth itself was about to swallow him.

Then Nonno heard what he knew the dog must have heard and he too became frightened. A low rumbling came rolling around him, as if some ancient monster was beginning to stir and grumble deep within the sea, just beyond his door. Then, it was as if the ground took up the complaint and the earth beneath his bed moaned painfully. As the groaning became louder, everything began to quiver and tremble. Small objects skittered across tables and shelves. The terrified dog howled loudly and the old man scrambled off his cot. He staggered toward the door, but the floor and furniture rolled around him and Nonno became so muddled in the dark that he found himself grasping at bare plaster where he was sure a door handle should have been. He barely had time to realize how topsy-turvy everything was before the roof and much of the walls of the dilapidated building collapsed on him. The old dog yelped once and then the howling stopped.

*

Upstairs at the Albergo di Santo Fico, Marta was awakened from a dreamless sleep by the sound of pictures dropping off the walls and crashing against the floor. The moon had set and the room was pitch black. The deep rumbling earth, the crashing pictures, her bed tossing back and forth – Marta became convinced someone was in her room attacking her and she sat up, her fists clenched and her arms swinging wildly to fend off an assault. But in an instant she came to herself and was out of bed and down the hall, shouting all the way.

'Carmen! Get out! Nina, hurry! Get up!'

In the darkness of the hall she heard Carmen scream, but could see nothing. She used the wall as a guide, hurried toward the sound, and ran straight into Carmen, who was bolting into the hall from her own room. Both of them tripped and fell over each other and became a tangle of limbs on a floor that rolled and pitched beneath them. Marta forced herself to her feet, pulled Carmen up, and started off in the direction of what she thought was Nina's room. But her face smashed into the plaster wall and she saw dizzying lights behind her eyes as she sank back to her knees. Carmen screamed louder. Suddenly, there were steady hands on their shoulders and Nina's voice commanded them over the groans of the wobbling villa.

'This way! Come with me!'

Nina led them down the trembling hall and all along the corridor while in adjacent rooms chairs and tables tap-danced madly across the hardwood floors. Marta and Carmen clung to Nina's thin nightgown and listened only to her soothing voice as it guided them through the black terror.

Down the hill at his little Fix-It shop, Topo slept peacefully, unaware that his family's penchant for collecting was about to do him in. The earthquake hit the cluttered Fix-It shop like a whirlwind hits a house of cards. In a matter of seconds shelves of containers, boxes of debris, years and generations of miscellaneous collecting showered down around him like a hailstorm of angry utensils. Discarded toasters, broken radios, obsolete thingamajigs and forsaken doohickeys all toppled from their precariously balanced pyramids and came crashing off their perches.

Topo scrabbled out of bed, groping for a light. His voice shrieked at a pitch usually heard only by dogs, 'Earthquake! Save me God! Earthquake!'

Leo stirred on the dusty sofa in the living room and discovered his room was raining small appliances as well, but his coma had been deeper. At Topo's second panicked screech of 'Earthquake!' Leo managed to wipe a line of drool off his cheek and sit up. He hadn't slept nearly long enough to actually sober up – only long enough to develop a massive headache and a ferocious thirst. Blinking at the light streaming in from Topo's bedroom he too became aware of objects crashing and collapsing around him. Topo was right. It was an earthquake.

'My God, Leo help,' came the new frantic cry from the bedroom. Leo could see his friend whirling around the room like a dervish, vainly trying to hold his film canisters in place. But in spite of his frantic efforts, canister after canister hit the floor with a cymbal crash. Then each flat can flew open and the spools wheeled themselves across the room. It was like a grotesque dance, the way Topo leapt about grabbing at his collapsing film empire. A few of the spools rolled out of the bedroom and across the living room floor leaving a shiny snail-trail of black celluloid behind. Leo almost wanted to laugh, but his head felt like his brain was three sizes too large for his skull.

With a gasp, the real peril of the earthquake hit Leo like a shot of dry cell voltage. He sprang from the sofa and bolted for the door, catching a medium-sized television that was dropping from a shelf as he raced past. The catch was instinctual and purely in self-defense, but from the bedroom Topo saw his friend save one of his only working televisions and was sincerely grateful for the help, until he watched Leo toss the TV over his shoulder and dash out the front door. Then the electricity went off.

Father Elio had to manage on his own. It didn't take much shaking and rumbling to rouse the old man; these days his sleep was fitful at best. At the first tremor he was sitting up on his cot. There was a door in his small room that led outside to the back of the church, but he ignored that way to safety and instead charged down the low corridor toward the kitchen. He heard things in the distance that made his heart ache.

Father Elio's hands fumbled along the stone walls of the ancient tunnel, stumbling blindly forward as if the terrible sounds echoing from the cathedral were pulling him. In the darkness ahead of him he heard explosions of glass crashing against stone floor and he prayed that some of the beautiful stained glass windows would be spared. Then a violent rending that sounded to Elio like a scream of pain shook the building far beyond the shaking of the earthquake. It was followed by the thunderous roar of a collapsing building and a tremor so violent it knocked Father Elio off his feet. Something was terribly wrong in the sanctuary. Crawling forward on his hands and knees, he began to cough and fight for air as the dark corridor was engulfed in a wave of thick, choking dust.

Leo ran so quickly up the narrow street he was unaware of when the quake actually stopped. From the tall houses that lined the corridor like sheer canyon walls, he could hear frightened voices crying and wailing in the darkness, calling desperately to loved ones, but he saw no people.

He stumbled and tripped a great deal as he raced up the hill, but not just from the remains of the alcohol that was rapidly sweating out of his system. The dark street was littered with broken crockery, the remnants of window boxes filled with flowers, and terra-cotta roof tiles that were shaken loose and crashed to the street. As chunks of dislodged debris fell out of the blackness, their shattering concussions on the cobblestones sent him dodging to one side or the other, often crashing into the ghostly white walls that defined his gauntlet. It was a good thing no one called for help because he had no intention of stopping.

Adrenaline carried Leo quite a ways up the hill, but by the time he reached the top his heart was pounding like an angry drum, his lungs burned, and he felt as if he might have thrown up had he not so effectively taken care of that earlier. But the quaking and rumbling had stopped; all that could be heard now were the whines and yowls of distant dogs and the intermittent wails of terrified people. These indistinct cries came from places beyond the edge of darkness and seemed far away and otherworldly.

Leo staggered his way around to the front of the hotel, trying to ignore his trembling legs, churning stomach, and the desire for cold beer and a cigarette. The moon was long down, but the sky was clear and the stars were close and bright, allowing almost enough light to make out ghostly shapes and phantom shadows in the darkness. When he had rounded the corner coming up the hill, he'd looked over the low wall and into the back garden of the hotel hoping to find three figures huddled by the chinaberry bush at the back gate, but everything was one great shifting shadow and he heard no sound. He moved across the empty piazza at the front of the hotel and still couldn't be sure of what was real and what wasn't. At least the hotel was standing, but the harder he strained to see, the less sure he was of what he saw. Where were they? Why weren't they outside? Why couldn't he hear them? If the roof had collapsed, then from the outside everything might appear normal, but Marta and the girls could be in their beds, buried under piles of beams and plaster and tile.

At the far end of the building – the side that overlooked

the bay — there was a wide staircase that led directly to the family's living quarters. As a boy Leo had raced up and down those stairs a thousand times and that was his route of choice now. He pushed through the gate and was fumbling his way across the verandah when he saw three ghostly apparitions clinging together like spirits floating slowly down the staircase. Nina led the way, her sure hands following the rails; Marta and Carmen still clung to her and gripped handfuls of each other's thin nightgowns.

'Marta . . . !'

Marta hated that she recognized his voice, but hated even more that she was glad to hear it.

'What do you want?'

'Are you all right?'

'Have you come to rescue me again? Last time you came by here in the middle of the night to do that, you were too late and I broke your nose. Go away or I'll break it again.'

Leo expected no less, but for Carmen and Nina their mother's cryptic remarks certainly raised questions. Both girls wanted to know more about failed rescues and broken noses, but Nina had a more urgent concern and she spoke directly to Leo.

'Have you seen Uncle Elio? I heard a big noise from the church. Can you see him?'

She may have spoken to Leo, but it was Marta who won the fearful, stumbling race across the suddenly treacherous piazza. Narrow white flashlight beams and broad golden glowing lanterns were appearing down the side streets of the village. Voices were calling out of the darkness; neighbors calling to neighbors in fear, or for help, or just to hear another voice.

Leo caught up with Marta at the church doors, which, of course, were open. It would never occur to Father Elio to lock any church door. When Leo pulled one of the great doors back he and Marta were greeted by a rolling wave of dust that poured out like a thick fog, spilling down the steps.

'Uncle Elio!' Marta screamed through the open door in spite of the choking dust. 'Uncle Elio . . . !' But the church was silent.

Marta threw herself into the black cloud of dust, but in just a few meters she was tripping and falling over unsteady mounds of broken plaster, jagged tiles, and splintered beams. She called for Father Elio, but her only reply was an occasional explosion of falling debris. Great chunks of plaster and tiles dropped from thirty meters over her head, bursting like bombs and refilling the dark air with more dust. Someone called her name, but the fine dry dirt filled her lungs and eyes and she lost all sense of direction. Scrambling across a mountain of shifting debris in what should have been the center aisle, Marta tripped over a plaster slab and landed hard against something jagged. She felt a searing pain in her hip and tried to call out, but she couldn't catch her breath. Time and direction blurred and her mind was filled with the image of her uncle buried beneath the wreckage of his church. She crawled forward, but again Marta heard her name being called from the bottom of a black well. She tried to answer, but all that came out was more choking and gagging. Something closed around her leg and pulled at her. She fought hard as she was dragged painfully back across the broken mounds of rubble; sinking deeper into a confused darkness, kicking with all her might at whatever gripped her leg. Suddenly everything seemed to give way. She was tossed and jostled in the air like a sack of potatoes and reluctantly she gave herself over to the spinning, tumbling fall. Wherever she was going, she would land eventually and deal with it then – and the blanket of dust swept over her and covered her mind.

Marta awoke on the steps of the church to stars shining out of the black sky. Carmen and Nina knelt beside her. Someone was coughing and gasping for air and she thought it was herself, but after a moment realized it was Leo. It was Leo who'd entered the crumbling cathedral, found her, fought her, and carried her out to safety – and she was stung by the thought that he finally got his rescue after all. She tried to speak, but her voice was thick with dust. She swallowed hard and tried again.

'Where's Uncle Elio?'

A thin voice called out of the darkness at the far corner of the building, 'Here . . . I'm here.'

The old priest was out of breath and covered with dirt, but he was alive and climbing the steps toward them. The three women collapsed on the exhausted old man, clinging to him as their tears smeared the dirt from their faces with the dirt on his.

'Something fell . . . The ceiling, I think . . . It has to be. I tried to turn on the lights, but I don't think we have electricity. Everything was dark. I had to go out through the garden. Some of the old wall has fallen, but I couldn't see . . . I couldn't see if . . . I couldn't see.'

Father Elio's dry voice was filled with dread. Everyone knew what it was that he couldn't see and what filled his heart with fear. If the garden wall collapsed, had it crushed the frail fig tree? Was the Miracle destroyed? But before anyone could respond, a high, frightened cry cut through the darkness.

'Father Elio!'

A lantern was running across the piazza toward them. When it reached the bottom step they could see that it was attached to Angelo de Parma's skinny grandson, Frankie. Barefoot and dressed only in his underwear, the boy was wild-eyed and out of breath.

'Father Elio! My grandfather told me to get you! Nonno's house fell in! He's buried! And his dog too!'

Elio struggled to his feet, rubbed his face harshly, and took a deep breath to clear his head – there would be much to do all over the village and that would keep him from thinking about . . . Don't think about it! Too much to do.

The old priest was amazingly calm as he quickly divided up chores for those around him. Leo would gather volunteers. Some of them would meet at Nonno's old shed down by the pier to begin digging and the rest would spread out to discover if more buildings had collapsed on their sleeping neighbors. There might be injuries. Many would be frightened and looking for refuge. Marta and the girls would open the hotel for everyone and would prepare coffee. There was much to do. But when they were ready to go, they discovered their lantern-bearer frozen like a statue.

At first Frankie was humiliated when he realized he was standing in front of Carmen Fortino in his underwear. Carmen, who was of course used to adolescent infatuation, perceived the boy's embarrassment and played on it for a moment out of habit. However, Frankie had discovered that if he held the lantern at just the right angle he could see many secret features of Carmen's body through her thin nightgown and he couldn't help but offer her an innocently lecherous grin. But before Carmen understood what was going on or Frankie could get what he considered a really good look, Father Elio was hurrying the boy back across the piazza toward the harbor road.

It didn't take long for word to spread throughout Santo Fico as to who had suffered what. There was an abundance of cuts and bruises, a fair amount of hysterics, and one suspected heart attack that turned out to be nervous indigestion. The injured and frightened, almost by instinct, began gathering in the piazza where they discovered candles and lanterns burning in every window of the hotel and they were drawn to it like moths. Marta and the girls had their hands full supplying coffee and tea and wine and whatever else a distraught neighbor might need.

It soon became obvious that everyone in the village, and probably the region, would have a fair amount of cleaning up to do. There was going to be a run on roof tiles for weeks to come. Fortunately for Santo Fico, it appeared that the only severe damage to buildings was Nonno's ancient shed and the church. But what had happened to the church was still unknown, and would remain so until sunlight. Father Elio refused to think about it; his only concern at the moment was Nonno.

A dozen workers in a variety of nightshirts moved with eerie slowness through the mound of rubble that Nonno and the gray dog had called home. The glow of kerosene lamps, with their tall shadows flickering against the back wall of Angelo de Parma's tall house, accentuated the ghostly quality. The men worked as quickly as they could, but they had to be careful. When the lights hit from a certain angle it appeared as though Angelo de Parma's great two-story back wall had shifted and was now leaning toward the sea. And, as if to thwart their efforts, great red tiles would occasionally slide off Angelo's roof and shatter on the cobblestones, landing dangerously close to workers.

As hard as Father Elio tried to put the fate of his beautiful little church out of his mind, images of the dust-clogged chapel and the terrible breach in the ancient garden wall attacked his brain. Every time a tile crashed near him he heard the terrible roar of his beautiful arched ceiling collapsing onto the mosaic floor. Stepping through the rubble of Nonno's room, he pictured the rubble of his garden wall. He was expecting punishment, but never this. This was too much.

They'd been working their way through the wreckage

for almost twenty minutes when Leo turned over a board and in the dim lamplight discovered a chunk of plaster that seemed to have a nose. As he bent down to inspect it, the chunk of plaster opened its eyes and blinked at him. Then it sort of smiled, and sort of wheezed, 'Hey, Nico.'

'Hey, Nonno . . . Here you are.'

Tears welled up in the dusty old eyes. 'I knew you'd find me . . . You're standing on my stomach.'

Leo called out. Others quickly gathered around and so began the slow process of digging him out. But Nonno called to Leo, 'Hey, Nico, you won't leave me, will you?'

'No, Nonno, I'll stay right here.'

But the old man wasn't convinced, and when Leo moved back to let the other workers in, he sobbed, 'It's not like the mountains, Nico! I didn't want to leave you! I swear to God I didn't! Please . . . Don't leave me here. Please don't leave me . . .'

No one had any notion of the storms that were swirling inside Nonno's head, but his panic was dangerous; every gesture he made came precariously close to knocking down the one remaining support wall. If it fell, a ton of ancient brick and plaster would slam down and press Nonno to the floor like a dry flower in a family Bible. Leo bent over his unexpected charge and spoke words to calm him.

'I'm here. Don't worry. I'll stay with you, but you have to hold still and let everybody work. Okay?'

'Okay.' And Nonno was calm again, but his eyes were still full of tears as he whispered just to Leo, 'I'm sorry about the mountains. I should have just crawled under the snow and stayed with you and your brothers. Everything's been bad since I left you. And now my house fell on me.'

'I know.'

'You won't leave me?'

'No. I'll stay.'

'Thank you. 'Cause when my house fell on me, I got scared. I think the gray dog's dead.'

'Don't worry. We'll make it okay.'

Stabilizing the house would take some time. Meanwhile, Angelo de Parma's roof tiles periodically dropping in like mortar shells was hindering the work. Something had to be done before somebody was brained. Lumber had to be gathered to brace the wall and also positioned to shield the rescuers and the defenseless Nonno. So half the workers scattered to gather boards and beams, while the other half stayed behind to protect the trapped old man. The protectors stood in the rubble and scanned Angelo de Parma's roof, brandishing garbage can lids to fend off the terra-cotta projectiles.

Father Elio asked Leo to take some men to the shed behind the church and retrieve some discarded lumber. When Leo suggested that it might be better for the old priest to take the men, he just shook his white head and said, 'I can't. I can't look. Not yet.'

Leo understood. But he'd made a promise to Nonno that he would stay close. At that moment, Frankie de Parma was sitting on a pile of the rubble with his skinny legs curled up into a ball and holding a garbage can lid over his head like an umbrella. In the debris at Frankie's feet Nonno's dusty face shone like a china plate as the two of them chatted. Nonno would be okay for a bit and the trip to the church and back would take only a few minutes, so Leo grabbed up a lantern, recruited a couple of other men, and ran up the hill toward the piazza.

He really did intend to return.

Ten

*I*n the darkness Leo couldn't tell if the damage to the church was better or worse than he'd imagined, and he was in no hurry to explore again – at least not through the front doors – so he directed their path across the steps and around to the north side. They passed a gaping hole in the garden wall; this had to be where Father Elio had made his scrambled escape.

The lumber was right where Father Elio had indicated and in a matter of minutes the men who accompanied Leo were hurrying back across the piazza balancing boards on sheets of plywood. Leo lingered behind on the pretext of searching for more lumber, but he had something else on his mind.

The thick garden wall showed no signs of buckling. It appeared as though most of the eastern section had simply gotten tired and decided to lie down. Leo climbed through the gap in the broken wall, afraid of how he would find the ancient fig tree on the other side. But the twisted old treasure was safe. The sudden slide of tumbling masonry had avoided the withered fig completely and the black stump and branches gleamed in the lamplight. Unhappily, the side of the cathedral that had been in the path of the toppling wall wasn't so lucky. Great chunks of its exterior had been cruelly battered and now the weight of much of the old garden wall rested against the side of the northern transept. With just the feeble light of his lantern, it didn't appear to Leo as though there was any serious damage, although from where he stood, much of the lower wall did seem to have taken on an unnatural, warped sort of posture. Leo pictured the other side of that wall and felt an involuntary shudder. He quickly groped his way across the brittle garden and entered the sanctuary.

Leo wasn't used to the cathedral at night. It was dark, and the cavernous space was alive with unnerving little noises. And instead of his lantern illuminating, its feeble light was swallowed up by hungry shadows, making it even more alien.

The largest pile of debris was mounded just inside the front doors and extended a full ten meters into the sanctuary. Beyond this heap, the wreckage gradually diminished, but still spread in every direction almost all the way to the altar. The mountain of debris on the floor was shocking, but what was even more astonishing was above him. Overhead, bright stars shone and twinkled against the clear black sky. Almost a third of that magnificent ceiling lay in ruins while what was left hung precariously, threatening with each aftershock to crash down on him. But still Leo gazed upward, bewitched by the serenity of the night sky. Of all the elements in the church, Leo had loved the ceiling the most. Now that it was spoiled, he was overwhelmed by the oddest sense of release. There was something strangely fulfilling about this yawning hole that joined the inside of the sanctuary to the expanse of creation that had always existed just outside, but never seemed to be considered. Churches were sanctums intentionally removed from the real world. They were meant to be more than just an earthly refuge; they were reflections of a promise that we might glimpse, but not attain – not in this lifetime. Now, as Leo stared up at the night sky, it occurred to him that he actually preferred the sanctuary this way. It was peaceful, and there was something wonderfully demystifying about it all.

He doubted if Father Elio would share his feelings, though; the old priest was going to be heartbroken. Too bad, he thought. Life is disappointment. Everyone else has to deal with the careless wounds life hands out, so why should Elio Caproni be any different? Because he's a priest? Leo figured out a long time ago that a person can run, or hide, or ignore the havoc of life for only so long. Permanent sanctuaries aren't allowed in this world – not in the obscurity of

Milano, or across the sea in Chicago, and certainly not here in insignificant Santo Fico. Calamity will find its way to you and, with an unforgiving fist, pound your door down – or in this case, your ceiling. This will break the old man's heart, but he'll survive. Leo had.

The floor trembled slightly beneath his feet. It wasn't much of a shake, just a tiny shudder. There had been a dozen small aftershocks in the last hour since the quake and although they weren't enough to do damage, they were certainly enough to set everyone's ragged nerves on edge. A few bricks dropped out of the darkness and crashed to the church floor, sending Leo scrambling out of the center of the room and back to the safety of the walls. Even for all of its irreverent spiritual implications, perhaps it wasn't a good idea to stand under that portion of the ceiling right now.

He was at the entry to the northern transept when either the flickering shadows of his lantern played tricks with Leo's eyes or he was struck with a horrifying sight. The blanket had fallen from the fresco and the faces on the wall stared out at Leo from odd angles and with expressions of what looked like mild surprise. The fresco had always possessed the remarkable ability of appearing three-dimensional, but in the dim light of his lantern the painting looked . . . well, rearranged. It was as if the earthquake had taken a few of the characters, shaken them around, and then set them down again in new positions, leaving them all slightly askew.

Leo crept slowly back into the small room, picking his steps carefully in the dim lamplight. He had to see the fresco more closely. A fine dust filled the air like a faint fog, but that didn't explain why the characters seemed so cockeyed. It was obvious that his assessment had been mistaken when he looked at the wall from the garden side. Outside, and in the darkness, it appeared as though the wall had taken a hammering, yes, but was still essentially sound. From the inside, even in the glow of the lantern, he could see that the lower wall had fractured and the weight of the upper section was slowly crumbling inward. The fresco wall was shattering before his eyes.

Another aftershock trembled beneath his feet and the fracture in the wall poured a stream of crumbling mortar onto the floor. Small rivulets of plaster dust rained down. Holding the lamp over his head, Leo discovered an ugly, gaping crack in the ceiling that ran the length of the short room. The transept was splitting in two from above as the supporting wall deteriorated. Every now and then the ceiling actually groaned, as if it could barely manage the strain of holding itself up. The faces in the fresco seemed to cry out to him, as though they also knew that the transept was doomed – maybe only minutes away from total collapse. Leo had visions of ending up like Nonno.

Nonno! He'd forgotten about Nonno! He had promised the old man he would stay. He should be back down at the pier right now. The faces on the wall were covered with dust and surprise, just like Nonno had been, but they couldn't be helped. The room was doomed and so were they.

As Leo turned to leave, a loud buzzing and a blinding flash of light startled him. The electric lights that pointed toward the fresco had unexpectedly burst on and then, just as quickly, they died. Father Elio must have tried to turn them on as he made his escape. After only seconds they glowed feebly again. They flickered several times, then slowly brightened until, after a few faltering surges, the two bulbs were shining steadily. The beams were nowhere near full strength, but at least he had light. From the cheers echoing in through the missing ceiling Leo concluded that the power, however feeble, was apparently back on in the whole village.

When he faced the fractured wall shining under the muted glare of the lamps, what he saw made his breath catch. He could feel his heart beat and in his ears was a buzz louder than the hum of the electric bulbs. His guilty dream had become substance. The buckling and bulging of the wall was forcing the top layers of the mural to pull away from their base. Like an aged photograph peels away from a yellowed page as it turns, both the thin *intonaco* and the thicker *arricio* layers of plaster were lifting away from the ancient weave of lath. The individual sections were separating like so many pieces of a jigsaw puzzle spreading across a strangely expanding table. Although a few smaller pieces had already broken away, fallen to the floor, and shattered like china, the major sections still clung to the cracked and splintered lattice by what appeared to be either sheer willpower or force of habit.

It was obvious that one of two things was shortly going to happen. Either a substantial aftershock was going to collapse the ceiling and destroy the fresco, or it was going to shake the damaged panels from the wall and they would be destroyed. In either case the fresco, like the ill-fated chamber that had been its home for over four hundred years, was doomed. If anything was going to be saved, Leo would have to act quickly.

There are some temptations that are so overwhelming that they don't require deliberation. We know the outcome before we ever begin the debate, but still we go through the mental gymnastics because we know that we should – we must, to continue living with ourselves. In the days to come, it would be these flimsy rationalizations that Leo would cling to in his attempts to justify what he knew he was about to do. In point of fact, he thought, it probably wasn't even his fault. It was all the fault of those two damn fat men from Roma who talked too much. This moment was merely harvesting the fruit of a seed that they had planted in his heart over twenty years ago.

It was the summer of his fourteenth year the day that an unfamiliar Lancia sedan pulled into the square. Leo and Topo were sitting in the center of the piazza with their feet dangling in the empty fountain, disputing the pros and cons of stealing some of Topo's father's cigarettes, taking them down to Brusco Point, and practicing smoking. The argument was going nowhere when the strange car circled the two boys and stopped in front of the hotel. Four fat passengers climbed out, spread a map across the hood, and stared at it. At last they folded it and entered the hotel. Although Topo begged Leo to let him do Franco's part, Leo knew that he would have to do it on his own. He did, however, agree to let Topo hang around – a decision he would forever regret.

Leo, dogged by Topo, found the party sitting at a table in the restaurant. As expected, the two bookish men (both short, round, and bald) and their wives (equally short and round, with mounds of spray-lacquered hair) were just another car of confused tourists headed for Follonica that somehow ended up in their dusty piazza. Leo was delighted to discover that they were actually rather eager to see and hear about the Miracle and the Mystery.

Everything remained monotonously usual until Leo took them inside the church to view the Mystery. He had barely begun his patter and turned on the lights when both men gasped. In unison, eyeglasses appeared from their pockets and they moved Leo out of the way for a better view. The confused boy didn't have a chance to tell them the full, miraculous story he had created because the two men became engrossed in their own hushed conversation. They asked Leo hard questions and he had trouble keeping up with their enthusiasm. They made him repeat certain sections of his story and then they would ignore him, brusquely turning their attention back to their own fervent discussion. They talked about things like 'three-point perspective' . . . 'naturalness of curve' . . . 'tone and hue' and other things that Leo didn't understand. At last their impatient wives gave them an ultimatum that could not be ignored and the quartet left the cathedral, paid Leo his fee plus a modest tip, climbed in their car, and drove off headed north.

That was the last Leo ever saw of them, but they had left something behind. They had spoken a great deal about 'the great Giotto' – a name that Leo and Topo immediately recognized as famous, but neither knew why. The fat men had also called the fresco 'an undiscovered treasure.' Most important, he had heard them use the phrase, 'could be worth a fortune.'

When the car had at last disappeared down the road, Topo burst into a whoop and a dance that Leo was certain would end with his friend wetting himself. Much to Leo's disappointment he realized that everything he had heard, Topo had also overheard, and Topo wanted to tell Franco and Marta immediately. Worse than that, he wanted to tell Father Elio and then run and tell his mother. The little blabbermouth couldn't wait until everyone in the entire village had heard the news – from him, personally.

But Topo suddenly discovered himself pressed back against the cool plaster wall of the church, his feet no longer quite touching the ground and Leo's fist pressing into his cheek. Leo's voice was low and, for a fourteen-year-old, remarkably frightening.

'If you ever tell anyone about this – One word, to anyone – and I'll kill you.'

Now, Topo didn't ever think that Leo would actually kill him. And Leo knew that he certainly wouldn't ever actually kill Topo, but both boys also knew that Leo meant the spirit of that threat probably more than he had ever meant anything in his life.

From time to time, Topo would try to talk to Leo about that phrase, 'could be worth a fortune,' but Leo always refused. It stayed a puzzle to Topo as to why Leo wouldn't discuss it. It was only later, after Leo was gone, after Topo had also become discontent with the meager life Santo Fico offered, and after he had become cynical enough to understand the hopelessness of his future that he began to understand the phrase 'could be worth a fortune.' It was hope. It was escape.

The floor shivered again and the room moaned, and over Leo's head, with sickening cracks and snaps, more dust rained down. If he was going to do it, it had to be now. He placed the lantern next to the wall and prayed that the wavering electric lights would stay on. Then, kneeling on the floor like a disciple at worship, Leo reached out and gently wrapped his fingers around a slab of broken plaster. The plaster was cool to the touch, and the painted surface, covered with a layer of fine dust, felt as smooth as velvet to his fingertips. It was a strangely thrilling sensation to actually touch a section of the vulnerable fresco and he discovered his hands were trembling. He felt as if he were touching a woman he had spent a lifetime longing for, but who was always out of reach and somehow beyond him. He thought of Marta, and he knew that if he hurried things, if he was clumsy or stupid, the moment would be over – spoiled forever. The fresco would reject him, crumble in his hands, fall and shatter on the floor. His hands were shaking.

'Slow down,' he told himself.

Wiping his sweating palms on his jacket, he again carefully gripped the panel that appeared to be in the most danger of falling – the center panel, the blessed Saint Francis himself reclining beneath the miraculous fig tree – and he pulled. The face of Saint Francis seemed to stare into Leo's eyes with what he had always felt was a strange look of perhaps sorrowful gratitude or maybe understanding or maybe just patience. But today what Leo saw was simply disappointment.

Unfortunately, as Leo pulled and the slab tore away from the wall, he was surprised that the panel's grip was so tenuous and he wasn't prepared for either its sudden release or its weight. He almost dropped it, but instead clutched it to his chest. He had it. He was holding it. Leo forgot to breathe as he caressed it and studied it in the dim light – not quite a meter wide and just over a meter tall – his own 'undiscovered treasure' that 'could be worth a fortune.' Cradling the slab of broken plaster like an injured child, he quickly made his way out the transept and around the corner to the garden door.

A pale glow shone in the eastern mountains and everything was bathed in a hint of pallid blue light. Dawn was still some time away, but it was quickly approaching and this was a job best performed in darkness. Finding a spot well away from the dangerous wall, he nestled his treasure in a clump of mint. A moment later he was back in the cathedral, kneeling before the fresco and patiently working his fingers under another panel.

This nervous work continued for too long, Leo thought, but it couldn't be hurried – prying and lifting section after section away from the wall and tenderly carrying it to a safe place among the herbs in the garden. Twice, aftershocks jarred the frail room as Leo was in the midst of his task.

After the first one, a large section of plaster fell from the ceiling, grazed the side of his head, and crashed into his shoulder. Instead of diving for the safety of the sanctuary, he had wrapped his body around his fragile cargo, trying to shield the painting from damage. But when he saw the size of the plaster that had crashed to the floor and almost split his skull, he determined that self-preservation is a valuable instinct and he should be willing to use it.

Leo noticed that as he worked his way up the wall, moving away from the fracture at the base, the fresco was less affected by the buckling and became more and more reluctant to be pried loose. His arms and shoulders ached and sweat stung his eyes as he worked on the massive tablet that was slowly allowing itself to be pried away. But the harder Leo worked, the more he feared the result of his efforts. What would actually happen when he finally pried such a large piece loose? Experience told him that it was going to come free quite suddenly and drop like granite toward the floor. How would he hold it, or balance it, or carry it to safety? By freeing a panel this large, all he was going to do was destroy it. He had just decided to stop and devise a more reasonable plan when the final aftershock hit.

The tremor was brief, but it was enough to pitch Leo's balance into the wall. His fingers were already wedged under the edges of the panel, and when he lurched forward he felt the fresco rip from its tenuous moorings, and a slight snapping sound accompanied a clean crack that shot directly up the center of the deep blue sky. Seconds later, when the tremor stopped, Leo discovered that his large panel had not only broken free, but now there were two of them. They slid toward the floor like twin toboggans and Leo smashed his face and body against the wall in a desperate attempt to pin the panels in place. His arms and back strained to support them and his legs began to cramp as he pressed his weight into the wall — it was obvious that gravity was going to win this battle. Then he heard someone entering the church.

'Woo-Whoo . . . Anybody here? Leo . . . Are you here?'

Topo's thin, whispered call filled Leo with ambivalence greater than any he'd ever known. Should he scream for joy or anger or help? The panels were separating along the newly cracked sky, splitting completely apart and slowly slipping down toward Leo's navel. He thrust his stomach harder against the wall to check the downward plunge and his dilemma was settled. He tried to sound casual, but right now his driving force was a desperation that was hard to hide.

'Here . . . I'm in here!'

He heard Topo stumbling through the garden and he prayed the clumsy little snoop wouldn't step on any of the rescued panels. He heard him tripping and falling over the debris as he entered the garden door. He heard him moving around behind him in the sanctuary. And then he heard him clucking his tongue in appalled condemnation.

'Oh, my God! Leo, you broke Saint Francis.'

Leo was glad he couldn't get his hands on the little rodent's neck right now.

'I didn't break Saint Francis, you idiot. There was an earthquake.'

'Does Father Elio know you did this? He's going to be so mad.'

'I didn't break it, damn it! I found it like this!'

The awkwardness of trying to support the sections of fresco and explain himself to Topo was more than Leo could manage. The two sections suddenly slipped farther and Leo mashed his pelvis painfully into the wall. Topo offered what he considered to be sound advice.

'Well . . . You better be careful and not drop those.'

Whether Topo would have eventually figured out Leo's dilemma on his own or not will never be known because Leo smashed his forehead against the wall and growled in such a horrifying way that Topo immediately understood and sprang to action. Together they lowered the panels to the floor.

The landscape outside was washed with the pale dawn as Topo surveyed Leo's efforts. Placed with meticulous care among bunches of rosemary, fennel, thyme, sage, and lavender were nine large sections of fresco that made up the majority of the Mystery. Scattered around them were a dozen smaller pieces. The small herb garden had become a surrealistic museum and it was all so incongruous and yet so perfectly serene, Topo couldn't speak, but Leo knew what he was thinking.

'The room is going to fall in. You can see that.'

Topo wandered around the garden shaking his head and clucking his tongue in disbelief. Leo remembered Topo's mother used to cluck her tongue like that.

'This was the only way to save it. You can see that.'

Topo scratched his head and sighed. He had to ask.

'Are you going to keep them?'

There was something about the stillness of the pale morning that made Leo's pause seem longer than it probably was. He knew in his heart from the beginning what he intended to do, but now Topo was asking him to say it out loud. He wanted Leo to admit that he was going to steal from the church; that he was going to take the only thing of any value in the whole town; admit that he was going to get enough money to leave Santo Fico and never come back.

'Yes.'

The gray stillness again covered the moment like a veil, but this time it was Topo who writhed silently on the horns of the dilemma. Leo knew what he was thinking as his little friend studied the ghostly chunks of broken fresco. The words of the two fat men from Roma echoed in his brain too. At last Topo sighed deeply.

'Well, I guess it's like my father used to say — Since the house is already on fire, we might as well stay warm.'

Leo's voice was no more than a whisper. 'There's an old door leaning against the shed behind the sanctuary.'

Topo was gone in an instant. Leo returned to the church and found the dirty blanket that Father Elio had used to cover and protect the Mystery for as long as he could remember. The lamps still shone on the sad wall at the end of the transept – now only a scar of naked plaster and broken lath. Leo thought it looked like Nonno, abandoned and confused. He pulled the plug of the extension cord and the lamps went out. Even though it cast the room in darkness

Leo knew the wall was still there, staring back at him open-faced, asking why. It would be good when the room finally collapsed.

When he scrambled back out to the garden Topo was lugging the old door across the broken wall and they immediately began piling the corpses of the Mystery onto it. Using the blanket for cushioning they tenderly folded it over each giant jigsaw puzzle piece as they stacked them in sturdy layers.

Then, as the eastern horizon showed the inescapable traces of first morning, they carried their treasure through the gap in the broken wall and around the corner of the church toward the piazza. The load was heavy, the door was wobbly, and as a team they were not a good match. They tried to work together, but Topo was too short for Leo and Leo was too tall for Topo. Topo took hurried, scurrying steps and Leo could only keep steady with a long swinging stride.

They stopped at the corner of the church while Leo ventured a furtive peek at the piazza. It was empty. After a few bickering whispers, they hurried across the square and made a quick right onto the street that led down the hill to the north coast road, then on to Leo Pizzola's farm and the old shepherd's hut by the sea.

Standing on the steps of the church, hidden in the shadows of the great doors, Marta watched her two childhood friends disappear around the corner with their peculiar freight and knew in her heart what they were doing without even having to look inside the church. And she cursed them for it. Cursing Leo Pizzola had almost become a habit, but this was different. She cursed him for what he was doing to the village and to the church. She cursed him for Topo too — always so willing to follow Leo anywhere. She cursed him for her uncle who didn't know how to curse. And she cursed him for herself because he had let her see his crime and now she would have to do something.

Eleven

*B*efore most of the people of Santo Fico bothered to notice that the sun was coming up, it already had. And as often happens, the horrors of the night weren't nearly so horrible once they were bathed in sunlight. There was damage, to be sure, but not as much as had been imagined in the darkness. Best of all, no one had died. Nonno was extracted from the ruins of his room with some cuts and bruises and an injury to his knee. He would limp and need a cane for a time, but the expectation was that he would be fine. In fact, many remarked that a limp and a cane might be, considering his age and eccentricities, just the right touch.

The real marvel of the night though was the old gray dog. As the workers cleared away the rubble of the room the dog was nowhere to be found, he seemed to have vanished. But just when it had been decided that the dog was buried too deep and they would have to retrieve his carcass later, the mutt crawled out from under Nonno's bed where it had been patiently hiding since the room collapsed. The dog yawned and stretched, then walked carefully through the opening that used to be the room's only door, and wandered off down the road looking for a familiar spot to relieve himself.

Candles in the windows of the Albergo di Santo Fico were finally extinguished and the last exhausted casualties of the night's ordeal straggled across the piazza to survey their own ruins and hopefully sleep half the day. And Marta could no longer avoid doing what she knew she had to do. She had to cross the piazza and enter the church again.

She set Nina to work upstairs putting their rooms back in order while she and Carmen attacked the disaster that was formerly her spotless kitchen. It would take days to put things back in order, weeks for the smells from the broken bottles of sauces and herbs to fade, and months to replace all the shattered crockery. She and Carmen worked side by side, both thankful that circumstances prevented them from having to mention the unpleasant Solly Puce affair of the previous evening – now so long ago. Besides, at the moment Marta was much more concerned with Uncle Elio than she was with her daughter's flirtation with a greasy postal carrier.

The eastern sky had been crimson gold when Marta stood at the hotel's front window and watched her uncle Elio trudge up the hill from the harbor. She had watched as he beheld his damaged cathedral for the first time in the morning light. Fully a third of the roof had simply vanished. Although the structure appeared as though a bomb exploded on top of it, everything else around the building was completely normal. Marta, like Father Elio, knew where the debris lay. She wanted to run to him and hold him so they could weep together. But she couldn't. She had seen Leo and Topo and she knew that what awaited him inside the church was a violation far greater than any pile of debris. She watched him sit on the edge of the fountain and bury his face in his hands. His poor broken church looked the way she imagined his poor heart must have felt. She thought of her father's old pistol hidden beneath her underwear in the bureau upstairs, and bullets, and what she would like to do to that damned Leo Pizzola – and that foolish little Topo too. Instead she watched her uncle wipe his eyes, struggle across the square, and disappear around the side of the church.

She waited for an hour. She wanted to give him privacy she told herself; some time to mourn. 'Give him a chance and maybe he'll come to the hotel,' she told herself. The real reason, of course, was that she couldn't bear to see the look on his face when he discovered the emptiness of the wall. But an hour was long enough and the time arrived when she had to make the walk across the piazza and see about her uncle. And as she left the hotel, again she thought of Leo Pizzola. She knew exactly where the pistol was, but she wasn't so sure about the bullets.

Marta entered the church through the kitchen the way she

always did, and from the moment she stepped through the door she knew that her uncle hadn't been back here. His kitchen was a smaller, simpler version of the disaster she had found in her own. Marta prayed that he might be in his bedroom. The night had been long and exhausting and maybe he was so worn out that he'd just gone back to his bed and was now asleep. Sleep would be the best thing for him right now. But when she peeked into his little cell and found the bed empty, she knew where he was.

As she made her way down the low passageway to the sanctuary, the sound of her feet scraping across the stones seemed intrusive. Just being there made her feel like a trespasser and she wanted to turn around and quietly leave, but couldn't.

The chapel did indeed look as if a bomb had exploded on the roof. The main devastation took place at the west end and the great mound of beams, bricks, plaster, and tile lay in front of the vestibule, with smaller shards of debris spreading out through much of the great hall. Broken glass crunched beneath her feet. The windows surrounding the room, both low and high, looked as if small boys had been throwing stones at the ancient leaded glass; none were completely broken out, but many of them had lost some pieces. What was amazing was that at the east end of the building, from the altar all the way to the end of the curved apse, was undamaged. The beautiful quatrefoil windows gleamed with the morning sun and were unharmed by anything more severe than a layer of dust. But what was most startling for Marta as she stepped out of the dark tunnel was the almost

painful amount of light that filled the room. The domed
ceiling that she had known all her life was now interrupted
by an astonishing patch of infinite blue sky that took up
much of the west end.

Father Elio sat on one of the wooden benches directly
across the room from her, his shoulders stooped, his hands
folded serenely in his lap. He might have been someone's
grandfather sitting patiently in some large station waiting for
a train, or perhaps a confused parishioner who arrived too
late for a mass that was already over. Daylight streamed in
through the hole in the roof and lit up the northern transept;
usually the most unnoticed corner, always cast in the darkest
shadows, but now every detail of the damaged little room
was visible. Plain to see was the split and sagging ceiling, the
fractured and collapsing northern wall, and the gaping gray
wound that leapt out like a scream.

But Father Elio wasn't looking at the transept or the vanished Mystery. He stared straight ahead, lost in some thought
and seemingly oblivious of Marta's presence. She was startled at how small her uncle seemed and how his white hair
shone in this light. She'd never noticed how translucent his
skin looked, an unhealthy white-gray that almost matched
his hair, and she wondered if it were merely a trick of the
light or perhaps just the effects of a layer of dust that covered everything, including her uncle.

He smiled as she sat next to him on the worn bench and
they sat for a moment in silence. Marta strained to think of
something, anything she might say that would help. She
knew he was going to be hurt again when she told him of

Leo and Topo. She wanted to shout their names at him. She wanted to take him by the hand and together they could march down the north coast road to that shepherd's hovel where she'd heard Leo was staying. Together they would beat him with sticks. They would bring the Mystery back home, and then Uncle Elio wouldn't be sad anymore and he wouldn't cry and Leo Pizzola would get what he deserved. But instead she sat in thick silence, unable to speak.

Father Elio spoke. His voice was raspy with fatigue and dry with dust and he had to clear his throat before any sound would even come out. Finally, he pointed in front of them and said, 'I always love the way those windows look in the morning light.'

The undamaged leaded windows at the east end of the building shone like kaleidoscopes, tossing gay colors and prism rainbows on the walls and floor. Marta joined him in studying the way the morning sun made the colored glass sparkle with an almost painful intensity.

'It hurts my eyes sometimes,' said Elio and he rubbed his eyes in a futile attempt to mask the tears. Marta put her arm around his shoulder, but said nothing. After a moment she could feel his breathing return, and after another moment he found his voice again.

'It's not right that others should be punished for my sin.'

'No one's being punished for anything. It was an earthquake, that's all.'

'No,' he whispered firmly. 'It was my sin. I knew I couldn't escape it, but I don't understand why . . . this?' And he lifted his arms and gestured toward the destruction around him, trying to express a confusion that was beyond words.

'Uncle Elio, you don't have sins and you're not being punished.'

'Not sins. Sin. One sin. One monstrous sin. You don't know.' The old man watched his own hands being wrung together and barely spoke above a shamed whisper. 'Many years ago . . . you weren't even born yet . . . I did a terrible, terrible thing. I knew then I shouldn't do it, but I wanted something. I wanted it more than . . . I wanted it too much. I thought it was a good thing, but I felt God turn away from me. This is my punishment.'

For the first time since Marta sat down, Elio dared to turn his eyes toward the sad gray wall and with her arm around him she could feel his breathing becoming labored again.

'Why would God take away such a thing as this? A painting does no harm. A painting cannot sin. A painting is innocent. Especially a painting like this, so . . . filled with His joy and spirit and . . . I don't understand. Why would God take it away? There must be a way of punishing me without this. I can accept that God has turned His back on me. I deserve it. I knew what I was doing. It was my sin alone. But, why this? I don't understand.'

Suddenly the old man sat up and gasped, captured by a moment of inspiration. 'Perhaps . . . an act of contrition. Some . . . penance.'

Marta didn't understand what he was talking about and tried to console him, but he only rambled more about 'his sin' and what he had to do to keep God from punishing her, and the girls, and all his friends in Santo Fico. She felt helpless patting his shoulder and offering flimsy encouragement, and feebly denying what she thought were just exhausted ramblings. But Father Elio was adamant that every heartache and catastrophe in Santo Fico was solely his fault and that included the disappearance of the Mystery. But what especially alarmed Marta was that as his anxiety grew, he became more and more convinced that he needed to perform some desperate act of atonement for his strange dark sin.

Now, Marta had never heard her uncle talk like this and the thought of him committing a sin was absolutely preposterous, much less a sin so wicked that it would turn God away from him. That was inconceivable. But his despair was so deep and his resolve to atone burned in him so fiercely that he frightened his niece when he suddenly gripped her arm and sat bolt upright.

'A fast!'

'A what?'

'A fast. I need to fast and pray.'

'For how long?'

'As long as it takes.'

The thought of this gaunt old man going without food was so ridiculous that it was more than Marta could accept, but there was a gleam in his eye that was, to her mind, deadly serious.

'Uncle Elio, you can't fast. You don't eat enough as it is.'

'An act of contrition!'

'But what's it going to accomplish?'

'Atonement! Maybe . . . I don't know. Maybe nothing. Maybe it will bring the spirit of God back to this place, to

Santo Fico. Maybe it will bring the people back to this church. Do you remember how this church used to be filled with people? You're probably too young. Once, there was a time, every seat was filled, every candle was lit, and the music . . . oh, the music . . . Maybe it will bring God back here . . . Maybe it will bring back the Mystery. I don't know. Maybe nothing. I don't know, but I have to try.'

Marta could see that the old man was determined, and it was the kind of determination that could kill him.

'Perhaps the Mystery isn't really gone.'

'No. It's gone. I spent an hour searching through the rubble on the floor. I thought, maybe, if I might find enough . . . maybe, it could be repaired. But I only found a few small, broken pieces. No it's gone. God has taken it.'

'Maybe it wasn't God.'

'What are you saying?'

'Maybe it was a person.'

The old priest's eyes grew wide, as he comprehended Marta's point. For the first time in her life Marta saw something that she didn't believe could exist. She saw anger cloud her uncle's face. 'A person took the Mystery . . . ?'

Marta felt on thin ice. She knew this was a moment that required artfulness. She didn't want to dismay him too much, so she chose her words carefully, keeping her tone simple and blameless – speaking as if she were comforting one of her girls when they were little and frightened.

'Yes. Possibly while you were gone, in the middle of the night someone came in here and stole it. It wasn't God that took it. It was probably a person. In fact, it was—'

Father Elio exploded at her, 'What are you talking about? Of course it was a person! Do you think I'm simpleminded? Do you think I supposed God's hand came down out of the sky when my back was turned and snatched it away to heaven through that hole in the roof? I'm old, but I'm not a fool! Do you think I'm a fool?'

His angry voice echoed around the sanctuary, bouncing off the stone walls, rattling the fragile windows, and disappearing through the cavity in the ceiling – then silence.

Marta was speechless and her uncle could see the fear and hurt in her eyes. In all her life he had never raised his voice to her. In all her life she had never seen him direct anger toward any living thing. The shock of his rage stung her and now she was the one who had trouble breathing because her heart was in her throat. She felt ridiculous and ashamed that she had treated him with such condescension, as if he were, indeed, simpleminded.

But Father Elio reached out and pulled her to him and kissed her tears and begged her forgiveness for raising his voice to her.

'I know that someone took the painting,' he said softly. 'The other explanation would have been a wonderful miracle, but my life has not . . . Well, I'm not touched by miracles. But don't you see? Whoever took the painting, they were only acting out God's will. If God had not wanted them to take the Mystery from this place, from my keeping, then it wouldn't have happened.'

'But sometimes people just . . . do bad things. Sometimes it has nothing to do with God.'

'I know that.' He chuckled ruefully. 'I've done that myself and this is my punishment.'

'Uncle Elio, if we were to find the person who took it—'

'No!' His voice was like the staccato report of a pistol. He caught himself, took a breath, and repeated softly, 'No . . . To have to face one of my children, after they have done something like this . . . To look in their eyes and know that they stole from God . . . No. Whoever did this, God is working in their lives too, and . . . and I don't want to know. I don't want the painting back. I don't want to know and I don't want it back! All I want . . . is . . .'

His voice trailed off and he again became lost in the sparkling windows at the end of the church. Marta stroked his hand.

'What do you want, Uncle Elio?'

He continued watching the colored window, his mind wandering around his own disheveled thoughts, until at last he said softly, 'I want God to love me again.'

'He does. God does love you.'

Elio smiled, and shook his head.

'Then He will,' Marta insisted. 'I promise you, He will.'

Father Elio's voice was so soft that even sitting at his shoulder Marta could barely hear him when he whispered to himself, 'Now, that would be a miracle.'

Twelve

*T*he shepherd's hut was stifling. Leo sat on the room's only chair, leaned his elbows on the only table, and let sweat drip off his nose and trickle through the bristles on his chin. He refused to open the door or the shutters on the windows to allow in the cooling sea breeze. That would be too dangerous. However unlikely, someone might pass by and look in. Better to swelter than run the risk of somebody accidentally discovering his crime. So he let his body slowly bake in the stone oven and his brain smoldered under the gaze of the saintly eyes staring back at him from the dirty cot across the room.

It was close to an hour since Topo had at last trudged back up the hill toward town. It had been over three hours since the two of them had fumbled awkwardly down the road, then huffed and puffed across the pastures with their prize. The trip had taken longer than either would have guessed. Loaded with broken plaster, the old door was not only heavier and more unwieldy than they imagined, but the discrepancy in their sizes became brutally wearing for both. To keep the sagging old door relatively level and prevent their delicate cargo from tumbling onto the road, Leo had to bend over at an angle that left his upper torso almost perpendicular to the ground and his knees oddly bowed. Topo, on the other hand, was forced to make up his portion of the discrepancy by lifting his end almost chest high and skipping along on his tiptoes.

When they had made their initial getaway, scampering across the piazza in the shadows of dawn, fear and a short-lived surge of adrenaline had given them the impression that they could carry their litter to Roma if necessary. But after a few minutes of maneuvering down the deserted north coast road, Topo's arms were shaking like leaves and Leo's lower back was screaming. They both wanted desperately to stop and rest, but for fear that someone might see them and guess what they had done, they kept up these contorted positions and hurried down the road as quickly as their mismatched legs could carry them.

It was only after they'd turned off the road at the opening in the old stone wall and disappeared onto the Pizzola 'estate' that they dared to collapse behind a row of cypress trees. They lay exhausted in the dry grass, panting and giggling – giddy in the confidence that the caper had been a success. Though neither mentioned it, both men sadly realized that their bodies were no longer able to keep up with their boyish enthusiasms.

The rest of their journey was accomplished in a prolonged series of short, furtive bursts of energy – each a bit shorter than the last. They staggered and rested their way past the boarded-up old house, past the unpruned olive grove, past the overgrown vineyard, past the Lombolos' curious horses, down the goat path, across the meadow, and all the way to the shepherd's hut overlooking the sea.

When they finally arrived both were completely spent, but still Leo doggedly demanded that they immediately store all the fragments of their treasure beneath his cot – all, save the figure of Saint Francis reclining beneath the tree. For some strange reason that Topo neither understood nor liked, Leo insisted upon placing that particular fragment on his cot with its back leaning against the wall. Topo found the image of Saint Francis sitting on Leo's filthy cot and staring back across the room at them unsettling. But Leo refused to move it; he just sat at the table and stared back at it.

It took over half an hour and a few liters of water for them to recover from their ordeal, but at last Topo had enough strength to pose a few questions he wanted answered. Like – How would they approach the selling of the fragments? Who should they contact? How much money were they going to get? Was this something they needed to mention in their next confession? Were they going to be dealing with criminals? Were they now gangsters? Where would they ever find an appropriate underworld person in Santo Fico? Would they have to leave the country or just the region? If they were caught, would they go to prison for a long time? Should the panels be sold all at once, as one fresco – or maybe individually, one at a time? Was it too late to take them back? Were they going to go to hell for this?

Leo was willing to weigh all of these questions, but any discussion would have to wait until Topo had worked his way through a series of alternating anxiety and exhilaration attacks. So Leo watched while the poor little fellow paced back and forth, his high-pitched voice questioning everything from their ill-conceived adventure to their ill-conceived births. He blasted Leo for ever going to America and then cursed him again for returning. He damned the two fat men from Roma who first mentioned the loathsome Giotto. He cursed and lamented and repented, all the while his arms flew about like lethal whirligigs, stabbing the air for emphasis. In the end, he just sat on the dirt floor in a corner, his back against the rough wall, knees pulled up under his chin, and rocked back and forth.

Finally, Topo quieted himself. He knew there was no taking it back; no undoing. It was done. At last he asked softly, 'I won't be able to live here anymore, will I?'

Leo shook his head.

After a moment Topo sighed. 'I could live in Firenze maybe . . . maybe Milano.'

'Milano's nice,' Leo replied.

'I think Roma would be too big. You know?'

Leo nodded.

Topo got to his feet and brushed himself off. 'I've gotta go home. The shop's a mess, but I've gotta get some sleep.' He stood by the door and stared at the face of the saint, who seemed to be looking in his direction, but not quite meeting his gaze. 'My God, Leo – what have we done?'

'We rescued it.'

Topo chuckled to himself. 'We did, didn't we. We rescued it.' And he was gone.

Once Leo was alone, he thought of his words to Topo – 'Milano's nice.' He was living in Milano when he went to his first museum. He didn't remember its name, but it was big. It was there that he saw a painted wooden panel that reminded him of the Mystery back in Santo Fico, but not as pretty. A small plaque explained that someone named Cimabue painted the wooden panel, '. . . in the Byzantine style.' It also said that Cimabue was the teacher of Giotto di Bondone. He remembered how the name Giotto leapt off the plaque at him. He knew that name. That was the name whispered by the two fat men from Roma. He asked a pretty girl in the gift shop what she knew about Giotto di Bondone and she told him that if he was interested in Giotto, then he needed go to a particular room on the far side of that museum.

What he found was a room filled from floor to ceiling with beautiful paintings. There were even frescoes painted on the ceiling, but he couldn't see them very well. The subject of all of the paintings was pretty much the life of Christ and some were even painted by the famous Giotto. But as beautiful as they were, he didn't see anything that he could connect to the Mystery back in Santo Fico.

When he went back to the gift shop he asked the pretty girl if there were any other museums in Milano that had any frescoes by Giotto and she suggested he look at some of the art books in the back of the shop. So, sitting there among racks of Michelangelo key chains and stacks of Leonardo da Vinci coffee mugs and Botticelli plates, Leo thumbed through rows of glossy art books. He was in the midst of a fervent prayer that he might never again hear the name Giotto when he saw something that took his breath away.

Staring at him from off a shiny page was the same boyish, melancholy face of Saint Francis that he had seen all his life – the sad, knowing eyes, the gentle mouth, and the look of eternal youth and innocence. It was the same face, the same robe, the same hair, but now there was no fig tree. This was a completely different wall painting than the Mystery of Santo Fico, but the same face. Across the page was another photograph of a different fresco, and again there was the same Saint Francis – his Saint Francis. The caption in the book even identified the character as Saint Francis, but neither fresco depicted him sitting casually beneath a fig tree. One was a mournful thing showing *The Death of Saint Francis*. The other was something called *The Apparition at Arles*, and, according to the book, the famous Giotto di Bondone painted both. Leo had found the link he needed to that phrase, 'could be worth a fortune.' He found it in the gentle face of the saint.

Leo spent the rest of that day wandering the halls of the

museum, but he wasn't interested in the paintings and statues anymore. He spent his time questioning everyone he could about the possible value of a work of art. Mostly he wanted to know how much a fresco by Giotto might be worth if it somehow happened to fall off a wall. By late afternoon he had made the guards nervous enough for them to suggest that it was time for him to go. And it was. He had learned all he needed.

Now, sixteen years later, sitting in the stifling stone hut and staring into those enigmatic plaster eyes that seemed to see something just over his shoulder, Leo was again plagued by 'could be worth a fortune.' He used his sleeve to wipe away the torrent of sweat that drenched his forehead, and when he looked down he discovered a dirty stain he'd just left on the arm of his linen jacket. The suit was ruined. He shouldn't have worn it yesterday morning. Was that just yesterday morning? He took off the tired jacket and thought of the little tailor shop off State Street. He'd had a date with some-one and needed something nice. Who was she? Women's faces catalogued through his mind like a Rolodex. It struck him as odd that he could remember the face of the tailor that sold it to him. He could even remember who was tend-ing bar the evening he strutted into the Chop House wearing his new linen suit for the first time, but he couldn't remem-ber the face of the woman on his arm. He couldn't remember any of their faces or their names. There had been lots of women. Why couldn't he remember them? He remembered his suit. To hell with it. With what they were going to get for the fresco, he could buy a closetful of linen suits.

Topo had actually raised a couple of good questions and so he tried to put his weary mind to some productive use. It was obvious that two things were going to be difficult. The first was finding the right person to handle the transaction. He knew guys who knew guys in Chicago – or maybe he just knew guys who said they knew guys. Once, in a bar, one of these marginal underworld guys, known as Sally Bones, was pointed out to him. Leo was disappointed to discover a small, nervous little fellow who probably dealt in cheap watches and fake jewelry. Leo thought Sally Bones looked like Topo after too much coffee. But to find a real fence in Italy, one who understood great art – because this was, no doubt, great art – they would probably have to go to Firenze, maybe even to Roma.

The other touchy part was going to be finding out how much to ask. Should they sell them individually or as a set? They might even want to break them up a bit more. A couple of quick shots with a hammer and they would have twice, three times as many little Giottos. Leo rejected that idea immediately. Also, how much is an original, undiscovered Giotto fresco worth on the open, or in this case the unopen, market? The original estimate of 'could be worth a fortune' was now a bit too vague. When it came time to actually talk to someone, Leo would have to have some reasonable figures in mind. Of course, yesterday at the hotel he'd done pretty well with, 'Oh, whatever you think is fair.'

A harsh pounding on the front door sent him spinning out

of his chair. It rattled everything in the room, most especially his fragile brain. It seemed as though the pounding might shatter the door and he almost called out angrily to Topo, but Topo would be home by now. And even if it were Topo, he would never pound on Leo's door with such ferocity. Thoughts buzzed around his fuzzy brain like fireflies, flashing in all directions at once and all too quick to grasp.

The painting! Saint Francis was resting comfortably on the cot, staring at something just beyond Leo's shoulder. The pounding began again, even more insistent, and suddenly, for the first time in his life, Leo knew where Saint Francis was looking and what he was thinking. The angelic saint was staring just beyond his shoulder at the door of the hut and he was thinking, 'Why don't you answer the door, Stupid!'

'Just a second!'

Leo rushed to the cot, laid the broken face of the saint flat, and threw a sheet over it.

When he opened the door and poked his head outside, the midday sun blinded him like a beacon, but Leo still almost made out the shape of Marta's hand an instant before it cracked across his cheek. The slap stung, but what genuinely hurt was banging the side of his head against the hut's stone wall trying to dodge her well-aimed palm.

'You rotten son of a bitch!'

Leo stepped outside and closed the door. Everything considered, he correctly appraised the situation remarkably fast.

'What the hell'd you do that for?'

'You know what I did that for, you rotten son of a bitch!'

Marta telegraphed her next roundhouse right and Leo was able to dodge this one. Confronted with the fury of Marta's rage, armed as she was with truth, and possessing the tenacity of an avenging angel, Leo chose the only safe course of action – lie as though your life depended on it.

'I have no idea what you're talking about,' he denied indignantly – maintaining his most sincere look of hurt bewilderment.

Marta's fury encompassed everything. It was that ridiculous look of innocence on Leo's long face, of course, but it was also dark years of disappointment, unspoken fears for her girls, a lifetime of hollow loneliness, and now the pain she felt from Uncle Elio. Everything swirled together and her brain crackled with electric blue flames. Leo watched a sort of madness enter her black eyes, as she screamed at him in tones that made him think his head was locked in a tightening vise. The sound made his teeth hurt. It seemed to Leo that Marta's fingernails were growing longer the closer she swung her claws toward his eyes. She struggled to express herself, but all that came out were spurts of shrieks and horrible sounds that, in better times, probably had some relationship to speech. At last, after pawing her feet in the dirt and sputtering like a demented coffeepot, she suddenly doubled her fist and hit Leo in the stomach. Strangely enough, this seemed to calm the moment as Leo bent over gasping for breath and Marta danced in small circles clutching the wrist she feared she had just broken.

When Leo was finally able to breathe again his aggravation with Marta became pointed and he dared to face her defiantly.

'What's the matter with you? Are you crazy? I don't know what you're talking about!'

Marta had determined that her wrist probably wasn't broken and she struggled against an impulse to kick him, but remained calm enough to speak.

'The Mystery! You stole the Mystery!'

Leo's jaw dropped almost to his chest and he stuttered in amazement, 'Some . . . somebody stole . . . the Mystery?' He knew he'd overdone it.

Marta hissed through clenched teeth, 'You stole it, you rotten son of a bitch!'

'Hey! Don't call me that. You knew my mother. That isn't nice to her memory. You shouldn't call me that.'

He was right. Leo's mother had been beautiful and kind and Marta had loved her like her own.

'And wouldn't she be proud of you now. Stealing from the church, you . . .'

She wanted to call him a bastard, but that cast aspersions on his mother *and* his father.

'You think I stole the Mystery from the church?'

'I know you stole it.'

Leo walked to his hut, threw open the door and stepped back contemptuously. 'Would you like to take a look for yourself?'

His heart pounded. If she went inside he was dead. She would have no qualms about sending him to jail if she had a chance. But Leo's bold stare and his belligerent challenge unnerved Marta and for a moment she doubted herself. If he had the fresco, would he offer to let her search for it? The dark room just beyond the opened door seemed shadowed and forbidding to her. There was something unexpectedly dangerous in this moment that Marta found unsettling. Her brain was telling her to just go inside the little pigsty, retrieve the fresco, and prove Leo Pizzola to be a liar up to his teeth. But there was something else in her heart, more mysterious and sinister, telling her to beware.

Leo had counted on her apprehension. He tested his advantage just a little.

'Well? Come on in.'

'Does it smell as bad as you?'

'I didn't steal the painting.' And he pulled the door closed with a secret sigh of relief.

'I saw you take it.'

Leo had been prepared to play this game as far as possible, but there was something in her quiet, controlled tone that told him she had just pitched a third strike. He managed to clear his throat with, 'You saw me . . . What does that mean?'

'I saw you and Topo carrying the pieces out of the church.'

Leo gazed out to sea and the moment hung in the air like one of the low clouds on the horizon. He was struck by how quiet everything was. There were no gulls crying loudly as they circled over the cliff. There were no cicadas screaming from the thistles in the fields. At this particular moment even the breeze stopped swirling around them; everything was still and his dream was over. He was tired and all he wanted was sleep.

'Okay. Fine. You saw us. Call the police.'

'I'm not going to call the police.'

'Okay. Fine. Don't call the police. I'll take it back to the church tomorrow.'

'You won't take it back to the church tomorrow.'

'Okay! Fine! I won't take it back tomorrow. I'll take it back to the church this afternoon!'

'You won't take it back to the church at all!'

'Okay! Fine! I won't . . . ! Would you tell me what the hell you want?'

'I want you to undo what you did!'

She hadn't really understood what she hoped to accomplish or even why she'd come here until this moment, but suddenly she knew. Leo had created this grief and he would fix it. How could he have been so selfish? Was he just pretending that he didn't understand?

'Do you have any idea what you've done?'

But Leo's dumb stare said it all – he honestly hadn't the least notion. And so she told him about finding Father Elio sitting alone in the church, staring at that blank wall. She told him of the old priest's tears and guilt, of how he blamed himself for the desecration, of how he felt that God was punishing him because he hadn't been a good enough priest or steward or something. God had taken the Mystery away from the village because of Father Elio's sin, whatever that meant. Father Elio knew this was a sign that God had abandoned him and it would take a miracle to restore God's love to his life. And she told him of the old man's determination to atone with an act of contrition – fasting and praying until God forgave him. This was as much as Marta could tell before anger took away her voice again and tears blurred her eyes.

Father Elio was a bigger fool than he had imagined, Leo thought to himself. Still, he didn't like the notion of the old man sitting around blaming himself and not eating.

'How long is he going to fast?'

'As long as it takes.'

Leo understood. The old fool was going to starve himself to death. No wonder Marta had attacked him.

'I told you I would bring it back.'

'He doesn't want it back! He can't stand the thought that anyone from Santo Fico would steal the Mystery. He prefers to believe that God took it.'

'But when he sees that a person took it—'

'He knows a person took it, damn it! He's not an idiot! Hell, in his heart he probably knows that it was you who took it! Don't you see? Somebody from the village taking the Mystery is just another proof that his life has been a failure. In his mind, you're just doing God's will to punish him. Don't bring it back! I mean it!' She shoved her finger into his chest like a dagger and her voice became an ominous whisper. 'If you bring it back, I *will* call the police.'

Leo looked around for something to kick. 'What the hell do you want me to do?'

'I want you to undo what you did. Make Uncle Elio know that God forgives him . . . and that He still loves him.'

'How the hell do I do that?'

'Make a miracle,' she said simply.

Even Marta was struck by the innocent sincerity of her

demand. She might just as easily have requested that he close the door, or stir the soup, or tie his shoe. But as soon as she said it, she knew that a miracle was exactly what she wanted, and now expected – or else.

Leo swallowed hard. He had heard her correctly and she meant it. He could see that she meant it. She expected him to make a miracle.

'How?'

'I don't know. You're the clever one.'

She abruptly turned and started back across the meadow, but she stopped. She stood for a moment with her back to him before slowly returning to face him. This time her voice was soft and sincere and she chose her words carefully.

'Leo, there's a lot . . . a lot of grief between us . . . you and me. Some of it . . . I don't know, maybe I . . . I don't know. But I tell you this from my heart – If Uncle Elio dies because of this, if he dies thinking that he's been deserted by God, I'll . . . I'll do something.'

She slowly pointed her finger at him again and Leo understood that he had just received a threat more dangerous than anything he'd ever faced before. She would do something and it would be terrible.

'You make a miracle.'

Then she turned again and headed back up the trail. Leo called after her.

'What should I do with the painting?'

Marta shrugged and called over her shoulder, 'Throw it in the sea for all I care. I never want to see it again.' And she was gone.

The first thing Leo did was open the door and all the shutters of the hut. There was no need to hide in the sweltering dark anymore. As far as Marta was concerned the fresco belonged to him. 'Throw it in the sea for all I care,' was what she said. The only witness to his crime never wanted to see it again. The treasure was once more his and this time with a crumb of backhanded approval. The sea breeze quickly filled and refreshed the room.

Leo went to the cot and pulled back the sheet, studied the panel for a moment, and for the first time in his life, he no longer cared what the saintly face was thinking. It didn't matter anymore. He placed the panel on the table in full view for anyone who happened by and then he collapsed on the cot. No one would happen by. He'd already had his visitor. And as he lay on the cot, enjoying the moments before sleep, he thought of Marta and her miracle. He knew it was going to be a challenge, but it was one he would gladly face. One miracle equaled one ticket out of Santo Fico . . . and wealth. He had no idea what he would do, but how hard could a miracle be, anyway?

Within minutes Leo was sound asleep and dreaming of Chicago, and baseball, and the cool green grass of Wrigley field.

Thirteen

By 1:30 of the next afternoon, Leo felt as if he had already performed a major miracle and any subsequent miracles would be child's play. He spent the morning keeping Topo from either killing himself or going to the police and confessing to every unsolved crime in Toscana.

As Leo explained to his guilt-ridden accomplice, it was God who had destroyed the wall, not them. 'After all,' Leo argued, 'if we hadn't saved the painting, it would have been crushed; gone forever.' So it was only logical: If God was going to destroy the painting, then God must have no more need for it. And if that was the case, shouldn't people be allowed to take advantage of what God no longer wanted? Wasn't Topo's own home and shop a testament to that sort of scavenger logic? On the other hand, spiritually speaking, perhaps God had a greater purpose in mind. Perhaps He wanted the painting to join the rest of the world so people everywhere could appreciate it. And, if either of these possibilities were true, could it not also be possible that God had intended for Leo and Topo to arrive at the church exactly when they did, precisely so they could rescue the painting? Hadn't they both prayed fervently for a long time that they should be allowed to escape Santo Fico? Who was to say that this was not the answer to their prayers? Did Topo really want to stand in the way of God's divine will?

By the time Leo was done with him, Topo was not only convinced of the soundness of both Leo's logic and theology, but was thinking that the town should be told of their good deed. They might receive a reward, or at least a testimonial, but Leo quickly persuaded him that this was perhaps going a bit too far. Then, once he felt that Topo was reasonably comfortable with the situation, it was time to move on to the more difficult task. He told Topo about his confrontation with Marta.

If Leo regarded Marta Caproni Fortino's strength of will with respect, Topo was absolutely cowed by it. He always had been. It wasn't that Marta had ever done anything to Topo, other than to occasionally give him a push or a solid punch in the arm when they were children. No, he was terrified of her potential – perhaps because she was a woman; perhaps because she was so remarkably beautiful; perhaps because she possessed those unknown dangers that he found so frightening and exciting.

When Leo told Topo that Marta had seen them leaving the church with the Mystery, and of Father Elio's reaction to the disappearance, and that Marta had threatened them with prison, he wasn't sure if his friend was going to cry or faint. Leo saw reflected in Topo's panicked eyes all the horrors he imagined awaiting him behind the cruel iron bars of prison. But by the afternoon, Leo began to make real progress. A major hurdle was Topo accepting that they weren't going to be thrown into a Siena prison for the remainder of their natural lives and that they were actually going to keep the painting, sell it, and make a fortune. The seeds Leo had planted in the morning hours establishing God's will on this subject finally blossomed in the afternoon and Topo even began to show small signs of enthusiasm about creating the proper miracle that would restore Father Elio's faith.

They spent the remainder of the afternoon at Topo's kitchen table, debating the merits of an assortment of possible divine events. They tried to keep their discussion on a respectfully high spiritual plane, confining any potential miracles to something with an established scriptural foundation, but their familiarity with biblical events was fairly random and what they could recall was sketchy at best. Consequently, they both kept unintentionally reverting to their most familiar exposures to things supernatural. As a result, Topo's miracles were too often reminiscent of science fiction movies of the 1950s, whereas Leo's miracles almost leapt off the pages of American tabloid newspapers – and unfortunately a couple of bottles of wine didn't help their inspiration or their temperament. By early evening a frightened and discouraged Topo suggested that it was time for Leo to go home.

The sun was passing from afternoon into evening when Leo stomped up the street leading away from Topo's shop. Who would have thought creating a miracle could be so difficult? At this point he wasn't sure who he was angriest with – Marta for her unreasonable demand that he produce a miracle, or Father Elio for his pointless hunger strike, or Topo for not asking him to stay for dinner. His frustrated march carried him halfway across the piazza before he noticed that he'd walked into the middle of a gauntlet.

Just ahead, Father Elio was on the steps of the church talking with Marta. The front doors of the church were open and it was evident that the old man had been hauling out the debris of the fractured roof. Apparently he wanted to continue his efforts, but no matter where the old priest turned, Marta stayed in front of him, holding out a basket that had to be filled with food and pleading for whatever was inside. Finally the old priest took Marta by the arm and gently turned her back toward the hotel. That's when they both saw Leo. Marta glared at him, but Father Elio smiled and waved as they descended the steps.

To make matters worse, Leo noticed Nonno sitting on the edge of the fountain. A wide bandage wrapped his forehead, there was an ugly bruise below one eye, and scratches, and he leaned on the newly borrowed cane as if he always had. The gray dog was asleep at his feet. Leo glanced at the old man out of the corner of his eye. Nonno was watching him and Leo could tell that the slightest provocation would bring him over. Any conversation with Nonno in the presence of Marta and Father Elio could prove awkward, and so he did what he could to ignore the old man.

Leo furrowed his brow as if he were the prisoner of deep thoughts and he walked with purposeful determination, his eyes locked on the cobblestones directly in front of his feet. He was sure that if he pretended he hadn't noticed them, he could make it across the piazza unaccosted. But also unfortunately for him, it occurred to Father Elio that a conversation with Leo might be the very thing to get Marta to stop pestering him. He loved his niece and he understood her concern, but the excellent smells emanating from that basket were beginning to test the resolve of his fast.

'Good evening, Leo.' The old man steered himself and Marta directly into Leo's path.

'Ahh! Hello . . .' Leo did his best impression of someone jolted out of some heavy deliberation. Marta simply sighed, shook her head, and made Leo feel exceptionally transparent.

At least Father Elio had accomplished his goal. Marta moved away from him and toward the hotel, but now he felt that some small talk was probably in order, so he asked Leo, 'How did your place do? I mean, with the earthquake the other night.'

'Oh, fine. Good . . . I was just, um . . . on my way . . .' Leo pointed down the north coast road and backed himself toward his destination. Marta not only didn't say a word, but refused to even look in his direction, which for some reason made Leo even more nervous. He was just about to turn and go when he was stopped by a familiar voice.

'Hey there, Nico.'

Nonno had left his perch on the fountain and was now, almost magically, standing at Leo's shoulder. He gave Leo a little wave, 'How you doin', Nico? Where'd you go the other night?'

Leo wanted to grab him and shake him until the few teeth he had left rattled – anything that would make him stop. Instead, he just gave a little nod and a feeble shrug.

'My house fell on me. Remember? You found me. Where'd you go? You promised you'd stay with me.'

The other night Father Elio had been so busy he hadn't noticed that Leo didn't return, but Marta knew where he was and Leo could feel her gaze turn to him. This was not good.

'I went to get some lumber so we could get you out.'

'You're a good boy, Nico. I thought you ran out on me. Maybe because of the mountains. But I didn't desert you. You know that! Even in the snow . . . when . . .'

The old man could tell he was getting jumbled. He had been told that he did that sometimes. So he just gave Leo a wink and a pat on the shoulder. 'My house fell on me, but you found me. Right?'

Leo shrugged again and tried to lose the image of Nonno's dusty face buried in the rubble with the dirt and blood and tears mingling with his trusting smile. He had deserted him, but he hadn't thought of it in those terms until now. Of course, Marta hadn't known about Nonno at all – until now, and the thought that Leo had abandoned that old man, buried in the rubble of his house, so he could steal the Mystery from the church, left her feeling a little sick. She wanted to hit him again, or scream at him some more, but she contented herself with just watching him fidget.

Father Elio was tired, so he bid them all good evening, explaining that it was time for him to go back to the church and pray. Marta nodded and as her uncle walked back toward the church she took a moment to catch Leo's eye. It was just a glance, but in her look Leo saw that there was something more than just anger. It was disgust. She stepped close to him and her voice was barely a whisper and as indifferent as a breeze.

'Three days. If you haven't done something to restore my uncle's faith in three days, I'm calling the police. Three days. Then, I'll do anything I have to do to make sure you're punished for what you've done. Three days.'

Without another look she strode across the piazza and disappeared into the hotel at about the same moment Father Elio vanished into the church. Leo was left alone in the center of the piazza with Nonno and the gray dog. He didn't want to look at Nonno because he knew if he did, the old man was going to talk to him and he especially didn't want to talk to him right now. He was too angry with the old fool for mentioning the other night in front of Marta, and he was also angry with Marta for her new ultimatum, and he was angry with himself for not yet having contrived a miracle that he could have tossed in her face. So, without acknowledging Nonno in any way, Leo walked across the piazza and down the street to the north coast road.

He was sorry about deserting the old man the other night, of course, and he was glad that he was all right, but Nonno was not his problem. All he had wanted to do was walk across the piazza! Why couldn't Nonno just shut up? Now, Marta was ready to serve him his head on a platter, roasted with sage and sweet basil, if he didn't make a miracle in three days. *Three days!* For the first time since he'd 'rescued' the fresco, he fancied he heard the clang of prison doors in that phrase – 'Three days!' He needed to think. He needed a miracle that couldn't be denied even by the biggest skeptic. He needed an event to happen in front of witnesses. He needed something unexpected, something impossible. He needed . . . He needed . . . He needed to know why the hell Nonno was following him down the north coast road!

They were all the way to the outskirts of Santo Fico before Leo noticed the shuffling sounds behind him. Nonno and that gray dog were following about twenty meters back. When Leo stopped and turned to them, they stopped – both looking casually preoccupied with something else. With renewed determination Leo turned and again walked down the road toward home, but he knew immediately that his personal nightmare and his damn dog were still following. So he stopped again. Nonno stopped also and busied himself by absently pushing pebbles off the road with his new cane, but the dog missed his cue and kept walking. When he discovered his error he went back and flopped down in the warm dust at Nonno's feet. Leo stomped back up the hill to them.

'What?'

Nonno truly didn't understand, and he shuffled innocently, looking for something to say.

'What is it?' stormed Leo.

'What is it? I don't know – What is it, Nico?'

'Look. I'm sorry about the other night. I'm sorry I didn't come back. I'm sorry!'

Nonno smiled and pushed Leo's shoulder playfully. 'Hey, that's okay. You're a good boy. You found me!'

'So, what is it? Why are you following me?'

Nonno thought hard for a moment before he said softly, 'My house fell on me the other night . . .'

'I know. I found you.'

Leo could tell that there was more to be said, but for some reason the old man didn't want to say it. It was as if there was something that Leo was supposed to know and Nonno was giving him a chance to say it first. But Leo had no idea what it was that Nonno wanted him to say and so the sun burned down on them as they stood in the road, each watching the other, waiting for the other to say this unspoken thing.

At last Nonno spoke. His eyes avoided Leo's and his voice was soft and hesitant.

'So . . . I don't have a place to stay anymore. Can I stay with you, Nico?'

He seemed ashamed and Leo felt worse about making the old man say those words out loud than he did about leaving him buried in the rubble. Buried in the destruction of his little room, Nonno had been a man trapped in a catastrophe, fighting for his life, but still a man. Even buried in the ruins, he had dignity. Now, he was a helpless old thing with a cane standing in the dust of the road asking for charity.

The words came out before Leo even had a chance to think, but they seemed an appropriate end for this day's fiasco.

'Sure. Come on.'

That night the shepherd's hut became more crowded than Leo could manage. It wasn't Nonno's fault. In fact, the old man turned out to be surprisingly good company. Once the fragments of the Mystery were safely stored under the bed and Nonno was finally allowed inside, Leo was amazed at how amiable the old man could be. Not only was Nonno surprisingly complimentary about every aspect of the ancient hovel and its bare surroundings, but he was especially grateful for the makeshift bed they created for him in the corner. The old man even offered to prepare their evening meal, and to Leo's delight, his new roommate turned out to be a surprisingly inventive cook.

No, it wasn't Nonno who strained the limits of hospitality. It was that skinny gray dog, who apparently assumed that Leo's invitation to Nonno was a package deal. Although Nonno swore that he not only never fed the dog but, in fact, had never even seen him eat anything, it was obvious that the dog was eating something. And whatever it was that the dog was eating, it didn't agree with him. Nonno's guess was grasshoppers, lizards, and scorpions. The bill of fare was irrelevant, because by about ten o'clock in the evening the dog's gas had become so potent that Leo stumbled from the small hut gagging for air, his eyes watering. Nonno followed him outside, apologizing for the cur's ill-mannered behavior. He was used to it, of course, but for strangers it was undoubtedly a bit thick.

What greeted them was a broad moonless sky carpeted with stars and a soft breeze off the sea. It was such a pleasant night that they built a small fire and brought some blankets outside. After a few minutes the dog sheepishly came out too and was forgiven, and then the three of them lay on the ground and stared up at the night sky. Conversation was sparse for a while, but eventually one comment led to another and before long they were discussing this and that. Nonno's memory and observations startled Leo. Up until then Leo had thought of Nonno as an eccentric to be barely tolerated, then brushed aside as you crossed the piazza. But to Leo's amazement, Nonno was not only interesting and pleasant company, but filled with stories and adventures. Only occasionally did he catch himself becoming disordered by memories of some vague and cryptic tragedy in some snowy mountains. For the most part he remained relatively lucid, although he did continue to call his host Nico.

It was probably almost midnight when Nonno told the strangest tale of all and yet the one that made the most sense. It was so simple, so logical. It was a variation on a story that Leo, and everyone else in the village, had heard many times before, but always in confused, disconnected fragments. Leo had never heard the old man put all the pieces together before. But now, listening to him tell the story by the campfire, Leo knew he had stumbled on to something exceptional. He had found his miracle.

Fourteen

For the first time in his life Elio Caproni was having trouble getting up in the morning. Early morning had always been his favorite time of day; he liked the freshness of the air, the cool emptiness of the piazza, and the blinding sparkle of the morning sun through the sanctuary's eastern windows. And then, there was that first cup of coffee — one of life's greatest pleasures.

But for the last few mornings all he wanted was to sleep. He wasn't waking refreshed and he had to force himself to pull back the covers and stumble to the kitchen. At first he thought it was because of the fast, but he had fasted before.

When he was a young man he had joined his predecessor, Father Luigi Scavio, in a fast that lasted two weeks. Maybe it was only ten days, but it was a long time and he could have gone longer, but Father Luigi was old and became too weak. Maybe that was it. Maybe now he was Father Luigi. Maybe now he was just too old to fast. These were not good thoughts to be waking up with and he tried to dismiss them. A cup of coffee and he would be fine.

And sure enough, within the hour (and after another cup of coffee) Father Elio was feeling better. What he needed was a bit of work to take his mind off things. So he spent this morning as he had the last two mornings, hauling the debris of the collapsed ceiling out the great front doors and piling it at the bottom of the steps. He was pleased to find that many of the roof tiles weren't damaged. In a few hours he was able to carry most of the remaining debris out and all that was left were some beams that he couldn't move. He would have to recruit help with them, but there was still a great deal of sweeping. He preferred doing this work in the cool of the morning because the days were so hot – even inside the cathedral, now that it had the gaping hole in the roof. He also confessed to himself that by working outside he didn't have to look at the way his beautiful little cathedral had suffered.

He was sweeping the front steps when he saw Maria Gamboni walking slowly across the piazza. This was odd because it wasn't one of Maria's usual confessional days and Father Elio hoped that Maria wasn't caught in the grip of some guilt attack and in need of an emergency confession.

He didn't want to go back inside. Now that the sun was shifting he wanted to go around to the north side and see if there was enough shade to work on the crumbled garden wall. Maybe she was just passing by on her way to somewhere else. But Maria walked slowly up to him and sat right down on the stone steps. So Father Elio put down his broom and sat next to her. Maria Gamboni had been a passionate fire of determined guilt for nearly thirty years and Father Elio wasn't prepared for this sad old woman who sat quietly next to him in the shade of the bell tower.

'What do I have to do, Father?'

'To do?' Father Elio repeated blankly.

'Why won't God honor my repentance?'

The question was so simple and profound Elio couldn't speak.

'I've prayed for forgiveness every day for thirty years. I've confessed my sins thousands of times. I've done my penance until my voice is hoarse and my knees are bleeding. You know this is true.'

He nodded. He did know this was true.

'So why won't God forgive me? What do I have to do? If my Rico isn't coming home, why can't I know this? If he is dead, why can't I know this? What does a person do when the only thing they love in the world refuses to love them back? What do I have to do to get God to listen to me, to forgive me?'

Father Elio sat for so long considering Maria Gamboni's questions, that if they were in the confessional, she would have thought him asleep again. But he wasn't asleep. He was astounded that she could speak his own thoughts and fears so eloquently. She could see his watery blue eyes were lost in her sad contemplation, but he also seemed lost for an answer.

Finally Maria rescued the awkward moment by pointing a bony finger across the piazza and exclaiming incredulously, 'Well, would you look at that? What on earth are they up to?'

The answer to this mundane question was no easier than her previous spiritual one. They watched in silence as Leo Pizzola entered the piazza from the old north coast road, followed by Nonno and then the gray dog. Leo seemed to be in a great hurry and tried to pull Nonno along, but the old man's new aristocratic limp refused to be rushed. When Leo saw Father Elio and Maria Gamboni watching from the church steps, he smiled and waved uncomfortably. Nonno wanted to tip his cap politely, but Leo impatiently guided the old man across the piazza toward the south road leading down the hill and out the other side of town.

When they were out of sight Maria made a clucking sound with her tongue and said only, 'Well, that's quite a pair.'

'Maria, about what you asked . . . I don't know what to tell you.'

The old lady stood up and dusted off her black dress. 'I know. It's okay. What would you know about God turning His back on someone? You're a priest. God loves you.'

She walked down the steps and called over her shoulder, 'See you on Thursday.'

Father Elio sat staring at the broom in his hands and

thinking about Maria Gamboni's words. What would he know about God turning his back on someone? He's a priest. God loves him.

Topo wasn't sure what upset him the most: that Leo believed Nonno's peculiar story or that he'd brought that smelly dog into his shop. That dog was looking for a place to pee. But when Topo was finally able to get his mind off the old dog sniffing around his boxes, crates, and pant leg long enough to listen to Nonno's story, he had to admit he was surprised by what he heard. For as long as he could remember, he'd heard stories about the mysterious history of Santo Fico, but the details of this particular incident Nonno told were new and intriguing . . .

It was in the winter of 1944, probably late January or early February, when Nonno had stumbled into Santo Fico from somewhere in the north. He was so gaunt and haggard that most of the villagers thought he wouldn't survive. In and out of a fever for a week, he raved about terrible things and most of what he said made little sense, but they pieced together that something terrible had happened to him with the Germans. They surmised that he'd been part of a band of anti-Fascists who were pursued by Nazis, driven into the Dolomite Mountains, and he was the lone survivor. How he managed to wander across half of Italy in the dead of winter was to remain forever a mystery.

To make matters worse, a month later a detachment of Germans was assigned to Santo Fico. They simply drove their trucks up the southern road one day, parked in the piazza, and moved into the hotel. They were part of a greater German force that had been sent to Italy to 'encourage' the heartsick forces of Il Duce. This small squad had been assigned to Santo Fico because of its quiet harbor and commanding view of the sea. Fortunately, the occupation didn't last long. The villagers did not like Santo Fico being occupied by the arrogant German soldiers who stayed wherever they chose, took whatever they wanted, and flirted with whomever they pleased. So the villagers fought back – in their own unique way.

According to Nonno, one night when naval and aerial bombardments were occurring all around the region, some of the men sneaked out and shut off all of the water. In the morning it was announced to the Germans that a stray bomb had destroyed the village well and every inhabitant of Santo Fico would undoubtedly die of thirst before it could be repaired. Of course, the villagers had stored away enough water to last them a month. They begged the Germans for help. In only a few days the thirsty Germans were gone and were never seen in Santo Fico again. The water was restored within twenty-four hours – all except the fountain.

Now according to Nonno, the fountain had its own ancient source, a source other than the main well and the water lines that supplied the village. The fountain dated back many centuries and its source was probably established when the cathedral was built – maybe even earlier. In 1944 there was only one very old man who knew where the pipes to the fountain originated and the night they shut down the water, it had been Nonno's job to accompany that old man and help him turn off the water to the fountain – which he did.

Unfortunately for the village, the old man who knew where the pipes to the fountain originated was very old indeed. Two days after their sabotage raid, he died. In the subsequent months, Nonno was of little help. He was not only a stranger to the region, but had only visited the forgotten water pipe once and that was on a moonless night. But, also, in those days his mind was even cloudier than now. So all memories of the old pipe remained vague and the ancient fountain remained dry – Santo Fico's only casualty of World War II.

At the time, there were certainly larger concerns than the fountain. It was wartime and things were hard. Then, as time passed, the cool water that had once flowed in the middle of the piazza became a topic for idle chat, then a fading memory, and eventually the notion of water in the fountain became only a fable that children joked about.

But for Nonno it was never a joke. For years he blamed himself, that he couldn't find where the old man had taken him that night in 1944. For years he combed the surrounding hills and firmly fixed his reputation as the official village idiot by continually insisting that one day he was going to make water in the town square. He still insisted, to the present day, that if he could find that unremembered place, he could restore the water to the fountain.

Topo looked from one expectant face to the other. It was an interesting tale, but he was totally baffled as to how Leo expected him to react.

But Leo smiled slyly and said, 'Wouldn't it be something if water did suddenly start flowing out of the fountain again? Maybe as Father Elio was sitting on the edge of the fountain . . . maybe praying that the water would return . . . and all of a sudden . . .'

Topo smiled and nodded. 'All of a sudden, water just starts flowing out of the fountain. That would be something all right. That would be . . .'

They shouted in unison, '. . . A miracle!'

Topo saw the beauty of this miracle immediately and the two men launched into their plan of attack. It all sounded exciting to Nonno too, but at the moment he just wanted to get that stupid dog outside before Topo noticed the puddle dripping from the soggy cardboard box containing the discarded parts for a belt sander.

It was true – about many things, Nonno was vague. Cloudy memories from an indistinct past drifted into smoky recollections of things best forgotten, and to say that he tended to become confused was an understatement. But about the water and the fountain, there were a few things of which Nonno was absolutely positive. The first was that the pipe was buried . . . maybe. He distinctly remembered digging. He wasn't completely clear if the digging came before they found the pipe, or after, or both. Just in case, Leo decided, they should probably carry a pick and shovel. The other point that was clear to Nonno was that the pipe was south of the village . . . Or, maybe he had just done most of his searching south of the village. But for some reason, 'south of the village' remained pertinent to his story. So with high expectations and appropriate tools, the trio set out.

When they had been sitting in Topo's cool shop, on the shady side of the old stone building, their endeavor sounded reasonable. By the time they were ten minutes down the road and the edge of the Toscana sun was cutting through their shirts, Topo, at least, was beginning to question the wisdom of the venture. And he didn't like carrying the shovel. He complained that the wooden handle was getting too hot and he just couldn't find a comfortable way to carry it, so Leo traded tools with him. But within a few minutes the pick was too heavy for Topo and he wanted his shovel back.

The two men were so completely absorbed in carping at each other that they didn't see the exact moment when Nonno, who had been leading them down the gravely road, suddenly stopped and held up his hand. They nearly walked into him. Whether the old man saw something, or remembered something, or smelled something on the wind, or just sensed the spirit of some previous adventure — whatever it might be, it was a mystical moment. They had just rounded the last turn in the road that took them out of a treacherous section of crags and cliffs. The dry heat almost crackled in the weeds and cicadas screamed what sounded like a warning. To their right a short field dropped steeply downhill to threatening cliffs and the sea. To their left, a sloping, tawny plane of thistles, cactus, and rocks stretched before them. Their narrow road continued for only another half kilometer before it turned inland and ran across those yellow-brown fields toward a grove of trees that, from this distance, was only a thin puff of green on the horizon.

Nonno gazed out at their options, scratching his white stubble, and mumbling to himself. All waited with expectation – even the dog. The old man was on to something. They waited for what seemed like a long time. Twice Topo started to speak, but both times Leo gave him a quick look and harsh gesture that told him not to interrupt Nonno's meditation. At last, the old man let out a sigh of understanding. He turned eastward and limped purposefully down into the weeds of the plain. Leo followed.

Topo followed too, but he was troubled. For many years Nonno and his old gray dog had been inseparable. Where one was, there was the other. People had always just assumed that the dog clung faithfully to Nonno's heels because that's the nature of the loyal beast. But now Topo was troubled. Was he the only one who noticed that the dog wandered out into the field to investigate a grasshopper just moments before Nonno received his inspiration? In Topo's mind it definitely raised a question: In this man-dog, master-beast relationship, just who was following whom?

And so the pattern was set for the rest of the day. Either Nonno or the dog would 'sense' something and they were off again. Often Nonno would stop and deliberate, study a rock, and debate if they should dig in that particular spot. He usually thought better of it and they moved on. But Topo made sure he kept his eyes open to see if he could catch the dog either nodding or shaking his head. On rare occasions Nonno would point his cane to a particular rock and that meant they were to turn the rock over and dig beneath it. Turning the rock over was Topo's least favorite part and then he was glad he had the shovel. He hated and feared snakes – black snakes in particular. As a boy, his mother used to tell the story of her younger brother being bitten by a black snake. She never tired of describing how he swelled up, turned blue, and then – with his eyes bulging – the boy babbled madness with a purple tongue and foam spewed from every orifice in his body (and other horrible symptoms that varied with her mood). Young Topo and his sisters often wondered at the inconsistency of the boy's afflictions and how much mad babbling he could have done at three years old, but the story did work its magic. The entire Pasolini family was terrified of snakes – a plight that Leo and Franco never tired of taking advantage of when they were growing up. If they could present a well-timed shriek of 'SNAKE!' along with the unexpected appearance of a wriggling length of garden hose, young Topo pretty much guaranteed at least a spastic leap, a girlish scream, and a torrent of curses and tears. Endless amusement.

By late afternoon, Leo and Topo both would have traded a healthy portion of their potential fortune for a tall glass of water, five minutes under a shady tree, or a hat. Then even the dog deserted them. It wasn't long after they saw him meander back across the plain toward the village that Nonno called it quits too. Topo was now totally convinced that, from the beginning, the dog had been calling the shots. But in fact, Leo had also grown discouraged with Nonno's perpetual chant of 'That looks familiar over there.' He began to wonder why everything that looked familiar was so far away. Why couldn't anything close ever look familiar? At last, the three of them went the way of the dog – dragging across the plain and then up the steep road to town.

They sat for a long time in Topo's cool shop, drinking water in silence. They had come close to making themselves sick with too much sun and heat, but at last Nonno said, 'You know, I haven't looked in a long time. But I think I remember something . . . I think we were farther away from the village.'

'How far?' Leo wanted to be supportive.

'Oh . . . Maybe across the fields, maybe . . . but, not as far as the trees. There weren't any trees . . . maybe.'

Thoughts of walking that far and carrying that shovel made Topo's head hurt. Luckily, Leo had a better idea.

'Tomorrow we should take the truck. And we'll go in the morning when it's cooler.'

'And you boys wear hats,' piped in Nonno.

'And tomorrow we'll take water,' added Leo.

Topo was too exhausted to speak or protest. He wanted to protest. He wanted to scream at Nonno that he was crazy. He wanted to tell Leo that when he volunteered 'the truck,' it was, in fact, his truck, and the thought of going through that inferno again was more than he could bear. He wanted to tell Leo to take the fresco back to the church, then go back to Chicago and leave him alone. He was tired and he needed to rest – especially since, apparently, he was going to have to do this all over again tomorrow.

The next day was better. They had the truck, they had

water, and they wore hats. Those parts were better. As far as Nonno being closer to remembering where he had gone on that moonless night in 1944 – that was still a little blurry.

The old man wanted to ride in the back with the dog. The dog liked to lean over the side with his nose into the wind, searching for mysterious smells. Nonno stood behind the cab, with his face also leaning into the wind, and scanned the horizon for the mysterious spot. The plan was to drive down the road, around the bend, and across the plain to the place Nonno indicated the day before. But it was slower going than anticipated, because every thirty meters Nonno would bang on the roof of the cab like a drum and shout, 'Stop! That place looks familiar.' The little truck would slide to a halt in a cloud of dust and they'd all pile out. They'd then tramp through the thistles and brambles, Topo's shovel ever poised, ready for a lurking black snake – waiting for Nonno's magical moment of clarity. Then, after twenty minutes or so, it was back to the truck to tear off down the road for another thirty meters before Nonno would once again bang his cane on his Fiat drum. They followed this ritual all the way down the hill, around the bend, and across the plain toward those trees that were slowly becoming more than just a low hedge along the horizon.

It was afternoon by the time the adventurers finally ran out of yellow-brown fields. The truck was parked at the final turn that carried the road away from the flat plains south of Santo Fico and curved into foothills that continued on toward the highway. Although neither Leo nor Topo noticed, they were parked in almost the exact spot where

Topo had parked and waited just hours before the earth-quake, when Leo demanded his vomit-stop on their way home from Grosseto. They might have noticed this coinci-dence, if they had stopped arguing long enough to look around. But the heat and the tension had finally become too much for them. That and an innocent comment by Nonno to which, well . . . to which Topo didn't react well at all.

Nonno had shouted and banged on their heads, as usual. They'd stopped the truck, as usual. As usual, they'd fol-lowed him out into the weeds. They'd waited patiently while, as usual, the old man scratched his stubbled chin and deliberated. Then Leo mentioned, quite casually, that they'd pretty much arrived at the trees and they were, more or less, running out of fields to search. Nonno looked around, con-sidered the truth of Leo's observation, and then replied softly, 'Maybe it was on the north side of the village.'

While Leo was stilled by this speculation, Topo went off like a Roman candle. He screamed at such a pitch, Leo thought the little fellow had actually, finally seen a snake. Topo stomped back toward the truck with the full intention of leaving his two companions (three if he counted the dog) to make their own way home. Leo chased him down and the two men launched into a fiery debate on many wide ranging subjects from childhood grudges to financial windfalls to mad schemes – none of which Nonno understood. So he ignored them.

Nonno was puzzled. How could he have remembered for so many years that the pipe was on the south side, if it was really to the north? He needed to sit down and think this over, so he looked around for an appropriate resting place and noticed a tall, thin rock that had apparently been recently tipped over. One end of the long stone was crusted with dirt where it had been buried and it lay next to a bowl-like impression in the earth. Nonno squinted at the rock and scratched his chin, trying to puzzle things through. He sat down on this stone that Leo had stumbled over a few nights earlier and studied the bowl-shaped indentation where it had once rested. A small flash of metal glinted in the sun. Something was buried there, so the old man scraped at the dry dirt with his finger.

'Well, what do you know about that,' he mumbled.

All of this was lost on Leo and Topo, and it was only because there was a lull in their shouting that they eventually heard Nonno talking to them at all. They were used to his incoherence, but his current observation struck them both as unusually odd and they responded almost in unison.

'What?'

'I said, it must be the trees. The trees couldn't have been this big then. Maybe they grew. But then again, maybe they were this big. Maybe I just didn't see them. It was dark, you know.' He sat on the rock, picking at something shiny in his hand.

'What about the trees?' Leo walked back to the distracted old man.

'I think those damn trees threw me off all these years. Maybe they weren't so big.' Nonno held up a tarnished old piece of metal. 'I found my watch. Doesn't work anymore. I lost it that night. I hunted all over for it, but it was dark.

When I finished burying the pipe, I pushed this rock up on
end as a marker. I must have pushed it right up on top of my
watch. Something knocked this rock over.'

Leo and Topo exchanged glances.

'You mean . . .?'

'Oh, yeah. This is the place. I never looked down here
because it's too close to the trees. Funny . . . I don't remember any trees. It musta been too dark. So . . . You wanna dig
here?'

Soon the three of them were standing over a hole that
revealed the remains of an antiquated clay pipe with two
full meters of it smashed to pieces and one end plugged with
rocks and all sorts of odd debris.

'This pipe is smashed,' observed Topo.

'You smashed the pipe,' noted Leo.

Nonno was grinning from ear to ear. 'Damn right we did.
This thing put up one hell of a fight. Took us a while too. All
we had were big rocks. You know, that pipe's old, but it's
tough.'

'You said you turned off a valve.'

'Did I say that? No, I don't think I said that. I said I
turned off the water. There wasn't a valve. We just smashed
it. Big rocks. Then, ah . . . ohhh . . . Water everywhere! I
thought I was gonna drown. We couldn't stop the water. So
I started jamming things up the pipe. I started with my hat.
Then my coat. That's when I took my watch out of my
pants. I didn't want to lose it. Then my pants went up the
pipe, but there was still water. That's when the old man
started taking his clothes off. We shoved all our clothes up

the pipe and it finally plugged up. But our clothes, they didn't want to stay. So I started shoving rocks and sticks and mud up the pipe. Then I put that one big rock in front of the end. That stopped it. Then I buried it and we sneaked back to the village – wet, covered with mud. All we had on were our shoes. It wasn't too cold, but the old man, he got sick. He died.'

They stared down in the hole.

'We're going to need a plumber for this, you know.' The edge in Topo's voice left no doubt that he blamed Leo for Nonno's having smashed the pipe.

'Ohhh, you're going to need a hell of a plumber. We smashed that son of a bitch.' Nonno laughed loudly.

Leo's mind raced – they could make this work. This afternoon Topo would drive into town and get a plumber to come back tomorrow. Get a plumber from Follonica . . . No! Follonica's too close. Topo should go all the way to Piombino and find a plumber who's never been to Santo Fico, a plumber nobody knows. Leo would dig out more of the pipe, then camouflage the hole. Tomorrow the plumber fixes the pipe, with a valve this time. Then with a bit of setup and good timing and luck, they turn the valve and – a miracle.

Nonno didn't understand any of what Leo and Topo were planning – he had his own plans.

'Wait until we go back and tell them. Wait till they hear we're going to turn the water back on!'

This could have been a disaster, but it was quickly explained to Nonno that the pipe, the water, and the fountain all had to stay a secret. It was going to be a surprise for everyone, especially Father Elio. In fact, he must never say anything to anyone, ever. Nonno understood. He liked secrets and he liked surprises and he especially liked Father Elio. They could count on him.

From her bedroom window, Marta watched the familiar little red truck move out onto the road in a cloud of dust and disappear into the trees. Topo was headed for the highway. She had watched them from her window, off and on, for most of the morning, and although Marta had no idea what Leo was up to, she didn't have good feelings about it.

Fifteen

*T*he next morning, bright and early, Leo, Topo, Nonno, and the gray dog sat in the shade of an oak tree and listened for the sound of a truck coming through the trees. The plumber that Topo found in Piombino promised he would drive down this road 'first thing' in the morning, but apparently pinning the plumber down to a more exact time was a losing battle. At least Topo had found a fellow who swore he didn't know anyone in Santo Fico, had never been to Santo Fico, and hoped never to go to Santo Fico. That was good, anyway.

The dog was the first to hear something. He lifted his

head off the ground and looked into the trees. By the time the other three could hear the faint growl of a truck coming down the road, the dog was already bored with it and had gone back to sleep.

The plumber's little truck sputtered to a halt in a haze of blue smoke and all three spectators stood in silent awe that the truck had actually made it all the way from Piombino. They also wondered if this plumber actually had a shop or just this beleaguered little truck. The back was filled with racks and shelves and bins, and they in turn were filled with every conceivable fashion of tool, pipe, clamp, bolt, and exotic plumbing implement imaginable. With all that equipment it was understandable why the axles and frame almost dragged on the ground. Or so they thought, until the door opened and the small truck groaned with painful relief as the short driver climbed out of the cab. The three observers all had concerns about the width of the door and the girth of their plumber. Leo couldn't recall ever having seen anyone who was actually as wide as they were tall, although admittedly, this cannonball with legs wasn't particularly tall. In fact, he was particularly short – he and Topo probably spoke eye-to-eye. And as they watched him pull a sack of tools from the back of his truck, it became apparent that there was not an ounce of what could be considered flab on this fellow. He was solid. And he was dark. His arms and face were close to the color of worn brown shoes. From where Leo stood, he couldn't tell if the man was weathered from the sun or just incredibly grimy.

He approached his three anxious helpers with a solid

rolling gait and a smile that lit up his face all the way to the top of his bald, brown head and asked simply, 'So where's this smashed pipe?'

Leo and Topo spun away from the approaching plumber almost simultaneously, as if they had been struck by a big stick. 'Over here . . . This way . . .' They quickly moved ahead and upwind of their plumber as they led him across the hot field toward the hole.

It's the nature of the world and the business of a plumber that occasionally they're forced to deal with situations that are, on a social level, unpleasant. Leo and Topo had no way of knowing what previous job this round man had performed – perhaps, even probably, it had been something disgusting. But the end result was certain – this poor honest laborer was encircled by an odor that was excessively ripe. Even Nonno, whose olfactory senses had already come into question as far as Leo was concerned, chose to keep his distance. Only the old gray dog seemed attracted to the plumber's powerful aroma. Of course, Nonno had seen that dog seek out rotting things lying in the sun, things that would make your stomach turn and your eyes water, and then that dog would flop down in the middle of it and roll with delight. So the dog's recommendation didn't count for much. Leo had a sense, however, that his pungent condition had nothing to do with any previous job and that this guy hadn't spent as much time in the sun as might be hoped.

But the fellow certainly knew his business. He stood at the edge of the hole for less than a minute before he assessed, 'This pipe's smashed.'

They were dealing with a professional. They nodded their agreement of his appraisal.

'So . . . you want me to replace it.'

It was not a question. It was a statement. This fellow not only grasped the predicament, but had the solution. They nodded at his conclusion.

'You want a valve?'

'Can you do that?' asked Leo.

'No problem. Two hours.'

'Is there anything we can do to help?'

'Yeah. Don't help.' The round plumber laughed hard. He'd used that line before.

Leo, Topo, Nonno, and the dog retreated from the edge of the hole while the plumber started about his business. They didn't want to get too far away because there was an element of interest in how this walking bowling ball was going to negotiate the hole. But then again, they didn't want to get too close because the wind might shift.

As it turned out, his agility was remarkable and the repair progressed with little difficulty. The only part of the operation that took any real time was when the plumber had to yank the two amateur saboteur's discarded clothes out of the pipe. The decades of pressure on the cloth and rocks and twigs and mud, compressed between the water on one side and the large rock on the other, had created an extremely effective plug. The sturdy plumber lay in the deepening muck, tugging, hacking, prying, puffing, and cursing for over thirty minutes before a wad of debris burst out of the pipe as if it had been shot from a fire hose. The water rushed out with such a surprising force that the hole quickly turned into an ever-deepening trough. The plumber managed to keep his head above the rising water and called out, 'If you still want to help, now would be a good time!'

Unfortunately, all this was more than the gray dog could stand. All he probably wanted was a drink of the cool brown water and whether he slipped or jumped would be debated later. The fact was that in a blink he was on top of the plumber and with his hind legs awkwardly wrapped around the poor man's shoulders, all paws paddled madly. After a few desperate moments of man and beast floundering in the muddy water, sometimes both completely submerged in the brew, Nonno unceremoniously dragged the dog to dry land and the plumber managed to screw the valve onto the newly threaded pipe. The torrent finally stopped and with a jolly laugh, the plumber climbed out for a moment to rest and dry off and also to allow the hole to drain. He actually seemed to have enjoyed the adventure and Leo couldn't help noting that his unexpected bath left him looking a shade or two lighter.

The lull was a handy time for Leo and Topo to coordinate their operation. The plumber assured them that the pipes would be connected in less than an hour. That would give Leo plenty of time to walk back to the village and get Father Elio out to the fountain. If Leo and Topo synchronized their watches, then Leo would have Father Elio praying at the exact moment that Topo turned the valve. Both agreed this was a good plan, but Nonno didn't like it. For some reason it was important to him that he turn the valve.

'I made the water go away, I must bring it back.'

Fine. Nonno turns the valve. But then the plumber had an objection to the plan too.

'You know, we don't know what's in the other half of that pipe. It could be clogged or broken anywhere between here and your fountain.'

Neither Leo, Topo, or Nonno had a solution for that, so they decided to ignore it. It was a good plan; an excellent plan. All they needed to do was synchronize their watches and decide on the exact minute. Then they were ready for Leo to go back to the village and prepare Father Elio for his miracle.

On his walk back to the village Leo had time to ponder something that he hadn't given much thought. How was he going to get Father Elio out to the fountain and praying for water at precisely 11:46 . . . No . . . 11:45. Topo was 11:46. Topo wanted that extra minute for a margin of error. That way Father Elio would be praying for a minute before the cool, clear water began miraculously trickling out of the cherub's jug and into the small marble top dish, cascading over the edge to the large second dish, and finally splashing merrily down into the empty pool. Leo liked the margin for error idea, even though he was sure Topo suggested it because he didn't trust Leo's American watch. But how was he going to get Father Elio praying for the fountain at 11:45?

By the time he was climbing the street leading to the piazza, Leo had a plan. Marta should do it. This whole dilemma was Marta's doing. She was the one who was unforgiving. She was the one with the spiteful words and the angry looks and snarling lip. It was for her uncle! Let her do it!

By the time he reached the top of the hill he had worked himself into a pretty good fume at Marta, so instead of walking on to the piazza, he took a sharp left that put him in the backyard of the hotel. He then just followed the enticing smells coming from the kitchen. Marta was at the stove stirring a large simmering pot of what smelled to be beef stock and Leo's stomach rumbled hungrily as he stood boldly in the doorway. He'd worked himself up for a fight and even rehearsed some potential dialogues in his mind, so he was completely disarmed when she looked over at him and said, 'You must be thirsty after that walk.'

He was. She nodded toward the sink and allowed him to fill a glass twice. Leo was thrown. Her attitude wasn't something that he could mistake as friendly, but she wasn't yelling at him – and he had walked right into her kitchen without even asking. And how did she know about his long walk?

She turned the fire down under the pot and invited him to join her at the kitchen table, and as he sat opposite her, all his instincts told him to beware of her hospitality – it could be a trap.

'So,' she began casually, 'have you decided it's time to tell me why you and Topo have been following that crazy old man around for the last two days? Or what you were digging for? Or where Topo went yesterday? Or why that white truck is parked across the fields by the trees? Or why my uncle still thinks that God has forsaken him? Or are you just going to tell me what you think I'm supposed to do about all of this?'

Leo remembered that the upper story of the hotel commanded a view of the southern plain unrivaled in Santo Fico and he asked, 'Have you told anyone about us being out there?'

'No.'

He breathed a sigh of relief. Then, since she asked, he told her everything.

When Leo left for his long walk back to the village, the plumber climbed back into the hole to complete the repair of the shattered pipe and work progressed nicely. Topo managed to make himself useful by fetching things from the truck as the plumber requested them: lengths of pipe, couplings, caulking, wrenches. Usually, by the third trip, he either hit upon the correct tool or one that the plumber could sort of make work. Plumbing equipment wasn't Topo's forte.

A half an hour passed before the jolly plumber called Topo over to the edge of the hole to once again express his worries about the other obstructions he found in the pipe. He seriously doubted whether the water would be able to flow through the old pipe all the way to the piazza.

'Maybe you boys should do this on another day, after these pipes have been tested,' he suggested.

Do it another day? Topo looked down the road. In the distance he could make out Leo climbing the hill toward the village. In a few minutes he would be there. There was no trying another day.

'No. It has to be today. Are you almost done?'

'Yeah. Maybe you can carry some of this stuff back to the truck?'

Nonno was looking for an excuse to get away from the wet dog, so he called out, 'I can do that.' And he began carrying tools and supplies back across the field to the plumber's shop on wheels.

The plumber shrugged. 'I'll finish this thing up, but you understand there's no guarantee about that fountain?'

Topo smiled and waved him onward with an air of jaunty confidence, but inside he was coming unstrung. It has to be okay, he thought as he carried a pipe cutter across the field. He sat down in the shade of the truck and tried to breathe slowly. In his mind he went over all the things Leo had said about why this plan would work. The first thing that came to mind was that they had a good plan – an excellent plan. This was going to be a miracle worth seeing. In fact, he wished he could be there to see it. This miracle would bring tears to the eyes of all who witnessed it. This miracle had definite possibilities. For instance, if tourists were willing to pay to hear religious stories, they might be willing to pay to hear this story. The town could still have the Miracle and the Mystery, only now it would be the Miracle of the Withered Fig and the Mysterious Waters of Santo Fico. And what if the miraculous waters were to someday heal some sick person? Then its fame would really spread. They could even bottle the water and sell it around the world, especially after a miracle like this . . . !

The voice of the plumber helped jolt him back to reality. 'Well, I think that's just about got it . . .'

Topo checked his watch as he walked back to the hole. They were ready and with twelve minutes to spare. The plumber was still hunched over his work, his hand resting gently on the pipe. He was frozen, concentrating intently on something. Topo wasn't sure what the plumber was waiting for, but he waited too. After a moment, the plumber shook his head dejectedly.

'Well, I told you, no guarantees. I don't feel anything.'

Topo was confused. 'What should you feel?'

'Water. I should feel the water rushing through the pipe.'

'But . . . But, you wouldn't feel that unless you turned on the valve, would you?'

The plumber stood up and began the challenging job of climbing out of the hole. 'Oh, I turned the valve on. It's on now. You can't test it without turning the valve on. But, like I said, there's no water going through the pipe. You got a clog.'

'The valve can't be on! It's not time! Not for . . .' Topo checked his watch, '. . . eleven minutes!'

The plumber was becoming as irritated with Topo as he was with the slippery sides of the hole.

'Look, it doesn't matter. The valve is on, but nothing's happening!'

Nonno, who was picking up a length of iron pipe to carry back to the truck, overheard the plumber's exasperated reply. The valve had been his job!

'No,' he shouted. 'I made the water go away and I bring it back! You promised, I turn the valve!'

Nonno swung around to Topo just as the plumber finally climbed out of the hole. The length of iron pipe chimed off his bald forehead like a Chinese gong and the jolly plumber went down like gravity's best friend.

Sitting at her kitchen table, Marta listened quietly as Leo told her the story: from when Nonno came to stay with him, to his tale of the war and the Germans, to the search across the plains, to the discovery of the watch and the pipe, to the arrival of the plumber, and finally all the way to his plan for her getting Father Elio sitting by the fountain and praying for water at precisely 11:45, in fourteen minutes – he told her everything. She looked at him for a long time. He could tell something was bothering her.

At last she asked incredulously, 'You're letting Nonno stay with you?'

'Yes.'

'And that dog?'

'Yes.'

Leo fought to maintain his composure. He wanted to throw his arms in the air, stomp up and down, and yell at her to stick to the subject – time was definitely a factor here. But he sat patiently and concentrated on breathing instead of screaming, and to his amazement, Marta smiled.

'Water . . . I like it.'

She liked it. She thought it was a good plan; well prepared, reasonable expectations, it even had the scriptural and historical validation of some prior miracles concerning water. She liked it. She would get Father Elio by the fountain, but with less than ten minutes to go they had better hurry.

Marta never made it to the church. When she and Leo came out of the hotel they found the piazza filling up with people. There were already over a dozen villagers gathered around the fountain, with more on the way, as word of the phenomenon spread. At the center of the crowd was Father Elio. And as Leo and Marta hurried across the piazza toward the priest, they heard a sound – something deep and guttural. It sounded like the wail of a melancholy tuba, with an oboe caught in its throat. The distinctly rude noise echoed around the piazza and all of the onlookers 'Ooohed' and 'Aahhed' and pointed at the dusty fountain. Marta gripped her bewildered uncle's arm fearfully.

'What is it? What's happening?'

'This is . . . strange. I don't know. Noises . . .' Father Elio could only shake his head. The explanation came from Maria Gamboni, who was hiding behind the old priest.

'It's a sign for me. I was coming across the piazza, I was on my way to the church. This isn't my day for confession, but I felt the need. So I was walking across the piazza to the church and all of a sudden the fountain called my name. It called to me! Twice! So I ran into the church and got Father Elio. Now, it only cries out in pain. But first it called my name. "Maria Gamboni! Maria Gamboni!" Twice! It called my name. Twice!'

From deep inside the fountain came another low, rumbling burp – rather like an entire brass section had gas. Marta heard Leo whisper to himself, 'I never should have left Topo alone.'

Obviously something had gone wrong, but maybe all was not lost. Someone just needed to seize the moment, so Marta shouted with great conviction, 'Uncle Elio, you must pray for the fountain!'

Leo was inspired by Marta's boldness and he quickly added his voice, 'Yes, Father Elio, please! You must pray for the fountain!' The ancient marble belched again. 'And quickly,' Leo added.

Both were astounded at how the cry was picked up by their frightened neighbors. In a matter of moments the piazza was filled with pleas for prayers from the venerable priest. He would drive away these evil spirits! He would make their fountain be quiet again!

Father Elio raised both his hands and held them sternly up to the offending fountain – much like Moses preparing to command the Red Sea. The crowd hushed and Father Elio's brows furrowed as he prepared a harsh prayer of reproach. He opened his mouth to speak, but from off in the distance came the insistent blare of a horn. With every second it got louder, until at last, the plumber's little white truck tore up the hill and skidded into the piazza, spilling plumbing supplies in every direction. In the back, Nonno and the gray dog peered over the cab like twin ambulance lights. The truck screeched to a stop between the fountain and the hotel and the engine died, just as . . .

The fountain belched again.

Leo, Marta, Father Elio, and everyone else in the piazza, or anywhere near the piazza, gathered around the truck. In the back Nonno sat beside the prone body of the plumber. He looked like he might be sleeping peacefully, except for the huge purple welt in the center of his forehead.

Topo stuttered in Leo's direction, 'I think we may need a doctor.'

'My God! What did you do to him?' asked Leo.

Topo shot Nonno a withering glare. Nonno looked to be on the verge of tears.

'He . . . bumped his head,' Topo offered weakly.

Nonno nodded gratefully. 'Really hard.'

The fountain belched twice, but no one noticed the appearance of tiny bits of mud that splattered the piazza cobblestones.

Father Elio stepped to the back of the truck and quickly took charge. In a matter of moments ice appeared from the hotel, then bandages, and then a glass of wine. In a short time the old priest had the plumber's wound swathed in cool towels, and to the relief of all, especially Nonno and Topo, the round fellow began to stir. Within a minute or two he was trying to get up, which was no mean feat under the best of conditions. Sitting up in the back of the truck, the poor plumber was dazed, but he was going to live. And after a moment of initial bewilderment, he fixed on Father Elio, who was sitting next to him, and gave the old priest a long, strange look – and Father Elio gave it right back to him. Finally the plumber broke the awkward silence.

'Hey . . . Father Elio. You look like hell. When'd you get so old?'

'Rico . . . ? Rico Gamboni?'

'Sure, who do you think?'

Everybody standing around the truck gasped and stepped back as if they'd met a ghost, for everyone knew the legend of the mysterious disappearance of Enrico Gamboni. If this dazed mound of humanity was actually Enrico Gamboni, then he was back from the dead. The plumber, though, was even more confused than the crowd. He looked around at the terrified faces, who watched him as if he were Lazarus stepping out of the tomb.

'Wait a second! This is Santo Fico, but . . . who are these people? What am I doing here?'

'Rico, do you know where you've been?' Father Elio asked as if he were questioning a dim child.

'Sure. I been . . . I been . . . I been . . . Where the hell have I been?'

'What do you remember?'

'I remember . . . I remember . . .' It was as if the fat plumber was reaching through a fog to put together some shadowy puzzle in his mind.

'I remember, I needed a new oil pump for the boat. I was gonna go to Grosseto, but as I was walking down to the bus, I had a hunch I should go to Follonica. So I did. But I couldn't find the pump in Follonica, so I took the bus to Piombino. Now, in Piombino, I went down to the harbor . . . and I was walking . . . someplace . . . and something fell on my head . . .' His voice trailed off as his huge sausage fingers gently touched a jagged scar along the top of his bald head. '. . . Something big.'

At that moment the fountain released an enormous rude belch and huge globs of foul-smelling mud spewed from the jug of the fat cherub who was balanced on the top dish. And then again. And again, even louder. And suddenly the top of the fountain became like an exploding volcano, showering globs of reeking mud and silt down on the crowd. The villagers screamed as the black ooze rained on them, and still with each unmannerly flatulence from the fountain, more mud and gunk shot into the air.

When he saw all this, Enrico Gamboni grabbed Topo by the shirt and pointed triumphantly at the geyser of mud showering the piazza and shouted, 'I told you, you got a clog!'

After a few more moments of violent burping the erupting fountain quieted and slowly the mud thinned to an oozing goo and then thinned again to a watery brown soup. Shortly all the eruptions stopped and only cool, clear water gushed merrily from the happy cherub's jug at the top of the fountain, filling his dish, and spilling into the larger dish, and then splashing into the empty, waiting pool.

Enrico Gamboni looked around the back of the pickup truck as if he'd just discovered himself sitting on the surface of the moon.

'Hey! Wait a second . . . Am I a plumber?'

Father Elio reached around behind himself and, after some struggle, pried Maria Gamboni's fingers loose from his black jacket. Her terrified eyes were like two great unblinking moons and, for the first time that Elio could recall, she was speechless. She was also a bit wary about getting too close to whatever it was in the back of the truck — either ghost or demon. But the priest put his arm around her trembling shoulders and firmly pulled her forward.

'Here's someone who would like to say hello.'

Maria waved her bony fingers weakly in the phantom's direction. Her voice was barely a whisper.

'Hello, Rico . . . Remember me?'

The plumber's face lit up like a rising moon. He climbed out of the truck and took Maria's quivering hand. 'Well, at last somebody who looks just the same. Still as pretty as ever.' Maria Gamboni actually blushed.

That afternoon the piazza was busier than it had been in many years. There was much to do. First of all, everybody in Santo Fico felt the need to help clean the mud and the decades of dirt from their fountain. Then, every man, woman, child, and dog in town needed to spend some time sitting on the edge of the fountain, dangling their feet in the water, walking out to the cascading dishes, touching it, tasting it. Young people, like Carmen and Nina and the de Parma grandchildren, needed to dance in the pool, splash one another, and kick water at passersby. And Nonno, with the old gray dog, needed to hold court at the edge of the fountain and explain a hundred times how he found his watch and repaired the pipe – occasionally adding how he turned the valve. Enrico Gamboni needed to be patted on the back, thanked for fixing the fountain, and welcomed home. Mostly it needed to be confirmed that he was flesh and not spirit – as if at his size there could be any doubt. Father Elio had not seen this much happiness in Santo Fico for many years. In fact, there were only three people who didn't seem to share in the joy of the day.

Topo left first. He muttered something about having work to do in his Fix-It shop. Then Marta went back into the hotel; she had beef stock on the stove. Leo tried to speak to Marta, but she was so disappointed she couldn't even glare in his direction. He wanted to tell her it wasn't his fault; and he wanted to shout after her that even she thought it was a good plan, but the piazza was too crowded.

Next to him, Enrico Gamboni still sat on the tailgate of the little white truck next to his reclaimed bride. Leo heard them talking softly to each other.

'You smell funny,' observed Maria.

'I've been a plumber.'

'Oh. Maybe that's it.'

'Is it bad?'

Maria gave him a sniff and thought for a moment, 'At least it's not fish.'

Leo was on his way home when Father Elio, sitting on the steps of the church, motioned him over. Leo wanted to go home, but he joined the old priest for a moment.

'Thank you for what you did.'

'I didn't do anything,' said Leo.

'Nonno says you did. I wanted to thank you.'

Father Elio patted Leo's arm and Leo noticed that the thin hand was trembling. The old man smiled at him, but Leo only saw gaunt cheekbones and dark circles under tired eyes. Marta's plea to save her uncle before it was too late echoed in his mind and Leo wanted to go home.

'I didn't do anything,' he snapped and abruptly started off down the street. The last thing he needed right now was Father Elio thanking him for anything.

But Elio called after him, 'Look at the happiness you brought. Look at the fountain. Look at the people. Look at Maria Gamboni. Look at the happiness you made.'

Leo just stomped down the street trying to ignore the old priest's words. He was in no mood to hear about any good deed or the happiness of Santo Fico, and he certainly didn't want Father Elio attributing it to him.

'Happiness,' he grumbled to himself. 'Let's see how happy Maria Gamboni is when she finds out her husband's got another wife and five kids in Piombino.'

Sixteen

*T*he next few days were difficult. Marta went to the church at least three times every day and even though her Uncle Elio always greeted her with a smile, she saw that he was weak. When he walked, his step was slow and his feet shuffled across the stones. When they talked, he was easily distracted and always seemed to be thinking of other things. But what frightened her most was the way he frowned at the plates piled with wonderful food she spent hours cooking. She filled her days wracking her brain trying to recall his favorite meals, but all of her efforts only made him unhappy. And so the third night after the episode with the fountain, she stopped bringing food and brought instead a large bowl of steaming vegetable broth and a glass of wine. It only took a few minutes of convincing before the old man accepted the broth and wine as merely variations of water. He hadn't disavowed water. He finished the entire bowl, drank the wine, and went to bed. That night he slept better than he had since the earthquake. Marta switched to broths.

Nina also began visiting her great-uncle more often. She missed her turns at bringing him his lunch tray. She always volunteered, but for some reason, her mother wanted to do it. Nina could do it next time, but when it became clear that next time would never arrive, Nina started dropping by the church for no reason. She couldn't see how thin and drawn her great-uncle had become of course, but she knew he wasn't well. She heard it in his voice. She had often heard sadness in his voice when he talked of God and she'd even asked him about it once, a long time ago. He had explained to her that he was never sad about God, but sometimes he became sad about himself because he had let God down so much. Nina had tried to argue this with him a number of times, but he always changed the subject. What the girl heard now wasn't just sadness, it was something else and it took a few days before she put a name to what she heard – despair. Her great-uncle Father Elio was giving up on something, but she didn't know what. She wanted to comfort him, but she didn't know how, so she prayed for the right words to say. Nina didn't begrudge her blindness – what would be the point? But now she longed to sit with her uncle Elio in the evening and read to him from a great book filled with some wisdom that would answer all the questions of his troubled heart and give him peace. But she had to content herself with just being with him and loving him.

Down the road at the shepherd's cottage by the sea, things weren't going much better for Leo. He avoided going into town because he didn't have any ideas for a new miracle and he couldn't face Marta. He also couldn't stop thinking about Father Elio. He hadn't understood why Marta was so desperate about the old man until he sat next to him on the steps of the church. Now, when he tried to sleep at night, Father Elio's hollow eyes faded in and out of the frozen face of Saint Francis and now both holy men stared out at him, accusingly, from the darkness of haunted dreams. He couldn't make them go away.

He was also having trouble living with Nonno. It wasn't Nonno's fault. In fact, since the water returned to the fountain, Nonno had been much better. He still spent his days sitting by the fountain, but now when people happened by they seemed much more willing to stop and sit and chat with the old man. And it seemed like almost everyone in Santo Fico happened by the resurrected fountain at least once a day. Groups of children were there almost all the time. True, there weren't that many children in Santo Fico, but those who were now seemed to live at the fountain, and Nonno had become their hero. Nonno loved the attention. And he loved the children.

Leo's problem was that the shepherd's hut was proving too small. It contained one pungent dog too many for Leo and he found himself spending more and more nights out-side. He would have said something to Nonno, but he'd never seen anyone come to love a hovel as quickly as Nonno and that dog took to that stone hut. It was as if the ancient builder, whoever he was, had that pair in mind. Leo decided that when he returned to America, he would leave the shep-herd's hut for Nonno and the dog. But for now, he found himself spending his days, and often his nights, wandering the land where he grew up – and had worked so hard to ignore since his return.

It started the morning after the fiasco at the fountain. Leo woke early and found himself in a terrible humor. He had spent a troubled night. How could such a wonderful plan go so terribly wrong? He had thought a walk before breakfast might calm him, and for no particular reason, his legs took him away from the cliffs and the sea and he followed the trails that led toward town – even though he knew that Santo Fico wasn't his destination. He stalked down one dusty trail after another, kicking at the clumps of tall grass, his mind lost in a labyrinth of frustrations. At one point he unexpect-edly came upon the herd of Lombolo horses that grazed his property. Both were startled, but Leo simply pulled off his hat, waved it in the air, and shouted angrily at them. The huge beasts flared their nostrils, bulged their eyes, pounded the soft earth with their sharp hooves, and ran away.

That was when he discovered he was across the path from the olive grove and he wandered into the grove for no particular reason. The gnarled old trees were familiar, but they had changed greatly. They were bigger, fuller, and sadder. He had never seen them so untended. He knew how they liked to look — trimmed and pruned, lean and tight. These trees sprouted long sucker branches that randomly shot toward the sky or hung almost to the ground. Leo picked one of the olives. It was small and hard. He knew that it wouldn't grow any larger. It would never fill with oil and juice, and become so full and ripe that it almost burst. These trees were thirsty. He imagined their old roots digging deeper and deeper into the sandy soil searching for water. But what water could be found was stolen by the sucker branches.

As he walked through the olive grove, Leo came upon an old pair of pruning shears sitting quite forgotten in a fork of one of the trees. They showed the rust of years. Leo imagined his father standing under that tree, using the shears. He imagined his aunt Sofia's strong, musical voice calling his father out of the field for dinner. Aunt Sofia — she had stayed with her dead sister's husband, and cared for him near the end. Leo imagined his father setting the shears down in the crook of the tree and walking slowly back to the house through a warm, crimson evening. His father would have had every intention of returning the next day to the shears because he was not a man who didn't take care of his tools. But no one returned and here the shears sat.

Leo studied the tree and he tried to imagine which branch his father might have been pruning. He picked one. He reached up and snipped it off. He liked the clean, sharp sound it made as the blade snapped through the branch. He liked the familiar pressure of the shears in his hand, and he liked the way the useless branch fell to the ground; so he snipped another. And so he began.

Leo used up the rest of his day in the olive grove, moving from tree to tree, doing again what he had done during the first half of his life, and what he had tried to deny during the second. That night he dreamed less.

The next day he awoke early again. This time he had no rage to work off, no frustration was vexing him – he just felt like going for a walk after breakfast. His stroll took him to the vineyard, and by some odd chance, he'd brought along his father's shears. But he discovered that the greatest need of the vineyard wasn't pruning. The thick twists of spiraled stems were healthy enough, but few tendrils trailed off and what branches had grown were thin and almost leafless. There would be no grapes this year. Vines are hearty plants that like the heat and grow well even in a dry, flinty ground, but this summer's drought was too much for even these tenacious old plants. The vines were dying of thirst.

But what broke Leo's heart were the rosebushes. At the head of every row of grapes was a single rosebush and they too were dying. They had been planted long before Leo was born and probably before his father's time as well. As a boy, he was told, 'The rose is like the grape, except the rose, it's more fragile, more sensitive to some of the ailments that also harm the grape. Whatever the vine might catch, the rose catches it first.' Leo learned that by watching the roses, the vine-tender had some warning of danger and precautions could be taken to protect the vines. He remembered how his mother loved her rosebushes. Just like the workers in the fields tending to the vines, his mother would be on her knees before the roses – turning the soil, feeding them, pruning their tiny branches.

'Snip above the five-leaf cluster if you want a flower,' she would say and his father would laugh.

'You love those roses more than the vines,' he would call to her from across the field.

And she would call back, 'When you have so many to tend to the vine, someone must be willing to love the rose.'

And when the vines were rich with leaves and the thick, full bunches of grapes dragged down near the ground, at the head of each row stood a guardian rosebush bursting with flowers – each bush a different color, and each color more vibrant than the last. And he remembered that his father would come out just after sunrise and cut armfuls of cool roses and take them back home to his mother.

'These fields are haunted,' Leo thought aloud and he knew that he had denied his ghosts as long as he could.

Leo pushed his way through the tall weeds at the top of the hill that was the highest point on the farm and went directly to an ancient pipe that seemed to sprout directly out of the ground. At the center of the old pipe was a rusted worm screw and the other end opened over a wooden trough that pointed down the hill and became lost in the overgrowth of weeds. With a bit of searching Leo found a short length of iron bar that was designed to be levered into the top of the worm screw, and then spent the next half hour tugging and pushing until, at last, the screw turned. Clear water shot through the cobwebs at the end of the pipe and washed down the dusty trough toward the bottom of the hill.

Leo used up the rest of the day with a shovel in his hand, racing along ancient ditches, trying to outrun the water that rushed down the hill to the olive orchard. Once he was there, he opened this gate or he shut that gate, skillfully diverting water from one row to another, until all the rows of olive trees were islands in a series of long, thin shimmering lakes. Then the race began again as the water tumbled through a new series of ditches, across the fields, and toward the vineyard.

At last, Leo sat on the bank of the irrigation ditch and watched the water roll by, just as he had when he was a boy. He watched the water disappear into the thirsty ground around the vines and the rosebushes. He watched the swifts dart overhead and chase the tiny insects that hovered above the water. In the afternoon, the Lombolo horses came by for a drink, but when they saw Leo sitting on the bank they kept their distance. When, after a safe minute, he didn't wave a hat or shout at them angrily, they came to the ditch and drank. Leo watched them drink. And he watched the swifts darting and diving through the air.

That evening Leo walked along the cliffs above the sea as he made his way back to the shepherd's hut. He knew he was making mistakes. He was pruning the olive trees in the wrong season. His watering was washing away too much topsoil around the vines. But he didn't care. He would do better tomorrow.

The smoke coming from the Pizzola place could be seen all

the way from the top of the north coast road. Topo was on his way to see Leo because he just couldn't stand the pressure and this whole miracle business was making his life far too complicated. Every time he even crossed the piazza, he could see Marta watching him from a hotel window and he could swear he saw prison bars reflected in her eyes. This whole thing was Leo's fault, but if Leo couldn't fix things, then it was up to Topo. He had an idea. They had tried Leo's miracles. Now maybe it was time to try one of his. Leo Pizzola wasn't the only one who could come up with miracles.

Topo forgot all of these concerns when he saw the great billows of black smoke rising from where he thought the Pizzola house to be. He hadn't planned on running, but he did. By the time he arrived at the sad old house he had slowed. The house wasn't burning, at least for the moment. The smoke came from farther down the trail, from the olive grove.

To his astonishment Topo found Leo hauling great cartloads of dried weeds and dead branches out from under the trees and across the path, well away from the grove. He stacked them in a pile near the edge of a large circle that he had cleared in the dry grass. Nonno stood on the bare dirt inside the circle, patiently and carefully feeding a roaring fire. He took debris from Leo's pile and, when he judged the time right, tossed it onto the blaze. The gray dog sat near a waiting garden hose that had been laid out just in case. As Topo walked by him, the dog gave him a reassuring blink – should the need arise, he was ready with the hose.

'Are you crazy? This is the wrong season to burn,' shouted

Topo above the roar of the flames. 'You burn in the fall. You could burn this whole place down.'

'We're being careful,' said Leo and he walked back to the olive grove. He didn't need to be reminded he was out of season.

Topo followed at his heels and he noticed that many of the trees seemed to be standing up straighter. They looked like olive trees again and many of the rows were raked clean. Topo liked what he saw; this was closer to the way it should be, but he was confused.

'Why are you doing this? I thought you wanted to sell this place.'

'I do,' Leo lied. 'Do you see a lot of buyers banging on the door? Nobody's going to buy it looking like this.'

That made sense to Topo and Leo was content that his friend had other things on his mind and didn't press the matter.

'I need to talk to you.'

Leo checked out Nonno's supply of fuel. He could take a break for a few minutes, so they found a shady spot beneath a tree. Topo glanced around to make sure that neither Nonno nor the dog could overhear.

'How's the fresco?'

'Fine.'

'Don't you think maybe you should move it? I mean, just while Nonno's staying there?'

'No. It's fine where it is,' Leo lied again. The truth was, his heart stopped every time Nonno came in the door. It was as if the fresco howled at him from beneath the cot. In fact, every time Nonno moved around the room, Leo was sure he was going to suddenly point at the bundle beneath the bed and exclaim, 'Hey! What's that? It looks like something you stole from a church!' The fact of the matter was, Leo was working hard to not think about frescoes, or fortunes, or miracles.

'I've got a plan,' Topo said, grinning slyly.

Well . . . It wouldn't hurt to listen.

The plan that Topo presented, Leo thought, was exactly the kind of plan Topo would devise. It was theatrical and flamboyant – filled with drama and spectacle. It had plot, a script, a cast, and special effects – and it was really pretty good. Topo's idea was deceptively straightforward. If the problem was that Father Elio felt God had rejected him because of some big, mysterious sin, then instead of trying to come up with things that would prove that God loved him, why not just have someone tell him that God still loved him? The miracle was not in the message, but in the messenger. It should be an angel, come down from heaven.

As Topo dramatically described the scene, Leo felt goose bumps roll down his arms. By the time the excited little fellow reached the story's denouement, he was having difficulty speaking because of the catch in his voice and even Leo found himself choking back a tear. When Topo was finished and they sat silently beneath the olive tree, Leo was convinced of two things: first, this was a good plan, perhaps the best – and second, if Guido Pasolini had grown up in Hollywood, he might have ruled the world.

For the plan to work, a number of things had to happen

and quickly. Topo talked about costumes and makeup, about special lighting, and a script – he would take care of all of these things. The one thing he couldn't do for the production (and he actually called it 'the production') was cast the role of the Angel. For that he needed Leo. The Angel was critical. She had to be angelic – which was to say, beautiful. She had to be someone that Father Elio wouldn't recognize – which was to say, someone who didn't attend church much. And, she had to be an actress. They both knew there was only one person in Santo Fico who could possibly fit this bill.

Seventeen

The small bell above the door that rang as he entered reminded Leo that he had been in Angelica Giancarlo's beauty shop before. Many years ago he had once delivered a message to his aunt Sofia, who used to have her hair straightened there when the small shop was still run by Angelica's mother. The delivery was hasty. There would have been no need for him to hang around, since Angelica had deserted Santo Fico a couple of years earlier. But now, so many years later, he still recognized the equipment: those turquoise and pink vinyl chairs with the chrome arms, the strange sink with hoses and a depression in the front, and those stands with helmets that looked like something out of an old science fiction movie. A caustic chemical odor still hung in the air and stung his nostrils and made his head light and his stomach heavy. It smelled like something that was probably harmful if you inhaled it long enough.

But his strongest memory of this place happened many years ago, outside, on the street. It was a thing that Leo would remember forever and yet he also knew that he would never mention it to anyone – even Angelica. He wouldn't know what to say.

It was November. A cold north rain had been battering the village for a week and for some forgotten reason Leo was late for school. Racing down the narrow, rain-slick streets he turned a corner and was met by an extraordinary sight. On the far side of the street a strange car was parked in front of the Giancarlo house. Any unknown car in Santo Fico was an event to be investigated, so naturally Leo slowed his pace. The small brown Fiat took up most of the street and even from where he stood, Leo could see that the back seat was loaded with luggage. A stranger wearing a dark suit and sporting a thin waxed mustache waited uncomfortably behind the wheel. Leo had no idea who he was, but he knew instantly that he hated him as much as he had ever hated anyone.

At the door of the house Angelica and her mother stood motionless in the biting wind and stinging rain, locked in an embrace that neither of them was willing to release. They wept bitterly. At last Angelica broke away, turned to an upstairs window, and stared at the streaked glass. Leo found it odd that she would stare at a black, empty window, but as he moved down the street, he became aware of a faint figure framed there. It was Angelica's father and the look on his face stopped Leo in his tracks. It was a face carved in stone; a face that only knew regret and it existed only to carry a pair of bottomless, anguished eyes. Leo had never seen such pain, and like a nightmare apparition, it made him think of death. He prayed he would never have anguished eyes look at him the way those eyes cried out to Angelica. But of course he did when he broke his own father's heart.

At last the statue face turned away from the window and then Angelica turned away too. She was climbing in the passenger door of the Fiat when she suddenly looked across the street – and there was Leo. He hadn't realized that he was so openly, shamelessly, staring at her, but he didn't care. All that mattered was Angelica was leaving and she was obviously unhappy. Both of these things filled the thirteen-year-old with longing and confusion, because at his age there was no difference between childish lust and love. He wasn't sure she even knew his name, but still he wanted to run to her and take her in his thin child's arms and protect her. And in the instant that their eyes met Leo pledged silent volumes concerning passion, acceptance, and forgiveness. Then she smiled at him. It was an adult smile of acknowledgment and gratitude for what his child's heart had declared. A moment later, the car door slammed shut, the brown Fiat sputtered to life, and

Angelica disappeared down the narrow street in a haze of exhaust.

This was all that Leo was to know of Angelica Giancarlo's puzzling departure. He often wondered if she remembered that day and him being there. And now he wondered what she might say to discover him standing in her beauty shop. He needn't have worried.

A moment later, when she swung through the sunflower print curtain that separated her small shop from the rest of the house and discovered Leo Pizzola smiling at her, Angelica's jaw dropped and she briefly lost all power of speech. Her mind raced – What on earth was he doing here? This was a grievous breach in the etiquette of their unspoken arrangement and for an instant she wanted to run from the room, but decided instead that she must face it out. She also decided that if he said anything, even the slightest hint of their secret and unacknowledged rendezvous at the swimming beach, she would slap his face and order him out of her shop. And she would never swim there again.

To her great relief, Leo was polite and respectful. He even called her 'Signorina Giancarlo' until she demurely gave him permission to address her as Angelica. He held his hat in his hand and stood respectfully, until she graciously invited him to sit. His eyes looked only at her eyes or at the floor and she never caught him glancing hungrily at other parts of her body, like most men did. He was more than polite; he was charming.

She did have a moment of serious misgivings when,

completely out of the blue, he respectfully asked, 'Do you attend mass regularly?'

Could she possibly have misread Leo Pizzola that drastically? Was he here to convince her to repent? Maybe he wanted her to go to church with him. So she cautiously admitted to him that, no, she didn't attend church on a regular basis . . . And yes, it had been some years since she had been to confession . . . And no, she would not say that she was close to Father Elio, although, of course, she had known him all her life and respected him greatly. In fact, she hadn't had an occasion to see Father Elio since she returned to Santo Fico some seven years ago.

'Our paths just don't seem to cross,' she said with an uncomfortable giggle.

Two people in Santo Fico not crossing paths in seven years is quite a feat, thought Leo, and he wondered if he could learn her secret.

When Leo explained to her about poor Father Elio's crisis of faith, it was obvious that her heart was touched. When Leo explained, in strictest confidence, the plan he and Guido Pasolini had in mind ('Who?' . . . 'Topo?' . . . 'Oh, Topo!'), she was inspired. And when Leo mentioned to her that they needed a beautiful actress to play the part of the Angel, she actually wept. He sat next to her on the tiny chrome and vinyl sofa for what seemed like a long time until Angelica was finally able to tell him that she would 'be honored to take on the role of the Angel to save dear Father Elio's faith.' And she meant it.

Leo assured her that Guido . . . er, Topo was taking care

of all of 'the production' details and he would get a script to her that afternoon. She and Topo could discuss costumes and makeup then. Leo could only imagine how much they would both enjoy that. He told her that the 'performance' would be that night in the grove behind the church, and then, after an odd exchange of bows, Leo departed.

If anyone in Santo Fico had a crisis with a toaster, radio, power drill, or any other appliance or contrivance that particular afternoon, they would have discovered the Pasolini Fix-It Shop closed for the day. Topo was a man finally following his true calling, but what worried Leo was his friend's sense of spectacle. What they needed was a poignant, uncomplicated little miracle. A Divine Being quietly appears in the forest and restores the simple faith of a defeated old priest. Leo feared Topo's approach fell somewhere between *Quo Vadis!* and *Ben Hur*. He also found a few things downright confusing.

'Why do you need all the extension cord?'

'To plug in the movie projector.'

'Why do you need a movie projector?'

'To run the movie.'

'Why are you going to run a movie?'

'To create the *unearthly light*, the *angelic glow*.'

'Won't it just look like a movie?'

'No. We use something black and white. Then we run the projector at a slow speed and blur the focus so everything's all fuzzy. Then, I slowly wiggle my fingers in front of the lens and that distorts everything more. Remember, we're projecting on tree branches and bushes. Nobody'll recognize anything. I still haven't picked what film to use. Something black and white. No subtitles, of course.'

'Oh, of course.'

'This needs a classic. *La Strada*! What do you think?'

Leo thought he liked the idea better when Topo was describing it under the olive tree. He weighed his words carefully. This was, after all, Topo's miracle and he didn't want to get in his way. Just because Leo didn't understand, that didn't mean it wouldn't work.

'Doesn't the movie projector make a lot of noise?'

Topo spun completely around and clapped his hands in the air. 'Blankets!'

'Blankets?'

'We wrap the projector in blankets. It's done all the time. All this stuff is done all the time.'

Leo shrugged and nodded as if he understood.

'Have you written anything for Angelica? She's expecting you any time now and she's nervous.'

It seemed to Leo that every time he mentioned Angelica Giancarlo's name, Topo became noticeably tense. And earlier, when he'd questioned Leo – in great detail – about his interview with her at the beauty shop, Topo had suddenly developed an uncharacteristic stutter. But now he just reached in his pocket, handed Leo a crumpled sheet of paper, and went back to digging through his film canisters. Leo read what was written and immediately felt better about the whole thing.

'Topo, this is . . . This is . . . good. This is kind of beautiful.'

Topo grunted and tore through more canisters looking for his Fellini section. 'Yeah. I'll take it over to Anga-Anga-Anga-elica's in a little bit . . . *La Strada* . . . That'll do the trick. You need to talk to Marta . . . Where's my Fellini!'

Going to the hotel wasn't nearly as foreboding as it had once been. Leo still wasn't sure what kind of reception he might receive, but Marta rarely greeted him with shocked outrage and shouting anymore. As he walked up the hill from the Fix-It shop, he tried to understand why she had become so thoroughly sour. Why she felt the way she did about him was, of course, all too clear, but it was more than that. Since he'd been around her, he'd seen that it went well beyond just disdain for him personally. She was bitter about life, and that troubled him.

As he passed a *vicolo*, the narrow passageway between two buildings, something caught the corner of his eye that made him stop and step back. At the other end of the tight alley Carmen was leaning against a wall while that strange greasy kid who brought the mail over from Grosseto leaned in on her. It wasn't a big mystery why she was hiding in the *vicolo*. Not only was she smoking, but also she was letting that boy put his hands on her. It was all done as adolescent trifling with lots of joking and pushing, but still, she was letting him touch her. In the brief moment that Leo observed them he could see that Carmen felt she was in control, but when she saw Leo watching her, her first reaction was fear. That passed quickly though and then she boldly returned Leo's gaze and puffed the cigarette. Her look was defiant, daring him to do or say something. Leo wasn't close enough to see that Carmen had

been crying. Solly Puce looked over too, and when he saw
Leo coldly staring at him he stepped away from Carmen,
hitched up his pants, went through an odd gyration that Leo
didn't understand, and shouted something unintelligible.

For all of the hard feelings and disappointments Leo felt
about Franco Fortino, still they had once been best friends
and this was Franco's older child. Leo knew in his heart that
he should walk down the alley and beat the crap out of that
creepy kid, just because that's what Franco would have
wanted him to do. But before he could move, Carmen tossed
her cigarette down, grabbed Solly by the shirt, and pulled
him around the corner. He could hear their laughter.

At the hotel Leo stood in the kitchen door and waited.
Marta wasn't there. He knocked and called her name and
was about to leave when Marta appeared at the top of the
stairs. She had the distracted manner of someone lost in
looking for something important.

'Oh, it's you. What? What do you want?'

'May I come in?'

'Sure. Yeah. What do you want?' She was agitated about
something and this time it wasn't him.

'I need you to bring Father Elio to the hotel tonight and
keep him here, away from the church, until about ten
o'clock.'

'Ten o'clock? That's late for him. I don't know . . . Why?
What are you doing?'

'Nothing. Don't worry. But tonight, sit at the table so you
can see the window. When we're ready, I'll come to the
window and wave at you. Then you let him go home.'

'How am I going to keep him here until ten o'clock?'

The question was rhetorical. There was something else on Marta's mind and as she walked him through the kitchen to the back door Leo hoped that she'd heard all he had said.

'Tell him there's something important you need to talk to him about.'

'Yeah. Okay. Talk about something important. Hey! Have you seen Carmen?'

Leo was halfway across the yard, but her frightened voice betrayed what was plaguing her mind. He thought of the beautiful Carmen with Solly Puce leaning up against her, rubbing his hand down her side and laughing wickedly in her ear and now he really wished he had beaten the boy when he had the chance.

'No . . . Well, I think maybe I saw her down the hill a few minutes ago.'

'Was she alone?'

'I don't know . . . I don't think so.'

Walking from the yard, Leo heard an old Vespa sputter to life down the hill. Everyone in the village knew the sound of that motor scooter.

Marta ran to the back fence and called down the empty alley, 'Carmen Fortino! You come back here! Carmen!'

The sound of the Vespa faded into the distance and Marta wanted to howl at the sky. Why had she fought with Carmen again? And about nothing! It was so stupid. If Carmen would come back right now she would tell her she was sorry. She would hold her in her arms like when she was little, or yell at her and shake her and then hug her – maybe all at the same time. As usual, the events of her life swirled madly around her, ignoring all of her attempts to order them, and she felt helpless.

Yes, she would talk to Father Elio tonight and it would be about something important.

Eighteen

*F*or the first time in many weeks, when the sun went down, a cool breeze rolled in off the sea and bumped into the mountains behind Santo Fico. It wasn't by any means cold, or even chilly – just cool. And it didn't affect much of anything except to give certain low gullies in the coastal hills a slight misty ground fog. Topo discovered this phenomenon as he was busy hiding his extension cords in the trees behind the church and he wanted to leap and shout for joy. Mist! Of course! What a marvelous special effect! For Topo, the appearance of mist was the next best thing to a heavenly endorsement of his miracle.

Marta had come by the church at about nine and asked her uncle Elio if she could talk to him about something that was troubling her, but she wanted him to come back to the hotel with her because she was waiting for Carmen to come home. Everything she said was true and Elio could see her distress, so he went along with her.

From the shadows at the corner of the south road, three lurking figures watched Marta and her uncle cross the piazza and disappear into the hotel. Then the lurkers, loaded with armfuls of equipment, dashed toward the back of the church. Topo carried his roll of extension cord directly to the church's kitchen door. He knew precisely where to plug it in because Father Elio always let him use the outlet just inside the door whenever he wanted to show his movies for the village. This time however, instead of running the cord back around to the piazza, Topo took it behind the church and disappeared into the trees.

Earlier in the afternoon, Topo and Leo had surveyed this grove of cedar, pine, and oak trees, looking for the perfect spot for an angelic encounter. Topo chose a small rise framed by three pine trees – it had a sort of cinemati- cally biblical quality. He also liked it because a massive clump of bushes at the foot of the rise made the mound inaccessible from the trail that Father Elio would have to follow. Topo didn't like the idea of Father Elio getting caught up in the moment and wanting to touch or talk to the Angel. This miracle wouldn't stand that kind of scrutiny. The bushes and the rise would be a perfect barrier and they were also good for what Topo had in mind for the 'special effects.' So it was to that place that Leo lugged the movie projector.

Angelica seemed to be having an awful time seeing in the dim light and she was terribly worried about her costume, and her make-up, and her hair, and remembering her lines. And since Topo was busy with other things, she requested Leo's assistance to help her negotiate a path through the bushes and up to the mount of the three pines. Leo had already come to the conclusion that their Angel was in serious need of glasses and just wouldn't admit it.

At the base of the rise, Topo was suffering through an old artistic quandary – how best to light a celestial vision. He'd just sort of taken it for granted that he would side light because that was traditional. But that was before there was this fantastic ground fog. Maybe back lighting? There was a lot of back lighting in modern movies and it would be a wonderful effect with the ground fog. After all, he wanted this to be a miracle! This had to be an angelic ascendancy! Topo had just decided on the ethereal power of back lighting when he glanced up the rise just as Angelica removed her dark cloak. The long, creamy nightgown they had chosen shimmered in the fading light and he recalled their afternoon together.

Topo had used alleys and back streets to get to Angelica's shop and even checked for prying eyes before he ducked inside. His secrecy had nothing to do with their project. In his mind there was something so overwhelmingly thrilling about Angelica Giancarlo that even visiting her house made him feel naughty and he feared for his reputation.

As he stood in Angelica's tiny shop, he suddenly realized that he had hardly ever spoken to this woman. Oh, as a child he'd followed her down the street laughing and imitating her voluptuous walk. He'd whistled at her from the top of the bell tower and then ducked down and giggled. He'd called suggestive things to her from a safe distance, and then run away. He'd sat in a dark movie theater and worshipped some veiled harem girl with incredible breasts. And as an adult he'd certainly fantasized that . . . Well . . . He'd certainly fantasized. But this didn't make them friends. Why did he think he knew her? He didn't know Angelica Giancarlo at all! But he was certain that she would know him! She would remember him! She wouldn't know his name, of course, but she would remember his childish taunts and his catcalls and the whistles and the gestures. Oh, my God, the gestures!

His stomach churned as he nervously stared at the faded sunflowers on the thin cotton curtain, watching for some fluttering that would signal her approach. What had ever possessed him to come here? She surely heard the bell above the door when he entered. In a moment Angelica Giancarlo was going to walk through that curtain, slap his face, and throw him into the street. And he would deserve it.

Topo was speculating as to whether he could quietly get back out the door and down the street before she saw him, when Angelica swung through the yellow curtain and suddenly they were standing face-to-face. Topo melted into her brown eyes and warm smile. He hadn't often been this close to her, not when he could actually look at her, and she was so much more beautiful than he'd imagined. Before she had a chance to notice that the poor man was a catatonic mute, Angelica was across the room and holding his hand.

'Hello, Guido,' she purred sweetly . . . Guiii-doow . . .' It's so good to see you. I think what you and Leo are doing for dear Father Elio is absolutely wonderful and I'm so honored that you thought of me. Did you know I used to be in the movies? Oh, of course you did . . . But that was so long ago . . .'

Topo needn't have worried about carrying his end of the conversation. And he didn't care anymore – she called him Guido. Of course, she said a great deal more and with great enthusiasm, but Topo didn't hear. She was so beautiful. And, although still taller than him, she wasn't as tall as he'd remembered. And she was plumper – not fat, just attractively plump. Quite attractive. And she was so kind and so sincere. And he loved the way she called him Guido.

She finally asked about a script and Topo pulled the crumpled paper from his pocket. Angelica sat on a small sofa, held the paper just in front of her nose, and slowly read. When she was done, she set the paper in her lap and began to sniff. She said the word, '*Beautiful*,' and then she sobbed. Topo quietly watched her weep, all the time wondering – where did she get that tissue?

When she finally recovered, she asked him about costumes and make-up and it became obvious to Topo that she valued his opinion. She spoke to him as if it were his decision as to what she should wear and how she should look. She had ideas about her hair, of course. It should swoop upward toward heaven, yet ring her head like a halo. She would take care of it – after all, hair was her business. As for costume, she had a half-dozen things that might do, but just couldn't decide. She said, 'After all, you're the director.' Then she took him by the hand and led him through the sunflower curtain.

After a short trip up some stairs, Topo found himself in the bedroom of Angelica Giancarlo. Spread across her bed were a variety of 'costumes.' She spoke quickly and with great enthusiasm, explaining that most of her choices were nightgowns and went through a rapid-fire list of their individual advantages and disadvantages. When Topo asked if she, '. . . might have something that was like . . . white and flowing,' she misinterpreted his question as disappointment. With apologies for her limited wardrobe she pulled him into her tiny closet where they stood with their bodies jammed together, while she nonchalantly showed him her racks of clothing. The musty smells of her closet, the exotic mixtures of perfumes and powders, and the closeness of Angelica's body made Topo both anxious and dizzy. He was almost relieved when they found nothing better in the tiny closet and finally returned to the bedroom and her original six choices.

Topo eliminated three right off, because the colors were wrong and Angelica was delighted at his decisiveness and discerning eye. But making the final decision was tough. So Angelica offered to show him how they looked.

Topo sat on a chair by the far wall while she went behind a changing screen in the corner and then, one by one, Angelica Giancarlo modeled each of the three nightgowns just for him. Topo's mouth was so dry he could barely speak and his hands sweated so much they almost dripped. At first Topo was worried that he might become obviously aroused in front of her and he'd brought no hat to set in his lap. But he soon discovered he was way too nervous for that — although this was by far the most provocative thing that had ever happened to him.

As Angelica stepped out from behind the screen and stood at the window, she would comment in offhand terms about how she felt each satiny, sheer slip affected her body. She talked matter-of-factly about color and length. Topo only nodded. She saved her favorite for last. It was a loose-fitting, floor-length, cream-colored little number of the sheerest silk. Topo, of course, knew only that it was kind of shiny. It had a yoked neck that exposed more than a hint of cleavage, but it also had tiny sleeves that made it somehow demure. She pointed all of this out before she changed into it, but when she stepped out from behind the screen and stood at the window, the sunlight shining in from behind made the gown all but disappear. Topo gazed in awe as Angelica posed and turned in front of him. She walked slowly back and forth in front of the window, completely oblivious of the effect of the sunlight on her silhouette.

'So? What do you think?'

'I like that one,' was the hoarse whisper. Topo heard the words and was pretty sure that it was he who had said them. It was settled. In a matter of moments he had recovered enough to assure her that her choices for everything — costume, hair, make-up — were all perfect.

'I trust you completely,' he said as he floated out of the shop. He ran all the way home without noticing the pavement, poured himself a large glass of wine, and then sat very still for a long time.

And now, as he stood at the bottom of the rise, with Angelica Giancarlo up there in her long creamy nightgown with the tiny sleeves, framed by the trees, Topo thought of her standing in front of that sunlit window. Back lighting was definitely out.

'Let's rehearse,' he suggested brightly and bounded back down the rise and began carefully wrapping the projector in the blanket.

'Leo, you walk up the trail like Father Elio and tell me when you get to the stump.'

They had decided that a particular broken stump was as close as Father Elio should get. So Leo walked some distance back down the dark trail, but he could still hear Topo's whispered voice through the trees.

'Are you ready, Angelica?'

'Ready.'

'Okay, Leo. Come on.'

Leo made his way up the trail, walking slowly, as he imagined Father Elio would, and as he approached the stump he said softly, 'Okay, I'm at the stump.'

At the crest of the rise in front of him, strange lights began to swirl and twist through the mist. The figure of a beautiful woman, with white-blond hair that circled her head like a halo, appeared before him. Her dress glowed and shimmered through the trees. The dim lights played around her, never holding still quite long enough for him to make out any details, but the effect was breathtaking. Her soothing voice came to him like music out of the darkness.

'Dear Father Elio . . . Do not despair . . . You are not alone . . . All mankind has sinned . . . Think not on the sin, but turn your heart to the mercy of the Father and the sacrifice of your Savior . . . God loves you, as he loves all his children, and no matter your sin, it is already forgiven . . . God forgave your sin ere you had the courage to ask it be forgiven . . . Dear Father Elio . . . Do not despair.'

Then the silver, shimmering vision reached her hands toward heaven just as the lights faded. And as magically as she had appeared, she was gone and Leo was alone in the forest. He was shaken. He had no idea that it would be this powerful. He had no idea Angelica's encouraging words would affect him so deeply. A small whisper called to him from the bushes.

'Well?'

He had trouble finding his voice. 'That was . . . That was . . . wonderful.'

'Could you hear the projector?'

'Maybe just a little, but . . . No. No, not really. It was . . . great! Can you do it like that again?'

'No problem. Angelica, that was wonderful. We're gonna do it just like that for Father Elio. Okay?'

From the dim shadows of the rise Angelica stepped from behind one of the pines, gave a little wave, and they heard a loud sniff. 'Okay. Anybody got a tissue?'

*

Marta had arranged things so that Father Elio was sitting at the kitchen table with his back to the window; from there he couldn't look out on the side yard. She'd just made coffee when Nina heard their voices in the kitchen and came downstairs and joined them at the table. She chatted with them for a while, but Nina's presence made her mother nervous. She had no fears of Nina accidentally seeing Leo through the window, of course, but if the gate squeaked or if Leo stepped on a dried branch, Nina would undoubtedly ask what that noise was and then Uncle Elio might turn to the window. So Marta suggested in an offhand way that Nina looked tired and should consider going to bed. The girl just laughed and said, 'If you want me to leave, Mother, just say so,' and she kissed them both good night and went upstairs.

Marta tried to talk about trivial things, but she was so anxious about Carmen that every sound seized her attention and she strained to hear the obnoxious sputter of a motor scooter. So, by the time Father Elio innocently asked about Carmen, poor Marta's nerves were as strained as her floodgates and the tears began to flow before her words did. He was Marta's uncle, but he was also her priest and it wasn't difficult for him to get her to talk. It was, however, difficult to tell which torment was filling Marta most — fear or anger. She was angry with Franco for dying so stupidly on that motorcycle with that woman riding with him, her arms locked around his chest. There was no reason to speak of her. She paid. She died too.

'But that damn Franco should be here now!' she railed. 'His daughter needs her father. Carmen won't listen to another woman, especially her mother. She needs a man to lay down the law. She needs her father! That damn Franco!'

And so it went for some time.

Father Elio listened. There was nothing for him to add. Marta was right. Franco was selfish; he always had been. And Marta was right about Carmen. It was obvious that the girl was dancing on tiptoes along the edge of a cliff with her eyes closed, just to prove she could do it. A father's stern voice or understanding love might help, but Franco was gone. Elio had an idea, but he knew Marta's feelings on this particular subject and so he remained silent while Marta fumed for close to an hour without rest. Then, when she finally stopped to take a breath, Father Elio ventured a thought.

'There might be one man Carmen would listen to.'

Marta had a feeling she knew where her uncle was going with this and she dreaded hearing what her heart already knew. But she asked anyway. 'Who?'

'Leo Pizzola.'

Marta replied with a short but heartfelt scream of terror as Leo Pizzola's face suddenly appeared in the window right over Uncle Elio's head.

Elio almost jumped out of his chair. He knew she might not react well to the mention of Leo Pizzola, but he hadn't expected her to scream at him.

'I'm sorry, I shouldn't have mentioned it.'

Leo gave Marta a quick wave and then he was gone.

'No, Uncle Elio, I'm sorry. That was silly. I guess I'm just tired.'

'Maybe I should go home.'

'It is getting late. Should I walk with you?'

'No. I'm fine. You wait here for Carmen.'

They exchanged kisses and an embrace and Marta sent her uncle out the back door to face alone whatever new miracle had been concocted for him. She knew that she should follow him. This whole miracle thing was her idea. She should try to protect him more. She should have questioned Leo more. But tonight she somehow didn't care and so she sat at the table with her cold coffee and waited. She wanted Carmen home. Where was she? Please, God, bring Carmen home safely.

The piazza was dark and empty and Father Elio's shuffling steps echoed around him. He hadn't been out this late in a long time. No wonder he was so tired. He couldn't let go of the image of Marta and her fears, so he stopped in the middle of the piazza to say a fervent prayer for Carmen's safe return home, and soon. Then, as the old priest groped his way up to the kitchen door at the back of the church, the oddest thing happened.

'. . . Elio Caproni . . .'

He thought that maybe it was the wind in the trees. It sounded like the breeze called his name. It was soft, almost inaudible, whatever it was. He shook his head. He was tired and hearing things – and he started back inside the kitchen door.

'. . . Elio Caproni . . .'

There it was again. Again, it sounded like his name, but it

wasn't the breeze. Who would whisper his name so softly, this late at night?

'Is someone there?'

He listened so carefully he was almost afraid to breathe. Silence. Just as he was giving up again, '. . . Elio Caproni . . .'

'Who's there? Who is it?'

He'd heard it for sure. Someone was whispering his name from the grove of trees behind the church. He crossed himself quickly and cursed all devils and evil demons. But what if someone needed him? What if someone was in trouble? Father Elio would never forgive himself if someone were hurt or in need and he turned his back on them out of fear. So the frightened old priest walked slowly toward the dark grove of trees – and the voice.

Leo moved back up the trail as silently as he could, pulling the old man deeper into the shadows of the forest. He stopped often to make sure Father Elio still followed and it occurred to him that this might not be such a good idea. His eerie, whispered calls through the mysterious forest were spooky even for him and he hoped he didn't give Father Elio a heart attack. It would not be good if their miracle was so effective it killed him.

'. . . Elio Caproni . . .' he whispered again.

Father Elio fearfully worked his way along the dark path he'd walked thousands of times, but always in the daytime. It was strange and a little ghostly at night. His legs were shaking and his mouth was dry, but with a trembling voice he managed to call out reassuringly, 'I can hear you, but I can't see you. Where are you? . . . Are you there?'

By now, Leo was crouched in the bushes beside Topo and he leaned into the darkness, straining to make out the figure of Father Elio approaching the stump. The old man was moving slowly, but Leo could see that he was almost there. He turned to Topo and whispered softly, 'Get ready.'

There were only two things that were different this time from when they had so effectively practiced their little pageant earlier. The first difference was a minor adjustment, hardly worth mentioning. It seems Topo had been troubled by Leo's offhand judgment that perhaps the projector had been a bit too loud. He knew he could do better. So he took the opportunity, while Leo was leading Father Elio up the forest path, to wrap the blanket just a little bit tighter around the projector – a minor thing.

The second factor was not so minor. In fact, it was life altering. While Leo went off to signal Marta and then lure Father Elio back up the path and while Topo rewrapped his projector, Angelica Giancarlo stood quietly in the dark at the top of the rise and waited. She waited patiently at the foot of the three pine trees and thought about the words she had just said and would shortly say again. And she thought about her life.

. . . *All mankind has sinned* . . . Angelica thought of her miserable years in Roma, years spent doing shameful things, just to get insignificant roles in embarrassing little movies . . . *Think not on the sin* . . . She thought about all the disgusting men she had been with for money. They all told her she was pretty . . . They all deserted her . . . *Turn your heart to the mercy of the Father* . . . She thought of the letter from her mother begging her to come home because her father's heart was broken . . . But she never saw him again after that day in the rain, when he turned his face away from the window . . . He died of his broken heart . . . *God loves you, as he loves all his children* . . . She thought of her baby, the baby she was carrying when she ran from her home, the baby she held in her arms only once before they took it away from her forever . . . It was a little girl . . . *God forgave your sin ere you had the courage to ask it be forgiven* . . . Angelica had wanted to wear her life like a beautiful ball gown of satin and lace. Now she saw that it had been a cheap and gaudy garment, crudely stitched with threads of vanity, self-ishness, illusions, stupidity, and lies . . . *Do not despair . . . No matter your sin, it is already forgiven . . . Do not despair . . . Dear . . . Angelica Giancarlo . . .*

Father Elio shuffled along the dirt trail, finally reaching the stump. Leo turned to Topo and whispered softly, 'Now.'

Topo flipped the switch. A brilliant light burst silently from the projector and was both softened and defused by Topo's fingers weaving hypnotically in front of the lens. This magical effect, however, lasted about two seconds before the new and improved blanket wrap jammed some cloth in the projector's gears. Then the film slowed to a crawl as the gears pulled the edge of the old blanket deeper and deeper into the machine. The film abruptly ground to a halt, freezing the action of *La Strada* on a single image. Topo's magic fingers left the lens uncovered as he clawed frantically at the blanket. The undiluted image shone brilliantly up the rise and framed poor Angelica

Giancarlo like truck headlights capturing a helpless doe on a dark road. The projector's beam pitched and rolled as first Topo and then Leo ripped and tore at the blanket.

The sight at the top of the rise was, in the truest sense of the word, fantastic. Angelica's shimmering gown and bleached hair glowed white in the naked glare of the light. Her arms reached up to the sky, as if she wanted to grip heaven and pull it down around her. Two huge and wet circles of black mascara filled the hollows of her eyes, making them bottomless holes, and from them black rivers streaked down her cheeks. Her red mouth was contorted into a cry of pain and her whole body was wracked with sobs. The image that flashed in that instant might have been the closing scene from *Oedipus Rex* and all the words Angelica could manage was an anguished wail of—

'God forgive my sins . . .!'

Then, just as the frozen image in the projector began to bubble and melt into a brown goo, this shrieking Angel lurched unsteadily down the hill toward the terrified priest. And the bloodcurdling cry began again—

'God forgive my . . .'

But Angelica didn't finish her second plea because her foot got caught in the extension cord that Topo had strung in front of her. In her blindness and desperation, Angelica's foot managed to pull the cord from the projector and everything suddenly went black. For its part, the extension cord managed to pitch poor, plump Angelica forward, sending her tumbling and rolling down the hill and into the bushes in front of Father Elio.

As for the effectiveness of Topo's miracle, Father Elio was well convinced that he'd seen an Angel – an Avenging Angel come for his soul. So, whether the old priest bravely stood his ground, or whether he was just too petrified with fear to move, will never be known. Whatever the case, he was still standing in the middle of the trail by the broken stump when Angelica Giancarlo crawled out of the bushes begging the forgiveness of God.

Father Elio helped the poor distraught thing to her feet. 'My goodness . . .' he stammered, 'it's . . . little Angelica Giancarlo!' He had known her all her life. He had christened Angelica. He had comforted her family through . . . the trouble. And he had buried her father. Now here she was, wandering through the dark forest in the middle of the night in her . . . my goodness . . . her pajamas? . . . babbling and crying and begging God's forgiveness. The whole thing astounded Father Elio. First the voice summoning him into the woods and now this. And that startling flash of summer lightning! Summer lightning this late in the season in weather that's turning cool is one thing, but to have the summer lightning appear as an enormous, grinning face of Anthony Quinn . . . Incredible! But Father Elio didn't have time to dwell on these phenomena. He had to get Angelica back to the church where he could calm her, and comfort her, and hear her confession. So the old priest led the sobbing woman back down the trail toward the church.

Leo and Topo crouched in the bushes and patiently waited for Father Elio and Angelica to enter the church before they quietly gathered up their miracle-making equipment and went home.

Later that night, upstairs at the Albergo di Santo Fico, terrible things were said. It was almost 2:00 A.M. before Carmen finally sneaked in the kitchen door, holding her shoes and tiptoeing across the tiles to the stairs. She was so intent on being quiet in the darkness she didn't notice the figure at the kitchen table watching her.

Earlier in the evening, shortly after Uncle Elio left, Marta grew tired of sitting in the kitchen and went upstairs — she thought she would be able to hear the motor scooter better from the balcony that wrapped around the southern end of the building. And so she was there, sitting outside, when she heard the commotion coming from somewhere in the trees behind the church. There was a brief flash of light that lasted only a few seconds and was accompanied by some wild shrieks; then nothing. Something told her that she'd witnessed yet another botched miracle, and her attention returned to the dark plain to the south where she strained to hear the sound of a scooter.

It was after ten o'clock when she went back inside and prepared for bed. She left her bedroom dark because she wanted to undress in front of her open windows. She wanted to hear that scooter chugging up the narrow road into town.

By eleven she lay down on her bed to wait. But soon her eyes were becoming heavy and she wanted to stop herself from falling asleep, so she went back down to the straight-backed chairs at the kitchen table. These guaranteed enough discomfort to keep her awake and she was still sitting at the kitchen table when her vigil finally ended.

As she watched her firstborn skulk through the kitchen shadows, Marta was filled with such joy and rage that she wanted to both weep and strangle the girl – simultaneously.

'Where have you been?'

Marta's voice reached through the darkness like an icy hand that gripped the girl by the scruff of the neck and jolted Carmen almost halfway up the stairs in one leap.

Carmen smelled of cigarettes and alcohol, her make-up was smeared, and her clothes were disheveled. When Marta asked her about it, Carmen told her mother that she'd been to Grosseto and her words slurred with drink as she declared defiantly that she was going to go again, any time she wanted. The argument escalated quickly into a fight. Marta warned her about the bars in Grosseto, about boys like Solly Puce, and about the price of stupidity. But Carmen laughed and told her mother that she could handle Solly Puce or any other boy and Marta believed her and was ashamed.

The things that Carmen and Marta shouted at each other were those terrible, cruel things that are said when a family battles – lies and truths twisted together with guilt and pain. They accused each other of crimes from years past, both real and imagined, and they each prophesied barren, loveless futures for the other. They said things that, in time to come, both would apologize for, both would forgive, and neither would ever forget. They could hear Nina crying in her bedroom, begging them to stop, but they didn't; they couldn't – their blood was raging too hot. It ended only when Carmen called her mother a disgraceful name and Marta slapped her daughter so hard her hand stung. But it wasn't Carmen who cried. Instead the girl glared at her mother with her chin high, daring her to slap again. It was Marta who burst into tears, ran down the stairs, and out into the night.

Only after she was gone did Carmen cry. She went to her room and sobbed and sobbed, but not for the slap. She had never felt such regret as she did for what she had said. It tore at her heart and the image of the dreadful pain in her mother's eyes seared her brain.

Now it was Carmen who lay in the dark and worried for her mother. Where could she have gone? Where could she run to in the middle of the night?

Leo had moved his blanket around to the west side of the hut so he would be shaded from the morning sun and that's why he didn't hear Marta approach. Only when she was pounding on the door with her fists and shouting his name did he rouse himself at about the same time Nonno opened the door with a lantern in his hand. Marta had forgotten that Nonno was living there and in the dim lantern light Leo could see that this midnight trip from town had apparently been impulsive. Her pale nightgown was torn and thistles clung to her hair and her bare arms showed scrapes from some painful falls. Her dirty face also showed the streaks of tears as she apologized to Nonno, 'I'm sorry . . . I need to talk to Leo.'

Nonno pointed toward where Leo was standing at the corner. Marta stepped away from the door apologizing, embarrassed at what the old man must think. 'I'm sorry . . . It's late . . .'

Nonno felt he should say something to the poor girl, but from the shadows at the corner he saw Leo shake his head, so he went back inside and closed the door.

Except for the distant murmur of the sea, it was quiet. Marta walked toward the cliff and Leo followed. He would wait until she was ready.

'I want you to . . . to do something for me. A favor.'

A favor? A favor is something one asks of a friend, Leo thought. These were hard words for Marta to speak.

'There's . . . this boy. He's . . . He's no good. Carmen . . . I think she's . . . I don't know if . . . she has or not.'

In the light of the waxing moon Leo could see Marta turn her face away from him. He could see the way she held herself, her arms clinched around her own shoulders in a despairing embrace. He could even see the way her chest and shoulders rose and fell as she tried to control her breathing. But he couldn't see her eyes and her eyes were what he needed to see.

'What do you want from me?'

He tried to make his voice as gentle as possible, but he regretted speaking even before he was done asking the question. He knew that the Marta he had known was gone. The girl had become a woman filled with bitterness, but tonight she was again different – more like a desperate animal drowning in a sea of despair and refusing to sink beneath the dark surface without a struggle.

'I don't know,' she shot back at him. 'Something! I want you to do something . . . or . . . or I swear, Leo . . .'

'What? You'll turn me into the police?'

'Maybe? I might!'

'Then do it! What do you want? Another miracle? I'm sorry, but I've still got my hands full with your last miracle, and I'm not having a lot of luck with that.'

'Talk to her! Just . . . talk to her!'

'Why?'

'Because! You owe me!' Marta's voice broke and Leo could see her bury her long fingers into her black mane of hair and then press, as if attempting to keep her head from exploding.

'. . . You stood in my bedroom, in the dark, the night before my wedding . . . and you said . . . things! You said things you had no right to say! You told me things . . . you shouldn't have! Not then! The night before my wedding! You owe me!'

'That was a long time ago,' Leo whispered.

'It was yesterday!'

She was crying and Leo found himself wanting to say things to her again. He wanted words that would explain that night and the years before that night, and the years since that night. But those words didn't exist. And so, because he didn't have words and she was in such pain, he reached out and touched her arm. But she pulled back as if he had burned her with a flame and he could see her hands held up to him, ordering him to stop.

'. . . Don't touch me . . . Don't . . .'

But there was no anger in her voice. Now it was the voice of a frightened girl, one he'd heard before. As he had stood in her bedroom so many years ago and said things he had no right to say, that was the voice that came pleading out of the darkness, 'Don't say that . . . Please stop . . .'

Marta wrapped the moonlight around her and calmed herself. When she spoke again it was as this new creature, this woman he'd come to know since his return.

'You had a friend once. You betrayed him. Carmen is his daughter. I want you to do this thing for Franco.' She turned and walked up the trail that would take her back to town and Leo was able to watch her shadowy form for a long time before it eventually disappeared into the moonlight.

Why the hell hadn't he stayed in Chicago?

Nineteen

The next morning began, as always, with a pale glow over the eastern mountains, which quickly turned to crimson as the sun approached. When it finally peeked over Santo Fico's edge of the world, the eastern half of the sky flared yellow-white and that brightness quickly spread as the sun climbed, until, at last, it lifted above the rim of the earth and rolled upward. Then the sky changed to a deep blue and all the fire was in the sun. It was a typical summer sunrise along this section of the Toscana coast. But those who rose to greet it found something new in the west. Clouds puffed slowly along the distant horizon, low and heavy. Also, the night before there had been a breeze that carried the smell of something new. Today there would be a heaviness to the hot air and for those who could read such signs, it was obvious that somewhere, not far away, storms were deciding which direction to go.

Marta slept late. When she'd returned home from her moon-lit dash down the coast, she was embarrassed to discover the way she looked and she was glad it had been too dark for Leo to see her like that – her wild hair, the scrapes, the torn nightgown, the dirt, and the tears. She sank into a warm bath and soaked much of it away. It was her mind that was still in torment as she slipped naked between the cool sheets. She was sure she wouldn't sleep; she wondered how she would ever sleep again. Then her head was on the pillow and almost instantly she was unconscious. When, at last, she rolled over again the sun was already high. She felt as if she had been given a powerful drug and she had to force herself out of the bed.

All the time she was dressing she wondered why she was hurrying. It was just another day. The regulars would be coming by for their morning coffee. She had enough fresh fruit. Nina was probably up and already at the *panetteria* picking up the breads. When she opened her bedroom door and smelled fresh-brewed coffee she knew that Carmen was up too and Marta wanted to go back inside her bedroom, close the door, and crawl back beneath the sheets. But she and Carmen were going to have to be around each other eventually. She prayed that Carmen would come to her first, and that she would say something that would make every-thing all right. It was unlikely, but it didn't hurt to pray.

The kitchen had been cleaned. It wasn't as if the place had been particularly messy, but with everything going on the night before, Marta had left many small chores to finish in the morning. Now, they were done; it must have been Carmen. Marta knew her stubborn daughter probably wasn't going to apologize, but the work she'd done in the kitchen said a great deal. Then the aroma of the coffee seized her and she poured a cup and was surprised to hear voices in the dining room. She slipped quietly through the swinging door and into a shadow at the back of the room.

Sitting at a table near the verandah doors, Leo Pizzola was drinking coffee and picking at some fresh fruit. Carmen leaned against the wall with her arms folded across her chest, listening to whatever it was Leo was saying, but her face was an enigmatic mask of disdain. Marta stood silently in the shadows, watching Leo casually explain something to Carmen and she wished she could make out his words, but he talked too softly. Then he finished talking and sipped his coffee, waiting for Carmen to respond. But when she did, Marta couldn't hear her either . . . so she slipped out of the shadow a bit.

The swinging door behind Marta suddenly whacked her on the behind and she squeaked as hot coffee slopped out of the cup and across her hand. Nina came through the door carrying a plate of bread and jam and apologizing to who-ever it was she had struck with the door. As Nina served Leo, Carmen approached Marta, looking uncomfortable —

nothing like the picture of defiance she'd presented just hours ago.

'He wants me to work for him.'

'What?'

'He says he needs to get his father's house cleaned up so he can sell it. He wants me to work for him, cleaning the house. I told him it was stupid. I told him you wouldn't allow it, but he said I should ask you anyway.'

Leo sat at the table, spreading jam across the thick bread and pointedly ignoring them.

'When does he want you to start?'

'Today.'

'Did he offer you a fair wage?'

'Yes.'

'I don't care. It's up to you. Do what you want.'

Marta put on her best air of nonchalant indifference and returned to the kitchen. Carmen was beyond bewildered, but money is money, so she went back and agreed to his proposal. Leo only nodded and plopped some coins on the table for breakfast, picked up his bread and jam, and walked from the hotel.

He crossed the piazza and was headed for home when something hissed at him. There was Marta, standing on the north side of the church, imitating a snake and waving him toward her. She pressed herself against the wall and refused to step beyond the corner where she might be seen from the hotel. It occurred to him that Marta must have run all the way from her kitchen, across the side yard, around the edge of the piazza, and circled around behind the church to have gotten there before him. She angrily motioned him to her again and he considered ignoring her and walking on home, but then she hissed once more — only a much more insistent sort of hiss this time. With a sigh, he walked to the corner of the church, but not quite close enough for her to actually get her hands on him and still remain concealed from the hotel.

'What do you think you're doing?' she demanded in a harsh whisper.

'Going home.'

Although Leo was sorry about whatever Marta was going through, he was also in no mood to be upbraided yet again this morning and so his voice was just as brusque as hers, and Marta was startled by his curtness.

'What do you think you're doing hiring Carmen to work at your house?'

'You told me to do something. I'm doing something.'

'What? Clean your house for you? That's not what I was talking about. What are you going to do?'

'I don't know yet. I haven't had a chance to think about it. I had a rough night.'

'Did you say anything to Carmen about my coming to see you?'

'Of course not.'

'Well, don't.'

'I wasn't going to.'

Behind Marta, down the north side of the church at the new break in the garden wall, an old gray head peeked out to investigate the snippy exchange. When Leo and then Marta turned and looked, Father Elio quickly ducked back out of sight, but after a moment he peeked out again. He was caught; there was no denying it.

'Good morning,' he offered weakly.

Leo and Marta returned a couple of feeble 'Good mornings,' and Marta shot a quick glance around the corner. Across the piazza, Carmen was wiping the tables on the hotel's verandah and chatting with Nina. Marta cursed to herself, hitched up her skirt, and ran back the way she came – hopping through piles of rubble like a rabbit. As she passed her uncle she couldn't think of anything to say so she just grinned rather stupidly before darting around the corner. Leo wanted to shout something sarcastic after her, but he was too tired to think of anything clever.

'Leo, could you help me with something?' asked Father Elio before disappearing back into the garden. Leo sighed again – he was never going to get home.

Leo found that Father Elio had been busy in the garden. All of the collapsed stones and bricks were carefully stacked and sorted according to type and size; all ready for some handy mason to reuse. And other than the collections of stone and brick, the garden was spotless. The broken fragments had all been removed and the plaster dust had been either swept away or worked into the soil. All the plants had been watered. Even the Miracle looked as if it had received a proper dusting; maybe even a polishing. All in all, the garden was as serene and inviting as ever.

But there was one sight that made Leo's heart pound and his blood run cold. The transept still stood! The north wall was cracked and near the base it had buckled slightly – but it still stood. In fact, in the bright morning light it looked damn solid! Leo had counted on that transept collapsing and it hadn't. Father Elio had gone inside and that meant that whatever he wanted Leo to help him with was inside the church. This was the last place he wanted to be and he was considering his chances of quietly slipping back through the broken garden wall when Father Elio called again from inside – 'You need to come in here.' It was as if the old man was reading his mind.

Inside, Leo was again astonished at how much Father Elio had accomplished. The church was spotless. If it weren't for the broken windows and the enormous hole in the ceiling, you couldn't tell that there had ever been a catastrophe. Father Elio was waiting for him in the damaged northern transept. The lights were on and in their glare Leo could see that the wall had been crushed at the base and the ceiling cracked, but the room was not going to fall. Father Elio had positioned a couple of two-by-fours at each of the corners to act as braces for a third two-by-four that was to span the top, in a puny attempt to hold up the sagging roof beams. All the boards were tilted at odd angles and Father Elio was obviously having trouble setting them in place.

But it wasn't the frailty of Father Elio's bracing that disturbed Leo. It was the wall. He couldn't recall ever seeing anything so markedly naked as the blank gray wall at the end of the transept. For all his life this wall had leapt out at him with colors and light and movement and faces and people he'd grown to know. He thought of them now – cramped and folded on top of each other, wrapped in an old blanket beneath a dirty cot in the shepherd's hut. The gray wall was dead now and didn't care anymore – that's what he told himself. He tried instead to think of the money for those meaningless hunks of painted plaster, but the naked wall stared at him like an accusation. He assured himself, there was nothing anyone could do to stop him. All he needed to do was steal Topo's truck and drive away. He could go to Roma or Milano – anywhere. Marta would have no way of finding him. It was so easy, all he had to do was leave. Why did he worry so much about Marta?

'What do you need, Father?'

Father Elio stood by one of the braces and tried to heft a short-handled sledgehammer.

'Every time I try to drive one of these braces into place, the other one tips over and then that cross beam falls on my head.'

'Here . . . You steady the other one.'

Leo took the hammer from the weak old hands and with Father Elio holding the opposite brace in position, Leo drove each one into place with just a few blows. The transept wasn't rebuilt yet, but the braces would help.

Father Elio patted Leo on the back and thanked him. And Leo thought, since the old priest doesn't feel the need to mention anything about the absent fresco, why should he? He tried to effect a good-bye, but Father Elio just kept following him – out the transept door and across the garden. Then the old man said something that caught Leo completely off guard.

'Marta isn't angry with you, you know.'

Sometimes a thing can come at you so unexpectedly that you don't have time to fashion a facade, and before you know it, the truth just spills out.

'Yes, she is and I don't care. A long time ago I did something stupid,' Leo confessed. 'If she wants to hate me, okay, fine. But she hates everything. I'm sorry Franco died. Excuse me, Father, but to hell with her.'

The old man sat down on one of his mounds of stones and scratched his head. 'A lot of things happened after you left. What happened between Marta and Franco wasn't good. Franco got everything he wanted. He got Marta. He got the hotel. He got beautiful children. And the more he got, the unhappier he became. Then, he got mean. He might have even hit her. I hope not, but maybe he did. He was cruel in many different ways – more painful, more lasting. I don't think Marta wants to be unhappy anymore, but it's become her way of life. It's hard to watch her struggle, isn't it?'

'You're her uncle, you're her priest – there must be something you can do to help her.'

'A long time ago, when I was at the university in Bologna, I took many wonderful classes. My favorite was the class about science. I wasn't good at it, but I loved that class. It taught me all about plants and animals, water and fish, air and birds. It taught me about clouds and storms. It taught me so many things, but one thing that it taught me . . . maybe the most important thing of all . . . it taught me about butterflies.

'God has a habit of working miracles all the time that we don't even see. Like butterflies. God works such a miracle in butterflies. He teaches us about our lives through them. Have you ever watched a butterfly break its way out of its cocoon? Oh, it's a terrible struggle. It appears to be agony . . . Maybe it is. Only the butterfly knows for sure. But one thing is certain – it's an exhausting struggle. The butterfly must break through the shell of its old life – this thing that, at one time, was strong enough to protect it from other bugs, birds, and lizards . . . all sorts of dangers. And other terrors too, like wind and rain – all the things that would have destroyed it because it was so fragile. But one day it knows that it's time to break through the cocoon. It wants to become a new thing, you see, and to do so it must break through that shell. But the cocoon isn't like a room with a door. It's something that the butterfly created herself, out of a single thread spun over time. Around and around herself the caterpillar wrapped that single thread, until it buried her. So, now she's a butterfly and she wants to be free . . . but she's trapped. And certain threads, threads that were spun with a certain . . . passion, they don't want to break. They cling to her and entangle her. And her struggle to free herself can be both frightening and inspiring. But for the butterfly, it's severe and unrelenting.

'As I watch a butterfly struggling and I pity her plight, sometimes I'm tempted to play the hand of God and reach down and help her. I could so easily pull open certain threads – just a few. It would make her struggle so much easier and she would never know. But I don't. Do you know why? Because I know it would destroy her. She would die. I learned this in the science class at the university. The butterfly has a . . . a . . .

thing in her stomach, I think. This . . . thing is full of a fluid that is meant to fill the veins of her butterfly wings. It's the pressure of the struggle and the squeezing to escape this prison cocoon of her own making that forces the fluid out of this . . . thing in her stomach, and into the veins of her wings. Without the fluid her wings would never expand and she would never fly. She would drop to the ground and die.

'Marta worked hard creating her shell. Now her time has come, and she will escape or she won't. But she must do it herself. We all must do it ourselves. That's God's plan.'

Carmen Fortino had been coming to the Pizzola farm for one thing or another all her life. Some of her earliest memories were of walking down the north coast road, holding her mother's hand until they turned down through the opening in the old stone fence. From there, Marta was too slow for Carmen because she had to carry Nina, who was still a baby – and the little girl liked to race ahead to find the road's deepest pools of fine dust to plop her bare feet in and pretend she was wading through warm puddles of her grandmother's lavender dusting powder. The walk was beautiful in those days. The weeds were kept low, there were flowers everywhere and they were always well watered. Her mother told her many times that Signora Pizzola loved flowers and when Marta was Carmen's age, she would often help her plant in the spring and fall. Signora Pizzola had been dead a long time, since her mother was a young girl, but her mother told her that Signore Pizzola would rather lose an arm than let his wife's flowers die. Carmen found that gruesome

The Miracles of Santo Fico

image thoroughly strange – after all, they were only flowers, and an arm was an arm.

Her mother was always respectful to Signore Pizzola, who was a tall man with a neatly trimmed white beard. He looked strong and he had a big laugh, but he didn't use it often and his eyes were usually sad. She remembered the old man's eyes when she saw Leo for the first time. As a little girl she liked sitting on the porch, sometimes on the old man's lap, and they would drink cold *limonata*. The old man liked it with a lot of sugar and so did she. She would sit and drink and her mother would talk to Signore Pizzola about people Carmen didn't know and things she didn't understand. Sometimes he would rock Nina and sing her funny songs that made her laugh or sleep and Carmen would go off and play with the goats. After Signore Pizzola died, she had no more reason to turn off the north coast road and wander down through the gate in the old stone fence.

In fact, she'd only returned once, although she would never have admitted it if anyone had ever asked – she was that ashamed. It had been over a year ago that Solly Puce had brought a bunch of his Grosseto friends over to Santo Fico. He said it was so they could go for a swim, but they never did. Instead they just sat on the beach and drank wine and talked dirty. Carmen didn't like them. She suspected they came to Santo Fico because Solly Puce had told them lies about her because they kept saying nasty things to her right in front of him and he let them. So she said cruel things about Solly's manliness to humiliate him and the other boys laughed harder.

When they'd drunk all their wine and run out of dirty jokes, they were at a loss for anything else to do, so Carmen suggested that they go to an old haunted house she knew about. She brought them to the Pizzola farm.

It had stood abandoned for some years. This was the first time Carmen had visited since even before Signore Pizzola died. The flowers had been replaced by weeds. The tile porch was empty and covered with dead leaves. The windows were dark and looked haunted – Carmen thought they looked like Signore Pizzola's sad eyes searching for a friend to come calling and drink some *limonata* and maybe make him laugh. But these were not friends she brought. Carmen hadn't even thought of throwing rocks until she heard the first stone smash through a window. She didn't like it. She told them to stop, but they wouldn't. They kept throwing rocks and smashing the windows. She screamed at them and ordered them away, but they just laughed and broke more windows. They left only because Carmen started throwing rocks at them. They rode out of town calling her ugly, drunken names and mocking her. She knew everyone heard them and she was ashamed. She didn't speak to Solly for two weeks.

Arriving now at the Pizzola house on this August morning, she found shutters covered the windows and the doors were boarded up as well. The trees surrounding the porch were already pruned back, and scattered around the front of the house large piles of dead branches, leaves, and weeds waited to be hauled to the field across from the olive grove and burned.

Leo was at the side of the house working with a hand scythe when he saw Carmen coming down the road. She walked briskly, her head held high, carrying a red and white checked cloth bundle under her arm, and for an instant he thought it was Marta, magically turned sixteen again. But Carmen's arrival meant he had to do something that he'd been avoiding and so he put down his scythe and went up onto the porch. Starting with the windows, he pulled at the weathered boards and tossed them one by one onto a waiting trash pile. By the time Carmen arrived at the porch, all the front windows had been cleared and Leo was tugging at the barricades covering the front door. She stood back and watched, unsure if he had even seen her. Rusty nails screeched and moaned as he pulled the boards back, but in a short time the door was clear and Leo tried the handle. Locked.

'You don't have a key? I thought this was your house.'

Leo turned cold eyes toward her and Carmen wished she had kept her mouth shut. He picked up a large terra-cotta pot and hefted it as if he were debating whether to toss it through a window or at her. But a key was hidden beneath the flowerpot, so he only moved it out of the way and set it back down. Leo slid the key into the lock and turned the handle. As the door creaked open, a wave of musty air greeted them, and Leo stepped back – politely allowing Carmen to enter first.

From the moment she entered, Carmen remembered why she loved the old Pizzola place. The rooms were open and inviting, with high ceilings and wide corridors. She passed through the entryway with its broad staircase leading to the rooms upstairs and entered the living room. The inside was dark and silent and the shadows made her anxious. Scattered around the gloom, pale mounds of furniture covered with white sheets gave the eerie appearance that the great room was filled with sleeping ghosts who were well content being left undisturbed. Even in the murky light she could see this was going to be a bigger cleaning job than she imagined. Cobwebs hung everywhere and in some places the dust was so thick that, with proper watering, she thought, plants could grow right out of the floor. And everywhere she stepped the crunch of broken glass under her feet pricked and scratched at her guilty conscience.

'You need to open the shutters . . .'

She was speaking to Leo of course, but when she turned she found she was alone in the large house. He was still on the porch and it occurred to her that she might not be the only one who was troubled by sleeping ghosts. But after a moment Leo abruptly moved into the room, began opening the wide, tall windows, and throwing back the shutters. Most of the front windows were broken out, as well as many on the south side.

'Looks like some kids had fun with the windows. I'll see if Topo can get me some glass next time I go into town.'

As Leo went through the house opening windows and shutters, Carmen followed him, listening to his orders about what he wanted done. He needn't have bothered. It was obvious. Then he was gone, as abruptly as he'd entered.

Carmen watched him from a kitchen window as he

returned to his scythe with a new ferocity and she wondered what terrible thing it was that he imagined he was hacking down.

Even though cleaning wasn't anything new to her, as she'd been helping at the hotel since she was small, this was the first time she'd cleaned anything that had been neglected for this many years. She didn't mind, however – she liked the house and she found that cleaning someone else's things was much more interesting than cleaning your own. And she was getting paid too. But the real fascination was Leo – this man who had been her father's best friend. There was just too much mystery surrounding him and her father and her mother. So as the morning progressed, with clocklike regularity, Carmen found more and more reasons to go outside and ask questions that might engage Leo in conversation, yet he persisted in ignoring her. She couldn't get him to either talk much or even enter the house. When questioned he simply called out a curt response from the yard and went right back to his work.

Around lunchtime Leo sat down on the edge of the porch with some bread and cheese, and so Carmen stopped her mopping, found the bundle Marta had given her as she was leaving the hotel, and went outside too. Leo was working on a loaf of semipetrified bread and a hunk of yellow cheese of questionable origin. Even though he used a knife to slice off thick slabs of cheese and lay them across slices of the crusty bread, the cheese still showed smudges of dirty fingerprints and other less identifiable things. He was washing it all down with water he would swig from an old wine bottle. To his credit, when Carmen joined him, he offered to share what he had, but she declined with a laugh, sat down on the edge of the porch not far from him, and unwrapped her bundle of red and white checked cloth. From within the parcel appeared grapes and oranges, carrots and radishes, hard-boiled eggs, slices of ham, cheeses, and two thick meatball sandwiches dripping with a red sauce – all neatly wrapped in brown waxed paper. Leo gazed at the girl's banquet longingly.

'My mother told me you probably wouldn't have any food fit to feed a pig, so she made enough for two.'

It didn't take Leo long to decide to swallow his pride rather than his stale bread and rancid cheese, and so the two sat on the edge of the porch, in the shade of a cork tree, and quietly feasted. They talked of small things – the view of the sea, the age of the trees, the names of the birds that flitted overhead – and little by little they began to know each other.

When the food was gone, mostly into Leo's stomach, he sat back and lit a cigarette. Now it was Carmen's turn to look on longingly.

'Can I have one of those?'

Leo studied her for a moment before he tossed her his cigarettes and matches.

'I thought you didn't approve of my smoking,' said Carmen as she lit her cigarette and tossed them back to Leo.

'Why would you think that?'

'The way you looked at me the other day when you saw me smoking.'

'Smoking's stupid. But when I saw you the other day, smoking was the least stupid thing you were doing.'

Carmen didn't like that kind of bluntness, especially from a man.

'Did you tell my mother?'

'What, that I saw you smoking?'

'Did you tell her that you saw me with Solly?'

'No.'

'Why not?'

'You're not my daughter. It's none of my business.'

For some reason that she didn't understand, Leo's words stung Carmen. Maybe because he was so cold in his not caring. Maybe because when she saw Leo she thought of her father. Hadn't they been best friends? Shouldn't she matter to him? Why didn't he behave like all the other boys? It occurred to her that maybe it was because he was a man and not a boy. She was used to boys.

'That's right. It's none of your business. You're not my father. My father's dead.'

'And you can thank your lucky stars for that.'

Carmen almost choked. How could he say something so cruel? How could he say that she should be glad her father was dead? It was terrible. It was horrible. She hated him for even thinking it.

'How dare you say that—'

He turned to her with a swiftness that left her startled, and although his voice remained low and calm, his eyes drilled into her and she was frightened.

'Because I knew your father, and if you think he would have put up with any of the crap you dish out, you're crazy. He would have slapped that cigarette out of your mouth so fast your head would have spun around three times. He hated to see women smoke. And if he had seen you with that kid the other day, you wouldn't be sitting down for a week, and that greasy little pimple who was feeling you up would be wondering if he'd ever walk again.'

It took Carmen a moment to realize that her jaw was hanging slack and she'd forgotten to breathe. She could feel a knot tightening in her throat and her eyes were stinging. Leo asked, 'Have you finished with the kitchen yet?'

The young girl heard herself mumble that she hadn't as she scrambled to pick up the remains of their lunch. She wanted to get back inside before he had a chance to see the tears she knew were only seconds away. When she was gone, Leo sat back and finished his cigarette. It was a start.

That afternoon Leo forced himself to go into the house a number of times. He would unexpectedly wander into the kitchen or living room to check on Carmen's progress. He didn't care how much she cleaned, of course, he just wanted to take opportunities to establish his authority. And over the course of that day she became somewhat respectful and sometimes actually even seemed anxious to please.

It was in the late afternoon that something happened that Leo couldn't have anticipated. He was throwing his piles of trash onto the cart – he'd already taken two loads to the fire pit across from the olive grove – when he happened to look up and see a figure approaching from out of the northwest. It was a rider on horseback and with the afternoon sun reflecting off the sea, the blinding light seemed to rest on the rider's shoulders. Leo recognized the visitor immediately

and strolled out to meet him. Carmen, who was on the porch
and also saw the rider, called to Leo.

'Who's that?'

'Paolo Lombolo. His family grazes some horses here.'

At nineteen years old, Paolo was the youngest of the four
Lombolo brothers and Leo's favorite. He was quiet, always
polite, and when he felt at ease he could often be funny. It
was his habit to ride down from his family's ranch once a
week and check on the horses. The Lombolos had a huge
ranch up the coast just south of Punta Ala, with many
orchards and vineyards, but Paolo loved the horses. When
he rode south he always kept his eyes open for Leo so he
could pass along his father's greetings.

Watching his young visitor ride out of the sun's glare
hurt Leo's eyes, so he turned his gaze back toward the house
and discovered Carmen was still on the porch. She might as
well have been turned to stone, she was that transfixed by
what she saw. Her eyes were filled with a wondrous sort of
terror. Leo looked back at what she was gaping at and he
tried to see what Carmen saw, but there was only Paolo
Lombolo astride his dappled mare, riding out of the sun.
And as the mare galloped up the slope, Paolo's long black
hair rose and fell across his tan shoulders in thick waves. He
sat tall on the horse and they seemed to move with one
motion. The sun burned across his bare arms and everything about him was cast in bronze and slow motion. To
Leo it may have just been Paolo Lombolo coming by to say
hello, but he could see in Carmen's face that to her it was
lightning shooting out of the west and scorching her heart.

Paolo finally slowed the mare to a walk and gave Leo a warm wave. From the shade of the porch Carmen studied the high cheekbones of his tanned face and the way his teeth shone white and his dark eyes smiled. From the corner of his eye Leo saw the girl suddenly turn and dart back into the house.

'Hello, Paolo.'

'Hello, Signore Pizzola. That looks like hard work. It must not be as hot here as it is at our place.'

'It's got to be done.'

'Did that earthquake leave you with more than you bargained for?'

Leo felt a quick electric shock shoot up his spine and tingle the hair on the back of his neck as he automatically thought of the fresco and he snapped back guiltily, 'No! What? What do you mean?'

'Did the earthquake do a lot of damage in the house?'

Leo tried to cover his paranoia with an equally nervous chuckle. 'No. Just time for a little cleaning up.'

'It's looking good,' said Paolo, nodding his approval. But the boy had other business on his mind and didn't seem to notice Leo's anxiety.

'My father wanted me to ask you a big favor. This heat is hurting our orchards and so all of our water has to go to the fields. He wants to ask if we might bring the rest of our horses down here? Just for a little while?'

'How many horses is that?'

'It's another six. I know it's a lot to ask, but my father's sure that it would only be for maybe a week or so. He swears that there are clouds in the west and he says he feels a heaviness in the air, and that means a storm is coming.'

'Bring your horses tomorrow and leave them as long as you need. I've opened the well at the top of the fields, so there's plenty of water.'

'Thank you. I'll tell my father. And I'll tell him about the work you're . . . doing . . . on . . . the house . . .' Paolo's voice trailed off as his attention was captured by something beyond Leo's shoulder. Carmen crossed the porch with a glass of water in each hand.

Now, Leo had watched Carmen strut around Santo Fico for weeks and he had watched her flirt dozens of times, with old men, young men, even little boys; anything male – just for practice. She'd even turned her flashing eyes and coy smile on him once or twice. But this girl who crossed the porch with the two glasses of water, Leo didn't recognize her – with her eyes cast to the ground and her small, shy steps. And when she held the water out to Leo, he saw something else in her face that he'd never seen before. Carmen was nervous.

'It's so hot, I thought you might like some water,' she said sweetly.

Leo was startled again by her gentleness. He took one of the glasses to drink, but Carmen cleared her throat and twitched her head slightly, yet emphatically, toward Paolo. Leo understood – how could he be so rude to his guest?

'Ehh . . . Paolo, would you like a drink of water?'

Carmen held the water up to him and smiled and Paolo Lombolo almost melted out of his saddle. His face, which had first gone ashen when he watched her cross the porch, now became so flushed that Leo worried about the boy's blood pressure. By now Leo was looking for his cues, so when Carmen turned to him again with her brow furrowed and lips pursed, he was on top of it.

'Paolo, have you met Carmen Fortino?'

Carmen smiled modestly. Paolo grinned like a moron, but it was obvious from his feeble grunts that the young rider wanted to speak – unfortunately, the complexity of language had momentarily escaped him.

'Carmen's helping me clean up the house.'

Paolo drained the glass of water without ever taking his eyes off her.

He mumbled a 'Thank you,' and politely handed the glass back to her.

'You're welcome,' she whispered hoarsely, staring at the mare's uninterested face.

Having accomplished this exchange, they each tried to think of something else to say, and failed. Leo held out his empty glass to Carmen also, but she ignored him and instead hurried back across the porch and disappeared into the house.

'So Paolo, we'll see you tomorrow with the horses?'

'Ah . . . Yes, signore, tomorrow . . .' Paolo seemed to study the patio's tile pattern for a long time before he asked with a casual nonchalance, 'Will she be here?'

'Probably.'

'Ah . . . Oh . . . Well . . . Tomorrow.'

Paolo turned the dappled mare back toward the sea and

rode off to check on his horses, but looked back over his shoulder no fewer than three times, trying to catch a glimpse of the beautiful girl in the house. Once he was completely gone from view Carmen casually returned to the porch and called to Leo.

'Did you say he was coming back tomorrow?'

'Did I? I think maybe . . . Why?'

'No reason.'

She gave her head an indifferent toss and turned to go and it was a wonderfully haughty exit – except she missed the front door by a full meter and bounced her face off the plaster wall. But still, she recovered quickly and hurried back inside.

For Leo, everything fell into place in an instant. It was like inspiration.

Twenty

*T*he next morning when Carmen arrived for work, Leo noticed a few changes. Most obvious was that the previous day's ragged cut-off shorts and old tank top had been replaced with a light billowy skirt and airy summer blouse. The folded bandanna that had so efficiently held her hair in place the day before was missing and instead a bright crimson ribbon held back her freshly washed hair. Also missing was the meager cloth bundle used for yesterday's lunch. Today Carmen lugged a wicker basket that took both arms to carry and Leo's stomach growled its anticipation.

Within their first hour, Leo was glad he'd gotten a full day's work out of her the day before because today she couldn't seem to stop cleaning the northwest windows. He also got the impression from Carmen's occasional caustic comment about her mother that she and Marta had crossed swords that morning. He wasn't surprised. He could imagine Marta's reaction when Carmen came downstairs, prepared for another day of grimy house cleaning, dressed like she was going to a birthday party. Then there was that wicker basket that Leo prayed contained lunch. It had been unexpectedly generous of Marta to prepare enough food for both of them the previous day and Leo was curious as to what story Carmen might have told that prompted Marta to prepare that suitcaseful of food. If Marta had thought Leo was a pig before . . . Oh, well . . . If his plans worked out he wouldn't have to deal with either of them much longer.

Leo tried to spend his morning working outside, but the unexpectedly helpless Carmen continually found herself in need of guidance – so every few minutes she wandered outside with a new silly question. Finally he had to find chores for himself inside, just to keep the girl busy. But what was worse, as she became comfortable around him, her questions became more personal. She wanted to know about her father, she wanted to know about her mother, and she wanted to know about them together, she wanted to know all kinds of things that Leo either didn't know or didn't want to talk about. Something was bothering Carmen and now, whatever it was, was also beginning to bother Leo. He tried to answer her questions, but it seemed that no matter what he said, Carmen was determined to turn or twist it into a snipe at her mother. They were working together in the living room when Carmen finally asked the oddest question of all and for Leo it was the last straw.

'You knew my father. Tell me the truth, okay? Did he seem . . . kind of dumb to you?'

'What! Are you crazy? No, he wasn't dumb. He was smart. Why would you ask a crazy question like that?'

'He married my mother. How smart could he have been to have married my mother?'

'What the hell's wrong with you?' Leo exploded. 'Why would you say a smart-aleck thing like that? All day you've been at your mother. Knock it off, okay?'

'Okay. I thought at least you'd understand.'

'Understand what?'

'You know how she is. I see how mean she treats you.'

'How your mother treats me is none of your damn business. Maybe she has her reasons. What's she ever done to you – except watch out for you and worry about you and want what's best for you?'

'How would she know what's best for me. She's never been anywhere and she's never done anything. She spent her whole stupid life in this stupid little town and she acts like she knows everything. She knows nothing.'

Leo stood motionless for a moment, as if he were lost in some difficult decision – and when he finally did move across the room it was so sudden, Carmen thought for a moment he was going to strike her. She was already backing up when he put his index finger on her chest and pushed. Carmen fell into the chair that was waiting behind her.

'Stay there.'

On the far side of the living room was an old cedar trunk covered with a lace shawl that stored the most meaningful of the Pizzola family treasures. It didn't contain ancestral jewels, or ancient deeds, forgotten land grants, or valuable coins. This chest was reserved for much more important treasures, those that are irreplaceable and beyond value – the shawl his great-grandmother wore on her wedding day, yellowed family pictures that dated back to the invention of the camera, precious letters, delicate baby clothes. It was a hodgepodge of cherished mementos whose origins were dim – but Leo knew them all. He knelt before the trunk and carefully dug through his past. He lifted out a large Bible that was so old the leather was turning to dust and Leo noticed that his hands were shaking as he set it gently on the floor. He was especially careful not to disturb any of the paper-thin flowers that had been gathered by generations of his family and pressed between the dry pages. Then he carefully lifted out three old magazines.

'At one time I'll bet every house in Santo Fico had at least one of these and most had a couple,' he muttered softly, talking half to himself and half to Carmen. 'I think we have the full collection.'

He closed the lid and carefully set the magazines on top. Then, with a sigh, Leo sat on the floor, put his back against the trunk, and began his story.

'A long time ago, way before you were born, when your

mother was just about your age, a whole bunch of people from Milano came here, to Santo Fico. They were fashion people from some magazine and they were here to take pictures. They were here for a few days and they stayed at the hotel. There was a photographer and people who took care of the clothes they brought, all kinds of people; I never could figure out what they all did. And three tall, beautiful, skinny women to wear the clothes. They went all over the town taking pictures. The harbor, the cliffs, the beach, the hotel, the church – all over the place.

'The first day they were here the photographer was sitting in front of the hotel when your mother came back from the church. She must have taken Father Elio his lunch or something. Now, she usually went around the back way to the kitchen, but the fashion people were here and she was curious, so that day she walked right across the piazza and in the front door of the hotel. And all the time she's walking across the piazza, this photographer is sitting at a table on the verandah and looking at your mother through his camera. But he doesn't take any pictures. He just keeps looking at her through the camera. Then he gets up and follows her right inside, still just looking through the camera.

'This photographer guy wants to use your mother in some of the pictures. Well, your grandpa said no, but your grandma said yes – and when this photographer told your grandpa about how much money they would pay your mama, he said yes too. So they took pictures of your mother for that fashion magazine. And when it came time for them to go back to Milano, your mama went with them. Come here.'

Carmen joined him on the floor and they used the trunk as a table. The magazines were yellowed around the edges and had obviously been perused many times, but they had also been handled carefully and were smooth and unwrinkled. The fashion pictures on the covers looked funny and out of style to Carmen, but she knew the names of the magazines. Inside were pictures of her mother. She was young and beautiful and she looked like Carmen.

'You haven't seen these? You've never heard about this?'

Carmen just shook her head and reverently turned the pages.

'She was gone for almost three months. Then, all of a sudden, she came home. She said she didn't like Milano. But when that photographer called, your grandma asked this guy why Marta came home and he told her that your mama said there was someone in Santo Fico she loved and she couldn't stand being away from him. The photographer told your grandma that your mother could have made a lot of money in Milano, maybe even been famous – but your mama knew all that before she came home.'

'She came back here because she loved my father?'

Leo only shrugged. 'I have to go into town. I'll be back later. If Paolo Lombolo comes by, tell him I need to talk to him.'

He left Carmen alone with the pictures of the beautiful young girl who might have been famous, but loved someone too much, and he appreciated that she was careful to not let any tears spill on the pages.

Outside, Leo headed up the path toward town. He had a

great deal to do and not much time. The air was thick and
sticky. Clouds were building in the west. There was going to
be a storm all right. Even he could see it.

For all his unpleasant traits, there was one area where Solly
Puce could never be faulted – punctuality. Some residents of
Santo Fico checked their clocks when they heard the sound
of the Vespa chugging up the hill – not to see what time it
was, but rather to make sure they were running accurately.
Solly took his job of hauling mail up and down the goat
trails of this section of the Toscana coast seriously. The fact
that so many of the tiny villages had incredibly beautiful
girls who were isolated and lonely was simply one of the
job's perks. So it was no surprise to anyone when at precisely 11:40 A.M., the Vespa spewed its trail of blue smoke
across the piazza and pulled to a halt in front of the Palazzo
Urbano – as usual.

Solly dug through the worn leather saddlebags on the back
of the scooter and glanced around the piazza. Usually on a day
like today, what with the heat, this square would be empty –
except, of course, for that screwy old man by the fountain
with his dog. But today, like every other day since the resur-
rection of that ridiculous geyser, there must have been more
than a dozen people either coming or going or gossiping by the
edge of the fountain, or playing dominoes at the verandah
tables of the hotel. The whole character of the piazza was different, Solly thought, all because of some dumb spray of
water. He liked it better before – dead. But for all these people,
Solly still couldn't find the one face he was looking for. Maybe

Carmen didn't hear the scooter. Impossible!

He found Santo Fico's packet of letters, magazines, and flyers and was carrying it into the Ufficio Postale when he noticed a sinister-looking guy leaning against the corner of the palazzo. The shifty little man was sucking on a toothpick and openly staring at him. Solly was struck with the notion that this short fellow with the weak chin and close-set eyes looked dangerous. But then, Solly thought most men, and a fair percentage of women as well, looked dangerous. As he entered the palazzo, he tossed his imaginary hair, rolled his shoulder, and shook his body into place and then he felt better. Even though it had long since become second nature, Solly still sensed his gyration announced to the world that he was not a fellow you wanted to mess with.

But when he came back outside, there was that short guy with the toothpick standing right by the Vespa.

'Nice scooter,' Topo observed dangerously.

Solly grunted and quickly placed the meager outgoing mail packet in the saddlebag, but the mousy fellow crowded in on him and Solly felt his mouth going dry. Topo spoke in a secretive whisper, the bent toothpick still in his mouth.

'Are you Solly Puce?'

Solly heard himself grunt an acknowledgment.

'I have a message for you from Carmen Fortino. She wants you to meet her tonight.'

'She wants to meet me?'

'Yeah. You know Brusco Point, north of town by the old wall?'

Solly nodded.

'Meet her there tonight at ten o'clock – sharp. No earlier, no later. Ten sharp.'

'Why?'

'Why?' The toothpick jumped from one corner of his mouth to the other in amazement. 'I heard you were smart. Why do you think a hot number like Carmen Fortino would want to meet a young stud like you at Brusco Point, by the old wall, at ten o'clock?'

'I thought she was mad at me after the other night . . .'

'Yeah, sure, that's why she wanted me to give you this message – because she's mad. You probably think, when a girl says no, she means no. Hey, it's up to you. Be at Brusco Point tonight at ten and be ready to be a man or don't. I think maybe she's too much woman for you, but it doesn't matter to me. I'm just the messenger boy.'

Topo hitched his pants the way Cagney used to and sauntered across the piazza. Solly Puce climbed back on his motor scooter and kicked it to life. His mind whirled with Topo's words as he tore out of town – 'Brusco Point . . . Ten o'clock . . . Too much woman . . . !'

As Topo rounded the corner by the hotel he gave Leo, who had secretly watched the whole exchange, a wink and a solid thumbs-up.

It was already after lunch by the time Leo was able to head back down the coast road. He clipped along at a brisk pace because he wasn't sure what time Paolo was bringing the horses. If he brought them while Leo was gone and didn't come by the house, or if he did and Carmen didn't tell him to wait, then he might have already left. And if Leo missed talking to Paolo, then everything would be ruined. He needn't have hurried.

As he approached the house he saw the dappled mare tied up under a tree and Carmen and Paolo sitting on the porch. Leo watched them for a moment. They talked easily with each other and laughed a great deal. That was good, but Leo suddenly had a new, more immediate concern. He had eyed that picnic basket all morning. Now, even from a distance, he could see its contents spread out before Carmen and Paolo. 'Oh, my God,' he gasped. 'She's given him my lunch!'

By the time he arrived at the porch Paolo was on his feet and greeting his host with a stiff formality. Everything was 'Signore' this and 'Signore' that – all that formality only made Leo feel old, and besides, they had eaten his lunch! He cringed as he poked through the remains of their feast. There had been two kinds of pasta, some sort of marinated shrimp, a torta, salad, bread, fruit, cookies, wine – although Carmen did point out some bread, a small wedge of cheese, and an orange that Leo was welcome to. She spoke with girl-ish delight of Paolo's ravenous appetite and Paolo raved that Carmen was a wonderful cook.

'My mother helped a little,' Carmen confessed and her eyes begged Leo to please shut up, which, of course, he did. And at last it dawned on him: This lunch had not, even for an instant, been prepared with him in mind. He should be grate-ful he got an orange.

The three of them spent a few pleasant moments chat-ting on the porch, but it was obvious that Leo's arrival had seriously dampened any glow that was sparking. Still he wasn't about to leave – not right now. He had things to do. Soon it was time for Paolo to ride north and for Carmen to return to her housecleaning. Leo walked Paolo over to the mare as Carmen gathered things in the basket and went inside.

'Carmen said you wanted to ask me something.'

Ask him something? He vaguely recalled saying something like that to Carmen before he left, but only as a means of getting Paolo to stay until he got back from town. Ask him something . . .

'Uh, yes. How . . . many horses did you say you were bringing today?'

'Six.'

'Oh, six!'

'Is that still all right? Is six too many?'

'No, no, no. Six is fine. By the way, Paolo . . .'

Leo became secretive and leaned in and Paolo could see that it was important Carmen not overhear what was about to be said man-to-man, even though she was already inside the house.

'. . . Did Carmen say anything about meeting you tonight at ten o'clock at Brusco Point?'

'No,' Paolo whispered.

'You swear to me, you didn't agree to meet her tonight at Brusco Point at ten o'clock?'

'No, signore, I swear it.'

'Do you know where it is? I mean, do you know Brusco Point . . . behind the old—?'

'Yes, signore, behind the old wall. I know Brusco Point. Why do you ask?'

'Oh, I heard a rumor in town this morning that Carmen was going to meet some boy at Brusco Point tonight at ten o'clock. The rumor was that this boy said he was going to . . . Well, never mind. Santo Fico is a small, stupid town with hundreds of stupid rumors every day. You know how it is. Anyway, Carmen's a big girl. I'm sure she can take care of herself if some greasy boy tries to . . . Well, never mind. Too bad she never had a father or even a big brother to protect her . . . Oh well, never mind. Thanks for coming by.'

Leo took the stunned boy by the arm and guided him to his saddle. Paolo mounted his horse out of sheer instinct, since his mind was a chaos of horrible images.

'Signore Pizzola,' he stammered. 'If you think there might be some danger for Carmen . . .'

'Danger? No. The whole thing's just a rumor. Besides, if that girl is crazy enough to go out tonight – at ten o'clock – to meet some wild, greasy, sex-starved kid – at Brusco Point, behind that old wall – then she deserves whatever happens to her. Listen, Paolo, you tell your father you can keep your horses here as long as you need to. Good-bye.'

Leo stepped away from the horse and gave its rump a swat. Up at the house Carmen was at the door, offering Paolo her smile and a wave of farewell. Leo watched his face as he rode away and thought to himself, it probably would have been kinder to the boy if he had just driven red-hot pokers through his ears and straight into his brain.

Once Paolo had disappeared down over the slope toward

the sea, Leo raised his arm in the air and shook his fist at where Paolo had been. Then he turned and stomped across the porch toward the house. Carmen had been standing at a window watching Paolo as long as she could, but when she saw Leo's fury and the way he stormed toward the house, she ran back to her broom. Leo stood in the doorway and glared at her and his voice boomed off the walls and rattled what windows were left.

'What exactly did he say to you, young woman?'

Carmen was staggered by his rage. 'Nothing . . . What . . . About what?'

'Don't lie to me! What plans did you two make?'

'None. No plans. What are you talking about?'

'Why would he tell me to remind you about Brusco Point, behind that old wall, at ten o'clock tonight?'

'I don't know. I don't know anything about it.'

'Carmen Fortino, swear to me you don't have any notions about sneaking out tonight and meeting that boy at Brusco Point, behind the old wall at ten o'clock!'

Carmen shook her head in terror. 'I swear.'

'Well, then . . . Good! We'll just let him go to Brusco Point tonight at ten o'clock and he can spend the night there. That'll give him the message he needs and then you won't be bothered by him again.'

The fear of never seeing Paolo Lombolo again glazed her eyes and it was obvious that Leo's performance was effective. His fear was that he had been too effective. Maybe he'd frightened her so much she hadn't understood the information she needed. So, just to make sure, he mumbled to himself one more time as he walked out the door, 'Brusco Point . . . behind the old wall . . . ten o'clock sharp . . . Indeed!'

He thought it might look odd if he immediately had to make another trip into town, so Leo worked around the house for a while. This also gave him a chance to change moods for Carmen. Within an hour she was convinced that any concerns he might have had about her sneaking out to meet Paolo Lombolo were quite forgotten and soon the soft music of her humming again filled whatever room she was in. Leo was sure that her cheerful humor was in anticipation of this evening, but he didn't care. He liked having her in the house. He liked the soft, rustling sounds she made as she moved from room to room, leaving a wake of spotless order behind her. Leo had never given much thought to children. What was the point? But today he found himself thinking, for no particular reason, 'She might have been my daughter. She could have been. And Nina too.' What surprised him most about these occasional fantastical thoughts about fatherhood and Carmen and Nina and what might have been was that they didn't bother him. In fact, he enjoyed them. He also liked the way Carmen would occasionally return to the cedar trunk. When she thought he wasn't looking she would thumb through the magazines for a moment, pore over a new picture of her mother, and then return to work.

Finally, enough time passed and it was safe for him to suddenly discover that he'd forgotten to 'order new glass for the windows,' and reluctantly trudge back up the road toward town.

*

He had put off confronting Marta as long as possible. Up until this point, if any pieces of his scheme had fallen through, then there would have been no need to speak to Marta at all. But so far everything had gone surprisingly well and now it was time to face her.

Marta wasn't thrilled with his request, but Leo stayed quietly seated at the table while she paced around the kitchen firing off questions he wasn't willing to answer. Why was it so important that Carmen sneak out tonight? Where was she going? Who was she meeting? Was he going to be there? What time would she be back? Leo knew that if she forced him to answer any of these particulars the whole thing would, most likely, go up in smoke.

'You told me to do something,' Leo finally snapped at her. He hadn't intended to be that harsh, but her belligerence was getting on his nerves. 'I'm doing something. I didn't hear you say, 'Do something, but get my permission first.' If you want me to mind my own business, that's fine with me.'

Leo sat back and waited.

'Just tell me if you're going to be there. I have to know someone is watching out for Carmen.'

'I'll be watching out for her.'

'Okay,' Marta said with a sigh of finality. 'But I'm going with you.'

Now it was Marta's turn to sit stoically at the table while Leo paced the kitchen, vigorously listing all the reasons why she should stay out of it.

In the end, they compromised. Leo agreed to let Marta come along with him and Marta agreed that she would remain silent and not interfere with whatever he had in mind. They would meet on the north coast road, by the gate in the stone fence, no later than 9:30.

Leo was at the door when he remembered something important.

'Do you still have your father's pistol?'

'Yes.'

'Bring it. And some bullets.'

Twenty-One

*T*he whole day felt strange. The rising humidity added to a general feeling of uneasiness and all day people found themselves glancing at the sky, not really knowing what they expected to find there. All day, people were plagued with restless feelings that they should bring something inside, or close something, shut something, lock something. The wind began to rise in the afternoon and people nodded their heads as if to say, 'See, I told you.'

The only person who was apparently oblivious of the approaching storm was Carmen Fortino. When she left the Pizzola farm that afternoon she commented proudly that between his work outside and hers inside, the place was beginning to look presentable and Leo had to agree. In two days the house and grounds were indeed transformed, but the thing Leo found most altered was Carmen's disposition. She was almost cheery.

Back at the hotel, Marta noticed the difference right away. She was standing at the sink washing tomatoes when Carmen entered the kitchen and gave her a spirited hello, stole one of the large tomatoes, and sat on the kitchen table to eat it. Marta could see her daughter studying her out of the corner of her eye and it made her uncomfortable. When she looked at her, Carmen only smiled strangely and continued to stare. Finally, Marta asked with a nervous giggle, 'What are you looking at? Why are you looking at me like that?'

'I was just looking at that dress. I like the little strawflowers. They're a good color for you. But I don't think it shows off your figure.'

'My figure? What figure? Two babies took care of my figure a long time ago.'

Carmen's laugh was so joyful it made Marta smile in spite of herself. 'You do too have a figure.'

She leapt off the table and in an instant she was pulling the old print dress from the back. The material tightened and clung around Marta's front. 'You see? There it is! Ay-yi-yi, look at that figure!'

Marta squealed with embarrassment at Carmen's teasing, but it was true. She still had a good figure. She laughed and tried to wriggle free, but it was out of the question since her hands were full of wet tomatoes.

'What are you doing? Let go! My goodness, what's got into you? Did you and Leo Pizzola spend all day drinking?'

Carmen let go of the dress and turned her attention to her mother's hair. She gently pushed a loose lock off her forehead.

'Why don't you wear your hair down sometimes? I'll bet it would be so pretty if you wore it down.'

Then Carmen did the most wonderful thing. She put her arms around Marta, leaned over, and kissed her mother on the cheek. And in an instant, she was bounding across the kitchen and up the stairs, humming all the way.

Marta stood at the sink trying to catch her breath. She couldn't swallow. She was having trouble seeing to wash the tomatoes. It had been many years since she'd allowed anyone to put their arms around her like that. And longer since she'd been kissed, even on the cheek. She stepped back and dried her eyes on a towel and her mind fought to deny what she felt.

'Foolishness . . . My figure . . . What figure?' she grumbled. 'This color looks good on me . . . Wear my hair down . . . Just to fall in the food,' she muttered. 'Get in my eyes . . . Make my neck all hot and sticky . . . Ridiculous,' she mumbled.

The window over the sink was open and the frame turned into the room. Marta could see her faint reflection in the glass. She was probably Carmen's age when she last wore her hair down.

Leo stood on the north coast road by the opening in the stone fence mentally kicking himself. Why hadn't he just asked Marta to give him the pistol that afternoon? Then he wouldn't be standing around waiting for her now. He hadn't told her where they were going. He could just leave right now and she would have no way of following. He didn't have his watch, but he was sure she was late because it was getting so dark. After studying the western horizon for a moment he concluded that it probably wasn't as late as it appeared. Black clouds were blocking the sunset. Still, he should have gotten the pistol in the afternoon.

At last a woman came walking down the road and she was carrying a small bundle – something wrapped in a shawl, but for some reason he couldn't be sure it was Marta. Something was different. Not until she was standing in front of him could he tell exactly what it was. It was her hair. Her hair was down. It flowed in gentle billows across her shoulders and around her neck as the wind from the west continued to rise. Leo hadn't realized it was so long and he'd forgotten how thick it was and how it shined.

She didn't like the way he was looking at her hair. 'So,' she said abruptly, 'where do we go from here?'

Leo pointed down the road to the north. 'Brusco Point. You're wearing your hair down.'

'So?'

'Nothing.'

She turned and started down the road. Leo caught the scent of her bath soap. It was lavender, or lilac, or something like that.

'You smell good.'

Marta stopped and faced him. Fortunately for Leo, she honestly hadn't heard what he said.

'What?'

'Nothing.'

She decided to let it go and started down the road ahead of him again. Leo noticed her dress. He hadn't seen that dress before and he wondered what kind of material it was. The cloth looked thin and smooth, but the color was so rich. It was amazing the way it appeared to be so loose and free and yet, at the same time, it seemed to cling to certain curves as she moved. Remarkable cloth. He caught up with her and they walked a ways together in silence.

'That's a pretty dress.'

Marta seriously deliberated just what he might have meant by that before she formulated an appropriate response.

'Thank you.'

After a moment Leo added, 'That color looks good on you.'

Marta hefted the bundle wrapped in the shawl. 'I'm carrying a loaded gun.'

They walked on toward Brusco Point in silence.

Brusco Point was less than half a kilometer down the road. It was a narrow point of land with sweeping views on three sides and gentle sandy trails that led down to a wonderful white sand beach. Sometime, many centuries ago, the Romans – or maybe even the Etruscans – had it in mind to build something at Brusco Point. If a person was willing to dig through the brambles and vines and thorny tendrils of wild berries, low stone foundations and other relics could still be found. But all that was visible to the casual visitor was an ancient stone wall about as tall as a man. It ran for a hundred meters across the point and then disappeared. Who built the wall, or even why, was lost forever.

Leo and Marta left the road at a well-worn trail that cut across the dunes and through clumps of razor grass as it wound down toward the beach. It was a difficult walk in the dark, especially on this night, with the wind picking up and blowing sand. Fortunately, a half-moon was rising over the mountains in the east. Although they walked in silence, both Leo and Marta were surprised at how little Brusco Point had changed. Leo felt he could almost walk the trail blindfolded, even after all these years. And although neither said anything, both were seized with the feeling that it was only last month that they had hurried across these dunes together to swim in the warm sea.

As they labored down the sandy slope, the stone wall on their right seemed to grow more distant. But when they reached the place where the dunes leveled out, the trail cut sharply to the right and entered a grove of cedar trees and thick bushes, and there was the wall again. The thicket pushed right up against the old cut stones. Before them, a gentle drop took the trail down to a wide expanse of wet beach washed flat by the pounding surf. Beyond that the sea stretched out toward a dark-clouded horizon. The grove of cedar trees offered some shelter from the wind, but the storm was moving inland quickly and flashes of lightning sparked in the distant darkness.

They sat silently on the warm sand trying to ignore the catalogue of memories this place brought to them. Marta sat up stiffly when she heard Leo chuckling to himself in the dark. She was sure he was laughing at her. She knew she should have tied her hair up. Here she was a grown woman, wearing her hair like a young girl, and she felt foolish.

'What are you laughing at?' she wanted to know.

'I was just thinking about how Topo used to steal his father's cigarettes and we'd come down here and practice smoking.'

The half-moon rose like a crescent lantern above the tops of the wind-bent cedars and cast enough pale light across the sand to make Leo and Marta feel suddenly exposed. So they moved back into the bushes in front of the stone wall where they could observe the trail and the beach, and still remain hidden. Their new sanctuary was cramped and they were forced to stand with their backs pushed against the wall and each other, but Leo assured Marta they wouldn't have to wait long. He had again become uncomfortably aware of the sweet flower fragrance of Marta's bath soap and she tried to ignore where her bare arm pressed against his back. She could feel him breathing. They waited. After only a few uneasy moments she demanded, 'How long before something happens?'

Leo had become used to the edge in her voice and tried to ignore it. 'I don't know what time it is. Ten minutes maybe.'

Even in the shadows of the bushes Marta could see the dark outline of Leo's face. He was watching the trail that wound across dunes coming down from the road, but she could see nothing. Now the trees began to toss as the wind continued to rise and still Leo stared at the dunes, looking for something in the darkness, and Marta could feel her hair on her shoulders. She was glad that when he had laughed, it wasn't at her and she too remembered when they came here to smoke. She remembered when they came here to swim. She especially remembered the last time, when Leo had refused to swim with her.

Marta didn't know she was going to speak until the words were already coming out of her mouth, but standing together in the shadows she knew she must. Much more in her heart than her head, she knew that if she didn't ask him now, in this instant, then she would never ask – she would never know. Sometimes the moment is just there and it's best if we don't think too much. Sometimes we have to push fear and pride out of the way and just let things fall where they will, because possibility, like the future, can vanish in an instant – forever. Marta didn't think all of this, of course, but she knew this was such a moment and she felt she might never have the courage again – so she spoke.

'Could I ask you something?' she whispered.

'Sure.'

Leo was prepared for another question about Carmen or maybe his plan for the evening, but he wasn't prepared for what she asked.

'The night before my wedding, when you came to my window, and you told me that you loved me . . . and you begged me to not marry Franco, but to run away with you – did you already know about Franco's whore in Grosseto?'

Leo hoped he hadn't heard her correctly, but he was sure he had. Her words were soft, almost a whisper, but she'd spoken the words right into his ear. He had heard her. There was no anger and he was struck by how impersonal the question sounded. Why did she ask? What did she want? Why couldn't Carmen arrive early? He had no idea what to say. Since Sofia de Salvio died on the back of Franco's motorcycle, tearing across the countryside in the middle of the night, and Marta called her Franco's whore, he assumed Franco's secret was out.

'Did you know about her then?'

'Yes.'

'That night, Franco got in a fight in Grosseto. Was it with you?'

'Yes.'

'Why?'

'We just fought sometimes.'

'Is that why you said all those things to me? Because you felt sorry for me?'

There was something wrong with her voice. She was asking him terrible questions, but she didn't sound angry or hurt or accusing. Her voice was soft and close to his ear. He wanted to see her face, but he couldn't turn. She was behind his shoulder, pressed too close in the darkness for him to see her eyes.

'Tell me. Was it because you felt sorry for me?'

Of course he had felt sorry for her. He had felt sorry for her since he was fourteen and Franco saw the way Leo looked at Marta. From the moment Leo had told Franco how he felt about Marta, he was sorry. Franco was his best friend and best friends tell each other things. But Leo didn't really know Franco – maybe no one did. Leo had no way of knowing that by telling Franco of his feelings for Marta, he would only stir something in Franco – not love, but greed. Franco was selfish. If Leo wanted Marta, then Franco wanted her too. And on that day began a competition that Leo would never understand, but it ended a friendship that had meant the world to him and also cost him the first and best love he would ever know.

For Franco, it was just another competition, but instead of a foot race, or swimming, or wrestling, the prize was a person. Leo knew he didn't stand a chance against the handsome, funny, charming Franco. But that night in Grosseto, the night before their wedding, Leo glimpsed the monster Franco would become. And he also saw Marta's future.

He and Topo had begged Franco to not go to Grosseto. But it was his party and so they sat at that table at Il Cavallo Morto, watching Franco drink and tease the inconsolable Sofia de Salvio. Everyone knew Franco preferred Sofia to Marta because she got drunk with him, and smoked, and laughed at his dirty jokes. But not that night, the night before his wedding. That night she sat on his lap and cried miserably and begged him to stay with her. Franco thought Leo was asleep with his head on the table when he whispered to Sofia that he would never leave her, but tomorrow he was going to 'marry the finest hotel, restaurant, and bar on the Toscana coast.' And then they both laughed at the big joke Franco was playing on Marta.

That was when Leo leapt across the table and tried to kill Franco.

It was as if, for the first time, he saw all the conceit and meanness that had always been in Franco, but hidden, or maybe just ignored. And in that instant, when he finally did recognize Franco, he also saw all the grief that would be Marta's future. My God, anyone would have felt sorry for her. But later that night, when he stood in her dark bedroom and finally spoke his heart, it had nothing to do with his rage at Franco or feeling sorry for Marta or even being drunk. He was sober. He just had to either confess what he felt or explode. Did he feel sorry for her? What could he say?

'Marta, this was years ago. What is it you want?'

'I want someone to finally be honest with me. I've spent so long with people lying to me, trying to protect me, and keeping secrets from me. My life hasn't . . . It wasn't good. I think maybe, it's time to let go of some of it. I just want someone to be honest with me. Did you say those things because you felt sorry for me?'

'No.'

Marta was quiet for a long time. Leo wished he had lied. He wished he had said, 'Yes, I said those things because Franco didn't love you. In the beginning he just wanted to beat me. In the end he just wanted the hotel. Yes, I felt sorry for you!' Leo wished he'd said that, but he hadn't. Instead he'd said, 'No.' And that meant that everything he swore to her in the dark had been true. Marta knew at last, and for sure, that Leo had loved her.

'Why did you wait until it was too late to tell me those things?'

'Because you loved Franco.'

Neither spoke for a long time. They stood in the darkness, so close they could feel the other breathing, and they waited for Carmen to arrive. The storm wind off the ocean was warm and strong. It blew the cedar trees and tossed leaves around them. The smell of rain was thick on the air. When Marta spoke again, her voice sounded distant to Leo, as if she'd gone somewhere far away.

'I remember coming here to swim. Do you?'

'Yes.'

'I remember one day we were supposed to go swimming down here, except something had happened. I didn't know what it was, but I felt it – it was between you and Franco. It was something bad. You said you couldn't go swimming. You had to go home. You had to work in the olive grove . . . and you were so angry. Do you remember?'

Leo remembered. He remembered the terrible, ugly stories Franco had told him that day about what he and Marta had done. He remembered his tears as Franco described Marta in his arms, kissing her and touching her. He remembered the shove, then the fists, the fight, and the names. He realized years later that Franco had lied about the whole thing, but the damage was done. In Leo's mind Marta belonged to Franco. Franco had won, and he had lost.

'I remember.'

'Everything was different after that day.'

'I know.'

'I wish we had gone swimming.'

'You were with Franco.'

'You were an idiot.'

Marta could feel Leo's breathing suddenly stop. His body tensed and he pressed back against the wall. She looked out into the darkness to where Leo was watching and saw a figure hurrying across the dunes toward the beach. It had to be Carmen. Leo whispered, 'It must be ten o'clock.'

After having waited in the thicket for so long, Marta was startled at how quickly the scene unfolded. As Carmen ran down the trail across the dunes, Marta became aware of the familiar and unpleasant putt-putt of a motor scooter out on the road. She could see the dim light of Solly Puce's Vespa stop and blink out as he parked at the top of the trail. Marta gave Leo's back a serious punch.

'Solly Puce? What's Solly Puce doing here!'

Leo gripped her shoulders tightly. 'The only reason you're here is because you promised to be quiet. Now shut up!'

Carmen ran down the trail and looked out toward the beach as the wind blew a light rain around her. Black clouds were now rolling in so quickly that the moonlight was having difficulty dodging them. It was as if this storm, which had been so patient and concealed beyond the horizon, was suddenly eager to crash upon the shore.

Carmen moved back from the beach to find shelter in the grove of cedars just as Solly Puce came bounding down the trail from the dunes. Carmen saw him at once, and although from where they were hiding Leo and Marta couldn't hear what was being said, it was clear that Carmen wasn't pleased to see Solly. It was also evident that Solly had taken Topo's advice to heart and he was there to prove to Carmen that he was a man to be reckoned with. The conversation didn't last long. Carmen ordered Solly away and Solly said something to Carmen that got his face slapped. The rain began to fall in earnest and the wind howled through the trees and their voices were only faint shouts as the words all blew away. Solly grabbed at Carmen. From the bushes it appeared to Marta that he tore her blouse. Carmen struck at him again, but he blocked her blow this time and they heard her cry out as he slapped her.

Marta wanted to run across the grove and join the fray — she and Carmen would show Solly Puce how it was done — but when she pushed forward Leo's arm shot across her body as a barricade. She wanted to shout at Leo to do something, to stop this, but he wasn't even watching. His eyes were focused up the beach to the north.

'Give me the pistol,' was all he said.

Her hands were trembling terribly as she unwrapped the shawl and placed the old revolver in Leo's hand. She was terrified that he was going to shoot Solly Puce, and she was terrified he wasn't. She prayed the old bullets would fire. At that moment, Carmen tried to run back toward the beach, but Solly caught her from behind. She kicked at him and they both fell to the sand.

Marta could hear Leo whispering something urgently to himself, but his eyes were still focused on the northern beach. Marta had had enough. She pushed Leo out of the way and started down toward the beach; this time he grabbed her, pulled her back, and clamped his hand over her mouth. Leo was prepared for whatever might happen. If Paolo Lombolo failed to appear Leo would have to either beat Solly Puce senseless or shoot the little bastard and bury his body in the dunes. At this point, he didn't care which. But Marta was right, the assault couldn't continue.

On the beach, Carmen's shouts were swallowed by the wind and the roar of the waves as Solly pushed her back on the sand. Leo had just decided he had waited as long as possible, when suddenly, and for no apparent reason, Solly stopped his attack. Then he stood up. Then he began backing away. From where she lay in the sand Carmen shouted something.

Marta's eyes grew wide as a great pale horse stormed over the edge of the beach and reared up. Leo thought it was wonderful that the lightning chose that moment to streak across the sky over their heads. Its thunder cracked the sky open and rain fell in torrents as the horseman moved steadily in on the retreating Solly until they reached the grove of cedars. Then the dark rider slipped his leg over the horse's neck, and without taking his eyes off the frightened postman, he slid from the mare's bare back to the ground. Leo was impressed with Paolo's coolness as he calmly took the time to tie the reins to a branch.

To his credit, Solly Puce stood his ground and even shouted a number of indistinguishable curses at the intruder. He was in the middle of performing one of his intimidating gyrations, when a fist shot out of the darkness and rechoreographed the routine. Instead of rolling his shoulder, Solly's head snapped back. Before he had a chance to recover or respond the fist was in his face again and bouncing painfully off his newly crushed nose. No one ever said Solly Puce was totally stupid and before the fist could flash out of the darkness a third time, Solly was on the trail across the dunes and headed at top speed for his trusty Vespa.

Leo finally relaxed his grip on Marta's mouth and she was able to whisper, 'Who is that?'

'Paolo Lombolo.'

'Ohh . . . My goodness, he's all grown up.'

Paolo went back to where Carmen lay sobbing in the wet sand. He picked her up and carried her back to the cedar grove.

It was hard to see them through the black rain, but Leo was sure they were near. Marta heard the pistol cock. My God, she thought, he's going to shoot them! Leo pulled Marta away from the wall, aimed the gun at the ground and fired twice.

Solly was halfway across the dunes when he heard the two gunshots. Positive that they came from the unknown horseman and were meant for the back of his head, he ran in blind panic back to his Vespa and tore off down the road.

Back at the beach, when Carmen heard the gunshots she gripped Paolo by the shirt and shouted, 'My God, he's got a gun!' She pulled Paolo across the grove and together they dove into the bushes at the base of the stone wall.

Leo and Marta barely saw them coming. They squeezed together against the wall as Carmen and Paolo took shelter in their bushes, less than a meter away.

Then the heart of the summer storm broke over their heads and Paolo put his arms around Carmen to shield her from the wind and rain and to comfort her fear. But in truth, the storm didn't frighten either of them – they had both been struck by lightning the day before. And fortunately, they never turned their faces away from each other, so they didn't see the two stonelike figures pressed against the wall behind them, their bodies squashed together, facing each other, afraid to move or even breathe. Leo looked over Marta's head or at the sky – anywhere but into her face. He had complete confidence that when they could move again, she was going to slap him hard or maybe punch him again. But when lightning flashed a brief white flare, he saw her dark eyes quietly watching him. When it was gone and they were surrounded by darkness again, he felt the side of her head touch his chest. He could smell her hair and he could feel her breathing.

The summer storm passed swifter than it arrived. The moon returned as the black clouds raced on toward the mountains in the southeast.

Paolo helped Carmen up, untied the mare, and swung easily up onto her back. Then in one smooth motion he lifted Carmen up in front of him. They rode up the trail across the dunes and at the road they turned south. From there they would let the horse slowly walk all the way to the front door of the hotel.

Leo and Marta decided it would be best if they took the route along the beach rather than risk being seen by Paolo and Carmen. So they followed the glistening sand and white surf until they reached the cliffs. There they took a familiar trail that led up through the boulders to the plateau that was the beginning of the Pizzola farm.

The moon was still bright as they crossed the fields and the roar of the breakers faded to a murmur behind them and Marta saw something at the top of the meadow that she hadn't seen in many years. A light was shining in a window of the Pizzola house. Leo was staying in the house. That was good. He should.

When they reached the dirt road that went up to the opening in the stone fence, Leo asked Marta if he should walk with her back to the hotel, but she told him that it wasn't necessary and they said good night. Before she left, Marta turned to him and said, 'Thank you for what you did for Carmen.' And then she took his face in her hands and she kissed him and it was more than a simple thank-you.

As he stood in the road watching Marta's form growing fainter in the moonlight, her voice called to him from the distance.

'It was never Franco.' Then she was gone.

That night Leo sat on the porch of his father's house for a long time before going inside. She had said, 'It was never Franco' – and he thought of those words, and about their years of growing up together. It was as if hundreds of tiny fragments of his life that had always been floating just in front of his eyes finally all converged and came together. He remembered all the mysterious looks that she had offered, but he thought he'd imagined . . . He remembered years of smiles that were meant for him, but he hadn't understood . . .

He remembered how she touched his hand or called his name or watched him play when she thought he didn't know . . . And he remembered his jealousy when she returned from Milano because of the boy that she didn't want to lose. It had been him. He was the boy. She *had* said he was an idiot.

At last he went upstairs and for the first time in many years he slept in his own bed in his own room. But that night Leo didn't dream about frescoes or Chicago or baseball or nameless women. That night he dreamt of when he was a boy, and he helped his father harvest the grapes.

Twenty-Two

*T*he next morning Father Elio awoke much later than usual and he discovered that he couldn't get out of bed. His legs didn't seem to want to work. During the night, a loud summer squall had wakened him and the flashes of lightning and rumbling thunder had left him unable to go back to sleep. He got up to see what damage the storm might have done to the church, what with that gaping hole in the roof.

What he found, to his delight, was that the storm had washed away much of the dust and dirt that his broom had been unable to capture. He wasn't sure what it would look like in the morning sunlight, but at that moment it was so clean it almost sparkled.

Then, since he was already awake, he turned out the lights in the church and went out to the garden. He sat on the stone ledge that surrounded the Miracle and leaned his back against the thin trunk of the old fig tree. This was his favorite place to pray, but he had become a bit nervous about sitting there ever since the earthquake collapsed part of the stone wall. It would be awful if someone happened by, saw him leaning against the fig tree, and thought he was pretending to be Saint Francis. Of course, he wasn't. He just loved leaning against the old tree, knowing that the blessed saint had done the same thing. That night after the storm he lost track of how long he sat and prayed. When he finally rose to return to bed, the joints in his legs were painful and his whole body felt chilled from the dampness.

It was only the most dedicated few who came to early mass, even on Sunday, and it was they who first began to worry about Father Elio. He was never late for mass and for him to miss a mass was unthinkable – especially a Sunday mass. But no one, not even Maria Gamboni, had the courage to go back to Father Elio's quarters to check on him. They were much less concerned for his privacy than they were fearful of what they might find. Angelica Giancarlo was the most disappointed of all. Not only was it a brand-new Sunday morning for her, but this was to be her first mass in many years. She was the one who finally made the trek across the piazza to the hotel and politely, almost shyly, told Marta her concerns.

Nina was the first to arrive. When she heard Angelica telling her mother that Father Elio wasn't at mass, Nina bolted from the kitchen and Marta had trouble catching her. Father Elio tried to pass the whole thing off as a slight chill, but his sallow color and sunken eyes frightened Marta. She left Nina sitting at his bedside holding his hand while she went to his kitchen and prepared a bowl of boiled oatmeal with a bit of milk and honey. When she brought it to him he tried to remind her of his fast, but Marta scolded him so harshly that she shocked both Elio and Nina. The old man finally allowed her to feed him a bit of the boiled oatmeal and almost at once he began commenting on how good it tasted. Marta made sure he ate the whole thing and when he was done Uncle Elio announced that he would like to take a nap – but for her to be sure to tell those he had disappointed that morning that he would be there for the evening mass. Then he closed his eyes. Nina held his hand until she was sure he was asleep.

How people might know these things is a mystery, but there is always a difference between a rumor and a surety. That Father Elio was ill was a surety. Who started spreading the word of his condition and his promise for an evening mass was unknown. It was probably either Maria Gamboni or the Saraceno sisters – it may have been both. Who it was didn't matter. The important thing was that by mid-morning word of Father Elio's condition had spread from door to door, leapt across streets from window to window, and scampered around corners until, at last, all of Santo Fico was buzzing.

By midday it was almost impossible to make a phone call into Santo Fico. The lines were all busy. As all this was going on, Father Elio slept for the rest of the day, the thick stone walls protecting him from the commotion going on outside.

By the afternoon, what began as a trickle had become a steady stream of cars and trucks bumping across the dry plains in the south and up the tortuous little road toward Santo Fico's piazza. Leo was on his way to the olive grove when he noticed the unusual cloud of dust hovering over the north coast road. It was only when he walked up to the opening in the stone fence that he discovered the line of slow-moving traffic working its way past his gate and up the hill. So he followed the parade into town.

It was at about this time that the first fishing trawlers started appearing on the northern and southern horizons. They all patiently and courteously waited their turn to enter the narrow jetty, but soon all the berths at the pier were filled. As more boats arrived, they dropped anchor in the little harbor and the occupants caught skiffs to the shore. By evening there was barely room to sit down in Santo Fico.

Father Elio was weak, but as the hour for evening mass approached he insisted that Nina help him from his bed. He'd promised an evening mass and he wouldn't disappoint them again. When he'd heard that Angelica Giancarlo was among those who had attended in the morning, his heart leapt for her. He would not fail her again.

For some odd reason, his kitchen seemed to be a hotbed of activity. Marta, Carmen, and Nina were there and although he was used to them being in his kitchen, it was rare to have them all there at the same time. On his pine table was a familiar tray with a large bowl of thick vegetable soup, fresh bread, and a glass of red wine. The smell of the broth was marvelous and he allowed himself to be bullied into eating again. And Leo kept turning up for some strange reason. Elio noticed that Marta's anger toward Leo seemed to have evaporated and was now being replaced by something else – but he tried not to show that he noticed. Then there was Carmen, whose attitude toward her mother also seemed to have experienced a drastic change. Carmen hung on her mother's every word and couldn't stop touching her. Then there was Topo, who never came near the church unless he wanted to borrow some electricity for his moving pictures. But today he apparently had a number of questions for Leo, so both men were popping in and out unexpectedly all afternoon.

Father Elio found the activity of his suddenly bustling little kitchen exciting, but confusing. He sat at the table nibbling the bread and picking at the soup, most of the time handicapped by the use of only one hand because Nina seemed unwilling to release the other one. So the two of them sat together like the calm eye of a quiet hurricane that swirled around them. Finally, he told them they had to leave. He'd eaten enough and he had to prepare for mass.

It was then that Father Elio made an odd request. He asked Leo to stay. He explained to Leo that he was still feeling a bit shaky and chilled. 'Besides,' he said, 'you were the best altar boy I ever had.'

Nina asked if she could stay also and he agreed, so the three of them went to the vestry where Elio discovered his vestments had already been laid out. Someone had cleaned and pressed them and Leo held the garments for the old priest as he had done when he was a boy. Neither of them spoke and both were pleased with how smoothly the ritual was performed. Then Nina helped her uncle down the few meters of stone corridor and a curious glow from within the church pulled the old priest forward.

When Father Elio stepped out of the corridor and stood in the doorway of the church his knees almost buckled beneath him. The odd glow he had seen came from hundreds of candles that filled the great room. There were candles in the candle stands that hung from the walls and piers. They gleamed from the great chandelier above the altar that had not been lit in decades. The candles in the great brass candelabrum that surrounded the altar glowed so brightly they almost hurt his eyes.

And everywhere were faces – hundreds and hundreds of faces. There were people everywhere – more people than lived in Santo Fico. People took up all the room on all the benches. People stood in the side aisles. People stood at the back. People stood in the choir. Everywhere he looked, there were silent smiling faces. And Father Elio knew all those smiling faces too, though most he had not seen for many years. Hundreds of faces that once lived in Santo Fico and then spread throughout the whole region. There were old and wrinkled faces that he recognized as companions of his youth. There were the middle-aged faces of those that he had married. There were the younger faces of those that he had christened. Everywhere were the faces of his family and neighbors – the faces of his life. There was Maria Gamboni sitting beside her retrieved love Enrico, the jolly plumber. There was Topo sitting beside Angelica Giancarlo, although her hair looked different. It was soft now, and sitting beside her was her mother. Father Elio hadn't seen Signora Giancarlo in church for many years. In a back corner was Nonno and beside him was the gray dog. Saint Francis would have liked having the dog in his church, thought Elio. And there was Angelo de Parma and his wife and his grand-children. Smiling in the front row was Carmen and there was a handsome young man beside her, holding her hand. And then there was Marta sitting in the front row and she was smiling too. Tears came to his eyes when he saw Marta's smile. Everyone was beaming and the room was so silent you could hear the candles burn.

Leo helped Father Elio up the stairs of the altar and then he took Nina to the front row. From where Father Elio stood at the altar he could see into the northern transept. The two display lights shone on a large sheet of plywood that leaned against the back wall and the broken pieces of the fresco covered the plywood like a giant jigsaw puzzle. From where he stood at the altar, and with the angle of the plywood, the benign face of Saint Francis seemed to be looking Elio right in the eyes and from that angle he also appeared to be smiling.

It had been Topo who had approached Leo earlier in the day and confessed that he no longer wanted his share of the fresco. He told Leo that he would help him with the miracles because he had said that he would – but Leo could have all the fresco money. Topo would be staying in Santo Fico a while longer. It seems that Angelica Giancarlo had asked him to come to her house for dinner next Friday. She wanted Guido to meet her mother. And they had even spoken of going into Follonica sometime to see a movie. She liked him.

'So, you can see,' Topo declared, 'it's impossible for me to make any plans on leaving Santo Fico right now – or maybe even anytime soon.'

The way Leo nodded his head slowly, weighing this bold pronouncement, made his little friend nervous.

'Well, I see,' said Leo. His voice was low and even. 'But, since you say you're willing to help me, then we still have one more job to do.'

It took them much of the afternoon to put all the pieces back in the small room where the painting had always belonged. Now the painting shone like a new jewel and few even knew of its short holiday. Leo stood in his place at the altar, behind Father Elio, and remained quiet and attentive, like the best altar boy in Santo Fico – while Father Elio performed the greatest mass of his life.

For those in the cathedral that night, it was like being one word in a great poem that had no end or a single note of music in an extraordinary chorale that rolled on forever. They were all part of a ritual and the ritual was sacred and it was timeless – and still Father Elio seemed to dedicate each word to each person, individually. He spoke of forgiveness. He spoke with simple words of everyone's need to accept what comes to them without recrimination or bitterness. Leo had to smile when the old man said softly, 'We should face our struggles with the courage of a butterfly.' Father Elio knew that for this particular mass, on this particular evening there was a spirit alive in his church that had not visited there for many years and he was filled with joy.

There were only two moments that were difficult for him. The Eucharist was exhausting. He had never performed the ceremony for so many people. Leo stayed at his side, supporting him and bringing more elements. Nina tried waiting with her mother, but she became concerned for her uncle. She sensed that the ceremony was taking too long and insisted that Uncle Elio wasn't strong enough. Finally she became so fretful that Marta had to take the girl to Father Elio's side where she gripped his arm and refused to leave him for the rest of the mass. Finally, Leo whispered to him that they had run out of Host and Father Elio sadly informed those that had yet to participate that they didn't have enough elements. But no one seemed to mind.

The other moment that was difficult for Elio was the plea of, 'Mea Culpa, Mea Culpa, Mea Maxima Culpa.' Everyone heard his hoarse voice crack when he implored God to forgive him, but none understood why this plea seemed to be wracked from the depth of his soul.

At last it was done.

His parishioners wiped their eyes and sat in silence. Nobody moved. The mass was over, but everyone felt there was more that must be expressed; only no one knew how to say what was in all their hearts. It was Angelica Giancarlo, with her background as an actress, who understood instinctively how to handle an awkward moment of such rich drama. She stood and applauded. At first most were shocked, but within seconds others understood the appropriateness of the gesture and they too rose to their feet. Many actually cheered.

Father Elio stood at the foot of the altar and raised his hand and waved to them and his lips moved silently. He wanted to say something, but instead he just sank to his knees and then fell to the ground. He lay on the cold stone floor with Nina still at his side, still clutching his hand.

It was Father Elio who begged not to be moved. For some reason it was important to him that he stay where he had collapsed, there at the foot of the altar. Topo brought pillows and a blanket from Father Elio's bedroom and they made him comfortable there on the stone floor. His congregation filed quietly, respectfully, past him – some wanted to touch his hand or whisper something special, but most were content with a simple wave good-bye. And soon they were alone. Marta and the girls and Leo and Topo sat with him throughout the night. They talked and laughed about many things while the candles burned down. Mostly, Elio reminisced. He spoke of people and events that they hadn't heard of and some they had. And so they whiled away the night with stories.

It was near dawn when Elio asked if he could be alone with Leo. There were a few protests about leaving him, but the old man was insistent and finally even Nina released his hand and allowed herself to be led away.

Leo sat beside the old man, wondering if the priest was finally going to chastise him about the fresco. But Father Elio had other things on his mind.

'You know, Leo, there are some things you should understand about your father. He forgave you for running away many years ago. He asked me to tell you that, when I thought you would be ready to hear it. I don't know if you're ready to hear it, but I'm running out of time when I'll be able to tell you.'

'You don't know what I did. When I ran away, I said terrible things just to hurt him. I deserted him.'

'I know. He forgave you.'

'I stole my mother's ring from him. I sold it and used the money to go to Milano.'

'I know. He told me. I remember when your Aunt Sofia found out that you had taken the ring. She said to him, *You should call the police. He stole from you. Your son's a thief.* I was there. I remember him looking at her and saying, *How can someone steal something that already belongs to him. That ring was always his. My son is young and he's foolish! My son is not a thief!* He forgave you years ago.'

'Did he also tell you that I struck him? That I knocked him to the ground? My God, I struck him in the face . . .'

'No. He didn't tell me that. But now I understand why he said that his worry was that you would not be able to forgive yourself. He forgave you everything. Let it go.'

'I *am* a thief, Father. I stole the fresco.'

'I know. And you brought it back. I never did understand why you took it.'

'Money. I wanted to sell it for a lot of money, so I could

run away again. I found out, many years ago that our fresco could be worth a fortune. It was painted by a famous artist.'

'Oh, yes, Giotto di Bondone.'

'You knew? All these years you knew? And you said nothing?'

'Leo, what kind of an idiot are you?'

Leo sighed. Maybe it was time he started considering everyone's assessment of his intellect. 'Apparently a big one. Why?'

'I can't believe that you told the story of the Miracle and the Mystery as many times as you did and you never figured it out. Leo, Giotto di Bondone died over two hundred years before this church was built and our fresco was painted.'

'Then . . . Then who did paint it?'

'Who knows.'

Father Elio reached up and rapped on Leo's forehead as if he were knocking on a door. 'Why do you think we call it the Mystery?' Considering the old priest's weakened condition, Leo was startled by how much his bony knuckles hurt – but he got the point. Elio smiled. 'Sometimes we have to just accept something as a mystery. Now Leo, I want to ask a big favor of you.'

'Anything.'

'I'm dying.'

The statement was so commonplace that Leo almost missed it and by the time he was coming back with his objections, Father Elio was already waving him off.

'Don't argue with a dying man. I'm dying and there isn't a priest . . . so, I want you to hear my confession.'

'Ohh . . . No, please, Father. We can get a priest. We can call Follonica, maybe Punta Ala. A priest could be here in no time.'

'I don't want to confess to a priest. I can't confess to a priest,' Elio declared harshly. He smiled at Leo, 'You were the best altar boy I ever had. I want you to hear my confession. Please.'

'What do I do?'

'Nothing. Just listen to me.' The old man's pale blue eyes flooded with tears even before he began to speak. His voice was a wrenching sob.

'I'm not a priest.'

Leo could tell that he mustn't speak. He must sit quietly and listen. Elio recovered his breathing and bit back his tears.

'I'm not a priest. I've never been a priest. When I went to the university in Bologna, I wasn't a good student. I tried. I really tried, but there was so much I didn't understand. Mathematics and science and history . . . mostly mathematics. At the end of my first year, they told me I wouldn't be coming back. Without the university, I wouldn't become a priest. They said I could try and take the test again in three years. The good cardinal at the university liked me and he got me a job.'

Elio chuckled ruefully to himself. 'He got me a job in a mortuary. I became an undertaker's assistant. For the next two years my job was to dress and prepare dead bodies for the coffin. I thought it was fitting work for me . . . dressing the dead. All I ever wanted in my life was to be a priest and come back to Santo Fico and live in this church. I may as well have been dead.

'One day an old priest died and they brought him to me. I wasn't even supposed to be working that day. But I was. Someone was supposed to bring by a nice suit for the priest to be buried in. But instead, someone brought two big suitcases. I never saw who left them. They just appeared. They were like trunks. They were filled with everything the old priest ever owned. All of his suits, and his robes, and his vestments . . . everything.

'I set the suitcases aside because someday soon, someone would come back for them. And after a few days, I moved them closer to the door. Then I moved them to the other room. Then, I took them home. The old priest and I were the same size . . . exactly the same size.

'At the end of the year, I did a terrible thing. I took those suitcases and I came home – back to Santo Fico. Then my lie began. I told everyone that I had been ordained. I wore the old priest's clothes. I was accepted. I thought if I was a good priest, my lies wouldn't matter. Now, I'm dying and I know they matter.'

Elio was done. He had confessed.

Leo cleared his throat, 'What do I do now?'

Elio smiled wearily. 'Tell me you absolve me of my sins.'

'I do. I do that. I absolve you of your sins.'

Elio patted Leo's hand. 'I wish it were that easy.'

There was a rapping at the side door and Topo's head poked into the room. His eyes were wide and he was actually trembling as he whispered, 'Excuse me, Father, but there's something out here you must see. It's the Miracle, Father, the tree . . . You need to see it. It's . . . amazing!'

Leo wanted to tell his friend to close the door and go away, but Elio calmed him. 'It's all right, Leo. Actually I would like to go out and sit beside the Miracle.'

So Leo put his arms beneath Father Elio and lifted him as he would a child. He was so light, the old man was. There was almost nothing to him. Leo carried him out the side door of the cathedral and into the garden.

Stepping outside, he found that besides Topo, Marta, Carmen, and Nina were also waiting there. Topo pointed in wonder at the withered fig. Silhouetted against a sky that showed the first, faint trace of an eastern glow, the smooth black trunk of the fig tree shimmered. Above it, from the two cracked and jagged stems, six leaves swayed gently in the morning breeze and below the leaves hung one full, ripe fig.

Leo carried Father Elio to the stone ledge beside the withered tree. Topo's voice was a hushed whisper. 'It's a miracle . . .'

Elio was also amazed and agreed with Topo's judgment, 'It is a miracle indeed,' said the old man as he reached up and brushed one of the green leaves with the back of his hand. 'It's a miracle that after all these years this tree would blossom again . . . with oak leaves.'

Leo looked closer at the Miracle. Apparently Topo had been unable to find the leaves of a fig tree on such short notice.

Father Elio gently gripped the ripe fig that hung over his head and tugged. Those standing near enough heard the frail thread that was holding it snap. The old man held the plump fig up and examined the thread that was dangling from the stem. 'And fruit too. Although after so many years it appears to be a bit stringy.' Elio smiled at Topo, who could only shrug, and Leo wanted to either throttle or hug his friend for his feeble, loving gesture.

Nina sat on the stone ledge next to her uncle. She took his hand and nestled her head against his chest as she had done so many times before and said softly, 'Topo just wanted you to have a miracle.' Then she leaned into him and whispered something else. But Elio didn't quite hear her words.

'What did you say?' he asked.

'I'm sorry you didn't get your miracle,' she repeated softly in his ear.

Her tender words hung in the air for a moment before they entered Elio's heart like a warm wind. The simplicity and innocence of her words swirled around his head. 'I'm sorry you didn't get your miracle.' The melody of her voice, the inflection, the innocent tone, her heartfelt love swept over him like a wave from the sea. 'I'm sorry you didn't get your miracle.' The beautiful honesty of Nina's love was like a key that he had been waiting for all his life. It was as if there had been bolts and shackles on his heart and Nina's words were a golden key that slid into an ancient lock and opened it. His life unfolded before him like a tapestry unrolling at his feet and for the first time he was able to step back away from the individual threads and he saw that the miracle that had been his life was depicted there. His life stretched out before him and for the first time he realized that it had all been a miracle – everything – every day –

every accident – every coincidence – every disappointment – every joy – all of it. If he had passed mathematics at
the university, he would have become a priest. If he had
become a priest, he never would have been assigned the
little, forgotten church at Santo Fico. It was a miracle. If he
had not agreed to cover for his friend who unexpectedly left
town, he would not have been at the mortuary when they
brought in the old priest and his suitcases. It was a miracle.
Angelica Giancarlo's renewed heart was a miracle. Enrico
Gamboni's homecoming and Maria's answered prayers were
miracles. Nonno was released from the guilt of his heart by
the water of the fountain. It was a miracle. The earthquake
was a miracle. Marta's smile and Carmen's love for her
mother were miracles. Leo's new heart was a miracle. All
around him was forgiveness and love and he understood
that these two things were always miracles. It was all a
miracle.

   In that instant of time Elio's life was spread out before
him like a brightly sewn tapestry and the richness of the
fabric and the intricacy of the weave filled his heart with joy.
All he had ever wanted in his life was to be an instrument of
God's will and he finally understood – he had been.

   He took Nina's face in his hands and kissed the tears from
both her eyes and sighed, 'It was all a miracle.'

   And then Elio leaned his white head back against the
trunk of the withered fig and he thought to himself, Perhaps
sleep wasn't the enemy after all. Perhaps, he thought, after
all these years, it has been nothing more than a patient friend,
and he closed his eyes.

Those around him could see in the pale dawn light a great sigh go out of him. Elio leaned against the withered fig as if he were napping and they all watched the peaceful old man beneath the tree – all except Nina. She sat next to him, still holding his warm hand and her face turned toward the rosy edge of the eastern mountains, where, at that moment, a sliver of gold streamed across the sky.

'Mama,' Nina said, softly blinking, 'is that the sun?'